RETURN OF THE RAVENS

JERRY AUTIERI

1

Three shadowed men blocked the path before Ulfrik. Their bodies coiled with explosive power as they treaded the narrow dirt strip, sunlight flickering across dull iron helmets and tattered gray furs. The darkness of the surrounding woods joined behind them, weaving the threatening shapes into a black mass. The lead man's eyes were lost in shadow, but a crooked nose split with a white scar dominated a tangle of brown beard and bent mouth. As he drew closer, his gnarled sword-hand flexed to the hilt bobbing at his side.

"They don't have to mean trouble," Ulfrik said as he extended his arm across Finn's chest. Finn bucked against it, his young and freckle-splattered face contorted into a scowl.

"And black clouds don't always mean rain, except when you're stranded outside with no shelter. Then you can count on a soaking."

A thin smile cracked Ulfrik's dour face, and he let his hand drop away to his own sword hilt. He lacked mail or hides for protection, not even a shield. Only long experience killing foemen offered him any defense. He set his feet wide and settled into the center of the path. Even birdsong fell away as he challenged the trio of shadows drawing upon him.

"Hail, friends," he said. "What good fortune it is to meet fellows on the road."

The lead man stopped and his two companions halted close behind so their bodies melded in the shadow like a single broad-shouldered beast. A patch of yellow light struck the leader's head, illuminating cold blue eyes and a wolfish smile.

"Good fortune, indeed, but for who it remains to be seen."

"You're Northmen," Ulfrik said, a hint of relief in his voice. He was still unsure of Frankish and Norse borders after his long absence. "Danes, from your accent I take it."

"Isn't it nice to find old friends?" The lead man's voice was rock-on-rock rough. "But this ain't a visit, brother. You're in my way on my road and there's a tax for that."

Ulfrik smiled and looked about as if only just realizing his place. "Have I not come into Hrolf the Strider's lands? If Hrolf collects a tax for this unused goat track, then he's far poorer than I recall."

"Ah, one for jokes are you? That's good, like it better than the ones that beg or piss themselves. All the same, friend," he warped the word like a curse, "I'll be taking swords and packs off you and your boy lover."

"I'm eighteen," Finn said.

"Not a boy," Ulfrik said.

"That's how you're going to play it?" The leader's sword hissed from its sheath, and his two companions in shadow slid their blades free. "Enjoy your laughs now, cause it ain't going to be funny when you're trying to hold your guts in."

Ulfrik drew his sword with lazy confidence, offering them a smirk. However, his stomach fluttered and hands grew cold. These were strong and young men built to withstand their own foolishness. Ulfrik, however, felt his age from the ache in his hips and legs to the burning twitch in his shoulder. A hundred battle scars raked him from the inside, tearing at his confidence like a hungry wolf.

"Three to two is a poor bet," Ulfrik said, ranging his sword at knot of enemy. "I've cut down twice as many enemies in one stroke. Better to stand aside and let us on our way."

The leader guffawed and his companions joined him. "Old man, you're so funny I may keep you around for some fun. Now put down the sword and do as I say."

Ulfrik burst into action, a lightning strike at the lead man's sword hand. The blade gouged a chunk of flesh from the knuckle, drawing a surprised scream. Finn wasted no time, darting into the underbrush lining the thin track.

"You dog-shit bastard!" The scar-nosed leader stepped back to parry Ulfrik's follow up strike, their blades clanging together as the two other's leapt to their brother's aid.

Pushing through, Ulfrik collided with the man behind the leader, a thick brute swathed in a wolf pelt and reeking of urine and sweat. He stepped on the man's foot then drove his shoulder into his chest, sending him toppling back. Ulfrik whirled in time to catch the leader's follow up strike with the blade of his sword.

Hurry up, Finn, he thought. The two of them had become a tight fighting team in the years spent as merchant ship guards. Ulfrik set himself as an anvil upon which Finn hammered their foes. Ulfrik's deep, mature strength and Finn's serpent-swift, precise strikes were natural compliments.

Re-emerging from the brush, all attention centered on Ulfrik, Finn plunged his sword into the kidney of one of the enemy. The yellow-haired brute's eyes flashed wide enough to show through the shadowed hollows of their sockets. His sword dropped as Finn shoved him forward into the leader, sending both off balance.

The remaining man slashed at Ulfrik's exposed leg, but he had left it out as bait. He stepped out of the blow but rounded his blade on the attacker, slamming against the helmet and spinning it on his head so the noseguard blocked his eye. He had hoped to kill with the strike, but had only disoriented the man. Ulfrik spun away, leaving this one for Finn.

His face was flushed red, camouflaging his freckles, and Finn pierced the hamstring of the man as he fumbled with his helmet. He screamed and grabbed his leg as he fell. A man on the ground in battle was as good as dead, and Ulfrik assured it with a quick stroke across the enemy's neck. Brilliant red sprayed across the dirt track and splattered Ulfrik's legs.

"Get him before he runs," Ulfrik's voice boomed, no longer the voice of a tired old man but once again that of the battlefield commander and jarl he once was. The leader had regained his footing and was already sprinting into the woods. Finn sprang after him like a hound after a boar.

Ulfrik had reclaimed his strength and battle sense out of the wreckage of his life, but his stamina for sprinting and chases never returned. His gait carried a slight limp now, and hard running was better left to younger men or moments when death loomed.

Following snapped branches and quivering underbrush, Ulfrik plodded toward Finn's hollering. The gleeful howl echoed off the pines trees whose roots threatened to trip the unwary. He dashed the final distance, finding Finn wresting the larger man. The two rolled over root and rock, neither having an advantage for long, though Finn had wound his hand into the enemy's hair and pulled hard.

He considered letting the battle play out, but the risk to Finn was too great. He stuck his sword into the ground and drew his knife. Approaching from behind, he worked the cold iron blade under the throat of the attacker.

"Don't struggle or you'll cut your own throat," Ulfrik said into the man's ear, spitting out the final word with disgust. "Friend."

The man released his grip on Finn, who scrambled out from underneath. His gray shirt has ridden up to his chest to reveal red scrapes across his belly.

"I'd have had him in another moment. Bastard was just fatter than I thought." Finn ran his arm under his nose. "Thanks for saving me the trouble."

"Alright, tax collector. I warned you about the odds. But you just saw an old man and kid lost on the road."

"Save your bloody talk." The man threw an elbow back into Ulfrik's gut that winded him, but the blade remained in place. Finn, now on his feet, had recovered his sword and jabbed the point into the man's thigh. He went still and remained seated in the dirt.

"Answer my questions," Ulfrik said. "Are these Hrolf the Strider's lands? How far are we from Rouen?"

The man struggled but Ulfrik dug the blade into the flesh. He could smell the grease of the man's hair. "You're on the border still. This is Frankish land."

"And who rules this place?"

"Count Amand."

Finn looked at Ulfrik expectantly, but the name meant nothing to him. He shrugged, then dug the blade harder and forcing the man to stand up. His legs were getting numb from crouching in the cold dirt. They rose with great care, Ulfrik for his sore legs and his prisoner for the edge at his neck.

"How many more in your bandit group? Tell me where they are so I can avoid killing the rest of them."

"It was just us."

"Liar." Ulfrik pulled the blade until blood trickled and the man bucked.

"Gods, it's true! We were headed to join the Count's army."

"You were Hrolf's men?"

The man waved his free hand. "No, Meldun Wood-Eye's men. Meldun died of fever so we left."

"But not to Hrolf? Why the Franks?"

"Because they're winning and the Count is hiring our people for a fair wage. Look, just free me. I've told you the truth, just like you asked. Ain't nothing else I know. You're right, we saw you for easy pickings and were wrong. That's all there is to it."

Ulfrik glanced at Finn, and he gave a slow nod. An angry fire warmed his belly, and Ulfrik's mouth pulled tight in anger. "The Franks are my sworn enemies, as are the dogs that sit under their tables and eat their scraps. You're life is done, you traitorous pig."

The man grabbed Ulfrik's arm but the knife cut into his neck. Hot blood poured over Ulfrik's hand as he sawed deep into the throat. A thick jet of blood sprouted and the man went limp with a gurgled curse. Ulfrik shoved him to the ground, tossing his knife aside and standing over the crumpled body.

Neither he nor Finn spoke as the spout of blood slowed to a trickle that the earth drank up. The forest sounds of cracking branches and distant birds filled their silence. When Ulfrik spoke, it was slow and sonorous.

"We are going back to war, Finn. The enemies here are fierce and do not deserve our mercy. They would offer none to us."

Finn shook his head, the flush still a red stain on his cheeks. His thin red beard did not conceal it.

"If Northmen are joining the ranks of the Franks instead of Hrolf, then it is a bad sign. I fear I may have taken you into a danger far greater than I had expected."

"It's alright, Ulfrik. I chose to accompany you."

They scavenged the bodies for useful items, each of them taking a helmet along with silver and supplies, then set out along the path again. Their long foot journey north had revealed a changed Frankia. He no longer understood it, and it had not welcomed him as he had dreamed it would. He feared the pile of dead Northmen behind him were only the first signs of something far worse.

2

Ulfrik sat on the mound of dirt, legs crossed, arm folded to his chest, one hand clamped tight over his mouth. His leg pumped with nervous energy as the red sun sagged behind the fat oak at the west. He studied it, a bead of sweat rolling down into his eye making him squint. The shadow of main trunk stood out in a stark V shape as the disk of light set behind it. He uncoiled at the sight, a heavy sigh of relief following.

"This is the right place," he said. "See the arrow shape against the setting sun?"

Finn, who was stripped to his waist and standing in a hole almost as deep, drove his shovel into the ground and paused to look. His face broke into a wide smile. "Hey, I see it. It's as straight as you said it would be."

"This is definitely the place. Keep digging."

"Are you going to help?"

"I'll carry the treasure, if that's what you're asking? You just dig."

Despite recognizing where he had buried his treasure, he still fretted for finding it. The memories were hazy, and he did not have his giant-sized second in command, Einar, at hand to remind him of what he had done. They had wasted days digging in spots that yielded nothing, or finding his treasure cache had been plundered.

Now he regretted not killing a slave to bury with the treasure, for without a guardian spirit the silver had fled him. They were still in Frankish territory, lands that had once been firmly under Hrolf. No doubt the greedy Franks had sought plunder caches and had cleared his away.

The small field was notable for a copse of aged oaks with straight trunks and the stream that gurgled behind them. Finn's shovel crunched against rocks and he cursed. Ulfrik constantly scanned the surroundings for followers, but only a gentle summer breeze stirred the grass into a thin whisper. When the shovel came down again, he heard a wooden thump.

"I've got something!" Finn tossed dirt out of the hole, then threw his shovel after it. He began to dig with his hands.

Ulfrik dropped down into the pit, his heart pounding.

"I recognize that box. Here let me help." He began digging out the small box, racing with Finn to extract the treasure. Relief spread through him as they worked it out of the ground, a fat worm twisting in the hole left beneath it. They lifted it together, though it was light and small enough to tuck beneath a single arm. Ulfrik could not remember what he had buried here, but from the size of the box it must have been jewelry.

"I can't wait to see a real treasure horde," Finn said as he pulled himself out of the hole. He extended his arm to Ulfrik, and helped haul him out. "This is so exciting."

"Gods, lad, don't piss yourself. This is a trifle of what I've buried in these lands, and even less of what I had buried in my hall." Ulfrik thought back to the banner he had flown at the siege of Paris, a red robe that he had taken from a slave who had turned out to be a Bishop. A king's fortune in jewels had been sewn into its hems, more wealth than even Hrolf the Strider had at the time. No one but he and Runa knew of that treasure.

The cover had been latched with a simple bolt which now rusted fought Ulfrik as he worked it open. When it snapped free, he carefully opened the top. Finn crowded at his shoulder, as if ready to dive head-first into whatever Ulfrik revealed.

"No," Ulfrik said. The box lid dropped into the dirt as he stared at the contents.

"Look at that," Finn said. "A gold chain."

"A single gold chain," Ulfrik said, fishing out the braided chain with his finger. He held it out as if it were a stinking fish. "I buried more than this."

"Well, it's got to be worth a lot." Finn reached out to touch it, and Ulfrik shoved the chain into his hands as if it were cursed. He turned back to the pit, hands on his hips looking down into it blackness. The final light of the day was fleeing and leaving a trail of shadow.

"Someone dug up the rest of it," Ulfrik said.

"There's nothing else in here but a red stone. Looks valuable." Sounds of Finn tapping the box followed, but Ulfrik remained staring into the pit.

"I remember now. There was an cross on the chain, set with red and white stones. There were supposed to be other things here too. Silver plates and cups. Why did the thieves not take the chain?"

Only the swishing of the grass answered him. He heard Finn stand, his knees cracking. "Maybe if they left some of the treasure behind they'd avoid the curse you left on it?"

"I didn't leave a curse on it."

"Thieves wouldn't know that. This is better than the other places we searched. This chain has got to be worth a herd of goats at least."

Ulfrik whirled on Finn. "A fucking herd of goats! I'm going to win back my lands and titles with a herd of goats?"

"I was just --"

Snatching the chain out of Finn's grip, Ulfrik thrust it skyward. "This is all you gods left behind for me? This is all that's left of my treasure? A chain worth a herd of goats?"

He flung it into the dirt, and Finn rushed after it. His freckled face, normally bright and open, was dark with shame. Finn rubbed the chain on his pants to clean the dirt away. Ulfrik stared after him, heaving as if he had been rowing at top speed.

Their silence was heavy and sullen, Finn burnishing the chain while Ulfrik stared in disbelief. It would have been easier to accept if thieves had taken everything or he had failed to remember where he had hid his treasure. Finding only a piece of it forced him to confront his poverty, and how much he had once possessed.

"Let me see that a moment." Ulfrik held out his hand for the chain. Finn did not turn to face him, but dropped it into his waiting palm. He bounced it a few times, feeling its weight and the warmth left from Finn's touch. "It's not so bad really. We'll hack it down to bits if we have to. It's a place to start."

"If this is only a part of your treasure, I can't imagine what the rest of it is like."

Ulfrik raised a brow at Finn. "You really have not seen much gold in your day?"

"Never until we joined the merchants, and never so much as this piece. It's the most gold in one spot I've ever seen."

"Then you're in for some pleasant surprises once we get our affairs in order." He draped the chain over Finn's neck. Though a strong youth he did not possess the same mass as Ulfrik, and the chain appeared huge around his neck. "You dug it up, so you enjoy wearing it until we need it and if we don't need it you keep it."

As Finn gawked at his award, Ulfrik combed through his options. He was not returning to his family without at least enough gold to provide for his own care and Finn's. Reasonably, the necklace he had just found would allow that much for a short time. But he needed mail coats, better helmets and shields if others were to seriously consider him a warrior much less a returning jarl. All of this required gold far in excess of one chain.

"If I go back to my family without gold, they will have to support me." Ulfrik said. Finn stopped petting the gold chain to look up at him.

"Shouldn't family do that for their own?"

"Not the family of a jarl. I don't know what has become of my wife and sons and stepdaughter. What if they need my aid, and I am unable to help them because I lack resources?"

"They've been without you all these years already."

"Alright, but think on this. I've been dead to them all these years. What then is the legal status of my gold? What if it has been divided among my sons and men? What if my former oath-hold Hrolf the

Strider laid claim to it? I need to secure what is mine before I tell the world I yet live. To do otherwise might risk me remaining in poverty."

Finn nodded, but Ulfrik had learned to recognize the difference between Finn's nod of agreement and his nod of patronization.

"You don't understand the world you are about to enter. Even if I were fine to stay as I am, others would not be so gracious. Men who once might have called me friend because of my gold and power would be just as glad to drive me under their boots when I am poor. And if you think it's all my pride, then consider the shame and sorrow my family would feel to see me a beggar not fit to lurk outside their hall. It's better I remain a rich ghost than a poor burden."

He also remembered Throst's lasts words to him, that Runa had sent him to his death. While he did not believe it, a fear lingered at the back of his mind and warned not to return home helpless. Such fears did not bear imparting to Finn, so he rubbed his mouth and kept silent.

Finn's posture relaxed and he nodded again, this time in agreement. "I understand. But what do we do?"

"There remains one place yet where my treasure should be intact. It's a long distance from here, and will be difficult to get. Yet it's our best choice." Finn gave him a puzzled look. "Remember, I was proclaimed dead and my head sent home. If I know my wife, she'd have burned that head and buried the ashes along with my treasures in sight of my hall. We're going to rob my own grave."

3

The burial mounds were gone.

Ulfrik crouched behind a tree at the edge of the clearing, the rough pine bark cool against his hand. Old stumps littered the expanse of field that led to the burial mound he had created for his wife's brother and dearest friend, Toki. He remembered clearing those trees to build Ravndal atop it's craggy perch and to deny enemies cover in an attack. Now he stared out of the forest where once Franks spied on his fortress and envied his power. The fortress Ravndal still remained, but yellow and blue pennants of the Franks fluttered above its black walls.

Two scars of earth jutted where Toki's mound and what he guessed had been his own stood. Grass like a young man's beard flecked the displaced ground, and the sun broke through the clouds as if to accent the insult.

"The farmer told the truth. Everything is gone," Finn said. He squatted beside Ulfrik, hugging another tree and scanning the wide field. "Is that Ravndal where you trapped the Franks?"

He nodded, words stuck in his throat. All the long trek north he had heard news from fellow travelers that the Franks had pushed the Northmen west toward the sea. Ravndal now went by its Frankish name of Randal and housed Frankish troops. The land had once been theirs, Ulfrik had seized it from them, and they had reclaimed. How much blood had watered these fields, he wondered, and to what end? The Northmen would reclaim it again and more Franks would die.

"There's people coming down from Ravndal," Finn said, tapping Ulfrik's leg. "We better pull back."

A thin line of black shapes ambled downslope, a wagon between them. They were safe at this distance, but Finn was right. There was nothing worth remaining to see. "Let's go back to the farm."

Though the Franks had reclaimed their lands, many farms still belonged to Northman families that agreed to pay the Frank's taxes. Some of the younger families, though Norse, had no memories of their ancestral homes and were forgetting the ways of their fathers. One such family managed a farm nearby and though they claimed to have liked Jarl Ulfrik Ormsson well enough they cared more about the land than who ruled in Ravndal. When asked about Ulfrik's family, they did not have much information. They only knew Runa the Bloody had taken her family west to join Hrolf the Strider and that the Franks occupied Ravndal thereafter. The eldest son, Gunnar the Black, was said to have disappeared.

"Do you think there's a chance the Franks left something behind?" Finn asked. They tramped through the pine forest, retracing their path back to the farm. The air was cool in the shade of the trees, and birds chirped in the branches above.

"They know what heroes carry into death and they would not leave a stone unturned. Those bastards piss themselves if a Northman even sets foot on one of their graves, but they don't fuss when digging up one of ours. I bet they scattered the bones." Ulfrik scowled at the thought of his brother Toki's bones being tossed out for wolves and dogs to gnaw, but he did not expect the Franks to respect the nobility of a fallen warrior.

After a long, brooding walk they escaped the woods and found the farmhouse. It was a typical A-frame home, gray with age and stained black with rain. New thatch glowed in the summer sun and a pleasant white smoke waved from the smoke-hole to spread the sweet scent of firewood. Outside one of the farmer's sons split logs while a stout brown dog began barking at Ulfrik and Finn. The son continued the work, but the doors of the barn opened in response and the white haired old farmer peered out. In their first meeting he had introduced himself as Gils.

Ulfrik waved in greeting and Gils stepped out, setting aside a pitchfork and wiping his hands on his pants. The son continued to chop wood, the logs splitting and falling to either side of the stump. The dogs tail began to wag, though he continued to bark.

"Saw what you wanted?" Gils asked as he approached, his white hair bright in the sun. The son stopped chopping to collect the logs.

"It was all true," Ulfrik said. "I should have saved myself the trouble."

Gils spit and shrugged. "You thinking of joining the Franks then?"

"We haven't decided." Ulfrik peered off into the distance. "The old jarl really has no more power here?"

"Gone for good, he is. This is Frank land now, and they're good enough if you give them what they ask. Don't really need the old jarl, do we?"

It was Ulfrik's turn to spit and shrug. "Mind if we camp on your farm tonight? Tomorrow we'll move on."

"Where to?"

Ulfrik shook his head and Gils frowned, but he turned to his son. "Tell your Ma Ulfar the White and Finn Langson will be our guests tonight."

Though no one would expect Ulfrik to be alive, he used a false name to ensure his memory was not raised, particularly on lands he once ruled.

Gils' son left without a word, pausing only to steal a glance at Ulfrik before he disappeared into the house. Gils pointed at the barn, "The house is full but you can sleep in the barn tonight."

They passed the rest of the day settling into a brooding silence while Ulfrik worked through his next steps. True to his word, Gils fed them a meal of chicken, onions, and beer. His two sons acted as if mute, sharing dark glances that Ulfrik did not trust. The wife and her two daughters chattered until Ulfrik's eardrums throbbed. When he and Finn settled into the barn for the night, he was glad for the silence.

They shared an empty stall, but the cow occupied the largest stall. "Even the cows live better than me," Ulfrik said, then laughed.

"Do you want me on first watch?" Finn asked as he spread his cloak out.

"Gils seems fine enough but his two sons are strange. Keep watch for trouble. Wake me at midnight or when you feel sleepy."

In the darkness, Ulfrik listened to crickets and the breathing of the cow. Silvery moonlight shined behind the cracks in the barn door planks. Before long he was drifting into sleep, visions of the defiled burial mounds filling his young dreams.

He jolted awake, cold and rough hands on his ankles and wrists.

There was no silvery moonlight now, but a harsh torchlight flooding the barn with heat. Strange men pinned him to the ground while others wrestled with Finn. A third man stuffed a rag into his mouth, while he felt cords tighten around his legs.

Wasting no time, he wrested a hand free and punched one of his assailants in the head. The man staggered back with a growl. Another man grabbed his free hand and forced it to his chest, then his two hands were wrapped in cord. In moments he was tied like a hog for the slaughter and laying face down on his cloak. Finn was similarly tied beside him, eyes wide with terror.

"Two swords, helmets, knives." One of the assailant's counted off their valuables. Ulfrik guessed a half dozen men filled the barn. The cow lowed in the stall beside him as someone invaded its space.

"Ah but look at this chain." Ulfrik heard their bags being dumped out and the clink of their meager treasures. "What's on them?"

Rough hands flipped Ulfrik over and he was looking into the smirking face of Gils son, the one who had been chopping wood. He frisked Ulfrik's body, finding the gold armband hidden under his shirt. He worked it off, then grabbed the silver Thor's hammer that Finn's mother and his lover, Gytha, had given him. It snapped off the cord and disappeared into the son's shirt.

"We've got everything. Let's get rid of them."

Ulfrik's heart beat against the base of his neck. Gils' sons worked with four other men to heave him off the ground and into the night. The man holding the torch aloft was Gils himself.

"Don't kill them," he warned the young thieves. "Drop them at the stream and cut them free."

"You worry too much, old man," said one of the strangers. "No one knows they were here but us."

The young men laughed and Gils repeated his admonition. A cart had been backed up to the barn with a horse ready to pull it. They tossed Ulfrik onto it like he was nothing more than a bale of hay. Finn followed on, crashing into Ulfrik's legs.

"Be back after dawn," said Gils' son as he took up the driver's seat with his brother. The four other strangers flanked the cart as it jerked to motion.

As the cart pulled forward Gils, his wife, and daughters turned to the inside of the barn. Ulfrik grunted and pulled at his bindings, but there was no slack. Knowing he had to conserve strength for the fight to come, he relaxed. Finn continued to wrestle as the cart trundled away from the farm, earning derisive laughter from their captor walking behind the cart.

Finn's eyes were bright with terror and when he stopped resisting he stared at Ulfrik. There was nothing either could do, but he offered him a slow nod of reassurance. Whatever lay ahead of them, panic and fear would not serve.

He closed his eyes and waited for the ride to end.

4

Runa sat at the edge of her bed and plucked at the wool blanket crumpled at its foot. Dark dreams fled from the sounds of morning and left her empty and tired. She rubbed her cold hand against her cheek to work away the vestiges of sleep. The space next to where she had slept had long been empty. As usual Konal had risen before her and was off with his so-called hirdmen. He would not waste the morning with sleep when fresh summer mead was in stock. He and his men would start on those casks before the first meal of the day.

The walls of her room were tightly fitted oak planks that allowed no light to seep inside. Still, she heard the voices in the main hall and the bustle outside the walls. Only a candle burned halfway to its iron holder cast any light and the tallow imparted a stale scent to the air. If she opened the door, the light from the main hall would flood her room, but she did not feel like greeting the surly folk this early in the day. Like Konal loved his mead, she loved her solitude.

Today was especially difficult for her. It was about this time when Ulfrik left her for the final journey. She remembered that day six years ago standing on the banks of the Seine, him preparing to sail south along some river to a place she never heard of before or since, and his solemn promise to return before Yule. He had kept the promise, but only his head had returned.

Runa fought the memories of that horrible day. Why had she insisted upon viewing the head? Why had they even sent it back, crushed as it was? Now that terrifying image was in her mind like a bloodstain that would never wash out.

Voices from the hall rose in laughter then died back to a murmur. She could not hide here all day. It would only sicken her. With a heavy sigh, she shoved off the bed again and exchanged her wool sleeping clothes for a plain green dress and white overdress. She combed her hair, but still refused to wear a head cover like other women. It was her last act of rebellion to leave her hair free, though now the tight ringlets of her hair were woven with gray.

On a whim she knelt on the floor and pulled a small chest out from beneath the bed. She held the key to its lock on her belt along with the other keys that symbolized her so-called authority of the household. In truth, Konal had allowed her nothing since marrying her. She twisted the key into the lock and was satisfied at the pop of the shank. Setting it aside, she raised the lid and stared at the contents.

She had not looked into this chest for years, at least since Gunnar's disappearance. Today she longed to touch something that took her to the past. Inside the chest were her final connection to Ulfrik. She realized it was foolish to hide them here, but sleeping over them each night lent her small satisfaction.

The first item she withdrew was her sax, a short sword that warriors wore at their laps and used for close quarters fighting. The old leather handle melded to her hand and to touch it sent her back through the years to the days when Ulfrik trained her in swordplay. She lifted away the loop holding it in the wood scabbard and pulled up the blade. Rust had claimed it and she regretted not caring for it properly. She had killed men with this weapon, and now it was rusted and useless, a mere relic of a forgotten time.

Just like me, she thought, then snapped it shut in the scabbard. She laid it aside, then dipped back into the chest.

In both hands she lifted out a faded red cloak. There was nothing special about this beyond the expense of the dye used to color it. A smile bloomed on her face as she felt along its hems. Sewn into the edges was a fortune in jewels, the treasure that had led Ulfrik to Frankia. So much fate was woven into the cloak, it had to have come from the hands of the Norns themselves. Konal and his now dead brother Kell had been searching for this treasure when Konal was shipwrecked on Runa's land.

As Fate decided, Ulfrik found the treasure and kept it secret from Konal. This was to be their safety, a vast fortune to be called upon when all other reserves failed. Though now Runa might have need, she could never allow Konal to discover she possessed this treasure. To her great sorrow, he was no longer the man she had admired and even loved for a short time. His discovering the truth of these gems would invite violence.

"What are you doing?"

Runa yelped with shock, dropping the cloak into the chest. She whirled on her knees, hand on her throat. "Konal!"

"And what other man would dare enter this room with you alone?" Konal's voice was raspy thin, like a man choked in smoke. He leaned against the door, which she had not even realized had opened. The terrible scars that marred his face and neck were white and red, as if a fiery finger had stirred the flesh. She had once looked past those scars, but now it was all she could see.

"I asked what you were doing." Konal stepped closer, his soft boots sliding across the packed dirt floor. "What's this?"

Runa's stomach burned and she shoved the cloak back into the chest, but Konal was more interested in the sword. He reached down and snatched it from her. She caught the scent of mead.

"A sword? What are you doing with this bit of junk?" He yanked it out of the scabbard and clicked his tongue at the rust. "Gods, woman, cut yourself with this and you'll die of the bending sickness."

She stood and with her foot pushed the chest beneath the bed, hoping to distract him from it. Now placing the cloak so openly made her blush with shame at her foolishness. "That is my sword. Give it back."

He raised a brow at her, tugging the blade completely free. The rust had crawled down its edges, ruining it for all but sentimental purposes. "This should be destroyed before it cuts someone. I'll take it to the blacksmith --"

"No you won't," Runa said, then grabbed for Konal's arm. "I'll keep it in the sheath, just return it now."

Pulling his arm away, he started to complain then paused. He examined the scabbard, and his mead-fogged mind seemed to assemble the true picture. He stiffened, slamming the blade back into the scabbard.

"You don't need a weapon to protect you. You've got me now."

"Please, just allow me to keep it. I never meant for you to see it. You won't be bothered by it again."

"Of course you didn't want me to see it. You think I don't know why you're looking at it today? Think I don't know what day this is? If you could see your sad face, you'd not ask me why I drink so much."

"You drink because you're a drunk, and you're too scared to do the fighting of a real man."

The hard words used to enrage him, but they had nothing kind to say to each other for years and insults had lost their bite. He weighed the sword in his palm and answered thoughtfully. "The rust can be scoured off, then I'll have the blade melted down for something more useful than a sentimental piece of trash."

"No you won't!" She struck his shoulder, hurting her hand more than anything. Since being forbidden to practice with weapons, she had lost her old strength. Konal laughed and held the blade away from himself.

"Ulfrik has been dead for years. No foolishness about this sword will bring him back. Put him behind you and act with more dignity. You used to have more pride in yourself."

"When I had something to be proud of. Now what do I have? I married a coward who fled Ravndal rather than fight, and now hides behind other men."

Konal's face reddened at that accusation. Runa still knew what words could cut him. "That's enough from you."

"Hardly enough. You shamed my children into leaving us."

"Gunnar left to avenge his father. It had nothing to do with me."

"And you refused to aid that vengeance. For the man who gave you a home and cared for your son like his own, you just turned your back."

"I'm warning you now, stop. You're getting carried away."

But Runa was not ready to stop. No matter how often they had this fight, she never felt as if she said it all. Today she would.

"I'll stop when I'm done. You took his hall, his gold, his glory, everything, and what did you do with it? Run at the first sign of danger."

"Hrolf recalled --"

"You ran because you didn't know what to do, and you still don't."

"Enough."

"You hide behind another man's glory and pretend this is all your doing."

He raised his hand, but she did not flinch. It hung cocked behind his head, ready to release.

"Today I remember the man who loved me and treated me like I was worth something more than a bauble in a treasure horde he happened to fall into. You don't deserve what you have. You didn't earn it and you nearly threw it all away. In your old age, you've become what you really were all along. A frightened little boy playing a man's part. What did I ever see in you? I wish Ulfrik could see --"

The backhand sprawled her across the bed. She expected it, went limp to absorb the force, but it still hurt. She crashed on her back and lay still, staring up at the rafters above. A tear slid from her eye and rolled into her ear.

Konal did not answer, and she heard him turn, then the crash of the sword thrown against the wall. She remained with her cheek throbbing, the tears rolling more freely now.

"What happened to me? Ulfrik, why did you have to go?"

5

Ulfrik sat up straighter when the wagon stopped, though Finn remained slumped in defeat. Dawn was still a thin white stain on the eastern sky, visible only through gaps in the forest canopy. The farmer's sons and their four accomplices carried Ulfrik and Finn out of the wagon and set them at the edge of the stream the farmer Gils had mentioned. With legs and arms bound and a spit soaked gag filling his mouth, Ulfrik had no opportunity to react. Despite dire appearances, Ulfrik did not mark these men for killers. They were opportunists and in some ways he could not blame them for their actions. He might have done something similar in the desperate days of his youth, and in fact had done far worse things.

That was not going to prevent him from taking a terrible revenge on these boys.

The taller of the two sons produced a knife and cut Ulfrik's leg bindings, then did the same for Finn. "The rest you'll have to figure out on your own," he said then laughed. All six of the men mounted the wagon and returned back into the early morning gloom of the woods. Ulfrik watched them disappear. Finn tried speak through his gag, but it was a muttered mess that Ulfrik shook his head at.

Without their captors to discourage him, Ulfrik knew he could work out of the ties. For one, his hands were bound in front of his body, and that was all he needed. He found a suitably sharp rock to begin sawing at the bindings. Finn's expression of amazement came through his gag, and he also located a rock by the stream. By the time dawn had painted the sky blue and awakened the woodland birds to their morning song, Ulfrik and Finn were free.

"I thought they would kill us," Finn said as he washed his face in the stream, crouched next to Ulfrik.

"If they wanted us dead, they'd have done it while we slept."

Finn fell quiet and scrubbed his face. Ulfrik cupped water and slurped, staring out of the side of his eye at Finn who remained staring into the clear steam. "I fell asleep. It's my fault were in this mess."

Ulfrik splashed water over his face. "I would agree with that."

"What are you going to do?"

"Follow the tracks back and recapture our belongings. Kill Gils' sons and rape his wife and daughters until they go mad. After that I'll probably burn Gils alive in his barn."

Ulfrik continued to scrub his face, letting Finn stare at him in stunned silence. As Ulfrik patted off his face with the hem of his cloak, Finn finally relented. "Well, I was asking what you were going to do about me, not our stuff."

"You? Well, mistakes happen. Sometimes our mistakes get us killed or worse. Just think of what a more ambitious man could've done with us. Have you seen a slave market before?" Finn shook his head. "Well today you could've been seeing one directly from the selling block. Fortunately, we were robbed by dumb farmers with no imagination. So take your lesson, because the next time we're probably not escaping this easily."

Finn's freckled face was sunburn red, and he lowered his head in shame. They continued to clean in the river, Finn clearly mulling his thoughts until he turned to Ulfrik again. "Are we really going to rape and kill?"

"Of course not. I used to rule these people, and I intend to rule them again. Make no mistake, we're getting our stuff back and if they give us a fight I've no hesitation to kill. But I just want what is mine returned, and have no interest in terrorizing them."

"You're taking this a lot better than I am."

"After all I've been through, this is not so bad. We'll wait until they think we've moved on, but by tomorrow night we'll have everything back. Mark my words."

Finn was restored to his good nature and the spring returned to his step. Ulfrik was glad for his company, and believed everything he had told Finn. Yet deep inside he burned to take revenge for the insult of being laid low by a farmer and his idiot sons. If they provoked him at all, blood would follow.

And he would not mind being provoked.

6

By the night of the second day after being robbed, Ulfrik and Finn crouched in silence behind trees surrounding Gils farm. He watched their stout dog with concern as it yipped and danced about the legs of Gils and his son. Though they remained upwind of the animal, hounds had uncanny danger sense and if exposed now Ulfrik's plans would fail. The sun had set and a bright yellow light flowed out of the open door to the family home. The four other men had not yet been seen, and Ulfrik figured they were friends summoned from neighboring farms. They would have all taken shares from their theft, but Ulfrik had plans to get them to return their spoils without having to track them down.

At last Gils, his son and dog all entered the home and closed their doors. Ulfrik crept back from the tree to where Finn waited in the rear, gesturing him near.

"They've gone inside for their meal and will be to bed soon after. Go back to the gully and kindle the fire, and I'll watch. If I call for you come running."

Finn nodded and slipped back into the trees. With their striking steel stolen along with everything else, they had to rely on dry kindling and friction to start a fire. Finn had been a woodsman with his father, and knew how to survive without any tools, a skill Ulfrik greatly valued. Tonight he needed fire and Finn would bring it.

He camped beside the tree and watched the house. It was a sedate evening with no noises coming from the house, nor any visitors approaching. As full dark drew over the landscape, the bright yellow thatch turned blue in the dim moonlight. Clouds hid the crescent moon from revealing their proximity. The dog barked but Gils shouted the animal to silence. Once the outline of yellow light shining around the door faded, Ulfrik knew they had retired for the night.

Threading a path halfway to Finn's position, he stopped and whispered his name. He did not want to travel woodland paths in the dark, fearing a turned ankle in the uneven ground. A small point of orange light answered, and grew larger as it bobbed in the dark. Finn arrived, husbanding the frail flame of the torch.

They took a looping approach to the barn. Once there, he unbarred the door and slipped inside while Finn waited, keeping the barn between him and the house. He had to let his eyes adjust to the dim light that entered from the open door. The stalls and miscellaneous barrels and straps were outlined in gossamer threads of blue light. He saw the outline of the cow's back, and used it to orient himself on the rest of the barn. As he felt along the walls, his hand located what he sought. He lifted the pitchfork off the wall peg, then slipped back to Finn.

"Start the fire," he said, and Finn held his torch to the thatch eaves.

Without oil to speed the flames, the fire took a long time to catch, then only as a smoldering bloom of orange cinders. He had to fan it to get it going, and the fire refused to spread.

"This is taking too long," Ulfrik said, waving at the nascent fire. "Smoke will scare the cow before the fire gets serious enough."

"The hay is drier inside," Finn said. "I know you didn't want to kill the cow, but this isn't working."

"Alright, let's do it. I'll lead the cow outside and you fire the barn."

"No," Finn disagreed. "If Gils sees the cow out of the barn, he'll know someone is nearby. With the cow at risk, even if he suspects someone nearby he will have to attempt a rescue."

Ulfrik waved Finn forward to the job. "Alright, these bastards brought this on themselves. You're right."

Finn's estimation was right and within moments of exiting the barn the dry hay inside roared into flame. They dashed toward the house, prepared to set up behind the door. As expected, the dog barked at their approach.

The cow cried out and was trying to kick free as flames rushed along the inside walls. The dog barked wildly and voices shouted inside. Ulfrik and Finn hid around the corner from the door, and it burst open with Gils at the lead.

"Fire!" he shouted. "Get buckets! Hurry!"

Ulfrik glanced behind, finding water barrels and buckets. Every farm collected rainwater as defense against fire, and he was standing in front of it. Without a word he grabbed Finn and the two looped around the far side as he heard Gils splashing a bucket into the water. He and Finn shared a relieved glance as Gils was too focused to notice them.

Now as the rest of the family roused from sleep, their shouts and screams reverberated through the walls. The dog barked furiously alongside them. Ulfrik tightened his grip on the pitchfork, then charged.

A form disappeared around the corner as he rushed out, but Gils wife was leaning into the barrel when Ulfrik appeared. He was on her before she could react, pushing her against the wall with the iron tines of the pitchfork. He smiled, "Remember me?"

The woman's eyes widened in fear and she screamed. As planned, Finn slipped around the corner and into the house.

The two sons and one of the daughters arrived with empty buckets and stopped short.

"Glad you showed up. Get your father. I think I left some of my belongings here."

The sons scowled and the mother whimpered. Ulfrik eased his pressure on her, just so she wouldn't accidentally puncture herself on the pitchfork.

Then the dog charged.

It bolted around the corner, snarling, teeth flashing with slobber as it leapt the final distance. Ulfrik spun the pitchfork around and braced his legs. He had anticipated the dog to act as it did, and the animal impaled itself on the waiting fork. It plowed him back with a horrible yelp. Ulfrik detested the sounds of a dying dog, for there were no creatures more loyal and less deserving of a bad death than a faithful hound. He dropped the skewered dog and stumbled away. The mother bolted and her two sons charged as the daughter shrieked.

Ulfrik hurled an empty bucket at one, sending him off track then slammed into the other son. His hands itched for a good fight and when his fist connected with the son's ribs he thrilled at the crack of bone and the painful cough. He drove his knee into the son's groin and tossed him aside like an old sack. The other son had recovered and squared off in a fighting stance. Ulfrik wasted no time, dodging in to strike. The son punched Ulfrik's head, staggering him, and followed up with a kick to his bad left leg. The pain shot his vision with white. The son recognized the weak spot and hit again.

Now rage bubbled over and Ulfrik charged low into the son's body, taking a beating on his head even as he slammed the son to the ground. Once atop him, he landed a withering punch to the son's face, followed by another, and one more until he heard Finn shouting his name.

"I've got Gils," Finn said over the screams of the women.

Ulfrik paused over the bloodied face of the son who stared hatefully back up at him. He shoved himself upright. Finn had gone into the home to find a weapon and now had returned with the other daughter and Gils, who he held hostage with a long knife to the throat. The old man stood stock still, frowning into the distance as if he were unaware of others.

"Good work," Ulfrik said. When he stepped toward Finn his leg buckled and the pain blinded him, though he marshaled a smile and steadied himself.

"Told you we should've killed them." The son who Ulfrik had just beaten sounded as if he were ready to cry.

"No doubt you should have," Ulfrik said. "But your chances for that are done."

"We don't have your gold," Gils said, still refusing to look at anyone. "So kill me if it'll make you feel better, but let my family go."

Inhaling the bittersweet scent of burning wood and thatch, Ulfrik smiled. "I burned down your barn, which makes me feel better. I don't believe anything you've said, Gils. That much gold is probably worth dying for just to pass it on to your family."

He grabbed the pitchfork and put his boot on the dog's corpse, yanking it free. One of the daughters sobbed at the sight. He pointed the bloody tines at the son on the ground. "I'll ask to return the gold to me one last time. I'm sure you had to divide it among your other friends. Also, my sword and my traveling pack, all of it I want back now. If you don't, I'll use this fork to pluck out this one's eyes. What do you say, Gils?"

"I don't have any of your belongings. That's the truth. The four others, they're Thorgest's men. He's the true power here. We owed him gold, so when you arrived we promised to hold you long enough for his men to get your stuff. I saved your lives, you know that? Told them I didn't want any death's on my head."

"And a bandit leader obliged?" Ulfrik's pitchfork did not waver.

"Not Thorgest, the four with my boys. I've known them since they were children, and they listen to me."

"Then they'll listen to you when you ask for my belongings."

Gils shrugged, and Finn dug the knife deeper. His two sons flinched, but Ulfrik touched the pitchfork to one's chest and they both subsided.

"Thorgest will have taken it from them by now.

Ulfrik stared at Finn, whose wide eyes indicated he was as nervous as the rest of Gils family. Ulfrik had expected his belongings to be divided up, but not to a bandit leader. He silently cursed this ill luck, grinding his teeth in frustration. Now he had a whole family as hostage and was no closer to reclaiming his belongings. He could walk away, claiming what he could find from Gils home. Yet his stolen sword was a beautiful weapon, made to his exact specifications. Also, it was no mean sum of gold that had been stolen and he would be hard pressed to the same find again. Walking away did not appeal. Striking at a bandit camp was equally foolish, if not deadly. He had no real options.

"Well, we'll arm ourselves with what you have around your home. You at least have an ax and Finn has found himself a fine knife. You've got to have other weapons at hand."

Gils seemed to relax, closing his eyes and slouching. The sound of the barn collapsing in flames shocked everyone, and all paused to listen to the flames crackle in the night.

Then Ulfrik pointed the pitchfork at the son on the ground. "And you can take us to Thorgest."

7

Ulfrik picked a gray day of drab light and woolly clouds to enact his plans for Thorgest's bandit camp. He and Finn studied the camp from the edge of the clearing, and Finn pointed at a flight of geese flying over the crude hall at the center of the field.

"That's a good sign," he said. "They're headed for us and are high in the sky."

Spitting on the ground, Ulfrik reached for the hammer amulet that was no longer at his neck but given to Thorgest as booty. He shook his head. "Forget the gods and their signs. It wasn't the gods that made the plans and laid the traps. That was us, so trust yourself most."

Finn's boyish smile remained undiminished. In the flat light of the afternoon his freckled face still seemed to shine with hope. "I do. This is going to make an amazing tale when it's done. Two against nine!"

"Gods, now that's a way to curse us. Don't say anything until this is done. You're ready to carry out what we've planned?"

"Been ready for days now." Finn rubbed his hands, and Ulfrik could not help but smile at the enthusiasm.

The wind had been still since morning but then started gusting after midday. Ulfrik worried it would ruin their bow shots, and seeing how Gils had only six serviceable arrows for his hunting bow they could not afford missed shots. Finn had a long knife and the bow. He had the keener vision and as a hunter was a deadlier shot. Ulfrik hefted an ax, a favored weapon of his giant friend Einar but an unwieldy tool in his own hands. Choices were limited to whatever they scavenged from Gils' farm.

"Let's get the girl and begin," Ulfrik said.

He shouldered the ax and led Finn back toward their small camp. For days they had hid on the outskirts of Thorgest's base, watching the bandit's activities. He had feared Gils' barn fire would have drawn their attention, but like all bandits after an easy haul they spent most of their days celebrating. They shared a few women for entertainment, at least by what he could see from outside the hall. They raised pigs and a goat, but otherwise did little else. These were opportunists and lay-abouts Ulfrik understood all too well. His only frustration was his lack of numbers, otherwise he would have had Thorgest's head by now. Thorgest, the bandit leader, made one obvious appearance to witness a brawl that had spilled out of his hall. He had a whore under one arm, Ulfrik's sword at his side, and Ulfrik's gold chain about his neck. That had been his sole showing, and while he was strong and scarred he was also bleary-eyed and careless.

He would soon be dead.

At camp Gils' youngest daughter sat tied to tree, gag still filling her mouth. Calling her the prettiest daughter stretched the compliment, for Ulfrik considered her only marginally better than ugly with thin brown hair and a protruding forehead. He assumed the bandits would covet her young flesh. He had not learned the girl's name, not wanting to put a real person to the tool he used her as. With luck she would survive, and he certainly planned on it. He had taken her hostage from Gils to ensure the farmer stayed quiet and did not betray them, and he had kept his word. The girl, too, remained docile when her gag was removed to eat and drink. He stood before her now, hands on his hips.

"Are you ready to earn back your freedom and return to your family?"

Her dark eyes were wide and she nodded furiously. Ulfrik smiled, and gestured to Finn who pulled out her gag and cut her free from the tree. He helped her stand and steadied her as she adjusted.

Ulfrik cupped her jaw and forced her to look at him.

"Here's what you'll do. Take this knife and hide it on your body. Go to Thorgest's camp and tell them you've escaped us. He'll press you about how you did it, so tell him you slipped us in the night and became lost. Here, tear your dress." Ulfrik grabbed her collar and tore the thin fabric to reveal the top of her cleavage. It was not as enticing as he had hoped. "Show him a bit of tit and you'll be on his bed straight away. That's when you call out for me and stab him. We'll rush in and finish the rest. You'll be safe to return home after that."

The girl stared at him in disbelief. Her trembling voice was barely audible. "You can kill all of them like that?"

"You'll have their attention. Three will be dead before they know it; three will die as they turn to face us; and three will die when they try to fight. That's nine dead. This is the only way girl. You ready?" He pressed into her hand the small knife he had taken from Gils farm and held it there. She continued to stare, her mouth struggling to form words.

Finn led her away and soon they were watching her approach the hall. She seemed tiny in the bland light. Two men appeared out of the shadows of the hall, one with a spear lowered. She started talking, and the men nodded, eventually taking her inside.

"How long before she betrays us to Thorgest?" Finn asked.

"The moment she realizes he has two teeth and smells like shit and ale, she'll be pointing the way to us. I just hope the bastard doesn't decide we can wait while he gets a better look at her body."

"I'll string the bow anyway." Finn put six arrows into the ground next to him as he readied his bow.

"Make every shot count," Ulfrik said. "I'll take up my position. Good luck."

They nodded at each other and Ulfrik looped around the far side of Thorgest's small hall. As expected, all nine men filed out of the hall with drawn swords or leveled spears. Some had grabbed shields and helmets, expecting an easy ambush of Ulfrik and Finn approaching the hall. Thorgest followed behind, Ulfrik's sword bright in his hand. He opened his mouth to bellow a challenge when Finn loosed his first arrow.

The lead man collapsed with an arrow in his chest, barely giving a shout. In the moment it took for the others to notice his death, a second man spun away with a grunt as an arrow caught him in the face. The seven men, crowded at the door as they were, jumbled into each other as some tried to duck back into the hall and others leapt for cover the opposite way. Another arrow took a man in the leg and he fell in the midst of them.

Ulfrik charged out of the cover, screaming with his ax held overhead. Thorgest had fallen back into his hall while the remaining men turned toward him. Five faces drawn stiff and white with fear turned toward him. The charge was suicide against prepared men, but they were confused and frightened. Finn dropped another man as Ulfrik closed on the targets.

"There's only two of them," shouted Thorgest from the safety of his hall door. "I've got this one. Take the bowman!"

Thorgest charged out with his shield in front of him. The four remaining men whirled with their shields. Finn's fifth arrow sank into one of the shields.

Cutting to the side, Ulfrik veered from Thorgest's charge and began running in the opposite direction. His leg pained him and he cursed laying a plan that required him to run. Finn had the much longer run, and the more dangerous part of the plan. Once he had dashed to his set spot at the edge of the woods he whirled back on Thorgest.

The bandit leader's fury was hot, having just lost four men. His face was red and lips curled back in a snarl as he hurtled forward. Ulfrik had the advantage of reach with the ax, and swept it at Thorgest's torso. A man can pull in his limbs or duck his head to avoid a blow, but no man can alter the trajectory of his body in flight. The ax swept into his side, the wedge-shaped head hooking him around his back like a fish on a gaff. He slewed to the side and crashed to his face. Ulfrik slid around Thorgest as he fell and now had the ax raised overhead.

"Stop!" was all the bandit leader could shout before the ax slammed down on his head. His skull split with a wet crack and a jet of blood arced onto Ulfrik's arms. He let the ax go and pound Thorgest into the ground.

"So I've stopped," he said over the corpse. "Now I'll have back what you've stolen."

He retrieved his sword and scabbard, then lifted the chain from Thorgest's neck after he had wrenched the ax out of Thorgest's skull. A search through his gore soaked clothes yielded the silver amulet of Thor's hammer given him by Gytha as well as two others. "Seems the Storm God had no affection for you," he said as he stashed the other amulets. He would have to return later, for now he had to help Finn.

He did not return the way he had come. Finn's final destination lied to the west, and Ulfrik loped through the trees to where he expected to find Finn celebrating his kills. There were no sounds of battle, which was encouraging, but he approached the area with caution. The small clearing appeared in the trees and he saw Finn against a tree with no one else. Before him, the covered pit they had dug for days was now open.

"It worked!" Ulfrik shouted, exiting from the trees. Finn waved a tired hand at him but said nothing. "That was brilliant shooting. Reminded me of my old friend Snorri in his younger days. That man could shoot. Let's see what you caught."

He jogged to the pit and looked inside. Four bodies were impaled on stakes, three were dead and another struggled in silence with a stake that had impaled him through his left side. "Hey, no need to let this one suffer."

Looking up at Finn he froze in horror.

Finn's clothes were soaked with blood. His freckles stood out in sharp contrast to the whiteness of his flesh. He gave a weak smile. "One of them threw a spear and cut my leg. It's not bad. What's wrong?"

Ulfrik schooled his expression, knowing full well any panic on his part would worsen Finn's condition. He drew a breath and smiled. "Seems like a scratch, but let's have a look at it."

"I almost missed the log we set over the pit. Could you imagine if I fell into my own trap?"

"I'd not let you live it down." Ulfrik gingerly peeled back Finn's shirt, finding the cut on his side and continuing around to his back."

"Wish I could've seen them fall in there, but I was busy running. Then a lucky bastard stuck my leg."

As far as Ulfrik could see, Finn's leg was unhurt. He gently leaned Finn forward and saw the ragged gash over his kidney. Had the throw been true, Finn would have died instantly.

"See it's not bad." Finn's voice was already weakening, as if he were falling asleep.

Ulfrik nodded as he stripped off his cloak to cut bandages. The wound was deep and long, flowing blood at a steady rate. Finn was right: the wound was not bad.

It was deadly.

8

Runa kept her head lowered in the hall, moving among servants whose expressions ranged from surprise to pity. The five hirdmen loafing at a table did not see her at all, drinking and either rolling dice or betting on their friends. Their brittle laughter made Runa's hands tremble with rage. There had been a time only six years past when she had been regarded with respect. Most of Ulfrik's hird had went to Einar's hold, and the men Konal recruited had been selected for their drinking tolerance rather than military power. She scowled at them lost in their gambling, her cheek stinging in answer.

"Lady Runa, your face?" A woman, Groa, who had been a servant to Runa since her time in Nye Grenner, intercepted Runa as she crossed the hall. She was a few years older than Runa, but toil had grayed her hair and lined her face. Her rough hand reached out to tilt Runa's head into the light, and she sucked her breath as it did.

"Not now," Runa said. "I just want to get some air."

Groa frowned. "How's your sight? Blurry?"

"No more so than yesterday. Please, I'll be fine. It looks worse than it feels." As if to deny Runa's lie a cold needle of pain raced across her throbbing cheek as she spoke.

They stared at each other while the rest of the servants flowed around them carrying out their chores. Groa's mouth formed unspoken words, the same protests she made every time Konal's rage ended in violence. Both knew all talk was pointless. Groa's eyes faltered and she relented, stepping aside. Runa patted her arm and continued out of the hall.

The sky was blanketed with woolly clouds and a cool wind lifted her hair over her face. Just the touch of it on her injured cheek elicited soreness. Their small fort consisted of the main hall, blacksmith, barracks, and a smattering of homes all ringed by a wooden palisade. The lands beyond were nominally under Konal's rule, but Hrolf the Strider was the true force from here to the sea, which was miles upon miles of land. Konalsvik, as it was called, hid far back behind the Frankish borders where Einar now held a larger, more important fortress. Hrolf understood Konal's true potential, and had kept him away from a position where his mistakes could cost him. A river flowed nearby, dumping into the Seine. It was about the only thing of importance in the area.

Runa folded her arms across her chest and shuffled down the main dirt road. A dog barked and children ran between buildings. The blacksmith's hammer clanged in the distance.

She hated her life. This morning had only served to deepen that hatred. Only her son her youngest son, Aren, remained with her now. Her eldest, Gunnar, was probably dead, having stolen a ship to search for his father and never returned. Hakon now fostered with Einar and made it clear he would never return to her side while Konal ruled. Her brother Toki's daughter, Kirsten, was given away in marriage at age thirteen and died with her first child the following year. Konal helped her endure all of this by drinking, bragging, and beating her when she reminded him of her unhappiness.

Fate was a strange thing, and her journey from a jarl's daughter, to a slave, to a jarl's wife, and finally a defeated old woman made no sense. Was this all that life meant?

She stood watching the playing children, the boys fighting mock battles with sticks while the girls cheered for their heroes. Her decision became clearer.

Divorce had never been a choice, not without family to support her. Einar would take her in, but with the Frankish border he would be pressed to his limit. While she could lean on him, she had to bring value to Einar's table. She also had to be certain Konal would not do something rash when confronted with her demands. She had never feared him to kill her, but his violence came easily these days.

A divorce would shame him, though it was her right if she chose it. Handled wrong, it could end in blood. The thought chilled her.

With Hakon now turned seventeen he was a man capable of accepting his inheritance. The jewels she had secreted all these years should pass to him, in part to aid his future and to support her after leaving Konal. Aren remained the problem, for he was not yet a man at age fifteen though some could argue it so. To get him from under Konal's control would be no easy thing. The law was clear enough that the father claimed the children. Yet if she could arrange to have him away when the time came, Aren might have a chance to avoid returning. Despite being his blood father, Aren did not love Konal and suffered under his demands for obedience in all matters.

No matter what happened, divorce was not a common thing for men of station. Common folk exercised their rights with less care for their reputations and standing. Though she knew another year living under Konal's unpredictable moods was not an option, humiliating him brought risks to not only herself but to her children. Even Einar would be caught in the backlash. She wondered if the guilt he felt for Ulfrik's death would be enough for him to endure a bad relationship with Konal.

The children's battle was ending, little bodies falling over in exaggerated death throes or little men dancing in victory. She smiled at them as she considered her next step. Einar would have to help her. Hakon fostered with him, learning the ways of leadership and battle. A visit to her son would be a good excuse to talk to Einar and determine where he stood.

The children scampered off and the wind gusted again, the scent of rain in the air. Like the children at play, Runa hoped to just disappear.

9

Runa had spent her day lost in idle thought, doing nothing more than wandering the confines of the hold. Women traded news and gossip freely with her, some staring intently at her bruised face while others strained to ignore it. Runa found their reactions interesting if pointless distractions from what bothered her. As the day closed she had to return to the hall and at least oversee the evening meal. She had avoided it all day, no doubt doubling the weaving that Groa and the other women would have to do without her. Now that people tottered off to their homes and hearth light shined from open doors, she had to return to Konal.

The clouds had broken up, never delivering the promised rain, and a balmy wind pushed her along the path as if shooing her home. Two men in dark cloaks and face-plated helmets waited at the hall doors, more attentive than usual. In fact, Runa paused at the way the two stared at her. She could see the whites of one man's eyes.

"I assure you it's me," she said with a small laugh. "Is something wrong?"

The two exchanged glances and Runa felt her stomach tighten at it. Her first thought was something had happened to Aren on his trip to Einar's hold, but then realized he had already been gone a week and ill news would have reached her already. Shaking her head to chase away the doubts, she proceeded up the path and between the guards. They let her pass, but as she entered they stopped another man approaching behind her and told him the hall was closed.

Inside the front room, she removed her cloak and hung it on a peg. The doors to the main hall hung open and a fire crackled in the hearth. The cooking pot not on its trestle, and no servants were preparing the evening meal. Looking to either side of the door, the benches and tables were still against the walls, and no one was present.

"I've been waiting for you. Come inside." Konal's voice was strained and thin as he tried to force it across the short hall. He sat at the high table, rigid and with both hands folded before him. He wore a clean red cloak, one Runa had not seen him wear before, and his clothes were fresh as opposed to his habit of wearing the same things for days on end.

"What's going on? Where is everyone? The evening meal?"

"I'm not hungry. I sent everyone away. You and I have some things to discuss. Come here."

Runa had known Konal for many years, and even with the changes age and alcohol had wrought upon him she had never seen a mood like this. He did not move as she approached, but yet seemed on the verge of an explosion. His terrible red and white scars stood out on his face and neck against the dancing hearth light, but more striking were his pale eyes sparking like flint. They never wavered from hers as she came to the table before him. He nodded toward the bench, and she sat as if she were lowering herself onto a trap.

"What is this, Konal? Are you trying to frighten me?"

"Why would time alone with me frighten you?"

"You almost knocked out my teeth when we were alone this morning. Maybe you want to finish the job." Runa put more bravado into her statement than she felt. He did not respond, but kept a serene yet arrogant smile like one of those Christian saints in a church tapestry.

"I did some thinking about this morning. Believe it or not, I do think about how we have come to be at each other's necks. I like it even less than you, and for all your self-pity you cannot see that I have made sacrifices for your benefit that you never recognize."

Runa turned aside and leaned away from the table. "This again? Yes, you ran to my side the moment Ulfrik was buried and yes you saved me the cruelty of widowhood. But I'd rather be a lonely widow than a married woman with a broken jaw."

Konal closed his eyes and inhaled, then slowly let out his breath. "This is not the discussion I want to have."

"Maybe it's what I want to discuss? Look at my face. The man I married would not have done this to me, but now this new Konal is all too ready to strike me for the slightest insult to his honor. I dared to look at a keepsake from my dead husband and that deserved violence? What if I should speak of him? Maybe you'd cut out my tongue?"

Runa watched the flush flow around Konal's scar tissue but he held the same arrogant smile, even if his nostrils flared to betray his anger. She knew he was on the brink of another outburst. However, were he to hit her again then she would have every ground for declaring divorce immediately. The hall might be empty, but people would be crowded outside to know what happened within it. She could make a case for public humiliation, and then Konal would have to consent to a divorce.

"As I said, I considered this morning. That sword bothered me, and not just for what it means to you. I know you wanted to believe Ulfrik lived even after seeing his head and hearing Einar's account of his death. When my brother, Kell, died I went through the same thing, but I moved beyond it as I thought you had. But this morning I was reminded that you still carry his memory."

"Is that so wrong? He was my husband for almost twenty years and the best man I ever knew."

She noticed Konal's hands were clamped tight on the table, and that they trembled. It was as if he were harboring a mouse beneath them that he feared to crush.

"I used to think he was the best man I ever knew, too. Until this morning."

They stared at each other, and his haughty smile shrank away. "Why this morning?"

"Because while you were gone I went back to our bed to clear away that rusted sword. While I was there, I thought of what else you might be hiding in that chest beneath the bed. The one you were so eager to keep me from seeing that you even goaded me into striking you. I took it to the blacksmith to break the lock and wasn't I surprised at what I found?"

"W-- What did you find?" Runa's eyes shifted to the red cloak draping Konal's shoulders. Her heart pounded against her ribs.

"Well, you're looking at it. A fine red cloak. I was disappointed there was nothing more. So I took it back to our bed and replaced it. But here's where Fate guided my hands. I think you know what I found next."

Runa wavered on her bench, a wave of weakness crashing over her. "There was nothing else to find."

"But there was more. As I folded the cloak I discovered something hard in its hem. I cut the edges of it and here's what tumbled out."

He lifted his cupped hands off the table and a pile of glittering, winking jewels sparked reflections under Konal's chin. She had not seen the gems since she and Ulfrik replaced them into the hem of a new cloak, and the memory of their brilliance paled beside reality. Even under these conditions they were breath-taking reds, blues, yellows, greens, and a few stones like clear ice. These were the gemstones prized off golden cross given from the King of Frankia as a gift to the King of England.

"At first I could not believe these were the same gems my brother and I had searched half the world to retrieve. After all, my dearest friend Ulfrik had told me himself that though Fate had delivered him the Bishop who possessed these treasures, he did not ever see them himself. These gems were to have been lost to time. But how does one forget such a pile of jewels? I have never seen the like since, and just like family I know my own when I see it. Dearest Ulfrik stole my treasure and lied to me and my brother about it. He let my brother go to his grave believing he had lost a king's fortune."

"You did lose it and Ulfrik found it. There is no law that he return it to you, not when you stole it to begin with."

His fist slammed the table and the stones leaped and jingled along with Runa who recoiled in shock. Her reflex was to still reach for the knife she had not carried in years.

"And you concealed it from me! Beneath my bed? I bet you had a fine laugh every morning, knowing the treasure I had spent half of my life seeking was hidden under my ass. Did you laugh well, dear wife?"

"No, it was not that. I held it for the future, for when we might need it."

"It's not for you to decide when I need it. This belongs to me and when I married you all that you possessed became part of my belongings. You knew that when you accepted my invitation to marriage. But you hid this ugly secret. Did you think I would rejoice one day when you finally decided to tell me? We're already lacking funds to outfit my men and fulfill my duties to Hrolf and Einar. Would we have to be hunting rats for our next meal before you parted with this secret? Or was it just another dear memory of Ulfrik?"

Runa bit her lip, knowing anything she might say could end badly for her. She had to swallow her pride and try to calm him. "I don't know when I would have shared it. I am ashamed now that you have discovered this."

She kept her eyes downcast and hands folded at her lap, all the while quivering at the potential for violence. The silence expanded, but she did not look up at him. She feared what his eyes might reveal. At last, he swept the gems into a bag and drew the string tight, then tossed them on the table. Again, she studied her lap while waiting for him to take his next move.

"What more have you hidden from me, I wonder. You've given me much to think about. For now, I will hold these gems safe from you or anyone else. I've no desire to have to split this fortune with Hrolf. But while I decide what to do, you must consider what else you need to tell me."

"There is nothing." She relented and met his gaze at last, tears welling in her eyes. She saw nothing but cold anger glaring back at her. She did not want to look at the bag of gems, but felt them pulling at her vision.

"How can I believe what you say anymore? You are to remain confined to the hall until I decide what's to be done. This sort of deceit tests the bonds of marriage."

He stood and took the bag of gems, then strode from the hall. As the doors slammed shut, Runa began to weep.

10

Ulfrik stopped the cart when Finn moaned. The track through the woods was so rutted and peppered with stones that even a slow pace could not prevent jostling. He jumped off the cart, patted the horse's neck, then went to check Finn. He lay on his back atop the meager bedding Ulfrik stole from the bandit camp. All it seemed to do was to worsen their battle against fleas, for Finn squirmed trying to itch himself against the floor of the cart.

"Don't do that," Ulfrik said as he mounted the cart. "You'll tear the stitches."

"Just kill me," Finn said, his eyes pressed shut and a slick of perspiration shining on his face. "Before the fleas do."

"Hold still, and I'll scratch your back. I've got to check your bandages anyway."

The flea bites were not as bad as Finn had made it seem, but Ulfrik dutifully scraped down his spotted back. He then unwrapped the brown stained cloth covering the spear wound. Ulfrik hissed at what he saw.

"When will it stop hurting? I feel like my side is on fire."

"I've got more ale here. If you can sit up and drink, it'll take the edge off."

He helped Finn raise his head then accept the ale skin. The cart had provisions for a few days for them and the horse, as well as a half cask of ale, all stolen from the bandit camp. The cart and horse were the same used to transport Ulfrik and Finn when they were first robbed. The women of the camp proved combative and he had to threaten them with death just to claim this meager haul. However, Gils daughter, frightened for her betrayal, had tried to make amends by carrying away additional supplies. She had even helped restrain Finn while Ulfrik stitched the wound. He repaid her with safe passage back home, but he did not dare risk Gils' hospitality again. One of his hot-headed sons would seek revenge. He half wondered if they followed him now.

"That goes down easily," Finn said, then wiped his thin beard with the back of his arm.

"Turn over so I can clean this." The wound was not deep, but the spear cut had torn and left a ragged rip that circled around to Finn's stomach. That had been a nightmare to stitch and he had done butcher's work at best. Finn would carry terrible scar.

Pouring the ale onto the wound, he patted it clean with a swatch of fresh cloth. Finn screamed as if branded, and Ulfrik stopped. "Why not call every wolf and thief in the forest to us? It's not like we can't handle them, after all."

"Gods, but that burns!"

"I never knew you for a weakling. Now keep quiet while I finish."

"I never had my back cut open then sewn shut."

Ulfrik worked in quiet anger. This was his fault for risking all for little gain. Had he risked his sole friend in all the circle of the world for cold metal? A sword and a chain of gold, no matter how fine, were no replacements for loyalty and friendship. He cursed his pride and the price Finn had paid for it. Worse still, Ulfrik suspected he had even hoped to impress Finn with this daring plan. He should have accepted his loss and counted his luck for not being murdered, then moved on. Yet he had to show off a clever plan. He shook his head in disgust.

Finn winced as Ulfrik worked, but otherwise held himself to low moans and grunts. When finished, Ulfrik pulled Finn's blanket over his naked skin then patted his back. Finn gingerly flipped to his uninjured side.

"Where are we going?"

Ulfrik stared at him, not having a clear answer himself. He had only thought to put distance between them and Gils farm. "Somewhere to get you help."

"I need help?"

"You have a fever. The wound is hot and red. It's beyond my skills to care for you. So, yes, you need a healer's attention."

Finn's usual smile fell and he swallowed. "I thought the weather was warm."

Ulfrik shook his head, then shifted on the cart to dangle his feet off the edge. The horse snorted and began to wander toward the track edge to poke its nose into the vegetation. The cart bumped and stopped as the horse settled into a place.

"There is no one in this land we can trust to deal honestly with us. Gils farm just showed us what simple trust earns a man."

"Should we seek your family? Certainly they can be trusted." Finn winced, then returned to resting on his stomach. Ulfrik looked from him and stared down the path they had left behind. The sun broke through branches to speckle the dirt track with brilliant yellow light.

"I don't know what condition my family is in. I'm not even sure where they are. I don't have time to search for them, not with you burning up."

"It's not so bad," Finn said, his voice filled with optimism. "I can hold on."

"Not so bad today. Tomorrow, it will be worse. The day after you won't know your own name. Then you'll die. We don't have time."

Finn did not answer, and Ulfrik sighed and leaned on his knees. The words had been harsh, but Finn needed to know how desperate their situation had become. Choices were slim, and there was only one Ulfrik knew he could make with certainty.

"We have a horse and I know these lands, which is better than we otherwise could have been. I don't know what the old nag can take, but I'll drive her into the dirt to get you help in time. I'll take you to Hrolf the Strider's hall. By horse it's two days away at most."

"But you said you didn't want to meet Hrolf without men at your back. What will happen if you go alone, with me not knowing my own name by that time?"

"I find out if Throst spoke the truth about Hrolf. He'll either kill me and you, or I'll appeal to our old bonds and get aid for you. He will help, if he is true."

"I thought you believed Throst? I don't want to get us both killed. There has to be a village on the way with decent people."

"How welcoming was your family of unannounced strangers, especially ones carrying weapons and wounded? Think on it. The world is fraught with dangers enough, so why invite more into your home?"

"Well, Christian priests?"

"They're not for our kind. Forget that. We are bound for Hrolf. He will help and I know where he is. Don't worry any more for it, and save your strength."

Ulfrik slid off the cart and pulled the horse back onto the track. He restarted their drive toward Hrolf, one that he had been making from the beginning. He had hoped his return from death would not place him into the same bonds he had before. But he had something greater to care for than his own worries.

He had Finn's life in the balance of his choices, and he was determined to choose correctly no matter what it meant for his own future.

11

Count Amand sank into the pillows of his elegantly carved chair, one of the few comforts that helped him endure these endless councils with subordinates. Would that he had sons to pass on the onerous duties of his role, he could spend more time enjoying the company of fine women at the courts in Paris. Yet God had set this cross for him to bear, and so he soldiered on no matter the cost to his pleasure. One day the King would recognize his considerable talent was wasted on guarding borders and recall him. For now, he smoothed his blue robe and adjusted the gold cross at this neck. Unlike other men of his age, he had kept a full head of hair which he let fall in curls to his shoulders. He was especially proud of his long and swooping mustache, and he stroked it as he awaited the start of this audience.

His Captain-At-Arms entered the chamber, drawing the attention of the servants flanking both sides of the room. He looked less imposing in his normal clothing than he did when adorned in mail and helmet, but that was the case for most men. His sword danced at his hip as he clomped across the wooden floor, foot falls reverberating against the stone walls, then knelt before Count Amand.

"My lord, the prisoners are all accounted for, but the one we discussed has been prepared for your review."

Amand reached out for a cup and a dutiful servant whisked a cool silver goblet into his hand. He sipped the wine, rolling its bitter notes on his tongue before swallowing. "Well, present him to me."

The captain's curly dark hair fell across his face as he lifted himself from his knee. His mustache was nearly as long as Count Amand's but not as gray. The captain beckoned men waiting outside the door, then returned to Count Amand's left side. His right side was left for his priest who would accompany the prisoner.

Entering first came two of Count Amand's guards, then came his burly Northman allies. These northern brutes and their armies had allied themselves to the Franks once they realized their kind were on the losing side. In the lead was Grimnr, a giant man of muscle and scars, with his long golden hair tied into a braid that hung to the small of his back. His eyes were small and thin but alive with keen intelligence and wit. Amand appreciated Grimnr's fierce sense of honor and his easy laugh. He moved like a wolf on the prowl, and the count did not doubt he was as dangerous as one. Behind him was his other Northman ally, Eskil. He was a head shorter than Grimnr, equally predatory but more like an owl than a wolf. His head was low to his shoulders and his clear eyes wide and alert, as if drinking in every detail. He had served Amand longer than Grimnr, but he trusted Eskil less.

Behind these two followed interpreters and at last was his priest and the Northman prisoner who was a boy no older than eight years by Amand's appraisal. At first sight he recognized the regal bearing in the child. His clear face was tipped back in defiance and his chest was puffed out, all like a miniature caricature of the Northman bravado. The priest guided him by the shoulders to stand between the two grown Northmen, but the boy pulled himself free and stood with arms folded across his chest.

Grimnr growled something in the bestial language of the Northmen, and the boy scowled at him. Amand could not conceive of a less elegant way of speaking. After a repeated command, Grimnr forced the boy to his knees. Amand gave slight smile. The boy had determination, an admirable quality though wasted on one in his position.

"I assume from the size of this captive he is a son of someone important? Don't tell me children are leading the barbarians now." Amand laughed at his own joke, his priest the only other to join him in it.

The Captain moved before Count Amand, bowing before he spoke. "Lord, our patrol overtook a traveling party of thirty Northmen yesterday. I will spare my Lord the details of the encounter, but we overcame the barbarians and captured this boy. We knew he was important from the way his companions guarded him. We not only captured him, but a chest of gold as well."

"Indeed God is good to us," Amand said. "So who is our young captive?"

Eskil shared a glance with Grimnr then stepped forward, bowing his head just enough to satisfy protocol. Amand stifled a sigh; these Northman can never be civilized only trained to not bite the hand that feeds them.

"He is Halfdan, son of Mord Guntherson," Eskil said.

Count Amand sat up straighter. "You mean Hrolf the Strider's second?"

"Mord's father is Gunther One-Eye, who is Hrolf's second. But Mord is as close to Hrolf as any man can be." Eskil looked at Grimnr, who shrugged.

"I don't know these men," Grimnr said. "I joined with you, Count Amand, not my countrymen."

The Captain stepped in front of the others again. "It was Mord's men we killed, Lord. I imagine they were returning with collected taxes or tribute, and for whatever reason his son was among them. The boy has refused to give us any details, though I can encourage that if you wish."

Amand waved away his captain's hint of torture and regarded the boy. He appeared to understand, but feigned indifference. Such a hostage was useful leverage. Maybe he could turn Mord on Hrolf, or at least convince him to stay at home when Count Amand's armies went to battle. God had put an important pawn into his hands, and he had to consider carefully what moves the piece could make for him.

"Yes, God is good," Amand said, more to himself than anyone else.

"Send word to Mord that we have his son and inform him Halfdan will be well cared for while I determine how to proceed. He has my word upon it. Of course, should Mord attempt any violence against us warn him I will rescind my word."

"Right away, my Lord." The Captain bowed with a flourish.

The boy, Halfdan, squinted at Amand as if daring him to do his worst.

"You have a strong spirit," the Count said with a smile. "Learn to hide it better or you will discover how easily it can be broken. You are not too young for that lesson, and I will be glad to teach it."

Halfdan's thin lips trembled, and Count Amand laughed.

12

As Ulfrik had expected, Finn was no longer coherent. His speech had been reduced to a rubble of grunts and moans, mostly elicited whenever the cart crossed a rut or hump which now felt like every foot of the miles they had covered. The gray sky sprinkled light rain on them as Ulfrik pulled up to Hrolf's town, known as XXXX. Seeing its high stockade walls atop a steep slope of earth returned a dozen memories to Ulfrik, some happy and others less so. He prayed for a happy day as he drove his cart toward the east gate.

"We're almost there," Ulfrik said over his shoulder to Finn. "Just hang on."

Finn answered him with parts of rowing song, then mumbled speech. Ulfrik shook his head and squinted at the shapes of men guarding the entrance. His horse had dutifully trudged the miles and never balked at putting in extra hours at dawn and or at day's end. Yet now it stopped short and neighed.

"What's the matter? Never seen a fortress before?" Ulfrik used his riding switch to tap its hindquarters. "Go on, and there will be better eating for you inside. Imagine a nice stable with golden hay. Go on, boy."

Ulfrik had never been good with animals. He had raised a hound once when one had been given as a gift, but the dog ran off in its first year. His face grew hot as he continued to goad the horse, until finally a strong whip got it moving again. He muttered to himself, and tried not to believe this was a bad sign. The cart lurched and rocked, this approach being heavily rutted from frequent use. However, no one else was on the trail today and the two guards flanking the gates leaned on their spears like bored children.

He had considered his approach to meeting Hrolf, from boldly announcing himself to approaching an intermediary like Gunther One-Eye. A bold announcement might end up in disbelief in his rise from death and approaching old friends would waste time. In the end, he chose to present himself directly to Hrolf and appeal for help. Finn did not have much time before his fever and infection ended in death.

The guards did not shift positions as he approached the gate, though two more interested men appeared atop the walls. The gates remained closed, which given the well-trodden path was unusual. He had passed a small village on the way in, all Northmen but none skilled in the kind of medicine Finn required. They claimed XXXX was an open fortress though recent desertions had made everyone cautious of strangers. They were not eager to for Ulfrik to stay and watched them leave with obvious relief.

Stopping before the guards, he looked at the two who continued to lean on their spears. A snigger echoed down from the men on the walls, and Ulfrik sighed.

"I seek aid from Hrolf the Strider," Ulfrik said. I wish passage through the gates. My friend is in grave need of medical aid."

The two guards exchanged sly looks and again more chuckles trickled down the walls. Ulfrik squinted up at the shadowed forms leaving over the palisade. At last one of the guards, a copper-bearded man with a fat mole on his cheek, straightened up and addressed him.

"The gates are closed. Franks are active. Go away."

Ulfrik rubbed the back of his neck and grimaced. "Then the village behind me should be empty, but they're fine. Please, let me pass."

"Hey stupid," said the other guard. "Thanks for the report but I think you just heard these gates are closed. Don't like the reason, go fuck yourself."

He glared at the guard, listening to the two men on the walls laugh. His throat constricted and he swallowed. "Hrolf has fallen on desperate times."

"What does that mean?" Mole-face said. "Gate's closed. Understand?"

Hands trembling, Ulfrik did not meet anyone's eyes but just watched his horse swish his tail and flick its ears. He had expected a return to Frankia to be difficult, and two men journeying alone to be dangerous. He had not expected to be humiliated by gate guards at the entrance to the very hall where he was once lauded as a hero.

"I understand what you want," he said at last. He reached into a pouch at his side and grabbed Finn's gold chain. Sorry Finn, he thought, but I need to use a bit of this to help you. I promise to get you a better chain to replace this. Then he pulled links of the chain and held these out on his palm. "You need this to open the gates."

The two guards shared a smile and Mole-face snatched it out of Ulfrik's hands. "That's a start. How about what else is in that sack?"

"You want all my gold to enter?" Ulfrik knew they were not letting him through the gate. To do so would risk Ulfrik's exposing their extortion to Hrolf. "The price is too high. I will travel elsewhere for help."

He picked up his switch to begin guiding his horse, but Mole-face grabbed it by the bridle. "You're not leaving until we get the rest of that gold."

Reaching for his sword, he froze when he heard a heavy thud behind him. He whirled to see an arrow next to Finn's prostrate body.

"Hand over the bag," called a guard from the wall and keep that sword sheathed. You may get away alive if you do."

Ulfrik stood facing Mole-Face and his smirking companion. "You are all a disgrace to the noble jarl you serve. Hrolf is a generous lord, and yet you steal from his people. You are scum."

"We're practical," said Mole-Face. "And you're a fucking stranger with a dying man in his wagon. You're probably one of the traitors gone over to bandits or the Franks and things went bad for you. So now you come crawling back here and expect to be welcomed? Surrender the gold and don't let me see you here again, or we'll fill your wagon with arrows."

Ulfrik threw the bag far to the side, hearing the gold clink in the grass. "If my friend dies because of you, I will cut out your hearts and feed them to pigs. Count on it."

"Be gone, old man," Mole-Face shoved his horse and it began side-stepping.

Trundling away with the derisive laughter fading behind him, Ulfrik brooded on his next steps. Finn began to moan and in a moment of clarity called out.

"Are we almost at Hrolf's? I...I'm on fire. I can't think. Hurry, please."

He closed his eyes and furrowed his brow. "Yes, we're almost inside. Just hold a little while longer."

13

Runa sat beside the loom, a basket of yellow thread on her lap. Groa worked next to her, feeding thread into the weight stones that she handed off to a young girl working the loom. Runa continued to stare into her lap, her mind not focused on anything. She felt Groa's glances as she worked, seeing from the corner of her eye gnarled hands moving up and down. The young girl mumbled something, but Runa did not answer.

Days had passed since Konal had discovered her gems and she still burned with anger and humiliation. She detested her foolishness for not giving the gems over to Hakon, who was now old enough to possess an inheritance. Now he might never possess the wealth his father had left for him. She shook her head and fished out a thread to begin creating embroideries for the cloth her women wove. She had done this all her life, and the movements were automatic. Her mind continued to spin in its own loathsome thoughts.

Konal emerged from their bedroom. She heard him yawning. It was midmorning and the shame of his late rising did not affect his mood. His raspy voice filled the hall. "Good morning! Seems another fine summer's day is underway."

Runa put her head down and continued to work, but the girl at the loom stopped to attended to Konal. "There is still food in the pot. I will heat it for you."

Groa continued to look at Runa, but she acted as if Konal had not spoken. Since his threat, he had behaved no differently than any other day, but she knew underneath his anger was hot. At night, he no longer reached for her, nor did he seek her company. They occupied the same bed as strangers.

"Runa, come sit with me while I eat."

"I'm not hungry."

She heard the bench drag along the floor, then silence. Groa stared at her, and finally Runa relented. Setting aside her thread and embroidery she took the seat Konal offered. The girl produced another bowl for her, and returned to heating the soup.

"There's much work to be done yet. A whole day of spinning wool lies ahead, and I don't have time to idle at the table."

Konal shrugged and asked, "When is Aren to return home? He has been gone overlong and I expect him to be by my side."

"Perhaps in another week."

"And Hakon?"

"Einar is fostering him, and decides when or if he may travel. Why do you care?"

"You don't need to know."

"They're my sons, of course I should know." Runa twisted on the bench, meeting his eyes for the first time in days. "Are you planning something special? You've never cared where either of them are."

" A lie," he said. The servant girl ladled hot soup into their bowls then slipped away like a doe fleeing the signs of a forest fire. Runa watched her and Groa gather their baskets and retreat from the hall. Konal snorted at their leaving. "Worrisome gossips, those two."

They ate in silence, the hall empty but for one of Konal's men seated with his head down at the far end of the hall. Too much salt had accumulated at the bottom of the bowl and Runa wrinkled her nose at the taste of it. Konal picked his up and drained it, then slammed it on that table.

"I've still not decided what to do. But I want Aren here at least before I make final choices."

Runa nodded and watched flecks of cabbage swirl in the last of her soup.

"I will be away for a few days." He stood and stretched again. "Try not to miss me."

"Where do you go?"

"A short patrol of the countryside. I don't expect trouble, but men will remain behind with you. I'll be leaving before sunset today."

She watched him stalk off to their bedroom to prepare. The hall was empty but for the one sleeping guard. She slumped at her bench and considered the opening this left for her. As far as she could determine Konal carried his newly discovered gems on himself at all times. Yet he would never risk bringing these into the field, which meant he would hide them before leaving. This was going to be her final chance to do anything before he decided upon whatever he intended to do about her so-called betrayal. Unless she took advantage of this, she would be at his mercy -- a quality in dwindling supply of late. Furthermore, his desire to have her sons with him on the day of his decision made Runa's throat constrict. A dozen terrible thoughts filled her imagination, and she shook her head to clear them.

She had to steal back her jewels and intercept Aren before his return. Together they would seek shelter with Einar, who also knew the history of these gems and what they had meant to Ulfrik. He would protect her out of a sense of duty and was the only person she trusted to not be tempted by the fortune she would be carrying.

Otherwise, to fail would bring disaster to not only herself but her children as well. She collected the bowls from the table and dropped them into a bucket as she left the hall. She had to find help to ensure she did not fail.

14

Ulfrik threw the last branch across the wagon, then stepped back to judge his success. At nine paces back he paused and folded his arms, satisfied the wagon melted into the underbrush off the side of the track. The late afternoon shadows cloaked it and overnight it would be invisible to human eyes. Wolves and bears would not roam so close to settlements, at least not in summer, yet the possibility existed. He had no answer for that problem. Too many other difficulties already pressed him from every side.

He returned to the cart and pulled off the branch he had just placed. Finn remained stripped to the waist, glistening with sweat, and resting on his stomach in the back of the cart. The bandages around his trunk showed brown spotting even though he had just changed them. The infection had been a violent red and even to brush the flesh made Finn moan. Ulfrik feared a critical line had been crossed and Finn could no longer be saved.

"I'll only be gone this night, and by tomorrow morning you'll be in Hrolf the Strider's hall or I'll be dead." Ulfrik patted Finn's calf. "In that case, we'll meet in the feasting hall where all heroes await Ragnarok."

"Who's Ragnar?" Finn's fever had rendered him senseless most of the time, though at least he still understood the gist of his condition which Ulfrik took for a positive sign.

"All the water and ale is an arm's reach away. Just sleep tonight." Ulfrik placed his sword next to Finn's side. "If you think you're dying, hold this when you do. You're a brave man, Finn the Red."

Ulfrik was surprised that Finn chuckled at his joke. His fever had turned his freckled face scarlet and Ulfrik had been calling him Red for a several days with no reaction. For a brief moment, he seemed to be his old self again.

"I'll be fine. Go on and be a hero," Finn said, stirring one arm dismissively. "Gods know I need one."

Ulfrik pulled himself up on the horse, inelegantly sliding over its back and nearly falling from it. The horse was a patient beast, and though he snorted and stepped he also calmed as Ulfrik patted his neck. Then he wound his hands into its mane and started for Hrolf's town. Approaching from the south gate this time, he wore his cloak with the hood drawn. As he hoped, other travelers were also headed for the gate. No one wanted to camp outside overnight, not if they had anything of value in their possession. With the sun low in west, only a few hours remained.

The guards here were less brutish and more akin to the professionals Ulfrik remembered. They questioned each person, searched their bags and took their weapons before allowing access for a small fee. On Ulfrik's turn, he kept his head down and allowed them to search his few packs and then held his cloak aside to reveal he had no weapons hidden. He pressed a silver coin into the guard's hand and he was waved through.

"How much easier was that?" he muttered to himself. "I'll have those four by their balls soon enough."

In truth, his current profile as an unarmed traveler was far less threatening than two armed men and a wagon. Desperation had caused him to forget that he might not appear as innocent to everyone as he actually was. A gray haired man on horseback was nothing to fear and so he passed beneath the gate without issue and emerged into the familiar roads of Hrolf's estate.

The horse knew to follow the road, which snaked uphill to Hrolf's magnificent hall. Now that he was inside, the issue of presenting himself to Hrolf was a new challenge. Despite the long, dull years he had to plan this moment, now that he was within reach of it he found all his plans lacking. Announcing himself outright might result in a challenge to his claims without ever seeing Hrolf. Who would believe a long-dead man returned to life? To sneak upon him could appear as if he were an enemy spy, which would be an even more disastrous outcome.

People hurried about in the last light of the day. Mothers stood in doorways calling their children home. Others rushed about their business, eager to arrive wherever they when. Ulfrik located a stables where the stable master accepted a handful of silver bits to care for the horse. Ulfrik took his pack while the stable master had his son take the horse. They exchanged pleasantries and Ulfrik shared news from the border. "Could I share a stall with my horse tonight?" Ulfrik asked.

The man thought about it. "Just this night, then be on your way in the morning."

Business concluded, the man and son left. An orange line now filled the western horizon and Ulfrik had only a half hour's worth of light to use. He tipped his pack over to reveal the few items he had taken with him for tonight's mission: an filthy cloak, old rune sticks from the bandits, and the same blindfold he had used to deceive Throst. A broken rake leaned against the wall, and Ulfrik snapped away the rake to use the handle as his walking stick. He only needed to hide his identity long enough to earn an audience with Hrolf. He gathered these together and made for the hall while enough light still allowed for travel on the paths. .

The grand hall sat atop a large hill and any hiding place had been cleared from it, save a large oak tree that towered over it like a protective hand. Ulfrik waited a safe distance behind a cooper's workshop, studying the men filing in for their evening meal. Hrolf would be inside with his family along with his trusted men like Gunther One-Eye. After all had passed inside, the guards surrounding the hall lit torches and settled in for their watches. Inside the faint sounds of song and laughter reached his ears. Ulfrik tied his blindfold, pulled up his hood, and took his stick, then stepped out toward the hall.

As expected the guards challenged him as he approached the doors. He could see out the bottom of his blindfold, and two feet in leather boots came into view.

"Hold, old man," said the closest guard. "You can't come this close to the hall."

"So this is the hall?" Ulfrik said, straining his voice to add age to it. "Then my visions have guided me correctly."

He heard the closest guard sigh, then he grabbed the walking stick. "You are blind? Then let me help your visions. Turn back and keep walking until you crash into the walls. Come morning someone will see you out the gates."

"No," Ulfrik protested. "The gods were clear, I have a message for a man inside this hall. His name is Balki Hard-Fighter."

Both guards grew quiet, and Ulfrik fought his smile as he waited for their response. At last the other guard stepped forward. "What do you want with Balki?"

"I don't know," Ulfrik said, turning up his free palm as if completely innocent. "The gods put that name into my head and said I should read him my rune sticks. When the gods make such commandments, I cannot disobey. I have to meet him."

Again more silence, but the other guard released his walking stick. "Well, I'm Balki. So what do you want to say to me?"

Iron scrapped as both guards loosened their swords. Ulfrik held up his hands. "Peace. Let me throw these runes and I will tell you what I see. That is all I want."

"You're not looking for silver, old man? I'm not paying for anything," Balki said.

Ulfrik shook his head and tossed his sticks. Feigning blindness he had to touch the layout carefully, noting the positions of the sticks, then he stroked the carved runes to "read" them. He made faces and sucked his breath at points, and he felt Balki and his companion draw closer. At last he struggled to his feet, and now both men assisted him. "This is a strange message. You have three daughters but no sons." He heard Balki inhale with surprise. He did not remember much about Balki other than he was a renowned fighter and had three girls as beautiful as they were clever. "Your youngest daughter -- is she eleven?"

"Thirteen. What of her?"

"I believe there is a boy that she keeps secret from you. She does not want to wed the man you've arranged for her, and tonight she and her secret boy, well, I'm not sure what they plan, but you need to stop it before it goes too far."

"By the gods," Balki said. "She's been a difficult girl these days. I just knew something like this was going on under my own nose. What else do you see?"

"That is all. I've come to say what the gods wanted you to know. I'm going back to the stables now. I'm much relieved."

Ulfrik turned to go, but the hand he expected grabbed his staff again. "Wait. If it's as you say, I need to go home right now. I'd like you to stay near, though. There is plenty to eat and drink inside, and Hrolf is a generous man. If you'll surrender your walking stick you can enter and enjoy a hot meal."

"That seems like too much trouble for you," Ulfrik said. "Besides, I'm a poor grub beside great men. I'd shame the jarl's hall."

"You'll be seated by the door. No one will notice you. Besides, I insist. Thorir here will see you inside while I go."

"If you insist, then I will comply." Ulfrik bowed and Throrir removed his walking stick, checked him for weapons, then guided him inside.

Scents of savory meats and smoke assailed him, along with a blast of warmth and raucous conversations. He acted intimidated, but Thorir just pulled him along to a table.

"What's your name, old man?" Thorir asked.

"Ulfar the White."

Thorir introduced him to his table mates, helped him to a seat, then returned outside. The men around him had only a few polite questions to ask, but soon were absorbed in their own conversations. Ulfrik sat patiently, hearing Hrolf's familiar laughter booming at the far end of the hall. He ate a stew of onions, spices and lamb, then washed it down with the smoothest ale he had tasted in years. By now Balki would be returning to reveal Ulfrik's lie, so he had to act fast.

He stood up and made as if he were going to the corner to urinate. His companions waved him off, not even realizing he was supposedly blind. Two other men were relieving themselves against the wall, and Ulfrik fit in between them. Using their bulk as cover, he removed his blindfold. As they moved off, he removed his gray outer cloak and revealed a second, cleaner one beneath. He pulled his hair back into a ponytail and tied it quickly with a bit of string. The men at their meals did not pay much attention, and those who noticed him assumed he belonged in the hall and their eyes slid past him.

Now he was a new man, and even if Balki returned he would not find a blind man in a gray cloak. He worked slowly toward Hrolf, leaning into the drunkest of conversations to laugh and joke with these men, who either were too drunk to notice him or simply shrugged him off. The high table was filled with familiar faces: the giant Gunther One-Eye sat at his right and a dozen other hirdmen surrounded him. His Frankish wife, Poppa, was like a lily wilting at his left hand and she ate with precision and delicacy. Her eyes were averted from all, but Hrolf often leaned to speak to her and her face brightened.

From the last table length he walked purposefully toward Hrolf. The men here were more alert, better trained, and were veterans. They noted Ulfrik's stride and his focus, and these men rose to intercept him. Ulfrik did not want violence. Only Hrolf's attention.

"Who the fuck are you?" The first man to stand in his way was not tall but broad-shouldered and packed with muscle. He butted right up against Ulfrik, and others closed down on him.

"Stand aside, Torfi," Ulfrik said. The man's heavy brows rose at the use of his name. "I've got business with Hrolf."

Now more men crowded him, and rough hands grabbed his sword arm. Ulfrik did not resist, but stared past all of them at Hrolf who was draining a silver-rimmed mug. When he finished he noticed the knot of men forming below his table and he leaned forward with a frown.

"What's going on there?"

The broad man, Torfi, faced Hrolf. "A stranger got in the hall and says he has business with you. He doesn't seem armed."

Hrolf and the rest of his table looked down. Gunther One-Eye stood, the scar tissue in his left eye twisting like a worm, and prepared to draw his sword.

"Do you recognize me, Hrolf?" Ulfrik's voice was clear and commanding, no longer the feigned voice of an old man. "It has been many years, but I've returned."

The front of the hall went still and silent while Hrolf studied him. Then his face turned white and his eyes widened. He shot to his feet and pointed.

"Seize him! Don't let him escape!"

Before he could say another word Ulfrik was face down on the floor with a boot on the back of his head and a sword-point between his shoulder-blades.

15

All Ulfrik could see were dozens of feet crowding him, and all he could hear was shouting. His arms were forced behind his back while the boot on his head drove his face into the hard-packed dirt of the floor. Straw pushed into his eyes and the scent of the ground filled his nose. Hands on his shoulders hauled him up, and another man pulled his head straight by yanking on his ponytail.

Hirdmen were rushing Hrolf's wife, Poppa, and his daughter to safety and both he and Gunther had drawn their swords. No others were allowed weapons but for Hrolf and his personal guard, but it was enough that the entire high table was brandishing sharpened iron. Hrolf stood a head taller than Gunther, and both were intimidating enough that Ulfrik doubted any single man could challenge them both. They stared down at him, Gunther's brow deeply furrowed in confusion but Hrolf's tight with revulsion. He bared his teeth then shoved the table aside.

"Bring that man to me." He held his sword low with both hands on the grip. In one strong flick he could cut Ulfrik's guts out.

Torfi cleared a path through the men while the one holding Ulfrik's arms shoved him forward. He stumbled up the high stage, but his captor held him up. Now he stood before Hrolf, and he smiled.

"Either you don't recognize me or Throst lied and you really did arrange to kill me." Ulfrik met Hrolf's clear, blue eyes and did not waver from them. He saw Gunther One-Eye lower his sword and stagger back. Hrolf's reaction was not as dramatic.

"You look and sound very much like a warrior I once held above many," he said, his sword now wavering. "But his men carried home his head and we buried it years ago. Whatever sorcery this is, you cannot be him."

"I am Ulfrik Ormsson. I did not die, but was taken against my will. I have spent all these years seeking to return to your side. Gunther has but one eye, yet he knows me." Ulfrik turned to Gunther, who stood with his hand on his chest and mouth open. He nodded to Ulfrik.

Hrolf lowered his sword. "How is this possible? Einar himself claimed to have witnessed your death."

"There is a long story to tell, and it will come in time. But first, I claim your hospitality. Please."

Shaking his head as if awakening from a dream, he waved at his men. "Release him. He....he is a friend. By the gods, is it really you?"

With the men withdrawn, Ulfrik immediately went to his knee before Hrolf. "I am Ulfrik Ormsson and I am honored to be welcomed to your hall again."

Hrolf lifted him up, and now his smile was wide and eyes nearly swimming with tears. He never knew Hrolf to be an actor, though his marriage to Poppa who was a Frankish noble woman might have taught him the skill. The emotion on his face was undoubtedly real, and not the expression of a man who would have had him murdered. Throst had been honest, and Ulfrik was both relieved and saddened to confirm it.

"What happened to you? You actually look good, if only older. By Odin's one eye, I can't believe you're standing here!" He enveloped Ulfrik in a crushing bear hug and the more sycophantic of Hrolf's men applauded. He smelled of ale and oil and the fine robes he wore were as smooth as a newborn's skin. He stepped back from Ulfrik to admire him, then presented him to Gunther, who had recovered from his shock and now stood straight again.

"Back from the dead? Now there's a trick I'll need to learn from you," said Gunther One-Eye. He also enveloped Ulfrik in a hug and slapped his back.

Ulfrik felt numb as more familiar faces greeted him, including Torfi who apologized for not recognizing him. The men cycled through and Ulfrik remembered what it felt like to be a hero and a man of standing. With Hrolf standing beside him, he felt as if again the world was within his grip. All he needed was a sword and a coat of mail, then give him an army and the enemy would fall. How he had missed this!

Yet when the greetings died down, he remembered Finn and his duty to him. All were still on their feet, but Ulfrik turned to Hrolf with his head lowered.

"I've no right to ask this of you, but I need an urgent favor."

Hrolf's easy smile vanished. He stared flatly at him, along with his closest men. Ulfrik licked his lips and pressed his request.

"I traveled with a companion, Finn Langson. His part in my story will become clear in time, but know that for now he has been gravely wounded fighting beside me. He is burning up with fever and I fear without expert aid he will die before the sun sets again. I beg you to welcome him to your hall and have him attended by your healers. He is like a son to me, and in fact I owe him a great debt. He's partly why I'm alive to stand before your this day."

When the reply was not immediate, Ulfrik raised his head to see Hrolf in thoughtful silence. Ulfrik swallowed, hoping he had not misread the situation and timed his request poorly. He silently cursed himself for being so rushed.

"Of course, I will see to your companion. I can dispatch men tonight if you will tell us where he is."

Ulfrik felt his legs weaken with relief. "Thank you. Of course, I will lead them direct to him. His need is great, or I would not have asked this of you now."

"Please stay with me while my men retrieve your friend. We know this land well enough that a description of his location is all we require." Hrolf looked to Gunther who began to select men for the job, then he gestured Ulfrik closer. "I want to know the details of your story, and there is much for me to share with you as well. But if your arrival here tonight is not the very working of the Fates then I don't know what it is. I need your help with something of tremendous importance and it requires the utmost secrecy."

"Anything, you must only say it. I am in your debt for the life of my friend."

Hrolf nodded and pulled him closer still. "This is not the place to discuss it. When the hall is cleared, I will speak with you. Also, not everyone here realizes who you are. Stay beside me, for I do not want your name and word of your return to spread. These hirdmen are close and I trust them, but the others at the far end might be less cautious."

"I go by Ulfar the White when I wish to remain unknown," Ulfrik said, and Hrolf nodded appreciatively. "But why must I remain secret?"

Leaning in conspiratorially, he whispered into Ulfrik's ear. "My son has been captured by the Franks. The gods have sent you to rescue him."

16

By late evening the hall had cleared, and those Hrolf did not trust with a secret were ejected to find another place to sleep off their ale. The hall echoed with the sounds of servants gathering buckets of plates and mugs and carrying them from the hall. Ulfrik sat at the high table overlooking the vast hall filled with milky smoke and bright with hearth fire. The last of the benches were pushed to the walls and several hirdmen who had drunk too much now snored on the floor where they had fallen. Hrolf's black dogs snuffed among them, ferreting out scraps of food as they searched.

Hrolf and Gunther One-Eye sat opposite him and a group of eight other men crowded around to hear Ulfrik's story. He left out no detail, recalling how Throst had awaited him atop the abandoned tower and of the ambush he had planned. Recalling his terrible fall from the tower, he held up his missing finger as evidence of that day when Throst hacked away his grip on the ledge. The rest of the tale held them spellbound, from the replacement of his body with a slave to life in Iceland and then the final battles with Audhild, Eldrid, and Gudrod.

"I lived more than a year with Finn and his mother, Gytha. It was a good and simple life, but it was not mine." Ulfrik held the amulet of

Thor's hammer that Gytha had bestowed on him the day he and Finn left. "We took a job rowing and guarding a merchant ship. Heidrek is the merchant's name, and I think you will find him a fair trader of rare goods from Iceland and the north. We idled for many months in England, and I saw what our people have built there in a place called York. It made me all the more anxious to return here."

"But you did not return to me right away," Hrolf said. "You should have come immediately."

Ulfrik shook his head, then told him of his revenge on Throst. When he described throwing Throst from the tower, Hrolf clapped in approval. Finally he told him of all his trials up to the moment when he fooled Balki into letting him in the hall. This account drew gusty laughter, not the least because Balki now sat among the other men with his face red.

"All daughters are trouble," he said. "It's too easy to scare a father to rash action."

Again more laughter around the table and Ulfrik patted Balki's shoulder.

Hrolf's mood had lightened but as the laughter ebbed he grew more solemn. "Now I should tell you what happened after your fall. It was not a good time for any of us. As I had expected, by winter after your death the Franks had attacked our borders in force. It was a mild winter, and so they harassed us until Spring when they launched full scale attacks. Of course, I was prepared on most of my borders, but not on yours. Your death left a hole I could not properly fill. In the end I sent Gunther One-Eye to restore order, but it was too late. Ravndal was surrounded and cut off. He had to break through to offer your family and men a means of retreat."

"How did that happen so fast?" Ulfrik could not imagine the fall of Ravndal, even though he saw the Frankish pennants over their walls.

"You did many good things in your time," Hrolf said, folding his arms. "But you had no plans for your own passing. When Einar returned he was too distracted with grief at your death and the murder of twenty men. He just was not capable of acting with the decisiveness needed. Your eldest son, Gunnar, flew into a rage at the news. He took your old ship, Raven's Talon, along with a crew of twenty young hotheads like himself and set out to find you. He has not returned and I fear he was lost in that effort."

Ulfrik blinked at the news and though Hrolf continued to speak he did not hear him. His chest hurt and a lump formed in his throat, he shielded his eyes fearing tears might disgrace him. However, Hrolf paused and leaned forward to place a hand on his shoulder. "I am sorry for my poor choice of words. Your son has been gone for so long, I forget that this is a fresh wound for you. He did the honorable thing, seeking vengeance for your death. If he did die in that adventure, then you will reunite with him in Valhalla. He will have died a hero."

Pausing to regain himself, Ulfrik raised his head and nodded. "It is grievous news, but there must be more for me to know. Please continue."

"My borders have shrank, as you've discovered, but the core of my lands are as strong as ever. My relationship with Poppa's family is good, though I had to at least become a Christian in name. So now don't speak to me about burning churches. Just do it and tell me you burned a very wealthy farm instead." All laughed and Ulfrik smiled, yet nothing lifted the weight of Gunnar's disappearance.

"Your wife remarried," Hrolf said suddenly. Ulfrik sat straight and swallowed, knowing this had to happen. "She grieved a year as custom dictated, but Konal Ketilsson took her in marriage. I awarded him a modest fort to guard the middle ground between the borders and us in Rouen. You man Einar, once he regained himself, has proved to be as able as you were. He has a much larger holding at the border, plugging the gaps. We are all free men, but Konal takes his direction from Einar."

A false smile trembled on Ulfrik's lips. Of course it was Konal. In light of everything, Ulfrik did not disagree with that choice. Aren was his son, after all, and Ulfrik dead to them. "My return is a complicated thing, isn't it?"

"In all my years, I've not had the dead return to claim their lands and families again. I agreed to that marriage and the division of those lands. As much as your return fills my heart with joy, I cannot take back my word."

"Of course not," Ulfrik said, dismissing the idea with a wave of his hand. "I think it best my family does not know of my return. At least for now."

Hrolf and Gunther shared a glance, then Hrolf stood. "The rest of you leave us now. I have private words for Ulfrik."

They waited in silence as the others shambled from the hall, a few stopping to rouse sleeping friends and escort them outside. When it was just Ulfrik with Hrolf and Gunther, he shifted on his bench to square off with them. "You want to discuss your son?"

"Yes, you remember my boy Vilhjalmer? He was a babe when you disappeared, but is not a hard-headed boy of eight years, though he considers himself ready to be king."

"So he takes after his father?" Ulfrik dared the joke and Hrolf paused, a flash of anger disappearing to a small chuckle.

"No one jokes with me anymore. I'd forgotten what that's like. But yes, he is royal blood to the core, though he takes after his mother's stubbornness." Hrolf rubbed his face and paused. Ulfrik used the moment to see what changes time had wrought upon Hrolf, yet he found him youthful and full of energy. His temples were gray and lines were thick on his brow and eyes, but the royal life agreed with him. He had not softened, for on his ring-laden hands fresh scars showed. For all that he was descended of a Norwegian noble he fought and bled with his men.

"He was to visit Mord Guntherson, who watches the southeastern borders for me. Well, the lad slipped away on an adventure with tribute collectors. By the time Mord had realized where he went, it was too late to recall them. It should have went well, but the Franks are active again. Their new Count Amand has been agitating action all across my front, typical of the new Frankish aggression. Anyway, they ambushed the patrol with my son. Of course they all died defending him, but in the end they captured Vilhjalmer."

"When did this happen?" Ulfrik looked to Gunther, whose one eye averted in shame. It was his son and Ulfrik's old friend Mord who had lost Hrolf's son to the enemy. The shame of it was impossible to shake.

"Merely a week ago." Hrolf leaned forward with a gleam in his eye.

"But my boy is smart. He has identified himself as Halfdan son of Mord and the Franks believe it."

"They don't know what your children look like?"

"I don't brook spies, though I am certain some have made it into my lands. In any case, all of our people look the same to these Franks. They think we're all yellow-haired, blue-eyed monsters distinguished only by our beards. Besides, I have a man on the inside of Amand's court and he will know to conceal Vilhjalmer's true name. So, for now, Count Amand thinks he has leverage on Mord and is pressuring Mord to spy on and eventually betray me."

Gunther One-Eye stood, his empty eye socket jumping with the twist of scared flesh. "My son has made a mistake and will pay for it. But he cannot act to free Vilhjalmer."

Hrolf gave a curt nod. "That will be your task. Eskil is the name of my man inside Amand's court. Our people, men who dare call themselves Northmen, have gone over to the Franks in the hundreds."

"They think we are doomed," added Gunther.

"Eskil poses as a leader of the Northmen under Count Amand. He has several others at work with him. I need you to go over to the Franks as if you were one of these traitors. Contact Eskil and he will arrange to help you deliver Vilhjalmer before his true name is revealed."

"Why not have Eskil free him?"

"It took years for Eskil to get into position and he feeds me the information I need to keep ahead of the Franks. Had you not shown up, I would have no choice but to pull him out with my son. Yet tonight the gods granted me the favor of your return. With Eskil's help, you will see my son home."

Ulfrik leaned back and stroked his beard. Hrolf was not asking him to do this, but ordering him as if his oath were still in place. Yet death should have broken those bonds, even if he had not truly been deceased. To undertake such a risk, he needed a reward beyond saving Finn's life.

"The gods do seem to have sent me in your time of need. But how can you be certain I am the right one for it?"

"You were ever good luck for me," Hrolf said, standing now. Ulfrik felt compelled to stand as well. Normally the tallest man in any group, he was dwarfed by both Hrolf and Gunther. "Look how you managed to appear within a sword's length of me in my own hall. You have shown another side that I did not know before. This is just the sort of guile needed to get close to my son and free him while leaving Eskil and his men intact."

Ulfrik pretended to consider his options. Hrolf's swagger faded and he glanced at Gunther for help.

"What do you want for it?" Gunther asked. His smile was a shade less than friendly.

"I want to be made whole. I will serve you again, Hrolf. I want my lands and men returned, my fortunes restored. Bring me back to life in truth."

Hrolf sighed and his posture relaxed. "For my son, it is a small price. I have no lands yet to give, but return Vilhjalmer to me and I swear that all that you had lost will be yours again. I cannot force your former wife, nor your children. But gold, land, and men are mine to give and I do so gladly. Do you swear to serve me as your jarl?"

Going to his knee, Ulfrik bowed his head with a smile. "My sword is yours to command. I swear on my life to deliver your son to your hearth."

Raising him up, Hrolf embraced him. "Welcome home, Ulfrik. But I fear I must send you into danger again at first light."

17

Ulfrik did not sleep well, despite the comfort and warmth of Hrolf's hall. He arose with the first crowing of roosters and stumbled outside to let the morning air refresh him. The guards at the door nodded as he walked down the path in the rose colored glow of morning. People were already about their business, moving between buildings or on the paths. Dogs barked and birds sang and the first plumes of hearth smoke fluttered out of smoke holes. Ulfrik had long missed scenes such as this, and it caused him to think of Ravndal. Realizing he would not see its hall again, he shoved the painful memory aside.

After lingering long enough to awaken, he turned back and ran into Gunther One-Eye who now stood in the door of the hall. The tall man rubbed his face, and wiped back a lock of grayed hair. "How did you sleep?" he asked.

"Not at all. Too much to think about. Has Finn been located yet?"

Gunther's single eye narrowed in confusion, but then he nodded. "Yes, your friend was well hidden but they found him. He's with a healer now, and we can visit him later. But let's walk a moment before we do."

They turned together and began to walk along the road. Despite their years of friendship, Ulfrik struggled with his words. "How is Mord holding up?"

A long sigh escaped Gunther and he seemed to shrink as they walked. "He blames himself, which he should. Now he is trapped into acting like a spy, and he is too simple-minded for that role."

"I remember him being a smart man. I'm sure he will fool this Count Amand long enough for me to get inside and rescue Vilhjalmer."

"Maybe. He is a loyal man, and I hate to see this shake his relationship with Hrolf."

"But Hrolf must understand what happened?"

"He let an eight year old boy slip him, Hrolf's only son. That's --" Gunther bit off his thoughts, and Ulfrik did not prod him. He understood exactly what Gunther feared, and he touched his Thor amulet for his old friend, Mord. They walked to a pen where pigs clustered around a feed bucket. They both leaned on the fence and watched the animals snort and shove their faces into the bucket.

"What about your family?" Gunther asked. "Your return is going to shock them, and will cause a lot of trouble. I don't know where Hrolf intends to find land to give you as a reward. He can't be thinking of taking it from Konal."

"I would not accept that," Ulfrik said. "Such a complication would be troublesome, to say the least."

"Worry for that when the time comes," Gunther said. "For now, think about how you'll get to Eskil and that plan."

"It's not much of a plan. I can't go to Eskil directly, since he's too highly placed and I'd just arouse suspicions. I'll work with a lesser known crew, find Eskil in secret, then we'll free Vilhjalmer."

"Plan's a bit spare, isn't it?"

"Why plan anything more detailed when we both know whatever I think of now will just be blown to shit once I get inside? Eskil will know the best way to Vilhjalmer and the best way out of that mess. I just have to link with him."

Gunther shrugged and they studied the pigs in silence. A young woman came to fetch the bucket but she melted away in shock when she discovered both Ulfrik and Gunther leaning on her fence.

"I see women still think you're ugly," Ulfrik said.

"Don't need to be handsome to get what I want."

They both laughed and Ulfrik watched the smallest pig finally get his place at the bucket. "I feel like that one, the little piglet scrambling after what everyone else has left me. I had it all, Gunther. Now it's gone."

"Maybe not all of it. Your family will welcome you back."

"They will, but what shall I be to them? A ghost returned from the dead? I knew their lives would have moved on without me, and that I could not force my way back to them. You want to know something, old friend? I don't think I returned for them, but for myself. For another chance at glory. I could've finished my days in Iceland with a good woman and no one would've been the wiser here. Maybe it would have even better for them."

"You do realize it can still be so?" Gunther had to turn to fix Ulfrik with his only eye. "Do this thing for Hrolf, and he'll give you a ship and crew and gold enough to make you a Christian King of Iceland."

The thought hit Ulfrik like an oar slamming across his shoulders. He pushed back from the fence and squared with Gunther, his mouth open.

"You never thought of it?" Gunther shook his head, his thin gray hair falling across his face. "You really do lust for glory."

"There's just not been a moment to think ahead, but you are right. I could return to Iceland a richer man and leave my old family in peace."

"Aye, and maybe it's better for them as you have said."

Ulfrik turned back to the pigs. They had scattered and the bucket lay tipped on its side. How much suffering would he cause Runa to suddenly reappear to her? Konal had loved her in the past, and Ulfrik believed after his apparent death they had found love together again. He could only complicate their lives in the worst way. Moreover, he was nothing now but a poor wanderer. What shame would he visit upon his sons to show up like this? He shook his head.

"Maybe it's best to move on after Hrolf's son is saved. Still, I would like to at least see my family one more time, even if only from a distance. I want to carry away a memory of them all in happiness.

Last I saw Runa, we had only recovered from a terrible argument the night before. I would like to replace that memory with a more pleasant one."

"You're good at moving in disguise. Last night you got close enough to give Hrolf a kiss before anyone stopped you. Maybe pay them a visit after this is done."

"No, I may have to leave quickly after that. I'd rather see them before I go. How far is their new home?"

"Hardly an afternoon's travel by horse. It's on the way to the Frankish border anyway. I won't mention that trip to Hrolf, if you choose to make it."

Ulfrik put his hand on Gunther's shoulder and squeezed. "Thank you for that. It will be good to see my family one last time before I leave them for good."

Gunther smiled. "Let's go see your friend, Finn, and let him know he'll be going home a richer man."

18

Ulfrik approached Konal's fortress with his heart beating and his breath ragged. He wore his now-perfected disguise of a traveling wise man. The sky above the dark stockade walls was gray and threatening rain. A low rumble of thunder rolled out of the distance, and the wind blew strong and cool against his face. He did not wear a blindfold, wanting only to glimpse his family a final time before moving on. All his wargear and weapons remained in keeping at the last farmhouse he visited. Unlike the situation at Gils farm, Gunther One-Eye had accompanied him and paid the farmers to care for Ulfrik and his belongings. The farm sat at the turning point south to Count Amand's lines and so he would have to backtrack to it, making the farm a logical place for them to part company.

"Eskil will not know you," Gunther told him before they parted. "But if you tell him that you've heard of dolphins in the mouth of the Seine, he will know you come from Hrolf."

"Do you know I have heard of dolphins in the mouth of the Seine?" Ulfrik laughed and he and Gunther embraced before parting. "Take good care of Finn for me. It pains him to not accompany me on this adventure, but promise him greater glories for when I return."

The giant that was Gunther One-Eye left him with a clap on the shoulder and directions to Einar's hold. Locals were headed in with trade goods, carts of empty barrels and crates as well as stacks of furs, and Ulfrik was placed among them for cover. Now they all approached the open gates, and the group's leader turned to Ulfrik. "One-Eye says you have business inside that requires secrecy. So you're my dumb brother come along for the ride. Just look at me if anyone asks you questions."

Ulfrik gave a curt nod and stared up at the guards studying them from the walls. None of them smiled, and a several set their bows in view.

"Never mind the show," said the leader. "Things are always tense on the border. They'll recognize us soon enough."

As promised the guards relaxed at their approach, and three men at the western gates inspected their wagons and waved them through. A guard looked Ulfrik over, but his eyes slid past in boredom. He still felt hot and weak for the scrutiny, and began to think this bid to see his family was foolish. He already could not stand to see Runa with Konal, and so settled for a chance to see Hakon along with Einar and Snorri. Once inside the walls, he realized getting close would be impossible without arousing suspicion. He cursed his stupidity.

The carts rolled toward the central square, bouncing along the black boards that lined the main roads. Ravndal had been the template for Einar's fort, which locals called Eyrafell. Ulfrik could guess at where buildings like the forge or smokehouse would be and find he had been correct. A strange sense of both returning home and being among enemies overcame him. He pulled his hood over his eyes and lowered his head.

"Here's where you should go do whatever you need," the leader said. "It's not a long visit today and we'll be heading back before sunset. Is an afternoon enough time to do your business?"

Ulfrik nodded, then slipped off cart and took up his walking stick. The leader turned his attention to his companions and they began to unload their goods. Ulfrik wandered off into a side alley, no one caring enough for the passing of an old man. He let his feet lead him, taking paths that were familiar but strange. Sometimes a path did not turn where it should have or there was no path at all. A curious old woman stopped him, the mother of the fletcher, and gossiped with him until he grew restless to leave. He did learn, however, that both Aren and Hakon were here together and that Aren was prone to wandering on his own.

No sooner did he learn this information when he rounded a corner into a side path and stood face to face with Snorri and Aren.

Despite the changes in both of them, recognition was immediate. Snorri was softer, more gaunt and stooped, but under wisps of gray hair and beneath wild brows stared out the intelligent and alert eyes of his oldest friend. His arm was locked with Aren's for support and his other spotted hand held a walking staff much like Ulfrik's own prop. Aren now stood at Snorri's height due to his stoop, and his face was wide and clear. A beard had begun to sketch onto his chin and jaw, auburn hair like Konal's in his youth. He looked directly into Ulfrik's eyes, his expression grave and his eyes radiating a fierce intelligence. Looking into them, Ulfrik saw fear, anger and disdain flash in their gray depths.

Pulling himself away was like tearing flesh from frozen iron, but he tucked his head down and immediately began walking in the opposite direction. His heart thudded and blood roared in his ears. Yet a simple word from Snorri arrested him.

"Lad?"

The voice had been clawed with age and pain, but it was Snorri's and it struck to Ulfrik's heart as sure as any arrow. His foot came down, but his other refused to move. Don't do this, he told himself. You've got to get away.

"It can't be true." Aren's voice had changed, now a young man's, but it was no less arresting. It was the voice of his son.

Aren grabbed his shoulder and tugged him around. "Who are you?"

Ulfrik did not resist, but let himself be spun around to face Aren. His raptor gaze searched him from head to foot as Snorri stumbled the short distance toward them.

"I know that face," Snorri said as he hobbled up to Ulfrik. "Why are you hiding it?"

"Take off this hood," Aren said, then pushed it back from Ulfrik's head. He peered at him with keen interest and nodded. "Speak."

"Are you so convinced of what you see?" Ulfrik asked them, his eyes not wavering from Aren's. In reply, Snorri collapsed forward and both he and Aren had to catch him before he fell.

"Lad, you are alive or I am dead. Which is it? I know who owns that voice and I knew his father as well. Tell an old man he has not lost himself to ancient memories."

Tears stood in Snorri's eyes, and Ulfrik blinked back his own. "I did not mean for us to meet again, at least not like this. But as fate has reunited us, then I will hide no more. I am Ulfrik."

Snorri stared at him with shimmering eyes, mouth open but wordless. Aren steadied Snorri, then gave Ulfrik a skeptical look. "I do not want to believe it's you, but I've not forgotten your voice nor your bearing. Are you really my father?"

"I was your father once. I raised you from birth as my own. There is a scar on your left foot from when a servant girl dropped a knife on it. You were only a child then but I'm sure you remember the pain. You cried for days after and refused to walk."

Aren hesitated then embraced Ulfrik, pinning his arms to his sides. The emotion behind that embrace surprised him, as Aren had always been a cool child so unlike the hot blood of either his mother or true father, Konal.

"I knew that head Einar returned with was not yours." Snorri now gripped Ulfrik's arms and his squeeze was feeble. "But he insisted you died, said Throst took him to find your body at the foot of the tower. What happened to you? Why has your hair turned so gray for one still young?"

Ulfrik laughed. "Would that I felt young, old friend. I survived the fall that Einar witnessed, but he was not shown my body until the next day. During that time, strange people found me and exchanged my body with a murdered slave's. They carried me off to Iceland, and it has taken me all these years to fight my way back home."

Both Snorri and Aren stared at him in awe and confusion. Aren's brow wrinkled and he cocked his head to the side. "There is much that makes no sense in that tale."

"Explaining it would make even less sense," Ulfrik said. "They were madmen and the tortures I endured under them aged me beyond my years."

"Whatever happened I am glad to have you back," Snorri said. "No matter what my heart told me, the truth was you've been dead these long years. Now I want to know all that I missed of your life."

Ulfrik shook his head. "There is no time, my old friend. I am not here to stay, but only to glimpse my family a final time before I leave."

Both Aren and Snorri stood back, blinking. Aren put his hand on his chest. "A final time? You can't leave. We need you. Mother needs you."

"She has Konal now, and my return would only complicate matters. It is best I remain dead to everyone, and let life here continue without the worry or shame of my presence. Look upon me, and you see all I possess. I can offer you nothing but more suffering. Let Runa and Konal live their days in peace."

"Konal is a beast," Aren said. "I've often thought of killing him myself."

"Aye, lad, he's not who you remember, nor is Runa. Both have been poison to each other and your memory is like a sword that cuts them both."

Now it was Ulfrik blinking in surprise. "Aren, Konal is your blood father. You can't mean what you say."

"I mean it," Aren said, exchanging a glance with Snorri. "And Snorri knows it is true. He beats my mother and spends his days drunk and angry. He is a disgrace to us, unable to do more than hide behind Einar and steal what glory he can."

"It's true, lad," Snorri said in a low voice. "Within a year after your death, he married Runa and fell into drinking and whoring. I don't begrudge a man these pursuits. I did enough in my youth. But it is all he does, and he does not lead well. Out of bonds of old friendship, Einar has carried him but now even those are sorely tested. The way he treats Runa, it's as if he never loved her but married her to spite your memory. It's a strange thing, for I know he was once sincere but something twisted him."

"Gunnar left to find you," Aren said. "Mother says he died in the search, but I think he gave up and refused to return and witness what Konal has become. The signs were on him even when Gunnar left. His tears at your funeral were strange. They fell true, but I don't believe from grief at your death."

Ulfrik stood in shock, unable to make sense of the hate flooding from both of them. He looked between them, their faces set in scowls of disgust.

"He beats her? Runa would never stand for it. Never. She would kill him first."

"Lad, your death went hard with her. The fire in her heart died, and fear replaced it. Gunnar's departure was the ax-blow that cut her down. She thinks only Konal can offer her a future, however black it might be. Without him, she has no family and no wealth. Einar would take her in, but a feud with Konal would invite Hrolf to intervene. She does not want to bring that trouble to him. Honestly, the Franks are worse than ever and Einar has no desire to seek more problems. So he turns his eye from it."

Rubbing the back of his neck, Ulfrik struggled to make sense of it all. What could have changed Konal into an animal? He had often spoken of his father as being mad. Perhaps such a madness now gripped him, a curse passed from father to son. It was all that made sense.

"So you can't leave," Aren said. "See Einar then arrange to meet Mother. Hakon is here, too. We will find a way to be a family again."

"Yes, I have to see this for myself. Runa cannot go on like this. And you two," Ulfrik pointed at both Snorri and Aren. "When did you become so close, strolling arm in arm like this? I remember neither of you caring much for the other."

"Time changes everything, lad." Snorri patted Aren's shoulder. "He's the smartest boy I've ever met, at least twice as clever as you were at this age. And people hate him for it. His own father can't stand a son smarter than himself. It's what scared me when he was young. Now I just know he's got a good head and there's nothing evil about it."

"I like to hear Snorri's stories," Aren said. "So we spend time together."

They stood facing each other at a sudden loss for words. Ulfrik looked around, the pathway clear of all but a boy and dog trotting along on their business. "I've got my duties to Hrolf, but when they are done, I will return."

"What has he got you mixed up with?" Snorri asked.

"Let's at least get out of the road while I tell you what I can."

They moved into the shade of a building, where Snorri settled on a stump and Ulfrik sat on an overturned bucket and Aren leaned against the wall. He told them of his revenge upon Throst, his misfortunes with Finn and the problems with Hrolf's son.

"So now you know all of what I do. Once I free Vilhjalmer, I have asked for lands and men. I thought I should forfeit that to leave you all in peace. Now I see I must pursue it. But both of you swear to me now that you shall not breath a word to anyone of my arrival and of what I've told you. No one, means Runa, Einar, and the dog in the corner of the hall. No. One. Swear it."

Both raised their hands and promised Ulfrik.

"I will return soon, and your lives will be better for it. This is what I swear to you. My family will not be made to live in fear and shame. I will not stand for it."

Both Aren and Snorri smiled. They embraced a final time and Ulfrik left them, resolved to set straight Konal and reclaim his wife.

19

Konal had kissed Runa farewell at the gates and left with thirty men, half of his standing force. They started out at dawn beneath puffy, pink clouds that rolled overhead like seals at play in the surf. Runa watched from the walls, waving dutifully with a stiff smile creasing her face. The wind caught her curly hair and blew it over her shoulders.

"Did you find out what I asked about last night?" she asked through her fake smile. Groa, who stood next her, holding her head cover tight against the breeze, simply nodded in affirmation. Runa's smile softened with a touch of the genuine. "Then we shall have much to discuss while spinning this afternoon."

Runa and Groa were assisted down the ladder by leather clad hirdmen. The ones left behind were Konal's most responsible men. Those Konal took with him were his fiercest drinking companions and while out on patrol they would no doubt protect the surrounding lands from excess ale or beer. She wished for once they would collide with a real enemy and settle all her issues. Fate was not so kind, and Konal was too canny to bring himself into any true danger.

Back at the hall, women had gathered baskets of wool and two girls were already with their distaffs spinning the wool into threads.

She waved them away. "Groa and I will take the easy work of spinning. You two are young enough for the looms."

She and Groa set their distaffs on their hips and began spinning wool. The two girls did not have enough thread with them, and had to fetch more. When they left, Runa waited a moment before turning to Groa. "Did you see it yourself?"

"Yes," Groa's voice came in a whisper. "Whatever it was, he stuck it in the well. There's a loose stone in there. He was leaned into it so far that I could've dumped him in it had I mind to."

"Murder has no part in my plans." Runa watched the wool pull tight as she lowered the weight stones, then studied the threads spinning together into tight strings. Her own heart felt as tight and twisted. "He is not a bad man, just lost. I want no more part of him."

Groa sniffed. "He beats you like a dog on some days then treats you like a Queen of the Franks. A dip in the well might be a good way to find himself."

"You're a loyal woman," she said. "You and I will be gone from all of this by tonight."

"What's he hiding in there? Treasure, I suppose."

Runa nodded, signaling with her eyes that hirdmen had wandered into the hall. Two of them sat on the far benches, setting aside their spears and falling into conversation. Their presence ended discussion of the evening's plans. After the girls returned and set the looms, the rest of the afternoon passed like any other. Once the evening meal had been finished and dishes were being cleared, Runa raised her brows at Groa who acknowledged by catching the attention of the other servants.

"See here," she shouted. "This whole table is stained. Who is supposed to be cleaning this?"

With attention distracted, Runa picked up a bucket and left. She wended her way down the tracks to the well. Men spared her nothing more than a glance, for she was only drawing water for the night's cleaning. After she lowered the bucket, she ducked her head inside. A mossy, damp scent filled her nose and each drip sounded like a roar with her head in the well. Immediately she discovered the flaw in her plans.

There was no light. Leaning into the well, everything melted into a thick brown smear and every rock disappeared. She fumbled with her hands, finding nothing, then had to back up to catch her breath. Evening light skimmed over the rooftops, nothing slanting down to illuminate the shadows. You foolish girl, she though. Should've come in the light to see what you're doing.

Not wanting to appear any more suspicious, she drew up the bucket of water and set it aside. It occurred that Konal placed this in the dark and would have had only torchlight. Therefore, the stone must be identified by touch. She leaned back in and felt around, coming back up empty. She tried twice more before a stone came free. It squeezed out of her hand and fell into the water with a splash. Hissing with fear, she reached inside to grasp the pouch. In one smooth move she withdrew from the well and stuck the pouch into her skirts. She then picked up her bucket and hurried back to the hall.

She and Groa waited until only three hirdmen remained, two of which were deep in conversation. Without having to speak, both of them knew the next steps in their plan. They transported their few belongings in baskets covered with the cloth woven during the day. Outside the hall they set aside the basket and pulled out travel packs. The sun had set but they had no worries of travel in darkness.

"The cart is ready?" Runa asked once they were away from the hall.

"And Soren is ready to drive us. I've already arranged as you asked. Once we're through the gates, then we are as good as gone."

Yet at the eastern gates they found them hanging open and a small group of men entering on horseback. They both stepped off the road, but when Runa recognized the front rider as he dismounted she put her hand to her mouth.

"Aren has returned," Groa said. "Was he supposed to?"

Runa shook her head and met her son while other men handled the horses. Something weighed on his mind, apparent to Runa from the slouch in his stance and cool reaction. They hugged, and over Aren's shoulder she saw Soren waiting on his cart.

"I did not expect you to meet me at the gate," Aren said as he pulled back from her. His eyes darted from Runa to her travel pack, then Groa, and his expression changed to shock. "What are you doing?"

Pulling him close as if to embrace him again, she whispered into his ear. "I've had all I can take. We are leaving while Konal is away. I wanted to keep you at Eyrafell with Hakon, but now you are here."

"You mustn't go," he said, grabbing her by both shoulders. "Endure Konal a while longer."

"What? Of all people, I thought you wanted to leave the most? You're not telling me something. I see it in your eyes."

She squeezed his shoulders and waited. He noticed her bruised face and turned aside in disgust.

"Gods, that is Konal's work?"

"Things are going to get worse," she said. "There's something you don't understand. Your return has fouled my plans, but Konal will be gone at least another day. We need to get to Einar before he is back."

"So, something I don't understand but you can't tell me more? I just have to trust you?" Aren raised his brow and Runa felt her cheeks warm in embarrassment. His smile was more of a wince as he brushed the hair from her bruised face. "You can't leave now. Everyone will see you leave, and travel at night is dangerous."

"We're going on Soren's cart, and he has a lantern. Only to the nearest farm and then on to Eyrafell in the morning." Aren was already shaking his head.

"Look around you," he said. "Every man is watching us. For tonight at least, you must remain. All I ask is you stay a while longer."

"I'm telling you, I don't know what your father will do when he returns."

"Don't call him that," he snapped. If they had remained unnoticed, now they had everyone studying them. Runa pulled back and Aren straightened himself. "I will protect you from whatever he will do to you. He will have to kill me to harm you. I swear it."

Runa's breath grew short and her lip began to tremble. "My dear son, you can't be with me always."

He took Runa's hands, and folded them in his own. "Tonight your plans are done. I have sworn a solemn oath to not reveal what I know, but I can tell you it will change your life. Just trust me, and within the week you will know everything."

She had never seen him so earnest, and her chances for escape had been foiled by his arrival. Too many eyes were upon her and Groa now. She nodded, then pointed with her chin at Soren. "Groa, tell him to wait on your plans. I m sorry."

Aren's square face was bright with happiness. "Konal will not hurt you again, and life is going to get better. I swear it upon my life."

"Do not make such oaths lightly," she said with a frown. "The gods may force you to make good upon it. Now take yourself to the hall with Groa. I have a small matter to attend to before joining you. And don't give me that look. I'm not sneaking away."

Waiting for them to leave, she withdrew the pouch of gems from her skirts. She did not know what secrets Aren held, but he was so convinced that she believed him. Since his youth, Aren always knew more than anyone. His mind was greater and deeper than any man's she had ever known, and he was still only fourteen years old. If he believed her life would change, he was likely right. She had to return the gems to hiding, since she did not know when she would have another chance. If Konal found his hole empty she would be in dire trouble.

At the well she leaned in and realized the stone was gone. It only just occurred to her now and panic filled her. He would know she had been here. She began to search for other stones, finding nothing suitable in the dirt beside the well. She leaned in again to search for another loose stone to replace the one she had dropped. When she slid back out of the well, she turned to face three men ringing her. She squealed if fright.

"What are you doing?" She summoned her best angry voice while slipping the pouch back into her skirt.

"Konal said to watch for anyone around the well. And look who we found."

"I am the jarl's wife! You'll all stand aside and leave me alone."

The men parted, smiling after her as she strode through them.

She had to flee now, or face the unthinkable at Konal's hands.

20

Ulfrik arrived at the border after dawn when the sky was the color of dying lavender. He emerged from the tree line, heavy pine scents clinging to him as he crossed the fields toward the stockade walls of the enemy camp. These were not built up on dirt mounds, but simple stockade fences demarcating lines that could not be crossed. "You can walk up to the fences," a local farmer had told him. "If you meet one of ours you can trade news, if you meet a Frank you can trade silver to walk away unharmed."

The Franks had pushed their borders beyond the Oise River and crushed the Northmen to the corridor around the Seine River then shoved them west toward distant Rouen. This land had been watered with the blood of both Frank and Northman too many times to count. Ulfrik guessed if he could part the stand of trees on the horizon he would see the smudged outline of his old enemy Clovis's fortress. He smiled without humor, certain Clovis's ghost laughed at him from whatever sad place Christians went after death. He would delight at seeing the land Ulfrik had annexed returned to his countrymen again.

The grass should be stained forever red, but the thick summer green carpet swished beneath his feet as he approached the first haphazard rows of fences. He could smell the mucky scents of the

Seine beyond them. Inhaling deep, he let out his breath slowly and checked that his sword was loose in its sheath before making his final approach. Dark figures lurked between the tall fences, and from the cut of their cloaks and the round shields some of them leaned upon he guessed them to be his own kind.

At a spear's throw away the men revealed themselves, seven all wearing simple wool shirts of white or gray and cloaks of deep blue or green now fouled with mud and other stains. They wore swords at their hips and a sax, the short thrusting swords for close fighting, hung at their laps. They ambled out with a carelessness so false Ulfrik suspected a trap. He paused and let his hand drop by his sword hilt, then he unslung the battered old shield at his back. It was painted in halves of black and yellow and was splintered and chipped from heavy use. Gunther had found it for him along with assorted other well-worn war gear to support his new persona.

The man in the lead saw Ulfrik's precaution and threw his head back in a laugh that sounded like a walrus. He wore a dented helmet but otherwise nothing more for defense. His hair was the color of straw and the same consistency, blowing out from under his helmet in clumps. An otherwise handsome face had been marred with pox scars, and a scraggly beard wagged as he laughed.

"I'm here to join Count Amand's forces," Ulfrik said. He set his hand on his hips and disregarded the leader recovering from his laughter. "Do any of you fools know where I can swear my oath?"

The men exchanged glances then stepped toward him, rolling their shoulders and necks. Ulfrik flicked his eyes between them but did not move. A crow cried overhead as if warning Ulfrik away from danger, but he paid it no mind. The gods send what signs they would, he had a task that unfortunately placed him in the path of fools.

"Hold on, this is too good," said the pox-scarred man. "Some old man strolls out of the forest with a broken shield and piss stained pants then expects to present himself to the Count." He scanned Ulfrik and recoiled as if he has sniffed spoiled milk. "Do you even know what you're doing?"

"I know I'm wasting my morning entertaining some goat-turd and his dog-fucking friends. If your man back there cracks his knuckles again I think he'll break his hand. Then how will he stroke your cock?"

Ulfrik stood as if he had just remarked on the weather rather than inciting seven men to murder.

The pox-scarred man glared as did his followers and his eyes narrowed. His hand came to rest on his sword hilt and he began to circle Ulfrik. "Those are some bold words from one old man. Do you imagine yourself a real killer, taking on all seven of us?"

"I was imagining myself talking to someone smarter. If you are the kind of men Count Amand employs, then maybe I was wrong coming here. You fools look like the kind to cut your own fingers off sharpening your swords. I suppose I'll be leaving."

"Not after those words," said the leader. He stood before Ulfrik and an odor like a midden pit assailed his nostrils. The man leaned in closer. "What's your name? I'd like to know who I'm beating into the ground."

"I'm Ulfar the White," Ulfrik said. "I shall guess your name as Thor Shit-Stink."

The man stared with his mouth half open, and then a sly smile emerged. "Gunnvald Hrethelson is my name. You'll learn to respect it."

"My sympathy to Hrethel for the tragedy of his son's life. I'll respect whoever earns it, and right now you've done nothing for it. Now either allow me through or draw that sword of yours and let's have a go."

Gunnvald's smile widened, flattening his pox scars, and he brushed aside a lock of straw-like hair. "Alright, you've made your insults and I like them. I'd be willing to consider you for my crew."

Ulfrik had remained as still as a stone, careful to keep any expression of concern from his face, but his brows raised at Gunnvald's statement. "I came to promise my sword to Count Amand. I heard he's the power here."

"We Northmen don't kneel to him, you oaf. We are sworn to Grimnr the Mountain, and he's paid by Count Amand for his loyalty. Don't you know anything?"

"So show me to Grimnr."

"You'll serve on my crew. That'll be good enough."

Ulfrik stared at Gunnvald and wished he had been warned of this structure in advance. Gunnvald might not be a fool but he was certainly unimportant and likely not close enough to Vilhjalmer to make serving him worthwhile. Still, he had only to find Eskil and Gunnvald's low status might actually benefit that effort. With nothing important to do, no one would miss Ulfrik while searching for Eskil.

"All right," Ulfrik said. "But I expect an equal share in spoils and whatever this Grimnr the Mountain is handing out."

"Not so fast," Gunnvald said. "Before I take you on, I want to know what I'm getting. You look a little too old for fighting, and you have to pay for those insults, too."

Smiling shyly, Ulfrik rubbed the back of his neck. "Well, those were some of my better ones. Glad they hit you hard. Like this."

He slammed his elbow into Gunnvald's face, the followed up with a kick to his shins that toppled him. He charged over Gunnvald's sprawled out body and slammed into the man behind him. He was a head shorter than Ulfrik but wide and swarthy like an old mooring post set into a muddy bank. He broke as easily as one, falling onto his back with a shout of surprise.

The first man to react grabbed Ulfrik's cloak, which had flown up behind him. Having expected some form of trouble, Ulfrik had fastened it with a simple antler pin that broke away when pulled. He whirled on the man standing flat-footed with a handful of green cloak. Ulfrik's fist plowed into his jaw, snapping the man's head around and knocking spit out of his mouth. Following up with a sharp jab to the man's gut to expel the breath from his lungs, and he collapsed.

Gunnvald was recovering, castling on hands and knees while cursing. Ulfrik whirled on two men who both sought to grapple him, but he leapt back out of their awkward grasping. He was laughing now. Even without his sword in hand, the battle lust he enjoyed in younger days was building in him again. Seven men to one were impossible odds, and he expected to be caught and beaten at any moment. Yet while it lasted his heart thrummed with battle song and he ached to draw his sword.

Another man got behind him and now Ulfrik was caught in a triangle of opponents closing on him. He bounced on the balls of his feet, raw-knuckled fists up. "All of you against me, is it? Need seven men to take on one old man?"

"Wait!"

The voice was deep and thick, and came from behind. When the two in front of him backed down, Ulfrik felt safe enough to turn. The man stood equal to Ulfrik in height but was nearly twice as wide. He had a protruding belly, a bald head fringed with long fly-away black hair, and fat, flat lips like a fish. He cracked the knuckles of his right hand.

"You had something to say about breaking my hand? I think you need to take back your words, or I'll stuff them back down your throat along with your teeth."

Ulfrik smiled. "Alright, Fish Face, let's settle up and then I can get on with kicking the rest of your friends back into the Seine."

The two squared off, and began to circle each other in a fighter's crouch. Gunnvald and his crew ringed them and chanted for their friend's victory. "Come on, Erp! Break the old man's back!," shouted one. "Break his arms like that last one you fought," cried another.

"Sounds like you've got a reputation, Fish Face."

"Stop calling me that."

They searched each other for openings, but while Erp stared at Ulfrik's eyes he watched Erp's middle. When Ulfrik tipped his head right as if preparing to lunge in that direction, he saw Erp shift with him. Instead he plunged in straight, swooping in with an upper cut to Erp's jaw. He had hoped to knock him out, but Erp's thick neck did not snap back hard enough. Instead he tumbled away with a roar.

Wasting no time, he pushed at Erp to get him on the ground, but he braced his legs and grappled Ulfrik waist. Crushed together, the two wrestled amid the cheering men. The grass dug up at their heels and Erp's hand worked down to Ulfrik's waist and threatened to pull down his pants. Ulfrik drove his knee into Erp's crotch, but missed the vitals and so their stalemate continued.

In a fight to the death they would have drawn knives to break the lock, but Ulfrik deemed he had wasted enough time and fell back on the next best move. He bit Erp's shoulder. Blood welled up in his mouth but Erp only grunted, punching Ulfrik's ribs now that he had shifted to bite him. Ulfrik tore at him like a dog until Erp began to shout and struggled free.

That was the break he needed. Once apart he punched Erp in the face, then hammered left and right until he stumbled onto his back. Ulfrik followed him down and continued to punch. Gunnvald and his crew moaned and tried to cheer on Erp, but he had given up under the flurry of punches and now guarded his face.

Pulled off by his shoulders, Gunnvald got between him and Erp. "Alright. You can fight! I see it now. Let's not kill each other."

Ulfrik wrestled out of the hold, then relaxed. He straightened his shirt and pulled up his pants. "You satisfied?"

Gunnvald's fist crashed into his left eye and his vision turned white. He staggered back, but no other blow followed.

"Now I'm satisfied." Gunnvald grabbed Ulfrik's cloak from the dirt and handed it back to him. "Welcome to my crew, Ulfar the White."

They grasped forearms and both smiled. In the background Ulfrik watched a man try to help Erp to his feet, but then be shoved away. Erp stood and his bloodied, swollen face met Ulfrik's. He drew a finger across his neck and pointed at him while Gunnvald's back was turned.

"You're going to be a great addition," Gunnvald said. "We could use fighter like you."

"I can't wait to start," Ulfrik said, all the while watching Erp storm away with his friends.

21

Ulfrik sank the cooking pot into the river, hauled up gritty water, then sloshed it in a circle. He rubbed the grit along the sides then dumped it back into the water. He repeated this twice more then skimmed the water to fill the pot with clear water and rinse it out. Setting it on the grass, he pulled out a linen towel and rubbed it dry, careful to get into the lip where rust had taken hold. The food cooked in this pot carried a metallic flavor that he attributed to poor maintenance. A crew's cooking pot was as important as their swords and mail, but Gunnvald and his men thought it a task beneath them. Ulfrik had been happy to take over the chore, if only to have an hour of peace.

The midmorning sun hid behind clouds, creating a pallid light that flattened distances and lowered his mood even lower. A black and white magpie hopped along the bank of the Seine, titling its head right and left as it studied Ulfrik.

"No scraps today," he said to the bird. "Maybe the Franks are feeling more generous in their fort. Go see them."

Shooing away the bird, it hopped a short distance then burst into flight. It actually winged to the northeast for Count Amand's fortress, and Ulfrik chuckled then returned to drying off the pot. After burnishing it and rubbing out the last bit of damp, he sat in the grass up from the river bank. The river water smell was thick in his nose as he watched men up the shore pulling up their eel traps. He had eaten eel for seven out of the eight days he had been on Gunnvald's crew and the thought of eating it again made his stomach ache.

He had to return the cooking pot and treat it with fish oil before rust set in despite his care. He mumbled to himself, "I feel like I'm here to care for this cooking pot. It's all I do."

Springing to his feet, he stared down at the pot. He imagined flinging it into the river, dashing for Amand's castle, then fighting inside to save Vilhjalmer. This long waiting combined with treatment little better than a servant from Gunnvald frustrated him. He was not sleeping at night, his mind churning plans to penetrate deeper into the territory. During the day he was busy with some aspect of camp life. He kicked a rock toward the river, then retrieved the pot and headed for camp. Gunnvald called his men a crew, but in truth they had no ship. He was little more than a bandit leader come to loaf on the front lines and avoid any real conflict.

At camp, he set the pot down and one of the men, Burr, was sitting by the remains of the campfire.

"Finish oiling this pot. I've got to go shit."

"You finish it. Ain't my job."

Ulfrik slapped Burr's head as he left him. "If I taste rust tonight I'm going to crown you with that pot."

While Gunnvald held the band together, Ulfrik could not help but take command naturally. Many of the men responded to his orders as if he had been leading them all along. This had chaffed Gunnvald, and Ulfrik was learning to subdue his tendency to give orders. So much of this life felt familiar, he struggled to remind himself he was fighting for the Franks now.

Once away from camp, he threaded his way toward the hall where Grimnr the Mountain made his residence. It sat outside the vast wooden walls of Count Amand's fortress, but close enough that he could retreat into it if threatened. No one challenged him as he moved between camps. Many Northman lived out of tents, though some had built crude homes. Those with ships stayed on them, meaning the impressive gathering of Northmen were scattered. Ulfrik noted this fact, for in an attack these forces would not mobilize together and loose the advantage of their numbers.

When he and Hrolf planned this rescue, both agreed that a methodical approach would serve best. Count Amand was satisfied to think he now had leverage over Mord and Gunther One-Eye, so Vilhjalmer was not in immediate danger. Yet the frustrating pace of trying to find Eskil increased his worry for the time he had to do this task. The risk someone would reveal Vilhjalmer or Amand would decide to trade his leverage increased with every day that expired. He had to connect with Eskil, but nothing was more likely to expose him as a spy than a newcomer asking everyone he met where Eskil could be found.

His wanderings took him to Grimnr's hall, and at last he did encounter resistance in the form of a brawny guard with a missing front tooth. "Hey, friend, out for a walk?"

This man was unlike Gunnvald and the dozens of other crews of opportunists. He carried himself with confidence, wore well-maintained mail, and wore a dull iron helmet with a decorated face plate. He was the kind of man Ulfrik would consider for his own guard.

"I'm new here and was hoping to see Grimnr the Mountain."

"Well, you were walking straight for his hall. Thing is, it doesn't work like that, friend. Times being what they are, the hall is closed to you."

Ulfrik smiled and stroked his beard. "Oh, I understand how that works. I hoped Grimnr would consider taking me on. Does he accept newcomers?"

The guard gave Ulfrik a quick look-over and tucked his head back as if discovering Ulfrik had been wearing no pants. "He's more about professionals, not men who went a-viking but washed up ashore instead."

"I'm professional, but I take your meaning. I know I don't look my best. Honestly, I've got stuck with Gunnvald Hrethelson when I showed up here. Do you know him?" The guard shook his head. "Why doesn't that surprise me? He's really just a bandit leader looking for easy loot. Grimnr is more likely to earn me gold and glory, where I think Gunnvald will see me on a hanging tree before long."

The guard was looking past Ulfrik and switching his weight from leg to leg. "Well, good luck with everything. Now get out of this area."

At that moment the doors of the hall opened and the man stepping into the dull light had to be Grimnr the Mountain. He was a giant man, at least as tall as his old friend Einar had been, with thick golden hair braided down to his waist. His full beard was interrupted by a criss-cross of scars that lined his face. Grimnr wore a wolf-pelt across his shoulders and his arms glittered with golden bands. Two lesser man followed along, hanging on his orders as he strode away.

"That's Grimnr?" Ulfrik asked.

"That's him."

"Does he rule all the Northmen in these camps? Is he the law-maker and gold-giver?"

"And he's Odin's third raven, too. Yes, he's our highest power after Count Amand. So now stop wasting my time, and move along. You can't linger here unless you've been summoned."

Nodding his thanks, Ulfrik turned back toward camp, weaving between buildings and tents. Now he knew what had to be done. As law-maker, Grimnr would hear disputes and settle all legal issues. While Gunnvald would oppose it, Ulfrik knew he had to get out from under him and into Grimnr's direct service. From there, Eskil and Vilhjalmer were only a short stretch away.

And from there he could reunite with Runa and settle matters with Konal.

A chicken wandered into his path and cried as he kicked past it. Someone cursed at him as he went, but he was not paying attention. He knew how to shake Gunnvald and get closer to Grimnr.

For that to happen, he had a busy day still ahead.

22

After the evening meal, Ulfrik tipped out the fish bones from his bowl into the midden pit at the edge of camp. The sunset was brilliant scarlet, a strange counterpoint to the weak light of the day. Clouds of rose colored fire rolled away over black treetops and a gentle breeze stirred the grass. All around him, orange lights of campfires flickered like candles. The sprawling Northman camps were settling in for the evening, but Ulfrik's was only just beginning.

He crossed paths with Burr on his way back. "No rust in the broth tonight. Good job."

"Go fuck a pig, Ulfar."

Ulfrik laughed, picking his teeth for a fish bone caught there. At least catfish was a relief from the steady diet of river eels.

Back at camp he approached Gunnvald. "A word alone?"

Gunnvald stood from his log seat, glanced at Erp whose swollen face looked even fatter in the odd shadows cast by the campfire. He led Ulfrik to the edge of the camp, his hand resting on the hilt of his sword. Still in plain view of the others, their hushed voices would not be heard. He raised his brows expectantly at Ulfrik.

"I know you've been good to me," Ulfrik said. "And I appreciate your letting me in. But this isn't the life I was expecting. Grimnr the

Mountain's hirdmen have the duties I want. No disrespect, but just watching these fences for Northman deserters is boring work."

"So you're hoping for something more likely to get you killed?" Gunnvald's pock scars were even deeper in the twilight shadows. He snorted a laugh and shook his head. "I never understood your kind, always ready to run out in front of an enemy spear for a moment of glory. All the skalds will tell you the greatest heroes are dead. That's you, Ulfar?"

"I'm afraid it is. I should've died with my oath-holder, but I lived and came here. We were not particular about which side of this conflict we fought for, just that we fought hard and for glory. Hrolf and his jarls want to sit behind their walls, and the Franks want to fight. So here I am, but I'm still sitting behind walls."

Gunnvald nodded as if he understood, but Ulfrik doubted the man had ever risked more than a nick for the sake of honor or glory. "I see how it is. You think if you get yourself killed in battle you're somehow honoring your old chief. Ulfar, if he's dead then he's gone to Valhalla and the Valkyries are pouring him mead and showing him their tits. He's not worried if you're dead or alive."

"I want to serve Grimnr the Mountain and I want you to speak for me when I ask to give my oath."

"Ah, well, that's complicated." Gunnvald sighed and folded his hands behind his back. "See, I consider you to be my man. You've been eating my food, drinking my ale, sleeping in my tent."

"I brought that tent myself."

"And I let you keep it. You see, I think you owe me something before you leave. Plus, you beat up my best friend and you owe him for those injuries. I just can't let you go without considering these facts."

"What are you asking of me?"

"A payment of gold to release you from my service. Now, unless I'm mistaken, you should have something like that on you. Am I right?" Gunnvald extended his hand and smiled.

"This should pay for all." Ulfrik slipped off the gold armband he had concealed beneath his shirt. He placed it in Gunnvald's hand, checking that Gunnvald's men witnessed it. He snatched it away into the shadows of his cloak.

"That'll pay for Erp's wounds and some of the food you've eaten. I'll have to consider the rest of the payment, and what buying out your oath should cost."

"What?" Ulfrik acted out indignation, though he had expected nothing less. "You promised I'd be released for a payment of gold?"

He grabbed Gunnvald's shirt and hauled him close, but Erp and others leapt up and drew their swords.

"I never said this band was payment for releasing you."

"And I never swore an oath to you! I should beat you senseless."

"But you won't because Erp will cut off your head." Ulfrik looked up to find himself surrounded by armed men, Erp's swollen face practically in his own.

"Let go of him." Erp sounded like he had wool in his mouth.

Shoving Gunnvald away, Ulfrik pointed at him. "This isn't finished."

"Be careful of your words, Ulfar. Do not threaten me or you will regret it."

Ulfrik pushed aside one of Gunnvald's crew and stormed off. Having expected just such a betrayal, he already had the next step in his plan prepared. He waited until the camp disappeared behind him, then circled back to the camp. Between the midden pit and the tents a small rise provided a place for him to lay flat and observe.

As expected, Gunnvald was coming out of his tent to speak with the others. Obviously he was filling them with lies about what had just transpired, but Ulfrik did not care. With the sun now set and darkness only relieved by campfires, he jogged hunched low toward the back of Gunnvald's tent. He listened at it, placing his hands on the dirty cloth to feel for heat or motions of anyone inside. With little time to spare he pulled up one of the rear stakes and shimmied under the tent. Inside was a mess of furs, broken weapons, a rack for his mail, and his bedding. Despite being the largest of all the tents in his camp, he had managed to crowd it with enough junk for it feel small. The front flap waved in the breeze, and Gunnvald and his crew were standing outside in conversation. They were too far off for the words to be more than mutterings, but Ulfrik froze when he thought one of the crew was looking at him.

He was still half outside the tent, looking like a turtle popping out of shell, while he searched for the location of his armband. Gunnvald's bedding was close to the rear wall of the tent by Ulfrik's left arm, and he noted how one corner of the blanket was folded back. He pushed it aside and discovered a small board under the bed. Smiling at his success, he flipped up the board to find his armband sitting atop a bag. Ulfrik lifted out the bag which sagged with the weight of its contents, then pulled out the sheathed dagger he had hidden in at his back.

The jewels on the sheath winked with reflections of the campfire outside. He had spent all day following one of Grimnr's guards waiting for his chance to lift this from him. He had paid a servant to spill Frankish wine on the guard, which was so poorly done it seemed more as if he had poured it on the guard's head. He hoped the servant appreciated the silver, for he would take a beating for his actions. Yet it had the intended effect. A man could bathe in ale and think nothing of it, but the foreign stench of Frankish wine was an insult. The guard went to the river and washed off the strange scent of wine. Ulfrik had plucked the dagger from his discarded clothes and now slipped it into Gunnvald's secret cache.

The board replaced and the bedding fixed as it had been, Ulfrik then slipped from the tent and set the stake back in place. As he glided away from the camp, he considered that he was turning out to be as good a thief as he was a warrior. Wouldn't that just make my family proud, he thought. A bit like proclaiming myself the best cheat in the land.

He stayed away until campfire began to wink out, and then he returned. The few men still awake regarded him coolly, but Gunnvald and Erp simply watched him retire to his tent. He lay awake, confident Gunnvald wouldn't discover the dagger but still worried for the success of his plan. At some point he did fall asleep, for roosters were crowing and a dim light shined through the thin fabric of his tent. He rose quickly, still dressed in his clothes of the prior day, and shot out from his tent. As usual, no one in

Gunnvald's crew was keen on early rising and Ulfrik used it to his advantage.

The camp was coming alive, and sleepy men tired from a night of standing watch paid him no heed as he sought the guard house. As expected, he was stopped before he could reach the front doors by a guard whose hair was nearly as white as snow with eyes to match. He barred Ulfrik with his arm, wearily addressing him.

"Hold on, where are you going in such haste?"

"I've got to speak to Vigrid, who is quartered in that building. I know who took his valuables."

The guard perked up, squinted at Ulfrik, then nodded. "Wait here."

Within moments six bleary-eyed men emerged from the barracks with the white-haired man pointing at Ulfrik. Vigrid was a slender man, with a fuzzy beard with made his head seem oversized for his body. He might topple over from the weight of it. Yet, all Ulfrik saw this morning was a hateful scowl that burned through Ulfrik as he charged straight for him.

"How do you know I've been robbed?" he snapped.

"Because I stole it from you."

The six men recoiled at the sudden honesty. Vigrid's shock wore off the fastest, and he grabbed Ulfrik by the shirt and cocked his fist. "So you're here to return it?"

"In a way," Ulfrik said, holding up his hands to show he intended no fight. "I was ordered to steal it from you. I'm new here, and Gunnvald Hrethelson took me on. Ever heard of him?"

"No," Vigrid said, still keeping his fist cocked.

"No wonder, since he's a gutless bandit living on the edge of the camps. He had me steal something of value to prove my worth to him. He also stripped me of a gold armband when he said your dagger was worthless."

"Worthless?" Vigrid's oversized head reddened and appeared about to pop off his shoulders. "That was given to me by Grimnr himself. It's worth more than that piss-pot would earn in a whole year."

"Look, I agree and I am no thief. I haven't slept since I took the dagger. I want you to have it back, and to accept my regrets for what I've done."

Vigrid held him, glaring into his eyes, but Ulfrik saw the corners soften. "Did you arrange to have that wine spilled on me?"

"So you'd go to the river to bathe. I know I couldn't stand the scent of Frankish wine in my hair and guessed the same was true for any man. I needed a way to get the dagger while you were not looking."

He let Ulfrik go and patted his shoulder. "Alright, then, take us to Gunnvald."

All of them barreled through the camp and arrived as Gunnvald was seating himself at his log by the expired campfire. His straw hair fell over his face as he snapped up at the sudden arrival of hirdmen. "What's this?"

"You've got my dagger," Vigrid said. "Had your lap dog steal it from me."

Gunnvald stared at Ulfrik and they locked eyes. He saw the realization dawn in Gunnvald's eyes and he grew still and cold. "It wasn't orders from me."

"But you have it," Vigrid said. "Is it in your tent?"

"I don't know." He never wavered from watching Ulfrik. "I suppose you're going to check."

Vigrid entered the tent and began throwing items out the flap, skins and bags followed by a shield and other junk. All of his crew came to watch, standing like children whose parents had just spoiled their games. Within moments Vigrid shouted and emerged with the dagger, Ulfrik's armband, and the heavy pouch.

"Look here! Want to tell me how this came into your possession?"

"Obviously it was planted. I never saw it before in my life."

Vigrid slammed his fist into Gunnvald's stomach, and he doubled over with a moan. Erp and a few others reached for their weapons, but Vigrid's friends had spears, alarm horns, and were also Grimnr the Mountain's hirdmen. Erp and the others checked themselves when the spear points lowered.

"Well, you slept on the fucking thing all night. Should've had time to get to know it. Listen, I don't know what sort of games are being played here. The whole thing smells like a whale carcass. Here's how it will be. I take my knife and whatever is in this bag, this armband goes back to your new recruit." Vigrid tossed Ulfrik the armband. "If I ever see you or your men within bow shot of the barracks you'll all be rounded up for thieving and hanged the next morning."

"I think we should bring this to Grimnr for judgment," Ulfrik said. "I want him to rule on my service to this band of thieves. They're claiming I owe gold to leave them."

"No need for that," Gunnvald said, raising his hands. "I don't want you about. Leave if that's your wish."

With everything settled, Ulfrik asked Vigrid to guarantee his safety while he collected his gear and broke down his tent. When all was ready, Ulfrik hefted his travel pack and nodded at his former companions.

"You're in charge of the cooking pot now," he said to Burr, who stared wide-eyed at him.

Gunnvald scowled, and Erp muttered through his fat lips, "You'll get yours soon enough, dead man."

Ulfrik smiled and waved at him as he left. Catching up to Vigrid, he tapped his shoulder. "I've nowhere to go now, and was wondering if you might recommend me to Grimnr's service?"

23

Count Amand stroked his swooping mustache as he stood before the broken body of the Northman. The dungeon was his least favorite place in all of his property and he hated time spent in its dark and musty confines. Yet it was the place where God's work was often accomplished and today was not different. His Captain-at-Arms, Remi, stood at attention beside him. The guard who had tortured the confession was a swarthy man with a jagged scar running from cheek to ear. He prodded the Northman on the table, eliciting a low moan from his bloodied mouth.

"This is terrible news," Count Amand said, more to himself than the others. No one could appreciate the weight of his position, particularly not after recent news.

"He's confessed to all of it, my Lord," said the guard. "Captain Remi was the witness."

"It's true, Lord," Remi said. "I've had a detail of spies watching the traitors for weeks and we know they are passing information back to their Northmen kin. This exercise was to make sure we had all the names we expected, and none more."

Amand nodded and touched the heavy gold cross at his chest. The Northman on the table was unfamiliar, but his face had been so ruined by his tortures that no one would recognize him again. On a bench beside the traitor sat pliers and a pile of bloodied and crushed teeth.

"And you are certain this betrayal is confined and not gone any higher?"

"Grimnr was not named, Lord," Remi answered. "We've watched him far more carefully than anyone, as he's quite popular with his kind. I believe his loyalty is solid."

Amand cleared his throat and his nostrils flared. "At least as long as we are paying him. His kind are like wolves that need a constant supply of fodder lest they turn on you."

"The Northman are barbarians, Lord. Not much else can be expected of their kind." Captain Remi took a poker form the brazier, and examined the orange glowing tip. Amand could feel the heat of it from where he stood. "I can ask this traitor to confirm for you."

"Heavens, put that away. I don't want to have to breath in the stink of burned flesh." Amand waved aside the brand and Remi stuck it back in the brazier with a petulant sigh. "You've no love of Grimnr, so if you say he is loyal then it must be so. I expect you'd want to see him hanged with his kin more than anyone."

"It would do my soul good, Lord. But unfortunately Grimnr appears completely unconnected to the spies. We'll continue to watch him, of course."

"Do that." Amand locked his hands behind his back and circled the table. The Northman stared up through his swollen face, attempting a glare but looking no more threatening than a beached porpoise. He waved his hand at the traitor. "Have the others missed this one?"

"We caught him returning from his meeting with Hrolf the Strider's men, and his companions were not expecting him until tonight. No one saw us bring him down here." Remi moved the guard aside with the back of his hand and stood next to the traitor. "I believe we've got all that we can from this one. He broke far more readily than expected. Not so much of the Northman bravery in him."

"They're all like that," Amand said. "Together they are brave but alone they're no bolder than children. You've recorded the names of the traitors?"

Remi nodded.

"Then finish this one, and round up the others."

Smiling, Remi drew his dagger and let the point hang over the Northman's eye. "Our Lord has promised an eye for an eye, you filth. Have you heard?"

The traitor tried to spit, but only succeeded in blowing a bloody glob onto his own beard. Amand watched Remi hold the man's head steady then slowly lower the dagger into the Northman's eye. The blade slid in with cruel deliberation and the Northman bucked and screamed. Remi did not increase his pace, but steadily pushed the blade deeper into the man's skull. Blood flowed out of the ruined hole and poured onto the floor. The other guard began to throw hay on the puddle of gore.

At last the Northman ceased bucking, but Remi twisted the blade to elicit a final cry from his victim. He hovered over the corpse for a moment, then pulled out the dagger and tossed it on the table with the Northman's teeth. Amand pitied Remi's hatred. Northmen had captured and raped his wife, costing her left eye in the violence of the act. She had been a beautiful and vibrant woman, probably a prospect for the courts of Paris, but the Northmen stole that from her and Remi seized every chance to enact revenge.

Amand cleared his throat, and Remi and the guard both straightened up. "Take as many men as you need. This will be a delicate matter for the Northmen. They will have to be given a trial to satisfy their sense of justice."

"I think --"

"I appreciate that a trial is not a strict necessity, Remi. But we have to massage our allies. They are a good fighters and I'd rather spend their lives fighting Hrolf than decent Franks. Remember we are not dealing with common criminals. Those names you collected are highly regarded by their fellows."

"Do you think the jarl's child, Halfdan, is in jeopardy?" Remi asked the question and Amand guessed his captain was suggesting a change of plans for the boy.

"You said the spies were sharing information on troop strength, plans, and whatnot. It's possible they had thought to free the boy. I know what you are suggesting, and right now I needn't do more than ensure the hostage remains under my own guards in my fortress."

Amand paused and stared at the corpse dripping out its lifeblood onto the floor. "Grimnr will have to be rewarded for his loyalty or else this may go poorly. I will increase his pay and provide him some gold from my personal belongings. Those Northmen put great pride in a gold ring or armband."

"I will get the men together and arrest the traitors."

"Be careful to make it quiet. I don't want to incite the Northmen to violence. I'll give them a trial by tonight and all of them will be hanged by morning."

Remi bowed and turned to leave. The guard waited for Count Amand.

"I honestly would have thought Grimnr would be the traitor," he said to the guard.

"He's a hard man, but true to his word. I'll give him that much, Lord." The guard began to clean up his torture instruments with no more concern than a servant cleaning up after a feast.

"Good to know. I thought as much for Eskil. It will be a shame to hang him, but since he leads the traitors he has left me no choice. His corpse will be on display tomorrow morning as a warning against treachery."

24

Runa and Aren ate alone in the hall. It was late morning, and Konal was still passed out in bed from a raucous night of drinking. The hall still had tables overturned and a bench smashed from the drunken brawl that had ensued with the patrol's return. The place smelled like smoke, ale, and urine and even with the front doors thrown open the breeze did nothing to relieve the stench.

All morning men woke up from their stupor and staggered out of the hall. Servants tried to repair what they could, but Runa had sent them way until later. Even Groa and her other women went elsewhere to complete their spinning for the day. Only she and Aren had any reason to be in this miserable hall, eating reheated mutton from the night before.

"Are you nervous?" Aren asked her without taking his eyes off his food.

"What do you think?"

"That you are expecting to die. What happened with Konal before you left?"

"He is your father, Aren. Use the proper respect when speaking of him."

She put her bowl down and faced him. One hand held his bowl

up to his mouth, but the other was balled into a white-knuckled fist on the table. He slurped the final broth then set the wooden bowl down with care. His wide face was red with anger, and she turned aside. They continued to eat in silence, only the sounds of people about their chores outside the hall filling the space between them.

"I know how much you loved your step-father. No one knows better than me." Runa paused to steady her voice. She found just mentioning his name under these circumstances brought tears to her eyes. "But in truth, Konal is your father no matter how much we both wished otherwise. Disrespecting your own father only brings you shame."

Aren held his characteristic silence. It was a trait of his that caused her a pang of fear. She never knew what he was thinking when he closed off others. Unlike herself or Konal, he did not spill his anger openly but kept it locked away. She wondered if one day all that he dammed inside his heart would burst out in a flurry of untamed violence. For all his cool exterior, she knew a seething fire burned under Aren's skin.

"You never answered my question," he said at last, the flush retreating from his face. He continued to swirl the residue in his bowl.

"I cannot tell you. Not now at least."

"Well, I can understand that problem."

She bit her lip and stood to collect their bowls. Had Konal been awake he would have chastised her for not acting like a jarl's wife, but the chore gave her a sense of purpose however feeble. Staking their bowls she carried them down from the high table to the bucket by the hearth. Aren had been back for three days now and refused to say what had happened at Eyrafell. Either Einar or Snorri had told him something that put him on edge, but she could not guess what it could be. She was grateful for something else to think about besides being caught returning the jewels and Konal's reaction. He still had to even act as if he knew what she had done, and maybe he did not. He and his men proceeded straight to a drunken feast.

The door to their room opened and Konal stood in the doorway. His eyes were bloodshot and his hair was a mess. He wore no shirt and his terrible red and white burn scars showed down to his chest and stomach. He smacked his lips and yawned.

"Gods, but I am thirsty. Water!"

The mention of water made Runa tense, and Aren stared at her with a raised brow. His keen, intelligent eyes seemed to read her thoughts, something he had been able to do since he was an infant. She instead focused on Konal, but he only staggered to the bench and sat with Aren. He threw his arm around him and hugged him close. It was Aren's moment to tense and he nearly fell over under his father's clumsy pawing.

"Where's everyone?" he said, peering around as if looking into the sun.

"I sent them home. Others are still probably asleep under the tables."

Konal laughed, a thin and wispy sound that lacked any joy. She fetched him a jug of water and mug, then went to the pot where the meat still simmered. As she ladled meat and broth into a bowl, the hall doors flung open and five men swept into the hall.

Runa spun toward them, the contents of the bowl spilling over onto her hand. She recognized three of the men as her own but the other two wore blue cloaks over mail shirts. Their boots and pants were splattered with mud and their mail jingled as they strode confidently into the hall. She glanced back at Konal who stared vacantly at the men. When she turned back, the two strangers were facing her and she inhaled in surprise.

"We have come with urgent news for you from Eyrafell." The first man, tall with piercing green eyes and a long, fuzzy brown beard, addressed her with a slight bow. She looked back at Konal, who still remained in a fog staring at them.

"There is bad news," the messenger continued. "Snorri has taken ill and will soon be on to Valhalla."

Her hand rose to her mouth and her stomach went cold. "How? Aren, you were just with him."

She heard Aren gasp and rise from his bench, but her eyes remained locked with the messenger. She did not know him, but she hardly spent time in Einar's hall to recognize any of his men. Something about him felt strange, however. His eyes seemed to flash another message at her.

"He was in good health only days ago," Aren said. He now joined Runa's side. "What happened?"

"He stumbled in the hall and struck his head," the messenger said. "He has been asking for Runa. He wants to see her before he dies."

"Then we shall go to him." Konal spoke up and all eyes turned to him. "He is an old friend."

"Jarl Einar has specified only Runa should come," the messenger said as he inclined his head to Konal. "He needs you here, for the Franks are hinting at a large scale action."

"Then how is it safe for my wife to travel?" Had Runa known better, she would have thought his question sincere from the care in her voice.

"We will escort her on horseback." The messenger indicated his partner. Konal snorted at this.

"Two of you? If I am not to come, then I insist I send my own guards."

"That's not necessary, Jarl Konal." Again the messenger glanced at Runa as he bowed. She felt as if he were warning her against the guards.

"Wouldn't that make us more obvious?" Runa asked. "Maybe it is better with only two."

"I insist." The finality of his words were like a hammer on metal.

"What about me?" Aren asked, rubbing his hands together.

The messenger appeared confused, looking at Runa with an expectant expression. She immediately grasped he did not know what to say.

"He should come as well," Runa said.

"He stays with me." Konal's whispering voice was stretched to its limits. He now stepped down from the high table, dragging his hand along it as he approached Aren. "He was just at Snorri's side, and if it is as they say, then travel is too dangerous for him. Do not contest me in this, Runa. I will not have it."

She knew better than to challenge him. If Snorri were on his death bed and asking for her, then she owed it to him to be at his side. He was like a father to her, as well as Ulfrik, and this news was one more twist to her heart she could not stand. Thinking of losing him at the moment she would need him most nearly brought tears to her eyes, but she shook the hair from her face and addressed the messenger.

"We should leave as soon as you are fed and your horses rested." The two men bowed and gave their thanks to her. Konal guided her away with a firm grip, his hoarse voice a wintry whisper.

"Give him my best," he said, not without a hint of sincerity. "But this has not spared you from your deceit. I know you were at the well, too."

Her stomach flopped and she felt ready to faint. She blinked at him, finding no words. What could be said? He sneered and released her.

"I will select the men to accompany you," he said, pausing at the doors from the hall. "Travel safely."

She watched him go, then Aren touched her arm. She jolted at the surprise, and Aren fell back.

"I don't trust this," he said, smoothing his hair after the shock of Runa's reaction. "Einar's messenger has more to say to you than he revealed. What will you do?"

"I'll get the rest out of him on the journey. Don't worry for me, but take care of yourself. I think your father is using you to ensure I return."

Aren swallowed and nodded slowly. "I know he is. I'm a hostage to my own father."

25

Runa and the messenger, who had given his name as Hrut Grisson, rode in a cart along the track to Eyrafell. The road was nothing more than ruts worn into the plains of grass from the frequent travel between the two fortresses. While they had thought to bring a horse for her, none had considered she did not know how to ride one. About three tries to get her on the beast convinced Konal to lend the cart. They had already been on the track for a day, and her back ached from the constant rattle and the poor sleep she had in the bed of the cart. Now fat rain clouds rolled over the horizon of dark trees and a strong breeze gusted across the grass. No birds dared fly in the wind, and so she had nothing to listen to beyond the wobbling and creaking of the cart's axle.

"My husband's guards are behind us now," she whispered to Hrut. "I think there is more for you to tell me?"

He shrugged, but checked over his shoulder. "We'll be at Eyrafell soon enough. What I have to say is best told there."

She folded her arms, but the cart struck a rock and the jolt nearly sent her to the ground. "Do you have to hit every obstacle?"

"Sorry, I don't often drive carts. It's a farmer's work."

Runa brooded in silence, staring into the glare of the eastern sun and hoping to see Eyrafell rise above the horizon. Hrut's secret ate at her heart like rat gnaws at sacks of grain.

"I can't wait. Tell me now." He shook his head. "Is it the presence of my husband's men?"

He nodded. "They'll have to go once we're at Eyrafell. They seem like good men, too bad."

"Too bad?"

"You'll see soon enough."

The rest of the trip was an endless procession of jolts and bumps and Hrut's maddening silence. Once Eyrafell came into view, Runa's heart nearly leapt from her chest. The gates hung open to welcome them. The men greeted Hrut and his companion, but frowned at the three other men Konal had assigned to be Runa's minders.

"We are here now," she said to Hrut. "Can you share you message."

"Snorri's not dying," he said. "But he and Einar desired a private meeting with you." He flashed his eyes at her three guards and realized now why Hrut regretted having them along.

"That was a terrible lie," she hissed at him. "Snorri is family."

He shrugged. "Wasn't my lie. What do we do with your guards?"

Runa stared at the three of them dismounting their horses and handing them over to stable hands. She bit her lip and considered. "Easy enough to slip them. I am not here as their prisoner, so they cannot follow me everywhere."

Hrut nodded in agreement. "I'll alert Einar of your arrival. Your son, Hakon, is eager to see you as well."

A whirlwind of feelings sped through Runa knowing Snorri was well and her son was present. The mystery of the entire adventure took her mind from the horrible weight of Konal's threat, even if only for this moment. Aren was still in his grip, and she would have to return for him. Yet still, something momentous was afoot and her heart raced in anticipation.

The arrival went as any one would expect. Bera, Einar's graceful wife and Runa's dear friend, came with her three daughters to welcome her. Konal's guards stayed at a close but respectful distance. Bera had seemed untouched by age with her hair full and lustrous and not lines on her plump face. She artfully ignored the bruises on

Runa's cheek and kissed her on the good one. "Be welcomed," she proclaimed warmly. As she hugged her, she whispered in her ear. "Why the guards?"

"Konal," she said, her eyes falling away. "I was hoping your daughters might entertain them long enough for me to meet with Snorri?"

They stared at each other, Bera's expression inscrutable, then she looped her arm into Runa's and laughed. "I see no harm in that. Snorri is anxious to see you."

For the next hour Runa and her guards were in the mead hall, where all the important men were conspicuously absent. Bera made small talk with her, but Runa did not hear it and smiled her way through the conversation. She was constantly scanning for the arrival of Snorri or Hakon, anyone who could reveal why she had been summoned. Bera's three daughters had taken up with the her guards and each was as charming and beautiful as their mother. A few well-timed giggles and several overlong stares had Konal's guards mystified.

Bera stood suddenly and spoke loud enough for Konal's men to hear. "You really must see these patterns my daughters have been weaving. They are quite clever. Come to the loom with me."

Only one of Runa's minders bothered to glance at her move toward the walls where the looms were set up. Bera pulled fabric out of the basket, and spoke under her breath. "Hrut should be outside the hall to take you to the men."

"Thank you, I hope Konal's guards won't raise a fuss."

"If they are any good, they will, and if I become angered at their behavior, I have two dozen men ready to restrain them." Bera smiled. "Go now and don't worry for your minders."

Outside the hall the night was cold for summer. The rain had not fallen from the clouds, but instead left the air wet and heavy. Hrut had a cloak prepared for her. "They are all gathered and ready for you."

Runa's heart was racing and she felt faint. She could not grasp what they had to reveal in such secrecy. Eyrafell was much like Ravndal had been, and she felt a familiarity as Hrut led her along the roads to a long barracks building in the shape of a ship's hull. Orange light flickered beyond the open door.

"Go inside," Hrut said. I will be out here if you need me again."

She crossed into the barracks, finding rows of beds with trunks and bags of gear, racks for shields and swords as well as stands for mail armor that she mistook for people in the dim light. The central area at the hearth held a long table with benches, and three men standing before it.

"Snorri, you scared me witless with that lie of being dead!" She crossed to the old man, who leaned heavily on his walking staff, and gave him a hug. His beard tickled her cheek as she did, reminding her of the ugly bruise she displayed there. As she pulled back, Snorri's cloudy eyes fell on it and his face folded up in anger.

"I'm sorry for the lie, girl. Judging by your face I was not mistaken in bringing you here."

"Mother, what happened?" Hakon pulled her into a hug, then brushed her hair over her ear.

"I didn't travel all this way to explain a bruise on my face. It's nothing, my son." She had not seen Hakon since Yule, and she studied him for new scars. He was the image of Ulfrik, though leaner and not as tall. His clear blue eyes were fierce and his golden hair had captured a wave from Runa's own tightly curled locks. Singular to him was a beak nose that lent a raptor-like cast to his face. He held her at arm's length now, examining her bruise and shaking his head.

"Sorry to bring you here under such deceit. We had urgent need of you and had to conceal our true purposes," Einar said. The giant man stood over her, and gently kissed her forehead. She remembered when he was only a round-headed, awkward boy who was too shy to speak to her. His mother, Gerdie, had been a friend to Runa during one of the worst periods of her life, and now he extended the same respect to her as his mother had.

"What could be so urgent and secretive?"

All three men shared a look, but Hakon's was most telling. A smile nearly exploded from his face, and thought the hearth fire burned strongly the light was still not enough to determine if those were tears in his eyes. He had always been her most emotional son, and the most needful of her support. She attributed it to being kidnapped in his youth.

"Come now," she said. "Don't look at each other, since it's me you want to tell. Someone just say it."

"I should be the one," Snorri said. "Since I'm breaking my promise. Did Aren say anything to you?"

Runa's mouth hung open, caught between a smile and a word. She shook her head, blinking.

Snorri adjusted his grip on the staff and Einar held his shoulder for support. Hakon took his mother's hand.

"It is as you always believed." His voice was low and rough with age, but his eyes glittered with vigor. "Ulfrik is not dead. He is alive, and visited both me and Aren only a week ago."

She heard the words. All three men watched her carefully, and Hakon squeezed her hand.

"Mother, are you alright? You look pale."

She opened her mouth. Nothing came out. Her entire body felt numb. Einar now stood beside her and began to guide her to a bench. She did not understand why they appeared so frightened.

"What do you mean he's alive?"

"It's what you think it is, lass. He has been gone but not dead all these years."

"You saw him?"

"Spoke to him, along with Aren."

The room grew dark for a moment and she was aware of hands holding her up.

"Mother, here drink something."

"He's alive?" she said in a tiny voice. "Why not come to me?"

"That's not a concern," Snorri said. "But right now he is in grave danger."

Runa looked right at Snorri's eyes, saw his solemn expression.

Then the world went dark.

26

Konal downed the last of the ale. It was harsh and bitter, the worst of a long series of bad kegs. He flung the horn aside, sending it crashing into the corner of his darkened hall. Servants jumped at the impact but none dared meet his eyes. Only that hag, Groa, stole a glance at him then turned aside. She had never liked him, and the feeling was mutual. All the old woman did was poison his wife against him. He should have driven her out long ago, and gods be damned if she had been a dear friend to Runa. A real friend does not poison marriages.

Hirdmen close to the high table raised their horns and toasted Konal's anger. He glared at them, but they were too drunk to notice his displeasure. Light and a cool breeze filtered in from the open smoke hole and front doors of the hall. Shadows flickered beyond the threshold, men passing on their duties. He rested his head in his hands and scowled at the open door. How he wished for such a simple life, uncomplicated with responsibilities and the demands of an oath-holder. He wished for the days when his twin brother, Kell, had been alive and the two sailed the oceans with naught but their crews and swords against the world.

Sighing heavily, he stared down the long empty board. He was alone here at the high table, as he had been for so many years. Runa may have slept beside him but her heart was forever lost in a dream of her dead husband. She had seen his head along with everyone else. Einar had witnessed the death. What more did the woman need? She had been keen to grab him as a drowning man grabs driftwood, but once she had felt safe again all the dissatisfaction began to surface. Was it not bad enough that fire had made him ugly on the outside, but that she had to make him ugly in his heart as well?

He clutched the gems at his belt and his frown deepened. A king's fortune now hung at his hip and his deceitful wife had hid it under his bed for all this time. Such an insult was staggering, but then to attempt to steal it again while he was gone. Had she lost her mind?

Men laughed and boasted, a few started a brawl that drew others to bet on victors. He was alone in the hall despite all these men. They did not care about him, only what gold and ale he could provide them mattered. When either was gone, he would be utterly friendless. Of course, the gems at his hip could prevent that, but converting these stones to something more easily spent would be difficult. Not many men could pay what these were worth, and the one who could, namely Hrolf the Strider, would put a claim on these treasures for himself. In fact, Konal did not doubt Hrolf would be tempted to kill him and take the treasure for himself. It was that valuable.

"Where's Aren?" He asked suddenly, then belched. To his shock, one of the servants hovering at the edge of his vision stepped forward with an answer.

"He said he was stepping outside for air, lord."

"Air? A man shouldn't have to go anywhere to find that." He slammed a palm on the table, and the front ranks of men turned on their benches to face him. He stared at them, their faces blurry and unclear. After another belch, he pointed at one gap-toothed man with a red cap. "Do you have to find air?"

The man's face fell at the question, but his companions began to snigger. "I never thought to look for it."

"He farts enough to keep himself in foul air all day," said the man beside him and the whole table erupted in laughter.

Konal slapped his hand on the table again. "That's right! I'm going to find my bastard son. He's right bastard too, but you all know that."

When he stood he stumbled, and his men laughed even harder. Along the way to the exit he bumped men and benches, but none dared do more than laugh or help him on his way. He passed the brawling men, their scuffle over and both sides nursing bloodied and swollen faces. He stopped at the obvious loser, his left eye swollen shut. "You look like my wife."

"Maybe he can warm your bed tonight," said one of the victors and more laughter exploded.

As Konal staggered outside he left his men in high spirits, proof that he was as good a leader as Ulfrik had ever been. "We didn't laugh this much under you," he muttered to himself. It was late afternoon and the sky above was dark and the western horizon stained orange. Over the tops of the stockade walls birds flew home for the night. Within the walls, people scurried to make the most of the last light of day. Konal wobbled down the tracks, people stepping out of his path with a bow and a word of greeting. He knew where Aren would be hiding. Same place every time.

Unsurprisingly he was at the stone Runa raised in memory of Ulfrik. He stood facing it, one hand touching the gray rock flecked with lichen and bird droppings. The runes graven into it followed a snake pattern and were strengthened with red pigment. Not many knew how to read runes, but he did and the words haunted him. <u>For Ulfrik Ormsson, a great hero and father and a terror to his enemies.</u> Aren's hand was tracing the serpent shape that contained the runes.

"Gods, Aren, he wasn't even your real father," Konal shouted as he staggered up to him. Aren bowed his head and did not answer. Konal stood behind him, unable to think of why he wanted to see his son.

"I had begun to forget what he looked like," he said, still not turning to face Konal. "His eyes were what I remembered best. Smart and alive, looking deep into your heart."

"What nonsense is this? You're looking at a rock. If I knew you and your mother would be crying over this pebble all the time I'd have never let you raise it. I should knock it over and put Ulfrik to rest."

"You tried to step into his shoes, but they did not fit. Not as a husband, a father, not even as jarl."

Through the thick fog of ale, Konal still felt the knife cut to his heart. He seized Aren by his arm and twisted him around, pulling his square face up to his own.

"You'd better take those words back."

"Or you'll break my arm or smash my face like Mother's? Do it, but it won't change the truth of what I said."

"And what did you say?" He twisted Aren's arm harder and he winced in pain but did not cry out. He bit his lip and squeezed his eyes shut as Konal pushed his arm to breaking. When he failed to relent, he released him. "I asked you a question."

"Are you too drunk to hear me? I said you cannot replace my true father nor replace Mother's true husband nor the people's true jarl. You are a fake, and always have been. That's why you're drunk all the time and why you hate everyone. You tried to steal a man's life and it failed."

"I did not steal anyone's life!" Konal's shouts drew others to stare at him, but he searched about as if to dare anyone to approach. People snapped their heads back to their own business. He stood over Aren, who clutched his arm and hung his head. He grabbed Aren's shirt and pointed a finger into his square face. "You are fourteen, and old enough to know words like those carry heavy consequences. You make such an accusation again in public and I will defend my honor."

Aren looked up in a sneer. "Defend your honor? Your honor is a little far gone for that."

He threw Aren against Ulfrik's memorial stone and he flattened against it. His face had gone white but he tilted his chin back defiantly, a look derived straight from Runa and one that set Konal's teeth on edge. A moment of clarity burned through the ale and he realized how much Aren understood his pain. Since the boy learned to speak he had always been saying things beyond his age, and seeing things no one should see. A fear gripped him at that thought. Did he know everything?

"This is ridiculous," Aren said, stepping away from the stone. "You're drunk. Go sleep it off and leave me alone."

As Aren walked past, Konal slammed his fist into Aren's gut. The boy doubled over and vomited out his dinner. Konal grabbed his thin hair and flung him back to onto the stone. "You think Ulfrik is your father? You want to be close to him? Let me help you."

Aren attempted to dart away, but Konal latched onto him with both hands and pressed him against the stone. Then he grabbed Aren's head by the hair and began to rub his face over the runes for Ulfrik's name. "This is where he is, son. Get close to him."

He smashed Aren's face against the rock, pulling his head back and slamming it again. Aren struggled and kicked, and it only drove him to slam harder. He smashed Aren's face until he lost count, stopping only when blood smeared the stone. He released Aren and let him collapse into a pile like a discarded cloak. His son remained balled up and shuddering with sobs. Konal looked about, discovering the area devoid of onlookers.

After catching his breath, he suddenly realized he had almost killed his son. His hands went cold and the drunken haze over his vision cleared. He bent over his son's body, hesitating to touch him. When his fingers were about to brush Aren's shoulder, his son whirled on him.

His face was swollen, lips broken and probably his nose as well. Blood flowed from both nostrils and his teeth were red with blood as he snarled. "Don't touch me! You are not my father! My father is alive and he will have revenge upon you for what you did to Mother and me!"

"I'm sorry," his voice was again a quiet, ragged whisper. "I shouldn't have --"

"He never died. That head was not his. He's with Einar now, and will be coming for you. Your face will be smashed on this rock. I swear it!"

Aren staggered to his feet and dashed away. Konal stood staring that the blood stains on the rock.

"Alive? That's not possible." But was it impossible? Runa had been summoned to Eyrafell and Aren had not been himself since returning from it. If Ulfrik were alive, he could not imagine the complications.

"You have to be dead," he said. He glanced at the memorial stone and his heart flipped in his chest. A bloody handprint covered the runes for "a terror to his enemies."

"And if you're not, then you must die again."

27

Runa sat on the bench, hand covering her mouth, and her head still swam from having passed out. Hakon sat pressed to her side, arm around her shoulder and hand on her knee. Snorri and Einar both sat on a bench across from her. As night deepened so did the wavering shadows of the hall, and to Runa all three men seemed to meld with the darkness as if all were a dream. Heads of men poked into the open door, but upon spotting them disappeared without a word.

Snorri had described every detail of Ulfrik's return and of the news he had shared. They now sat in thoughtful silence, and Runa imagined imprisonment in Iceland. The place had been legend as far as she had known, and traders spoke of it being out of reach of normal ships. Yet Ulfrik had lived there all these long years, and had found his way back to her. The feelings swirling in her heart were a confusion of joy, sadness, anger, and dozens of other sensations she could not identify. As Hakon held her and smiled, she decided to follow his lead and be happy Ulfrik was alive.

"I don't know the details of Ulfrik's task, but Hrolf sent him in disguise to join Count Amand's forces," Snorri said. "After rescuing Vilhjalmer he expects lands and gold as a reward, and I've no idea what that means for his decisions about you. But I told him about

Konal and he had that look we all know so well. He's not going to let it pass."

Runa felt heat on her face and studied her lap rather than meet anyone's gaze. "I never expected to be judged for what I did. I thought him dead."

"Not judge you, Mother," Hakon said, squeezing her shoulders. "But free you from this shameful life Konal has brought you. Look at your face. Father would go mad at seeing that bruise."

She smiled weakly. "I'm not sure that's what I want to happen."

"We're getting ahead of the matter," Einar said. The giant man folded his muscular arms across his chest, gold armbands and rings glinting in the hearth light. "Only days ago my men were sent to contact spies in Count Amand's forces. This is a regular meeting that happens every month. They collect the information and send it back to Hrolf. This time, however, after they had received the latest news from the spies matters worsened."

Runa stared at him, eyes searching between Einar and Snorri. "How so?"

Einar leaned forward on his knees. "The spies were being followed by Count Amand's men. We did not see if Hrolf's spies were overcome, but we are certain they are known to Count Amand."

"Ulfrik is to contact these spies, but in their last report they made no mention of him," Snorri added.

"They would not know to expect him," Einar continued. "Nor did my men know to ask after him. But now that we are sure Count Amand's men are following the spies, Ulfrik may be in danger."

Runa did not feel fear, only anger. Her fist tightened and she narrowed her eyes trying to recall Ulfrik's face. *The moment I learn you are alive,* she thought, *is the same moment I'm warned you may die?*

"Why are you telling me this?" she asked, a whisper thin and hoarse enough to sound like Konal. "If he must die again, I do not want to suffer the same pain twice."

"You can help him," Einar said.

"Carry this news to Jarl Hrolf, girl." Snorri stood from the bench, wrestling with his staff. He hobbled over to settle beside her so she was now pressed between him and Hakon. "If he knows his son and spies are in danger, he will take action."

"I still don't know why it should be me. Why torment me with this worry?"

"Girl, Hrolf has a soft place in his heart for you." Snorri patted her knee. "You're also a lot better looking than the lot of us."

"It's likely Hrolf might do nothing at all with this news," Einar said. "In fact, any action is dangerous. Maybe Amand plans to let the spies continue, maybe feeding them wrong information. In that time his son might be freed."

"But his men would be doomed," Runa said. Einar shrugged. For her own children's safety she had let far more than a half dozen men die.

"I could not sway him," Hakon said. "I'm too inexperienced in some people's eyes. Otherwise I'd go in your place, Mother."

"He thinks he's ready to rule Paris," Snorri added dryly. "You know Einar cannot leave with the Franks acting up all along the border. I'm too old. There's only one choice that makes any sense."

"Me," she said softly. "I have to at least convince Hrolf to send warning to Ulfrik."

"It would risk exposing him, and could spell his death and a worse fate for Vilhjalmer," said Einar.

"Or it could save Ulfrik. And you'll forgive me for not caring a whit if Vilhjalmer lives or dies."

Einar laughed. "Oh, he won't die but would be a sword over Hrolf's neck. That's his only son!"

Surrounded by the men dearest to her heart, entrusted with securing Ulfrik's safety, the choice did not even figure into her mind. "I have to leave immediately, but Konal has sent guards to watch me."

"I was surprised at that," Einar said, rising from the bench with a sigh. "I will detain them, and send my own with you. It is important that this be kept a strict secret among us alone. Not even my wife knows why we are meeting tonight. The fewer people who know, the better we can protect Ulfrik."

"Aren knows, and he is trapped with Konal." She looked up at Einar and his lips were tight. No one spoke for long moments.

"I have no right to interfere with Konal," Einar said. "Delaying his men from their orders is insulting enough. He's done nothing wrong."

"Do you see my mother's face?" Hakon leapt from the bench, fists balled at his sides. "You're telling me that's not wrong?"

Einar stared at Runa. "What a man does with his wife under his own roof is not my business. If your mother sought my help, I'd lend it to her, but I've not heard a complaint."

"But with my father returned things will be different," Hakon said, looking between Runa and Konal.

"Oh, lad, things will be much different," Snorri said. "But that's a worry for another day. For now, we need to get your mother on the road to Hrolf."

"Travel down the Seine is still the swiftest and safest method for traveling west. You'll leave at dawn with a full crew. They will see you to Hrolf, and home again."

"I can't go home again," she said, striking her palm with her fist. "Get my son away from Konal, and I will remain here until Ulfrik returns."

They all lingered in silence, Einar nodding then leaving the hall. Hakon returned to her side and draped a consoling arm around her. Snorri remained standing but averting his eyes to the distance.

"Aren is Konal's son," he said. "Until he is a man, his father decides everything for him."

"I'll not have him be a hostage, and you know that's what Konal will do the moment he learns Ulfrik is alive." Runa stood and faced Snorri. "So make him a man and get him away."

28

Ulfrik and Grimnr's hirdmen spent their time in drills, patrols, or idling in Grimnr's hall. A cold night was settling on the camp, but Ulfrik's waist burned from the rigors of a full day of shield wall practice. The bench he sat upon was unforgiving and he yearned to lay out flat. Yet with his new sword brothers at his side, he could do little more than smile through the soreness and wish he were younger. The hall was spacious and smoky, lined with banners of a dozen petty chiefs all subordinated to Grimnr's standard of a black wolf head on a red background. Grimnr's table was set higher than any other Ulfrik had seen, as high as his knee. That table was empty now, but a row of mugs and drinking horns spread out before his seat and solemnly awaited use.

The drinking started early, with a tasty ale in strong supply this night. A plump serving girl worked a newly tapped cask, snatching up one mug or horn after the next and refilling it until suds overflowed onto her hands. Vigrid sat next to him and ensured he never had an empty horn.

"A hard day's work is rewarded with a hard night's drinking," he said, slapping Ulfrik's shoulder.

"A fine way to end the day," he said. "But without something in my belly I'll be under the table before the sun sets."

His protests brought laughter and another full mug that slid across the board to slosh its contents over its rim. Though he spoke lightly, the truth of his predictions began to manifest in dizziness and a warm glow on his face.

"You're the new man," Vigrid said. "And we haven't seen how well you drink."

"You can tell a lot about a man by how he holds his drink," said another man with bushy eyebrows from across the board.

"Oh yes," Vigrid agreed. "I think you can tell quite a bit. Here, I'll match you this one."

Raising a mug to Ulfrik's horn, there was nothing to do but put it back. The drink went down easier than the last, and the pain in his back diminished with each mug. Others cheered them on and clapped as they finished. Before Ulfrik could belch, a fresh horn of frothing ale was shoved into his hand.

This continued until he was surrounded by the rest of the hirdmen, each cheering his drinking. He did not notice Grimnr's entrance until the crowd parted for his arrival.

Ulfrik liked Grimnr the Mountain. True to his name, he was a giant to rival Hrolf or Einar, and he wore his hair in a long braid to his waist. It was an impractical style, Ulfrik thought, prone to being grabbed in battle, but Grimnr had the scars to show he had survived whatever the shield wall had thrust at him. The day Ulfrik stood before him and met with approval a tingle of pride ran up Ulfrik's back. Such a feeling was rare in him, but Grimnr had a natural charisma that made men want to follow.

In another life Ulfrik would have liked to call him a friend, but instead he lied to Grimnr about every detail of his history and searched for weaknesses he might exploit if he ever had to kill Grimnr. Fate was unkind.

His ponderous bulk shoved through the gathered crowd and the bench across from Ulfrik cleared. He settled on it, a wolfish expression on his face, then leaned across the table.

"You've made a strong showing in drills these last few days. Heard you kick down shield walls like opening the door to a mead hall."

"A lifetime of practice does it," Ulfrik said. The crowd's boisterous laughter softened and many struggled forward to hear the answer.

"Aye, no lie in that," Grimnr said. The plump serving girl set two mugs of ale before him then shrank away. He did not acknowledge the drink, but studied Ulfrik. "I have to wonder why I've not heard of Ulfar the White before today."

"You have," Ulfrik said. "I met you five days ago."

He burst out laughing at his own joke, but no one else followed. He was already feeling weak from too much ale on an empty stomach, and his bad joke alerted him to be more cautious with his words.

"Your name has reached my ears at least once for each of these days," Grimnr said. He looked at him with a gimlet eye. "It seems in battle there's little you can't do, and your sword brothers are mightily impressed. So let's see how a battle of drinks goes for you."

He shoved one of the mugs across the table at him, ale splashing over the side. The surrounding hirdmen clapped and began to place their bets.

"Vigrid has already poured me three mugs in a row. I feel like crawling under the table."

"Three mugs?" Grimnr's lip curled in a sneer, then downed the mug before him. "I've had two already. Now it's fair. We begin."

He slammed the board and a roar went up from the hirdmen. Ulfrik found himself staring at his mug while Grimnr chugged a fresh refill. Vigrid prodded his shoulder. "Drink, you fool. I'll keep the ale flowing."

He slugged the ale down, spilling as much as he could without being called a cheat. True to his word, Vigrid had a mug ready when he was done with the last. Three mugs later the room began to swim and after another two he fell forward on the table.

Rather than cheers he found himself being hauled onto the board. There was no sound but for the rasp of a dagger clearing its sheath. Grimnr held him down, his face red and frowning.

They know who I am, Ulfrik thought as Grimnr's massive hand crushed his neck. They're going to kill me right here.

The dagger point was at his eye and Grimnr snarled. "What's your real name?"

"Ulfar the White," Ulfrik managed to say through the choke hold. He tried to punch Grimnr but discovered men pinned both arms and legs to the table. He was as good as tied down.

Grimnr released his hold, then backhanded him hard enough for Ulfrik to see stars. He repeated the same question and Ulfrik gave the same answer.

"Where are you from? Who did you last serve?" The men dragged him up while the questions fired at him. His legs were like wilted stems and he collapsed. Rough hands hauled him upright and Grimnr appeared before him, dagger in hand. "Answer my questions."

"I served Leif the Unlucky. I am from Trodheim in Norway." He gave the answers he and Gunther One-Eye had prepared. Leif had been a real jarl who had died in battle along with most of his crew.

Grimnr growled in frustration, then Ulfrik was being shoved through the throng. They punched him in the gut, clapped him in the head, or beat his face as they cycled him through the crowd. Each one asked the same questions Grimnr had, and as drunk as he was Ulfrik held on to the lie. They had attempted to weaken his mind, and now they weakened his body as well. He crashed to the floor when a flurry of kicks landed all over. He crumpled into a ball to protect his face and body.

"Let me through." He heard Grimnr's voice, then felt his massive hands fall on his shoulders and flip him to his back. "Get his arms and legs."

He was held like a hunter's prized boar between two men. Grimnr guided him to the hearth where hot embers glowed. Ulfrik struggled as they set his head beside the fire, the heat scorching the right side of his face. He vomited and it hissed as the puddle flowed into the fire. Grimnr's hand pushed his face onto the hot rock of the hearth and it scorched his cheek. With his other hand Grimnr drew out a burning brand from the fire.

The searing heat was inches from Ulfrik's face, making his eyes water. The more he struggled the harder Grimnr pressed his head.

"Last time, or I burn out your eye. Who do you serve?"

"You!"

"What's your real name?" The brand thrust closer and Ulfrik squeezed his eyes shut.

"Ulfar the White!"

Grimnr roared and Ulfrik braced for the flames. Then he heard a wooden clunk and sparks landed by his face. He opened his eyes as Grimnr released him, then he slid to the floor.

Someone doused him in cold water and a cheer went up. Leaning against the hot stones of the hearth, he looked up at a smiling Grimnr. Behind him, the hirdmen were giving approving nods.

Holding out his hand, Grimnr said, "Sorry about that, Ulfar. I had to know if you were honest. Trouble with spies recently. You understand."

Ulfrik nodded, water running off his face as he sat. He took Grimnr's hand and the giant man pulled him up to a crushing bear hug.

"Ulfar is one of us today," he proclaimed. The hirdmen cheered and clapped Ulfrik on the back, each friendly hit like a hammer against his weary flesh.

Despite everything he laughed and accepted the welcome. He had succeeded in becoming a member of Grimnr's hird, and the sensation of success was warm spot in his chest.

Yet somewhere beneath the thick blanket of drunkenness and pain, Grimnr's words began to bore home. Trouble with spies, he had said. As Ulfrik accepted his welcome, his mind drifted to worry for Vilhjalmer. He had to find Eskil before he was subjected to something worse than Ulfrik had endured.

Outwardly he smiled at his sword brothers, yet in his heart he cursed his foolish pride. The time he had to finish this task had shortened to nothing, and he had to complete it as soon as eyes were off of him. Unfortunately, he realized he had put too many eyes on himself.

Secrecy and deceit had never been his strongest skills, and now he had to execute flawlessly or become a causality of his own vanity

29

Runa stood outside Hrolf the Strider's mead hall as a drizzle pattered atop her hood. The two guards at the door pulled into their cloaks and folded the material over the shafts of their spears. Both were young enough to be her sons and both appeared miserable. Runa shifted her weight, tapped her foot, and shot a frustrated look at the half of Einar's crew that remained with her outside. She understood that a woman was not accorded the same respect as a warrior, but to be made to stand in the rain while others entreated Hrolf for an audience on her behalf was shameful. There had been a time when Hrolf's doors swung open to her without effort, but now status and power kept his doors shut against all no matter how old the relationship.

Rain dripped off the edge of her hood and onto her nose. She snorted it away and it was as if that blew open the hall doors. Her men reappeared and were smiling. "He'll see you," said Reist, the hovedsmann of Einar's ship that had ferried her down the Seine. As the leader of the crew, it had been his duty to present to Hrolf even if Runa was a jarl's wife.

"About time," she muttered, pushing past Hrolf's guards. "The rain is getting worse and I'm cold enough."

Inside the front room guards checked her escorts who willingly surrendered swords and daggers. As a woman she was spared the attention and was first to be shown inside. The humid warmth inside the main hall clasped her face as she entered. Hrolf was sitting at his high table, his mousy wife Poppa at his left and the giant Gunther One-Eye at his right. None of them smiled and Hrolf's usual charm was as scare as his manners had become. She noted how his golden-ringed fingers absently thrummed the table.

After bowing to Hrolf and receiving his permission to speak, she looked over her shoulder to Reist, then back to Hrolf. His expression was stern and inscrutable. She knew the pain of a kidnapped son and what it did to a man's heart, but she almost felt anger from his stare. She could not understand how a simple audience could irritate him so, particularly since a man of his station did not need to grant it. Swallowing, she raised head back and spoke clearly.

"Jarl Hrolf, I know this will seem a strange request, but we should speak privately."

His thrumming fingers stilled and Poppa sniffed, only Gunther One-Eye smiled slightly. The scar tissue in his eye socket twitched as leaned toward Hrolf to whisper something. He broke his cold gaze from Runa then spoke in low tones to Poppa, whose face grew more offended at each word. At last, she huffed and stomped from the hall, a dozen maids and servants scurrying after her.

She turned to Reist. "Thank you for all you have done, but my business with Hrolf is not for your ears. Please await me outside."

Having just complained about standing in the rain, she wondered if Reist would resent her for sending him back into it. Yet he only acknowledged the order with a nod and left without complaint. Now she stood with Hrolf and Gunther, feeling no bigger than a mouse standing beneath the two tallest men she had ever known.

"I know why you are here," Hrolf said, his voice toneless. "But in case I am mistaken, tell me why you have sought this audience with your jarl."

"Ulfrik is alive and a man he traveled with named Finn is recovering here." Hrolf's eyebrows raised and his clear eyes widened, but he did not move. Gunther One-Eye shook his head and laughed silently. "I tell you this so you know I understand the task you set for Ulfrik."

"You do?" he asked as if inquiring about nothing more pressing than the weather. "How did you come by that knowledge?"

She told him of Ulfrik's visit with Snorri, and Hrolf's expression shaded from mild irritation to red-faced anger. His voice did not betray his mood, remaining as level as before. "So you are here to see Finn, I assume, and learn what you can of your husband's life these years we thought him dead?"

"I would like that, Jarl Hrolf, but there is more urgent news relating to Ulfrik and Vilhjalmer." He leaned forward and spread his hands to indicate she should share. Licking her lips, she described all Einar and Snorri had told her about Count Amand's men and what Einar feared may happen. Hrolf listened dispassionately, and Runa stumbled more than once wondering how he maintained such a distance when depicting the threats to his own son. When finished, she waited for him to agree. Instead he fell back in thought, steepling his fingers before his lips.

After an uncomfortably long silence, he sat up straighter and met her eyes. "This is dire news, and I am grateful for the haste and care taken to deliver it to me. Who else knows of Ulfrik's task?"

"None but my sons, Snorri, and Einar. Snorri would not have betrayed his promise to Ulfrik had he not learned your spies were followed by Count Amand's men."

"You are certain they will not speak to anyone else?"

"They place their honor above all. You know this to be true, Jarl Hrolf."

He nodded appreciatively. "Aren? He is young yet, maybe inclined to tell his love this great secret?"

Runa suppressed a laugh, for Aren was nothing if not a complete failure with girls. "He is wise beyond his years, and would never speak such a crucial secret to anyone."

He stared at her a while longer before speaking. "You have done me a great service. I will have a slave see to your comfort while you are here and put servants at your command."

"Is that all? What are you going to do with the news?"

Gunther One-Eye slowly nodded his head as Hrolf smiled at her like she were a precocious child. "I will consider what is best for my son. I expect you to observe strict silence on this as well. Not even my dearest wife knows what has happened. She still thinks Vilhjalmer is with Mord and I do not want her informed otherwise."

"I understand that, lord. But Ulfrik's life is in danger and if he acts while Count Amand is searching for spies it could be doom for both your son and my husband. You must send word to him."

She expected him to explode in fury, but instead his shoulders fell forward and a glimpse of the old Hrolf glimmered in his troubled expression. With a touch to his shoulder from Gunther the iron returned to his voice.

"I appreciate your concerns and how hard it is to learn Ulfrik lives but is in danger. Do not think I would entrust him to this task if I did not believe him capable of facing whatever the Fates have planned for him. This is the life of my son and the future of my kingdom we are discussing. I have placed it all in Ulfrik's hands and I know I have not misjudged him. If you knew the details of what he survived to return to us, then you would not fear his safety. He will succeed."

"But I don't know the details," she said with forcefulness she regretted. Hrolf and Gunther both leaned back in surprise. "At the very least he must be alerted to the threat. Don't leave it to the gods to decide, for they have ever loved to toy with my husband."

"I will consider what you have said." Hrolf stood to signal the end of his patience. Runa's pulse throbbed in her neck and her hands trembled. This was not enough. She had to be sure Ulfrik was safe, and if Hrolf would not act then she would.

"Do not consider, but act. How long can you delay before he is discovered? What will happen to him and your son?"

Hrolf's face turned red and he pressed his lips together. Gunther One-Eye stepped down from the high table to gently take her by the arm. "You're cold and tired from your trip. News like this must hit hard. Take a rest and you will feel better."

"What? I'm not so helpless that I have to lie down. Do you take me for one of those delicate flowers the Franks so love, that all my petals will fall at the first strong wind? We have to do something about this news today. You must see that?"

Gunther nodded, but his grip on her shoulder tightened. Her eyes widened at him, then she turned to Hrolf. His face was still red and he leaned on the table with both fists. "What happened to your face?"

The shift in topic threw her. The shame of her beating was the last thing she wanted to describe to Hrolf. Reflexively she pulled her curly hair over the bruise. "It is nothing."

"I understand a lot of nothing happens in Konal's hall."

Runa gasped. How could he know such details and why would a great jarl concern himself with the details?

He smiled at her reaction. "Yes, I know the hearts of all my men. What they fear, what they love, who they know and where they travel. It has grown harder over the years, but key men I make a habit to watch. I wonder what Konal will ask you when you return? What will you tell him?"

"That I went to visit Einar as I said I would." Her voice shrank and she did not even convince herself.

"Of course, but he will discover your visit here sooner rather than later. Maybe he already knows? Then he will beat you until you relent."

"He would not do that," she said, her voice diminishing. "And I would never tell him the truth."

"A common belief until the pain becomes too much," Hrolf said. His expression shifted from anger to concern. "But he'd have it out of you and then what would he do knowing Ulfrik lives? Of all the people to fear his return, Konal has the most cause for it. He took Ulfrik's wife and home, assumed Ulfrik's life for his own. It was all honestly done under the assumption Ulfrik was dead. But now questions will arise. He might panic and word of Ulfrik's return and his mission might leak. Such starling news may travel faster than anyone might expect straight to Count Amand's ears. What of Ulfrik's safety then?"

"That will not happen," Runa said, tipping her head back in defiance yet realizing her assurances meant nothing.

"Of course it will not." Hrolf smiled and extended a hand to her.

"You will remain my guest until Ulfrik returns. I will send word back to Einar for you, and instructions that will guarantee he does not repeat what he knows."

"You can't do that," she stepped toward him but Gunther held her back. "Konal will know something is amiss and take it out on my son."

"Leave your son and Konal to me. For now, I will keep you with Finn and he will tell you the details of Ulfrik's story."

Gunther tugged her arm and she lowered her head and nodded. Further arguments would bring nothing good. "Please tell me you will keep Ulfrik safe."

"He will do that himself, and return my son. Have no fear for it."

Runa nodded, but she did fear. In her heart, she knew the gods looked down and laughed at the small hopes of mortal men. They would be entertained before men realized their dreams.

30

Konal sat alone in his hall, unwashed, hands still flaked with Aren's blood days after smashing his son's face against Ulfrik's memorial stone. Rain pelted the roof and thrummed on the hide cover over the smoke hole. A leak caused the hearth beneath to hiss and steam, mimicking the state of Konal's thoughts. He was all heat and vapor since Aren stunned him with the news of Ulfrik's return. Not a single thought remained whole in his mind, nor could he string them together to make sense.

Everyone had quit him, either at his own command or through his vile cursing. Groa, the old bitch, led a revolt of the free women and now only slaves remained in his presence. A single slave, an old Frankish man with a shaved head, lurked at the end of the hall to attend him. Otherwise, he had spent the last three days alone in gloomy silence. The hirdmen took meals at their barracks, and sent food to him at the hall. A plate of cold pork sat before him, untouched from the night before. All he needed was a keg of ale to keep him alive.

The regret for beating Aren was overwhelming. He was a strange child, but was Konal's only remaining kin. Why had he abused him? Aren held onto Ulfrik's memory as if he were the greatest man who had ever lived. The boy just did not understand the truth and never would. Ulfrik had poisoned Konal's own son against him, ensuring years after his death that Aren still held him in higher regard than his own blood father. Every time Aren praised Ulfrik's memory he wanted to crush it out. Every time Aren's face glowed at some account of Ulfrik's life he wanted to smash it down. Every time, Konal's hands itched to grab Ulfrik's ghost and throttle it out of all memory. Yet Ulfrik had been dead, and the living were all he had in reach, so they bore the burden of his ire.

He tottered out of his chair, stumbling through the hall as he had three nights before. The old slave stood as he approached, but he continued past until he crashed out into the rain. Puddles spread like brown lakes across the center of his hold. People remained indoors, but Konal found the cold rain welcoming. He wandered through the muddy tracks until he came to a barracks. Inside, he found men passing time with gambling and drinking. All fell silent at his arrival.

"Find my son. Bring him to the hall."

He did not await acknowledgment but returned to the hall to await the completion of his orders. Back inside he sloughed off his cloak by the fire, removed his boots, and stretched his legs out on the high table. He let his clothes drip into small puddles beneath his seat. He was dozing when the hall doors burst open and three men dragged Aren inside.

Fighting all the way across the hall, the three hirdmen left a trail of rain water behind as they deposited Aren at Konal's feet. The bedraggled men stood over the prone form, frowning. Konal set his feet on the ground and leaned across the table.

"Where did you find him?" His voice was a strained, thin whisper.

"With the cooper," answered one of the men.

"Groa's husband," Konal said. "Of course she would shelter him. You may all return to whatever games you were playing."

He watched them leave, ignoring the dripping, heaving form beneath him. Konal wondered if anyone had been keeping look-out duty, particularly in the rain when no one wanted the task. He needed to get back on these men, but not before he dealt with more pressing concerns.

"Stand up," he said. "I didn't break your legs."

Aren stirred, reluctant to obey but eventually staggering to his feet. His hair was flattened to his head and plastered to his face, which he kept lowered. Rain water ran from his cloak into a puddle at his feet.

"Get out of that cloak and dry off. You look as if you just pissed yourself."

When Aren did nothing, Konal stood and fetched a dry cloak left against the wall. He approached Aren and began to remove his cloak, but his son pulled back.

"As you wish," Konal said, dropping the fresh cloak on a table. He turned back toward his own bench. "I've given thought to what you told me the last time we spoke."

"Is that what you call it?" Aren asked, head still lowered. "We were speaking to each other?"

"You've got a right to be mad." Konal strained to fill his voice, but his burn wounds forever rendered his voice thin and weak. "I took a heavy hand with you. But you know better than to bait me with your praise for Ulfrik. There is so much history you don't understand, but how could you?"

"So I deserved to have my teeth broken and face smashed?" Aren raised his head to match Konal's gaze. His square face was rounded with swelling, and brown scabs crisscrossed his forehead and nose. He flashed a wicked smile to reveal his front tooth had been broken in half. "Was I not ugly enough without this?"

"It's not so bad," Konal lied. The damage he saw filled him with self-loathing, but he would not reveal that to his son. "Since you're not a fighter, you'll need a few scars to give you some presence with your men. The broken tooth will do."

Aren laughed without humor. "I hope you die. Do you know that? I beg the gods to kill you."

"That saddens me. I wish things had been different between us. You are my only blood in this world. You look just like my father, but you've got my brother's mind. Kell was as clever as you are, maybe more so. He was the better part of me, and I the worst part of him. Maybe his death is why I've become what I am."

"Is there a point to this, Father?" Aren's eyes were small behind swollen flesh, but glittered with hatred.

"Tell me everything you know about Ulfrik. Where is he now?"

Aren recoiled as if struck and turned his head aside. Konal waited. He had to know the details surrounding Ulfrik's return and what he planned. Whatever Aren knew had to be told. "I'll get it out of you one way or another. Besides, you've already told me the most important thing, so what is it to tell me more?"

"I don't know much," Aren said, his shoulders dropping. "But here is what I know."

Konal then listened to the most fascinating account of survival he had ever heard. That Ulfrik could survive a fall from a high tower then imprisonment in Iceland was proof of his hardiness. Konal had grown to despise a great many things about Ulfrik over the years, but he had nothing but respect for his stamina.

"So he left for the Franks right away. Never met with Einar?"

"Not that I know. Neither Einar nor Hakon ever spoke to me about the return of my father."

Konal's fist clenched at Aren's use of the word "father" for Ulfrik, but he had to dig deeper. "And your mother? She has been called to visit Snorri upon his deathbed. Do you think it means Ulfrik has returned?"

"You now know as much as I do. May I leave?"

"No," Konal slammed his fist on the table, causing Aren to flinch. Beneath the table Konal's other hand touched the bag of jewels at his side. "Did Ulfrik say what his intentions were in returning? You said he planned to kill me. Why?"

Aren's swollen face blanked and he stared as if he did not understand the question. "That was just my anger at you. He said he only wanted to fulfill Hrolf's task and take his reward in gold, then leave."

"He would not ask anything of me or his former wife?"

"Nothing he told me."

The lie was plain to Konal. Aren was the smartest boy he had ever known, but was still a boy who did not understand guile as well as a man. He was a perfect copy of Konal's father, right down to the habit of rubbing his nose when lying. Aren dragged the back of his hand under his nose as he repeated his lie.

"Ulfrik will not come for you. He said to appear to Mother would be too disturbing and that returning was a mistake."

"And those threats to my life were your own words and not his?" Aren nodded. "Besides Hrolf, no one but you and Snorri know Ulfrik has returned?"

"Those are all who know." Aren did not touch his nose.

Konal sat back and waved Aren away. "Go back to standing in the rain, if that's your wish. You've told me what I need to know."

"You will not say anything about this?"

"Of course not." Konal resisted his own temptation to touch his nose. "I've no desire to bring more pain to your mother."

Aren left, his sopping cloak dragging up days old straw from the floor as he went. The hall doors opened to hissing rain and Aren disappeared into it. Konal sat still, waiting until Aren put distance from the hall.

Then he exploded with anger, flipping the table and sending his dish of uneaten food crashing to the floor. The slave cowered in the corner while Konal flung mugs, plates, jugs, anything that came to hand. He raged until he was out of breath, then collapsed onto a bench.

Ulfrik had defied death. If he was back in Frankia then it meant he had already taken his revenge on Throst.

And if Ulfrik had killed Throst, without a doubt he would have discovered Konal's hand in the plot to kill him.

It felt as if ages had passed since he set those plans in motion. Throst was eager for revenge, and Konal was tired of being left to guard Ulfrik's family and treasures while he played at being a hero to his people. Now he realized Ulfrik had him guarding the jewels he now had at his hip, a new insult after so many years. Ulfrik understood how he tormented Konal, forcing him to guard his wife, a woman he had never stopped loving, and then returning long enough to make love to her before his next adventure. His own son called Ulfrik father before Konal's eyes. The shame and humiliation had burned him worse than the flames that had marred his face.

When the opportunity to betray Ulfrik to Throst arose, he could not resist. Ulfrik would die and Konal could assume the life he had stolen from him. For the love of the gods, he had seen Ulfrik's head and heard Einar's account! How could Ulfrik be alive today?

Of course Ulfrik knew the truth and the only thing preventing him from killing Konal was Hrolf's task. Konal had not fought a real battle in more than a decade. Despite the Franks being only a short distance downriver, he had managed to avoid combat of any sort. Ulfrik, however, had evidently kept his skills sharp over the years. A fight between the two of them would fare poorly for Konal, and he could not allow it come to that.

Only three people knew of Ulfrik's return: Hrolf who he could not influence, Aren who he controlled, and Snorri who would help Ulfrik fulfill his revenge.

Snorri had to be handled. If Runa was with him on his deathbed, then he might confess what he knows. It could be played off as the ramblings of a dying man, but Konal had to be sure he did not repeat the story to Einar and Hakon.

After Snorri, he had to ensure Ulfrik failed in his task. That would be more dangerous to Konal, but to let Ulfrik return would be even more ruinous. He would visit Count Amand and inform him of the spy in his midst. He just had to keep his motions secret from Hrolf, which would be made easier by disguising his travels as a visit to Eyrafell.

From there, Ulfrik would at last truly die once exposed to the Franks. He would remain blameless and Runa would be none the wiser. He had to act now and ensure Ulfrik did not live another day.

31

Two days after Ulfrik's grilling at the hands of his fellow hirdmen, rain drenched the camp. Standing in the door frame of Grimnr's hall he listened to the rain slashing into the well-churned mud. The continual splashing of the puddles obscured the ground. Though it was summer the rain had cooled the air and he pinned a dark green cloak over his shoulder.

"Glad you did not pull guard duty?" One of the hirdmen appeared behind his shoulder to stare outside with him. Ulfrik glanced back at the man.

"Of course, but I've got work at the blacksmith's today."

"In this rain? Raynor won't be banging iron in weather like this. He'll be in bed and on top of that young wife of his."

The man chuckled as did a few others nearby. Ulfrik smiled and rubbed his face. "I promised to help him with heavy lifting today. When has rain ever been a reason to not honor your word?"

The hirdman patted his shoulder. "You should learn to give your word less often, Ulfar. I suppose you must at least allow Raynor the chance to send you away."

He placed all his weapons and anything that would rust by the trunk given to him when he joined Grimnr's hird. He had the honor of serving Grimnr in his hall, and so had a place in the front room to sleep and store his belongings. Nine other men shared the space with him, and so he feared nothing but rolling over onto one of them in his sleep. None would touch his gold, war gear, or anything else. As he had been told, only women were shared among the hirdmen but all other property was private. On this rainy day, only Grimnr had the luxury of women for his bed.

Taking the ragged sealskin cloak Gytha, Finn's mother, had bestowed on him years ago he stepped out into the rain. He had to find Eskil today, and set solid plans for rescuing Vilhjalmer. The rain pounded on the cloak, rolling off with ease. He needed sealskin boots to match, but had not be so fortunate in his travels, therefore water sloshed into his feet as he splashed through the puddles.

He had learned Eskil was well placed with Count Amand, on par with Grimnr in his status though nowhere near him in terms of command. Count Amand prized him for his tactical advice and insight into the finer aspects of the Northman culture. Ulfrik had been loath to inquire too deeply for fear of eliciting attention, but in recent days he had heard rumors among Grimnr's hirdmen that spies were uncovered in Eskil's command. He had to begin his dialog with Eskil before Count Amand turned his attention to him.

Across the muddy drilling grounds he crossed into camp territory he had yet to visit. These tents and buildings were closer to Count Amand's walled fortress, and Eskil was said to keep his hall here. Fortunately Raynor's forge was on the way and so if anyone watched him they would see Ulfrik headed to where he claimed to be going. As expected the forge was dark, so he detoured around it and passed into the tents and buildings.

Only fools and people with no choice were out in this rain, so he had no one to ask for Eskil's location. Further up between two buildings he saw what appeared to be a guard huddled against a wall. He approached the man directly, calling him as he closed. The man peeked up from behind a brown cloak that shielded him from the rain.

"Hail, friend," Ulfrik said as the guard stared at him. "I am from Grimnr's camp and looking for Eskil's crew. I hear they are based over here."

The guard stared at him under a furrowed brow. "Who did you say you were?"

"I didn't say. I'm looking for Eskil's crew." The guard shoved off the wall and Ulfrik saw his hand slide beneath his cloak for his sword hilt. Apparently the rumors about Eskil had some men on edge, and he had to calm the situation before it got worse. He dropped his voice, barely audible over the hiss of the rain. "Is it true what they say about them? Do you think there are spies among them?"

The guard's expression did not change. Ulfrik glanced around, and saw no one coming to the guard's aid.

"There might be some truth to that," the guard said. Emerging from the shelter of the wall, rain pounded the guard that wreathed him in a white spray. He peered at Ulfrik. "I asked for your name."

"What are you guarding?" Ulfrik countered, searching about and finding nothing worth posting a guard.

"Eskil and his crew."

The two of them stared at each other without expression. The guard flicked his eyes to the left then Ulfrik saw it. A row of spears had been set up around a hall and heads were thrust atop them. In the distance they were scraggly black and gray globs with matted hair. Ulfrik swallowed, not knowing which head was Eskil's but certain all of Hrolf's spies were represented. He turned back to the guard.

"I don't think they'll be escaping any time soon," Ulfrik said. "Unless you expect the heads to float way."

"Grimnr is interested to see who comes asking for Eskil or catch anyone wanting to take down those heads."

They locked eyes.

The guard jerked his hand to draw the sword, but Ulfrik saw it first. He slammed into the guard, thumping him into the wall and pinning his sword arm against it. The guard began to scream but Ulfrik wrapped his hands around the guard's throat and dragged him from the wall and splashed down into a puddle. He drove his thumbs into the guard's windpipe and his eyes popped in terror. However, the rain had made everything slick and his hands slipped enough to let the guard gasp a breath, prolonging the kill.

A warm feeling spread on his thigh, then realization struck. Without releasing his choke hold, he looked down to see the guard had pulled a dagger and cut his leg. With his one hand he shoved the guard's face into the puddle while his other hand sought the blade. Once he had it, he held it firm while pressing the guard's head into the water. The guard bucked and struggled but his face was completely in the water and the moment he dropped his dagger Ulfrik pressed his head deep into the mud.

The guard drowned in the muck, kicking out with a last bubbling breath. Ulfrik held the head longer to ensure death, then pulled the body out of the sucking mud and rolled it next to the wall. He pressed against it, hands trembling both from the effort and fear. Their struggle had lasted a moment, and the roar of the downpour had obscured most of the commotion. He most feared the crash against the building but no one came to investigate.

His own leg had not been cut badly, but his pants were torn and blood mingled with rain to flow freely into the mud. Explaining how he cut himself without any weapons was going to take a bit of storytelling. The guard next to him had a head full of tan mud and his eyes stared horrified into the falling rain. Ulfrik closed them and put the guard's hand upon his sword, then whispered beside his ear. "You died fulfilling your duty. Go on to the feasting hall, and await me there. It is a sad day when a loyal man must die alone in the mud."

The scene had to appear like a robbery, something Gunnvald's crew would commit. He flipped the body over and stabbed the dagger into the guard's kidney. The wound was a certain kill that did not produce much blood, which he did not want splashed on him. He did not trust the rain to wash it away. He then took all the valuables from the guard: his rings, a silver armband, a small pouch of hack silver, and three gold coins. These he concealed in his cloak and would dispose of later.

He then dashed away, mud splattering his pants as he rain. The blood from his cut leg spread in a dark stain. Once out of sight he altered his path back toward Raynor's forge, and from there retraced his path to Grimnr's hall. His heart pounded, more from knowing Eskil had been executed than for fear of killing the guard. Despite the setback he had garnered useful information. Count Amand was on alert for spies, which meant he had to be more cautious than he had been since arriving at camp. Also, he counted himself lucky to have not located Eskil earlier or his own head would be on a spear as well. Without help, however, freeing Vilhjalmer would be all the more difficult. If only he could send word back to Hrolf, he might have a chance. A distracting attack on the Franks would cover a breakout, though the timing would have to be perfect.

As he closed the final distance to the hall, he snorted at his hubris. He was planning as if Vilhjalmer had already been contacted. The location of Hrolf's son still remained unknown. Amand's fort was the logical place, but getting inside to investigate would be challenging. Ulfrik had never been much for sly infiltrations, having left those tasks to younger and more talented men.

Entering into the dry warmth of the hall, men paused to stare at him. Vigrid, who was now is best friend in this crew, laughed. "Did a horse drag you back? And what happened to your leg?"

Ulfrik rolled his eyes as he stripped off the sealskin cloak, which had done nothing to keep him dry after he had fallen in his fight with the guard. "Raynor was in his house and I don't think he wanted to be disturbed. I decided to do some of the work I had promised on my own. I bumped into a blade and cut my legs for my troubles, then I took a spill outside the forge. The god of the forge did not want me around without Raynor there, so I returned."

Vigrid slapped his back. "You look like a rat. Get out of these clothes and warm up next to the hearth."

Stripping away his clothing, he tossed them into a pile. As he set his boots beside the hearth, Vigrid began to help lay out his other soaked clothes. Ulfrik's heart came to his throat when he found Vigrid staring at the guard's stolen wealth that had fallen out of the pile.

"What's this?" he asked, and stared expectantly at Ulfrik.

32

Ulfrik awakened the next day after a fitful night's sleep. His clothes were still by the fire, stiff and caked with mud that flaked off on the hearthstones. Few of the men were awake, as most had passed a dull night of rain with heavy drinking. Vigrid stood in the door, staring outside at the clear dawn. Water still dripped from the frame but the rain had ceased in the deep of the night. Ulfrik was still awake when it had stopped.

Vigrid had accepted Ulfrik's excuses for the wealth he had hidden on himself. After confronting him with an armband and ring, Ulfrik kept his reactions cool. "The armband is too tight, so I take it off when I work. The ring belonged to my wife when she was still alive. Too valuable to wear it."

"She had fat fingers?" Vigrid asked, holding the ring up to the light.

"You fool. It was a man's ring I got on raid and gave to her. She wore it on a chain."

Ulfrik collected the belongings from Vigrid then tossed them back on the pile of clothes as if nothing mattered. Today, he would be certain to lose the ring rather than risk someone identifying it. The armband was plain enough to keep but the ring had delicate snake patterns engraved into it.

"Who has the morning watch?" Vigrid asked. "Is it you, Ulfar?"

Lost in his thoughts, Ulfrik did not answer to his false name until Vigrid called him again. "I think I've got drills today, but I still need to see Raynor about yesterday. I should probably visit him before the day gets started. Will you cover for me?"

Vigrid shook his head. "I don't owe you anything. If Grimnr asks I'll tell him your shirking your duty to plow a Frankish girl. I bet that's what you're after. Raynor's an excuse."

The idea was useful, so rather than deny Vigrid he smiled as if he had been unmasked. "I won't be long, but that depends on what I find at the forge."

"Miss the drills and you'll not be seeing that forge for a good while." Vigrid winked at Ulfrik as he dressed.

Without the rain to worry about, he strapped on his swords and daggers. His confidence increased feeling the weight of sharp iron. He was going to hunt for Vilhjalmer today, and had to be prepared to exploit any opportunity. At this point his only plan was to find a plan and run with it. He hated to operate blind, but with Eskil's death he was without eyes.

Halfway to Raynor's forge he turned for the river. He squatted down with other men along the bank and washed the mud out of his hair. While he combed it, he used the moment to toss the ring into the water. He followed it up with a few rocks to make it seem he had only been idly skipping stones. Then he walked up the banks toward Count Amand's fortress.

No one challenged him from the river approach. He had no direct access to the walled fortress from this side. However, ships were unloading cargoes of crates and barrels and placing them onto carts. Watching the crew at work, he carefully approached the carts and pretended to admire the horses. Never much for animals, his pats on their flanks made them snort and sidestep. He drew a curse from a man standing in the other cart.

"Don't scare the horses, man! You want them to run off?" The man had belly that filled out a white shirt, and beneath a floppy red cap gray hair flowed into a braid tied at the back of his head. A pink scar sat diagonally across his face.

"Sorry, I just like horses."

"Maybe you like them too much? Seems you make them feel strange." The man began to thrust his hips back and forth, drawing laughter from his crew. Ulfrik smiled and his face grew hot.

"Alright, I take your meaning. I'll get out of the way."

The fat man nodded and Ulfrik began to move off, but he was not as fast as he could be. He glanced at the fat man as he continued past, and he pressed back a smile when the fat man called him again.

"If you've got nothing better to do than look for horses to fuck, why not put in some honest work here. I'd like to get this cargo out fast, so I can get under sail before noon. Want to earn a few silver bits?"

Ulfrik rubbed the back of his neck and squinted up at the early morning sun. "I actually have drills this morning. Not sure I have time."

The fat man shrugged. "Off you go, then. Wouldn't want to interfere with your drilling."

"Well, I could help a short time."

"Right," the fat man said. "You see the ship. Carry off the barrels and stack them on the carts. Don't touch the horses again."

He fell into line with the other crew and spent a solid half hour off-loading the cargo. By the end he had sweat a V shape into his brown shirt and his brow glistened. The fat man paid him three silver bits, a pittance for the work but Ulfrik was not after silver.

"All of this is going to Count Amand? That's a lot of beer. What about the crates?"

"Crates are mix of things to keep a fortress running. Not really for you to know, is it?" The fat man raised a brow at him as he pressed the silver into Ulfrik's palm.

"Thanks for the silver. It's a bit thin for the work I did. Do you need help unloading?"

The fat man was turning away then paused. "You after more silver? We unload just inside the gates, and my crew can handle that. No sense my paying you for it."

"Actually I was just hoping to ride on the cart. I have to go back that way for my drills, and a spot of rest would do me alright. By the time we get there, I might pitch in a bit to repay your kindness."

The fat man smiled, his pink scar bending with it. "Ride with barrels."

The cart ride was short and once inside Count Amand's fortress, he began to study every detail of its layout while helping the crew offload their cargo. The only gate was heavily guarded by Franks. No Northmen made it this far into the fortress. Of course, with a proper disguise Franks and Northmen were hard to tell apart. The main building was constructed of stone with wood outbuilding and towers. No telling where Vilhjalmer could be inside the place, or even under it. He guessed the towers were more likely than a dungeon.

"That's all there is," the fat man said. "Thanks for your help. We've got to clear out now."

They clasped arms and Ulfrik followed behind as they made for the gates. The Franks were idle and inattentive during this routine. The Northmen crew filed out without a glance from anyone. Ulfrik used the moment to slip into the shadow of the walls, and he waited while the gates dragged shut.

He was locked inside Count Amand's fortress, fully armed, and out of place. "Great plan. Your head is water-logged from yesterday," he whispered to himself.

The goods they had delivered were stacked to the side of the open courtyard. Servants in plain clothes carried away the smaller casks and crates, while teams worked on the larger ones. He watched them for a short time, all of the servants intent upon their jobs. He decided the best approach was to act as if he belonged here. Stealth would draw suspicion, but walking boldly across the courtyard would promote confidence Ulfrik was at home.

He strode toward the pile of trade goods, back straight, head up, then lifted one of the casks. As one servant approached, he met the man's eye and nodded to him. The servant's brow furrowed but he nodded back and continued his business. He shouldered the cask and followed the line of servants carrying goods into the fortress.

The heavy scent of cheese filled his nose as he followed the front man through a short hall into a storeroom. He set the cask beside the others, the servants there uninterested in him, and turned to follow the same man out. Once in the short hall, he was alone but for the man in front. Frankish conversations carried from a room to his left. He turned back to head deeper into the fortress.

Pausing at a corner he listened for activity on the other side, and hearing none he rounded it. A woman stood in his path holding a broom. They both startled at each other, though Ulfrik regained himself faster.

The woman was young and slender. Lustrous brown hair flowed out from beneath a white head cover and wide green eyes stared at him from beneath thin brows. She touched her chest in surprise, but when Ulfrik smiled she relaxed and returned the same.

"I did not hear you there," he said in broken Frankish. Never talented with languages, he was only regaining his ability with Frankish after years of disuse.

The woman blushed and shook her head as if to say all was fine. She stood to the side as if to let him pass. Behind her was an open door where light glared into the room. A table and benches had been shoved to the walls and stubs of candles showed the room was in current use. From the filled spear racks Ulfrik determined it was a guard room and the open area beyond was the inner courtyard. He might find the tower entrances there, but his presence would be questioned no matter how confidently he behaved.

Unless he had an escort.

"Actually, I'm new to the Count's service," he said to the girl. She continued to smile and she tilted her head to the side to expose her graceful neck. He paused in confusion, unprepared for her interest. "Well, you seem friendly enough. I'm looking for the captain of the guard and was told to find him in the tower. Which one is that?"

Without a word, she tugged his sleeve and walked him out into the courtyard. Despite the warm glow of her interest, he remained alert for a trap. A square of trampled grass that now had been churned to mud after the rain filled the inner courtyard. The girl pointed diagonally across to a square log tower. She smiled at him and drew closer, and he was about to thank her when doors to his right swung open.

Grimnr emerged with five other men. Not time to back into the doorway, the two of them locked eyes.

Ulfrik grabbed the girl on instinct, but in the same moment Grimnr's eyes softened and a wolfish smile pushed his scars aside.

"I have to ask how you got in here," Grimnr said as he crossed the distance. "But I don't have to ask why."

Nervous laughter came unbidden, and he tugged the Frank girl closer. She did not resist and let her arm slip about his waist. "I was hoping to keep this secret a little while longer."

I was actually hoping to ride this chance to the end, he thought, but then you showed up.

"Yeah, well, I'll let you in on a secret," Grimnr said as he stood beside him. "The whore rides any Northman cock she thinks will take her out of this place. Forget her."

He pulled the woman's hand from Ulfrik, and firmly set her aside. He guided Ulfrik by the shoulder and resumed walking. The four other men behind him were unfamiliar, and though they displayed gold armbands and jeweled rings all of them appeared bored with Grimnr's talk. Ulfrik glanced back at the girl, who dragged her broom in defeat back into the guard room.

"How did you find her?"

"Did you see that slim waist and fair skin? Not too hard to find that, is it?"

Grimnr laughed. They continued under the gates of the inner courtyard and now passed the stack of cargo, of which only a few barrels remained.

"Well, she doesn't leave this fortress, so how did you find her?" Grimnr was not looking at Ulfrik but signaling guards in the tower to open the gates.

"Merchants at the river docks sometimes hire help to unload and deliver their goods. I thought to make some extra coin, seeing how we've not had any action since I've been here."

They passed beneath the gate and outside the four other men parted with a short wave, heading into what had formerly been Eskil's portion of the camp. Grimnr studied him, the morning sun filling his predatory face with shadow. "Don't take any more work unless you speak to me first. Nothing wrong with making side money, but I need to know where you are always. Forget the whore, too. I'll make sure you don't go lonely for too long."

"As you say." Ulfrik inclined his head and Grimnr patted his shoulder. They both headed back toward his hall.

"Also, you'll be the first to know, and I think you'll like this news."

"Really, what would it be?" A burning sensation already ignited in his gut, but he smiled as they wove between the tents and buildings.

"Just finished a council with Count Amand. I got him to see that we need to shake up the enemy and let them know we're here. If we continue to hide we're giving them time to strengthen their defense. Besides, Count Amand has an important hostage that so far has done us no good that I've seen."

"A hostage?" Ulfrik tried to sound conversational, but his heart bounced off the bottom of his throat.

"Son of Hrolf's right hand, Mord Guntherson. A true Northman's son, that boy. I admire his fight. Anyway, that's not a concern of yours. We're marching to war, boy!"

"We are? Great." Ulfrik's weak enthusiasm made no mark on Grimnr. "Who are we attacking."

"We're stabbing right at the heart of their defense, show them we can hit wherever we want. You will be right up front with me to see it too. We're going to lure out and ambush that giant bastard, Einar Snorrason, and I'm going to nail his head over my hall door."

33

Ulfrik lay in the wet grass, mud clinging to his back. Clouds scudded through a blue sky while black dots of birds wheeling high above floated through his vision. His body ached and his arms throbbed. He blinked hard to clear his head from the ringing. The dark shape of a man loomed over him.

"What happened to Ulfar the Invincible?" the man asked as he extended a hand to help him up. "Am I'm fighting a child?"

White pain lanced through his leg as he stood, memories of wounds dealt long ago. He limped a moment, then picked his shield and sword out of the grass. "Sorry, Narfi, I think I got sick in the rain yesterday. Feel like I've got ice in my blood."

Narfi, Ulfrik's sparring partner, shook his shaggy head. All around them pairs of men practiced fighting with sword, spear, and ax. All were invigorated with Grimnr's announcement of the upcoming attack. Grimnr's personal hirdmen had to be in top form and he expected the most kills to come from his own. "You will capture Einar's standard and I will take his head," Grimnr had said to the unanimous roars of his men.

"You don't look well," Narfi agreed. "But the enemy doesn't care how you feel. Put up your shield."

His ax clanged down on the metal boss at the shield's center,

Ulfrik barely blocking the strike. His hand went numb but he held firm. The hird practiced for blood, and stories of men losing limbs or lives were fresh in the minds of the group. He considered such deadly practice wasteful, but also agreed that practicing with edged weapons garnered the best results.

He just did not want to fight for blood when his heart and mind were in another place.

Swiping under the shield, Narfi danced away but Ulfrik closed the gap. He drove with his shield and crowded Narfi. Ax and spear fighters hated close fights. Worse for Narfi, he had failed to lodge his ax in the shield which was the weapon's primary role. Despite what some men believed, the ax was a support weapon for hooking or negating a shield for a spear or sword to exploit. Narfi was of the school that mistook it for a primary weapon.

"You want to give up now?" Ulfrik asked as he shoved Narfi back, who braced against the shield with the haft of his ax.

"And miss the chance to give you this?" Narfi stepped back to let Ulfrik's force carry him forward. As Ulfrik fell, Narfi rammed the haft into his side and knocked the wind from him.

"Bastard!" Ulfrik shouted. He stumbled to avoid Narfi's follow up, but the ax was already swinging for his trunk as if he were a tree to be felled.

He imagined allowing the blow to land, to crash through his side straight to his spine. He would not need to struggle any more, nor face Einar in battle or fight to reclaim what he once possessed. No more impossible battles. No more of anything but his reward in the feasting hall.

"Gods, Ulfar!" Narfi pulled his strike, and the ax hit him flat.

Ulfrik collapsed forward and landed face-down in the mud.

"You could have stepped out of that," Narfi yelled at him. "I almost killed you!"

"I really don't feel well."

He remained in the mud, the cold damp seeping between his mail. At last Narfi squatted beside him, his voice softer. "Maybe you should save yourself for the battle. Here, give me your arm."

Again Narfi assisted him to his feet, and Ulfrik kept his head lowered as he felt other eyes upon him. "Thanks, I'll be fine with some rest. Besides, I've got to get the mud out of these links or all my mail will be rust come the real fight."

Hobbling off toward a barracks house, he ignored the men watching him. He understood their fear, knowing in two day's time they would be fighting shoulder to shoulder with him and their lives depended on each man being his strongest. If Ulfar the White was not ready to fight, then he would be a burden at best and a threat at worst.

Outside the barracks Ulfrik found the barrels for cleaning mail. When a man wore his armor all day, the constant movement caused enough abrasion between links to work out rust. Now that his armor was plugged with mud, no normal wear would sufficiently clean it. He would have to spend the majority of the day getting it back in shape. In one barrel was stored rainwater for rinsing off the dirt, and another barrel was half filled with coarse sand. After drying the mail he would seal it in the sand barrel and roll it around the field for an hour until the sand worked off rust and absorbed moisture between the links. Finally he would wax the armor to protect it from new rust.

After he pulled off his mail and straightened his clothes, he leaned on the water barrel. The thought of fighting Einar made him weak. He could think of no way out of the battle, which added nothing to his cause but increased his risk. After being caught in Amand's fortress, another absence would be conspicuous enough for Grimnr to send men after him.

"Don't vomit in the water." As if summoned by the thought of him, Grimnr appeared behind Ulfrik. The tall man padded up behind him as silent as a wolf on the prowl. Ulfrik whirled to find him at arm's length, his long braid falling out of a dented helmet and his wide shoulders pulling his mail shirt tight across his chest.

"I'm sorry about practice. Just not feeling well."

"I saw Narfi flatten you. Very unlike what I've seen so far." He leaned next to the barrel beside Ulfrik and folded his arms to watch the others practice in the distance.

"Good thing Narfi can handle his ax, or I'd be in two pieces."

"Only the most skilled warriors belong in my hird." They both fell into silence as observed the sparing practice, the distant clang and shout carrying over the field. Behind them, dirty tents trembled with the morning breeze. Grimnr shifted and spoke again. "Get your rest, Ulfar. You only need enough practice to learn how to fight with this crew, and the battle is at least a week away yet. We have to settle the details with Mord."

The mention of Mord made Ulfrik stand straighter. "You're going to use his son against him?"

Grimnr nodded. "Like I said, Count Amand has held the boy prisoner long enough without making a demand. If he keeps waiting Mord will just have another son and forget this one." He laughed and Ulfrik forced himself to match it. "We go tomorrow to plan the attack. Three jarls form the bulwark of Hrolf the Striders' defense. Einar Snorrason, Mord Guntherson, and Ull the Strong. Behind these three the defense weakens, except to the north where Hrolf has concentrated strength against threats there. We will entice these jarls to battle with Mord's aid, then be certain he takes the center line. Mord will betray his fellows when we attack, holding back his men to let us crush the separated forces of Einar and Ull. The bulwark will be smashed open and we can march straight to Rouen and kick that giant troll back to Norway."

The description gave Ulfrik an ache in his stomach. "Will Mord be willing to become an oath-breaker to Hrolf and will his men follow him?"

"I don't know," Grimnr said, squinting into the distance. "He seems prepared to do anything to regain his son. This meeting will tell us much, and whether we can trust him."

"What if he doesn't bend? What of his son?"

"Count Amand wants to keep the boy. Maybe he's sad he only has daughters wasting away in Paris. I think Amand will keep him to check Mord. I'd counsel him to ransom the boy for gold enough to buy more warriors, then we'd keep Mord in check permanently after we cut off his head."

Ulfrik nodded and considered the situation. The time for feeling sick had past him, and now he needed a new plan. Mord's best choice would be to play along and get Hrolf's son back. He could enlist

Hrolf's authority if his own men bridled against the betrayal. He could also alert Einar and Ull to arrive under strength to prevent total destruction, but then risked not fulfilling his bargain and losing the chance at Vilhjalmer's return.

Worse still for Ulfrik, if Mord succeeded he would have achieved nothing and be left to return to Runa with nothing more than what he carried on his back. He had to be the one to save Vilhjalmer and not Mord. Still, with Eskil dead he was in a far more precarious position. He needed to get this message to Hrolf, and ask for more aid or at least cover for his escape with Vilhjalmer.

The only chance he had at getting his message out would be to pass it directly to Mord. He stood directly in front of Grimnr, who did not stir but merely let his eyes drift to meet Ulfrik's.

"I want to go with you on this meeting with Mord. I want to see him for myself, and get the measure of the man we're entrusting to deliver our victory."

Grimnr raised a brow. "I don't see why you need to know."

"This is not my first battle. I've years of experience, more than I'd like to admit. When you parley before the battle, you bring men with you to see the enemy up close and advise you. Why should this be any different? Besides, I don't need to drill with these men. I've fought beside enough strangers to learn how to adapt. Take me to the meeting for my experience and use me for more than just swinging a sword."

Grimnr's tongue probed his cheek as he stared at Ulfrik. The silence grew, but neither man backed away. Grimnr shrugged.

"All true. An extra set of wise old eyes is always valuable. Be ready to leave tomorrow."

Slapping Ulfrik on the shoulder, Grimnr left him. Ulfrik leaned over the barrel, his mouth dry. In the dark water his reflection wavered like a fleeting ghost. He had to rescue Vilhjalmer before the battle, or only a future of landless poverty awaited him. He kicked the barrel, swirling his reflection into a scattering of meaningless color.

34

Ulfrik knew the meeting ground well. He had fought dozens of battles with the Franks over this stretch of plains, from skirmishes to clashes of shield walls that watered the earth with blood. Once again, men would stand shield to shield, braced rank upon rank for the enemy charge, and spend their lives for an empty plain. Flesh would be laid out for the ravens and soon white bones would dot the green grass. With each step he took over this ground, he imagined the face of a fallen sword brother beneath his foot. All across this rocky, rolling stretch a man's ghost haunted the spot he exhaled a final breath.

Within another week, if the Franks had their way, the plains would have a host of Northman ghosts to add to its inhabitants.

The Franks rode horses, twenty well-armored men with a surfeit of weapons surrounding the bulk of Count Amand. Grimnr and his small retinue followed on foot. The Count employed Grimnr and his loose army of Northmen, but Ulfrik surmised he did not enjoy their company. Amand's disgusted glances revealed a haughty disdain common among the noble Franks. Such an attitude was not unwarranted, Ulfrik thought, for when not fighting amongst themselves they proved redoubtable enemies. The Count, however, did not exhibit much to justify his arrogance other than a fine swooping mustache and a glittering gold cross at his chest. He was gray and soft, unlikely to have ever fought a real battle. Ulfrik wished for a chance to knock him from his horse and introduce him to the mud.

The midday sun hid behind dark clouds, a bad sign that Grimnr brooded upon for the entire morning. "Something'll go wrong with Mord. I feel it," he had said that morning, and repeated the same dirge for most of the trek to the meeting place. The brooding did not fit Ulfrik's expectation of Grimnr, but his furrowed brow did not release even as they closed the final distance to Mord.

Ulfrik could not see Mord and his men when the leading Franks called a halt. Despite all that depended on the outcome of today's meeting, Ulfrik still anticipated seeing how Mord had changed over the years. Mord, Gunther One-Eye's only son, had been sent to foster with him during the siege of Paris. He had proved an able man and fast learner. They had grown in friendship after Mord completed his fosterage, and Ulfrik counted him a worthy successor to his father's legacy.

"Grimnr, we need you up front," called one of the Franks. He stomped forward to join with other Franks, every motion like a petulant child about to throw a tantrum.

"Does he always take signs so seriously?" Ulfrik took the moment to ask Vigrid, who was also selected to be part of Grimnr's personal guards.

"Two things Grimnr respects are signs from the gods and a strong enemy."

"But dark clouds are common enough."

Vigrid shook his head. "Not on the day of an important undertaking, and not when they come from the south and head for the north. That is a bad sign."

"Maybe in his village," Ulfrik said. "I've never heard of such a thing."

They waited for the initial meetings to complete, then were led to the center field. Franks had started construction of a pavilion, little more than five poles to stretch out a white and blue striped cloth against the intermittent sunlight. As they pulled the ropes tight and spiked them into the muddy ground, Ulfrik stepped to the side to seek Mord.

He stood at the fore of his twenty warriors, all in dark furs and well-worn chain shirts. Their eyes glared out from beneath plain iron helmets with wide nose guards. Their hostility was written in their postures, and hands rested on weapons and flexed as if ready to draw. Mord himself had not changed much over the years. He was never a tall man, nothing like his father, but he filled out his armor with a strong body. He still wore his blond beard short but his hair had grown longer, a splash of yellow flowing over powerful shoulders. When his eyes met Ulfrik's they seemed clouded with thought until they widened in recognition.

Ulfrik worried Mord had not been told of his return from supposed death, but from the swiftness of his recovery Ulfrik assumed he knew. Mord's eyes glided off him with no more curiosity than if he had seen a deer wander across the background.

As Count Amand and his captain fussed over proper seating and Mord's crew snickered at them, Ulfrik studied how to best pass his message to Mord. When all were finally called to their positions, Ulfrik again met Mord's eyes. He raised his brows at Mord and inclined his head slightly. He then shifted his eyes to one of Mord's men, hoping that he understood that man would receive his message. Mord gave no reaction, but instead took a stool set out beside Count Amand.

The meeting started with Count Amand delivering a windy speech about cooperation and the benefits of joining Frankia. The words tumbled through Ulfrik's ears without leaving a mark. He positioned himself at the back of Grimnr's guard, letting the three other men stand before him. Vigrid had offered him his spot beside Grimnr but he refused. He now waited, staring at Grimnr's thick braid wagging from beneath his helmet. He chimed in whenever Count Amand prompted him, but his role at this point was otherwise unimportant. No tactics were discussed, which would be Grimnr's place.

Ulfrik began slipping back toward Mord's line. More words slithered out of Amand's mouth, but Ulfrik only made a pretense of listening. His head was filled with his own message, which had to be delivered with the sharpness and precision of a master archer's arrow. He slid ever closer to the edge of his own side like ice melting on a cool spring day. Mord ignored him, but he could not resist glancing at him enough for Amand to absently follow it back to Ulfrik.

"What if Einar and Ull won't play along?" Mord's statement was as clear as a spear hurled at Ulfrik's feet. His emphasis on that question was subtle and his glance at Ulfrik fleeting, but the message was clear. Einar and Ull would not be blindsided. Knowing this thawed the ice around Ulfrik's heart, yet he still had to get his news into Mord's ears. A considerably harder task when not being permitted to speak.

"If you expect your son returned, then you will make them comply," Count Amand said with a dismissive flip of his hand. "Grimnr can advise you on ways to convince them. He has a way with words your kind understands."

Ulfrik took a larger step toward his target.

"How do I know my son is alive?" Mord asked. "You should have taken him to me as proof."

Another step closer.

"You have my solemn word before God that your son is in perfect health. My priest cares for both his body and spirit, and I daresay he is enjoying his time in my home."

A final step and the man at the end of Mord's line looked askance at Ulfrik.

"Words to your god mean nothing to me." Mord spit on the ground. "Without proof my son lives, you'll get nothing from me. Don't you know how this works?"

Count Amand gave Grimnr a withering look, then turned to Mord. "I thought your people put great stock in personal oaths. As one warrior to another, I am being honest with you."

Ulfrik nodded to Mord's man, a solid fellow with dark skin and his front teeth missing. His voice was a harsh whisper. "Hey, are you the one they say lost his teeth trying to fuck a horse?"

"What?" The man's face twisted into a scowl and his fists balled.

"Horse kicked you in the face, did it? And here you thought animals would be easier than women. I bet that was a shock."

"You dog shit!"

Flinging himself at the man before he could draw his weapon, Ulfrik plowed him backward. He followed up with a punch to the man's gut, hoping to wind him. Breath like stale cheese expelled into Ulfrik's face, but he shoved the man onto the ground and followed atop him. He sought to turn the brawl into a wrestling match.

Men from both sides skittered aside and shouted. Ulfrik gave the man an opening to recover, and then he wrapped the man in a headlock. Sliding to the mud beside him, he hissed into the man's ear. "I have a message for Mord. You must pass it to him in secret after this meeting."

The man elbowed him and growled. Ulfrik tightened his lock and shook him. "Eskil and all his men are dead. Send help to get the son out."

It was all he could say before others crowded them and began to pull them apart. He released the man, his eyes wide with shock and his hair wild and twisted from the fight. Ulfrik glared at him and nodded. The man blinked but nodded as well, kicking back.

The warm feeling of success vanished back into cold fear when Ulfrik looked up. Franks and Northmen were fighting, and not just with fists. Count Amand had retreated behind a wall of Frankish guards. Grimnr and Mord were peeling apart combatants. Men slugged each other and others crossed swords. Grimnr howled like the wolf he resembled, calling for peace. For all his size Mord demonstrated his strength tearing men from battle. In the confusion, Ulfrik again looked to the man he had targeted.

"You must get that message through." The man stood and again nodded.

The brawl ended when Grimnr and Mord had settled the last stubborn few. When all was done, one of Grimnr's guards lay dead. Ulfrik had not even learned the man's name. A dagger stuck out of his belly and blood flowed in a red stream into the grass.

"I knew this would be a bloody day," Grimnr said through

clenched teeth. "Look at this. Mord, you give me the bastard who did this to my man or it's you who'll answer."

Mord bristled, scowled at Ulfrik, then wheeled on his men. They lined up like naughty children and he pulled their hands out one at a time until a thin, copper haired man turned up a bloody palm. Mord yanked him out of line and thrust him at Grimnr.

"Blood for blood." Grimnr pulled his sax from its sheath, and before the copper haired man could protest the blade rammed into his gut. He moaned and crumpled to the ground, Grimnr tearing his short sword from the body. He pointed the bloodied blade at the line of Mord's men, his face dark red and deep-lined with hate. He walked down the row toward Ulfrik, stopping just before him.

"You filth aren't worth the life of one of my camp whores."

Without warning, he plunged the gory sword into another man's throat.

A dark-skinned man with his front teeth missing.

"That evens it up," Grimnr said as the man to whom Ulfrik had delivered his message gurgled his final breath through his punctured throat.

Roars on both sides went up, weapons flew from sheaths and shields faced enemies. Mord shouted for peace at his own men and Count Amand was forced to stand before his Franks and stand them down. The flare of anger lasted only moments, but to Ulfrik it felt as if a decade had passed. He fixed on the man at his feet, his blood dark and thick beneath his head.

When all had stood down, Mord approached Grimnr in barely controlled rage. "This one started the fight." He thrust a finger at Ulfrik. "You should give him to me and then we'll call this done."

"I'll give you back your life, little man, for insulting me with your threat."

More explosive cursing ensued, but Mord and Grimnr stared each other down until Count Amand intervened. "Enough, Grimnr, we've done enough damage for one day. Take your dead and let us be gone."

Amand turned to Mord, his flowing mustache wagging as he spoke. "If you want to see your son alive, then comply with my plans. I'll give you another week to make your decision, but if you insist on being difficult then I will send one part of your son home for every day you delay until I have only his head to cut off."

Before they broke off, Ulfrik tried to catch Mord's eyes but he had turned aside without a word.

Grimnr's omen had been right. He left the dead man in the grass.

35

Konal awoke face-down on the high table and those of his guard that had not drank with him were arrayed before him. Their faces were stern in the thin light of the morning falling through the smoke hole.

"Ten men from Hrolf's hall have arrived, and they have a message for you."

Konal thought his guard had repeated that same sentence at least twice but could not be certain. He struggled to see him clearly through blurry vision. His head hurt and eyes throbbed. His thin voice was even more strained and ragged after days of constant drinking. "What's the message?"

His guards shifted their weight, a few shook their heads. The lead man chewed his lip before answering. "I think they want to speak to you directly. Do you need a moment to prepare?"

"Prepare what?"

Someone in the shadows snickered and Konal stared into the blank corners of his hall. "Something funny? I'm dying of thirst. Someone get me water and send Hrolf's men inside. Why've you kept them waiting?"

The guard bowed and left with the others. Konal waited for an old Frank slave to pour water into his mug, then gulped it down.

Slamming it on the table, he pointed for a refill. This one he did not drink, but splashed on his face. Blowing away the water that ran into his mouth, his flesh prickled with cool air. When he opened his eyes, Hrolf's messengers were already filing into his hall after surrendering their weapons at the door. The low murmur of deep voices filled the hall as they clustered at the far end. Konal sat straighter and smoothed his beard, which dripped water onto his chest. A pungent odor hit his nose, and glancing at his feet he found a puddle of vomit.

The crowd of men walked with straight backs and eyes bright with purpose. Konal felt like crawling beneath his table in their presence. Even the lowliest of Hrolf's servants carried themselves like jarls and his guards carried themselves like kings. The leader had a strong, weathered face, deeply lined, and a hooked nose with a red scar on its bridge. He bowed crisply, helmet tucked beneath his arm and clean blue cloak flipped over his shoulder. A silver pin glinted in the thin light of the hall.

"Jarl Konal, I am Magnus the Stone, and I come with an urgent message from Jarl Hrolf."

His eyes were a clear blue, a stark contrast to his dark hair. Konal envied his rugged looks, his own face a ravaged landscape of burn scars that no woman had dared overlook. Not even Runa could see past them now. She figured his heart was as scared and ruined as his face. His hand touched the jewels hanging at the pouch at his waist and he squeeze it. The contents were as hard as his own heart and no less cold.

"Jarl Konal, are you feeling unwell?"

Magnus came back into focus. He shook his head, hearing more snickers from the dark corners of his hall. "I think I'm still drunk. You and your men have traveled long, so be seated and refreshed."

Magnus inclined his head with a feeble smile, but remained standing. The remainder of Hrolf's men settled on benches and waited to be served. Konal waved his servant toward the ale casks and the old slave began to fill mugs.

"Your wife is currently a guest at of my lord. I assume you know this."

Heat flared in his belly and he scowled. "I know but don't understand why. She was summoned to attend a dying friend at Eyrafell. I sent her with three guards and they returned to tell me she had slipped them while Einar detained them. All seemed rather strange to me. Has she offended Hrolf?"

He knew full well what had happened, and knowing it had set him on his weeklong drinking binge. Snorri had alerted Runa to Ulfrik's return and she sought protection with Hrolf.

"I cannot speak to the reasons. Forgive me." Again Magnus bowed and Konal smiled at his manners. It has been years since anyone had demonstrated manners before him. "Your wife is well but unhappy."

The heat in his gut roared hot, and he leaned across the table as he spoke. "What is she unhappy about?"

"She longs for her youngest son, Aren. Hrolf decided the boy should attend her while she relaxes at his hall."

Konal slouched and let a breath escape. Suddenly aware of the dozens of eyes studying him, he sat up again. "My son has already been away too long. I wish him to remain by my side. Send my regrets to Jarl Hrolf."

"I'm afraid you will have to keep your regrets." Magnus' smile was as hard as rock. Now Konal understood his name. "Aren will accompany us and in due time he will return with your wife."

He found himself on his feet, his face hot and fists clenched. "Fuck Hrolf! Aren belongs here. Did Hrolf's instructions include killing me to take my son? If you hope to carry them out, then be ready to do just that."

Konal's wretched, strained voice still managed to shock the hall. The visitors lowered their mugs and looked to Magnus, whose flinty eyes did not falter. Konal's men, the ones awake and not sunk in drunken slumber, recoiled from him.

"Jarl Konal," Magnus said in a calm voice. "May I speak with you privately? There is more to my message and you may change your choice of words for Jarl Hrolf once you've heard it."

The cool delivery mollified Konal though he glared to ensure his own men did not think him weak. With a grunt he motioned Magnus toward a side door in the hall. Outside the morning air smelled of earth and people criss-crossed the center square about their morning chores. He watched a young woman straining to carry a bucket of water from the well, a puppy dancing around her feet. Did such pleasant scenes take place in his fort? He had stopped seeing them years ago.

"Are we safe so close to the hall?" Magnus asked. Konal shook his head and they began to walk toward the center of the training field.

"Unless Loki sends are raven to listen on us, we're safe from others out here." Konal rubbed his face, trying to force away the fog of ale that clung to him.

"Jarl Konal, you and I have not met before, but I understand your situation quite clearly."

Konal stared at him, and Magnus only smiled. "You do?"

"Of course you have learned by now why your wife shelters with Hrolf. It's bit of shocking news, is it not?"

"You're talking about Ulfrik?"

Magnus nodded. "Your wife is mad with worry for her son. She believes you'll use him against her. She has been agitating to contact Ulfrik, probably because she believes he will counter whatever you intend to do. Therefore, to keep her happy and to distract her from thinking too much of Ulfrik on his important mission, Jarl Hrolf wants Aren at her side."

"That's asking a lot of a man. My son is my only kin, and you think I'll just give him over to the bastard who stole him from me?"

Magnus the Stone's face cracked with a smile. "Sending Aren back will keep Hrolf satisfied his son's rescue will go as planned. He is anxious about the length of time without news, but trusts Ulfrik will succeed. Your wife is filling him with doubts, and we don't want that to happen."

Konal frowned. "We? Why do you care?"

"I am here on Hrolf's behalf but I am sworn to a man who has helped you extensively with...certain things." Magnus cleared his throat, and Konal's eyes widened in understanding.

"What's the rest of your message?"

"It is best for everyone that Ulfrik does not succeed in his mission. In fact, he must fail if you are to keep your wife and family, all that you had sacrificed your honor to obtain."

"My honor is fine," Konal said, his voice harsh and strained. "How do you know all of this?"

"That is not as important as solving the problems Ulfrik's return has created for everyone. Plans are falling apart, Konal, yours in particular. Too many people know Ulfrik lives, but it will matter little if the Franks catch him at his task. They'll behead him for real this time. You should take your ship and a strong crew up the Seine. It's the fastest route and time is crucial. Find a man called Grimnr the Giant and inform him that Ulfar the White is really Ulfrik Ormsson and then reveal his mission."

"What if they don't believe me?"

Magnus shrugged. "Be convincing. I am only a messenger, and not a mighty jarl like you. I'm sure you can get your point across."

"What happens if I succeed? What if Hrolf finds out I ruined his son's escape?"

"His son will be freed, no fear. We've handled Hrolf for you before, and can do it again. Now don't wait. We take Aren today and you leave on this task at the same time. We will cover your tracks."

Konal and Magnus stared at each other as the rest of the fort inhabitants went about their business. Konal broke first. "I was thinking of doing this myself, anyway. Now I know I have support, it makes it easier."

"Do whatever needs to be done to ensure Ulfrik never returns," Magnus said. He leaned in closer. "If Grimnr won't believe you, then put a knife in Ulfrik's back. Just don't let him return alive and everyone wins."

36

Four days after returning to the Frankish camp, Ulfrik left his guard post at the side of Grimnr's hall. A half moon painted the camp with silvery light, enough to navigate the path to Count Amand's stronghold. His mail shirt weighed on his shoulders as slipped from shadow to shadow, sword slapping on his hip as he moved. Being freshly scoured mail, he feared a gleam from it would betray him, yet to blacken it would condemn him if caught by others. He had to look natural while so many Franks were suspicious of their Northman mercenaries. Being his most valued possession, he could not leave it behind.

He paused at a building, standing behind a buttress that leaned against the outer wall, and two Franks in their blue and white surcoats passed him. It was early evening yet, when most had settled for the night but not all. He had chosen the earlier part of the night for his plan, needing most of the darkness to make his escape. When the Franks passed, he slipped out again at a quick but confident pace. He had a field to cross and running would only attract attention.

Vilhjalmer was leaving with him this night, even if he had to fight his way out of the camp with only his sword and shield.

After the disaster with Mord, he had expected Grimnr to be furious with him but instead he had been pleased. "Good job showing those whelps who they are up against," he had said, emphasizing it with a slap on the back. Grimnr had been more upset with Count Amand failing to bring the hostage, which apparently Grimnr had advised him to do.

The breakdown in negotiations had been skillfully done. He gave credit to Mord's quick thinking, rejecting the deal but still leaving the possibility open and therefore keeping Count Amand's interest in his hostage's value. Combined with the muddy conditions from the heavy rains, an attack was not probable in the near term. After recovering from the shock of his failure, Ulfrik understood he had one chance to get Vilhjalmer out, and he took it this night.

Arriving at the walls of Count Amand's fort, he paused to study side walls where a wooden tower monitored that section. Hiding in the deep shadows of a tree, he closed his gray cloak tight on his throat. The rope hung over the side wall, as he had instructed the girl. Days ago, he returned to the fortress to find the Frank servant who had been so eager to know him. At first he thought she was dumb, for she never spoke, then she displayed her severed tongue. He promised to deliver her from the Franks and give her a place of honor in his hall if she would help with Vilhjalmer's escape. The rope dangling before him was either a sign of her complicity or treachery.

Ready to learn which it was, he hauled on the rope and found it strong enough to support him. His mail coat dragged at him, but he mounted the wall, dangled from the other side, and dropped into shadow. His legs sparked with pain and he grunted, but when he stood nothing moved. The outer court was empty, but the door to the storeroom hung open, a deeper black against the gray and silver colors of night. Straightening with a wince, he walked confidently through the door, hand beside his sword.

The Frank girl waited inside, leaping up like a child ready for her gift. Her white head cover was gone and her thick, shining hair flowed around sparkling green eyes. In the gloom her flesh appeared as clear and white as milk. Despite the tension, he felt a rush of heat to his face when she slid into his arms. He whispered to her in his halting Frankish. "You did well. Take me to the boy now. You will be rewarded like a queen."

She grabbed his cloak and threaded him through the halls without any light. Ulfrik focused on his breathing and keeping pace with the girl. She stopped him at a room, then motioned he should wait outside the door. She slipped into the room, and he waited in darkness until he feared his thudding heart would alert the entire building. Yet she returned with a smile and held the door open. Dazzling yellow light from lamps hit her, and they flitted through the room that smelled of sweat. Popping out the opposite door, they then emerged closer to the tower entrance she had shown him before. She pointed at the door, and tugged him forward.

"You want me to go first?" Ulfrik glanced between her and the door, and she nodded then tapped his sword.

Loosening the blade in its sheath, he clung to the shadow as he made for the tower. The door was unlocked, and inside two men sat at a table with mugs in their hands. They looked at him without surprise, one raising his eyebrow.

"I'm here to bring the boy his meal," he said. The guards frowned.

"What are you doing?" One asked as he rose from his seat. Ulfrik chose his dagger for its quick draw and the cramped size of the room. Tearing it from its sheath at his hip, he drove it into the standing guard's throat. Hot blood flooded over his hand and he shoved the body to the floor. The other man remained stunned, a spot of his companion's blood hanging from his nose. The moment of hesitation cost the other guard his life. Ulfrik planted the dagger into the base of his neck while clamping his bloodied hand over the guard's mouth. The guard struggled, kicking a leg out and knocking the mugs from the table. Ulfrik felt the pulse ebb as the man slouched forward, and he guided the dead guard's head to the table. Cleaning his hand and dagger on the seated guard's shirt, he found the stairs up.

Leading with his dagger he climbed through an empty room to reach the third floor of the tower. At the landing a bar hung across a door confronted him and a guard sat slouched over a small table, head buried in his arm. A candle dwindled to a nub beside his arm. Ulfrik got behind him and steadied his hands, then snatched up the guard's head by the hair and cut his throat with a quick slash. The man died without a sound, blowing out breath that smelled like blood. Ulfrik put him back into position, then lifted the bar from the door.

"Vilhjalmer?" he said into the darkness. "I've been sent by your father. I'm here to get you out."

The boy sprang from the darkness, eyes wide and eager. "You know my real name? How do I know you are from my father?"

"I just killed everyone in this tower, which should tell you enough." He reached out with his bloodied hand, and then hesitated to frighten Vilhjalmer. To his credit, he did not flinch at the gore.

"The priest was making me pray every day. I'm ready to leave." He stepped out into the shallow ring of light from the wavering candle.

Ulfrik had not seen him since he was a babe, but he had his mother's strong nose and jaw. In his eyes and bearing he was all his father. No more time remained for comparisons, and Ulfrik knelt beside him. "Stay quiet and close to me. We're leaving with a Frank girl who wants to help us. By dawn we will be safely away, now come on and do as I say."

Leading the way down the steep stairs, the floor moaned as if trying to rouse itself from sleep and warn the fortress. At the bottom, the blood of the dead guards had spread into glittering pools of deep scarlet and the room flooded with the coppery tang of blood. He checked the door, peering outside for anyone approaching. Satisfied they had an opening, he grabbed Vilhjalmer's wrist and dashed across the short courtyard to the door where the mute girl waited. She wrinkled her nose at the sight of blood.

"Was there going to be another way to do this? Show us the way out, and we'll be gone by dawn."

She led them deeper into the fortress's lower levels. Twice they had to jump into rooms to let a servant pass, but otherwise the fortress was asleep. Exiting out of the rear fortress, they came to a smaller gate that had only a single guard posted. He paced in a circle, arms folded into his cloak and his spear and shield leaning against the wall. The Frank girl motioned them to wait, and she walked openly to the guard. Initial surprise changed to delight when he saw the girl approach. She went up to him, lifted onto her toes and planted a kiss on his cheek. He grabbed her close and his hands began sliding down her back.

"You're getting an education tonight," Ulfrik whispered to Vilhjalmer.

"My father does that to our servants," he replied, clinging close to Ulfrik's side.

"Not what I need to think of right now. Stay here. She's giving us an opening."

The girl had already faced the man's back to Ulfrik and was leaning against the wall as the guard fumbled with his belt. The fourth man tonight died as Ulfrik clamped one had to the guard's mouth and drove the dagger into his kidney. He caught his fall, then dragged the body into the shadows by the wall. The girl looked on with no expression and Ulfrik felt a chill. She had no love for her own people. Maybe they had cut out her tongue and earned her hatred. For a moment he saw a spark of cold fire in her eye, but he had no patience to consider it.

"Looks like you're no stranger to the guards back here," Ulfrik said. "Get the gate open and I'll get the boy. Outside the gate, we're going to walk very calmly to the edge of camp and then we'll slip away. Just don't act like you're running and we should not attract attention.

She gave him a nod then he fetched Vilhjalmer. "Don't worry about stabbing the man in the back," he said to Ulfrik. "My uncle Gunther One-Eye says sometimes a man has to be killed any way he can be and it's not dishonorable."

"Your uncle just likes killing. Now let's go. Stay close and you'll be seeing him by tomorrow."

The gate swung open to the camp. At the heart of two armies of Franks and Northmen, Amand did not waste resources on extra guards. They walked calmly into the night across the short open field toward the first line of tents that showed gray in the moonlight. He put his clean hand on the girl's shoulder and squeezed it. "Almost home. You'll have a place of honor in my hall, trust me."

At the line of tents two men appeared out of the darkness. Both first looked to the Frank girl, the lead man's smile failing. "You've already got company for tonight? We were hoping for some private time."

Ice poured through Ulfrik's heart. In the moonlight he recognized the pox-scarred face of the speaking man as Gunnvald Hrethelson, and standing beside him was the pot-bellied, fish-lipped bruiser Erp. Despite his dull wits, Erp's dark eyes widened in recognition, flitting between him, Vilhjalmer, and the girl.

Ulfrik reached for his sword. Gunnvald and Erp did the same. The blades hummed in the night and moonlight flashed from Gunnvald's sword.

"Ulfar the White and a young boy coming from the fortress. How wonderful, Erp. We've found the last of Eskil's spies."

37

"Vilhjalmer, run for the edge of camp then for the trees. Climb one and wait for me there." Ulfrik guided Hrolf's son to his side, then gave him a gentle push to begin running. Watching both Gunnvald and Erp spreading out, he hoped Vilhjalmer could slip them. Their blades trembled with moonlight and but their eyes displayed their hesitation. The Frank girl quavered at the edge of his vision.

"If you think we're going to fight you to the death," Gunnvald said. "You're mistaken. We've seen your work and don't like our chances. Besides, you're wearing mail."

"Maybe I'm not offering you a choice," Ulfrik said, gripping the sword with both hands and holding it low. He felt a tug at his side and glanced down to see Vilhjalmer had pulled out his dagger.

"In the name of my father, High King Hrolf the Strider, put down your swords." Vilhjalmer leveled the dagger still stained with blood.

"Is that who you are?" Gunnvald asked, face bright with delight. "Erp, get us some help to take the brat captive. I smell a reward in the air."

Ulfrik leapt forward, blade low for a gut strike on Erp, but Gunnvald struck the sword aside and Erp scrambled back to begin shouting. His voice was booming and strong. He cupped one hand to his mouth and called to the tents around him. "Help! Prisoner's escaping. Hurry!"

The Frank girl screamed then darted away. As Ulfrik recovered his balance he raised his blade to strike Gunnvald, but then another shape intervened. Vilhjalmer charged Gunnvald with his dagger overhead, screaming with all the rage of an eight year old boy. Ulfrik pulled his strike, and Gunnvald did likewise, yet Vilhjalmer slashed with unskilled fury. Gunnvald backed up and left himself open.

Ulfrik pierced Gunnvald's side and spun him back. He cursed the poor strike, as now Gunnvald screamed with agony and put a hand over the bleeding wound. Before he could finish him, Ulfrik again had to pull back his strike as Vilhjalmer leapt in with his dagger. The blade plunged into Gunnvald's thigh.

"Run, Vilhjalmer! Or kill him! Just don't let him scream more!"

The suck of mud behind him alerted Ulfrik to step right, and Erp's blade swished through empty air. The pot-bellied man had slashed as if trying to split a tree in a single strike, and when nothing resisted he stumbled forward.

Ulfrik hacked across Erp's back, but his cloak and fur vest prevented the edge from biting flesh. Instead he collapsed into the mud. Gunnvald struggled to his feet, then pointed his sword at Vilhjalmer. "You little bastard, stop or I'll forget that your worth a ransom."

"I said run!" Ulfrik collared Vilhjalmer and yanked him aside. The boy squealed, but Ulfrik had no time left to consider him. Gunnvald shouted and slashed, striking the mail on his shoulder with a crunch of iron.

The longer the fight lasted, the less chance he had of escaping before others interfered. Determined to finish the fight, he slammed Gunnvald in the head with his left fist. Pain lanced up his arm as Ulfrik's knuckles connected with Gunnvald's temple, but the blow staggered his opponent. He plunged his blade to the hilt through Gunnvald's stomach.

His pock-scarred face went white and his death scream echoed in the night. He took Ulfrik's sword to the ground as he folded forward and collapsed.

Weaponless, he whirled on Erp who despite everything had not retreated. His fish-like lips were taut with a smile. "Looks like more reward for me."

Vilhjalmer had lost his dagger, and now Erp held it to the boy's throat. Ulfrik straightened himself and snorted. "You're going to kill him? Amand will hang you for that even if I let you live."

"You got no weapon, fool." Erp's smile widened.

"Sure I do. Here's the sword you dropped to grab the boy and the knife. You're a real help, Erp. Couldn't have succeeded without you."

Erp's face dropped and he tried to step on his discarded blade. Ulfrik never intended to grab it. He balled a fist and braced it in his other hand. When Erp stretched to slam his foot on the weapon Ulfrik hammered with his braced fist on top of Erp's head. It snapped forward into his chest and he lost grip on Vilhjalmer and his dagger. Ulfrik's knee flew up into his face, smashing his teeth but cutting Ulfrik's skin through his pants. The fat man flipped back and a final shove from Ulfrik sprawled him.

"Now I'll take that sword." He snatched it out of the mud, and just as Erp rose he flicked it across his neck sending him back down with a jet of blood pumping an arm's length into the air.

He threw the blade aside, and took Vilhjalmer by the shoulder. He did not have to look around to know armed men circled them. Four already converged on them with spear points flickering in the moonlight.

"Why didn't you run?"

"A jarl's son does not flee from battle."

Ulfrik stared at him, then at the semi circle of men tightening their distance. "Put up your hands," said one of them. Ulfrik complied.

"That's very noble," Ulfrik said. Vilhjalmer beamed at him. "And quite stupid. Once I return you to your father, I'm going to knock sense into your head."

"You wouldn't dare."

"You'll prefer my lessons to your father's, I can promise you that much."

The first arrivals closed on them. Ulfrik began to concoct excuses, but as another man arrived with a struggling woman in his arms he realized excuses would not help. The guard shoved the woman toward them, her full and lustrous brown hair flying across her face. When she regained herself, she pushed it back and blazing green eyes glared out at him. She let out a low moan and pointed at Ulfrik.

"At least the gods were kind enough to send a traitor with no tongue." Ulfrik smiled down at Vilhjalmer, who stood with both hands on his hips as if surveying his troops.

"This was a good start, but we'll have to try again."

Ulfrik nodded, then one of the guards drove his spear butt into Ulfrik's gut and he collapsed to the blood soaked earth.

38

Runa stood when the hall door opened. Rosy light of early morning filled the square and two figures of perfect black hovered at the center. One was the a slender woman, a head shorter than the male figure beside her. She gestured the man inside with a slight bow, and he nodded silently. The woman stepped back and closed the doors, revealing the man.

Light from the smoke hole and the crackling hearth reasserted its claim on the small hall and the shadow of the man revealed Aren standing with a pack slung over his shoulder. The lift of joy Runa experienced flooded away when Aren stepped closer. His wide, square face was lumpy with bruises. Brown scabs surrounded by halos of angry red skin raked across his forehead and cheeks. His lips were livid black and bags under both eyes were heavy with bruises. Worst still, when he smiled his front tooth was broken in half.

He stopped and let his pack drop, then smiled. "Thank you for calling for me."

She raced to him, sweeping him into her arms, tears plucking at her eyes. He flinched when she touched his face, but she could not help it. Under all this damage was her son, but she could not believe it. "Your father?"

"Konal did this," Aren corrected. "I was at my father's memorial stone. Konal was drunk. I angered him and paid the price."

A tear streaked down her cheek as she examined his face. "I'm so sorry." The words felt thick and stupid but anything more would unleash a flood of tears.

"It's not your fault." He gently pushed her back, reminding Runa how little he cared for displays of emotion. "He is never going to hurt either one of us again."

His eyes brightened with hope and a thin smile stretched his bruised lips. The innocent hope in his expression drew out the tears she had struggled against, and she turned aside to conceal them. She walked toward the back of the small hall that had been a comfortable prison since her arrival. Other than taking meals in Hrolf's magnificent hall she never left this place.

"You should have told me about Ulfrik. I would have taken you with me and saved you this beating."

Aren gave a quiet laugh. "No, what you would have done is angered Konal enough to beat you bloody and have him prevent either of us from leaving. Besides, at that time I had sworn to Father not reveal his return to anyone, especially you."

Runa's heart fell at the words and she whirled on him, tears cold against her cheeks. "Why? Of all the people who visit, it should have been me. I'm his wife!"

"You're Konal's wife," Aren said. He retrieved his pack from the ground and looked around for a spot to store it while Runa stood without an answer. Her face heated at the obvious statement.

"Not any longer. With you here, when your father returns I will declare myself divorced from Konal. The shame he has caused me is known widely enough. No one will dispute my claim."

Aren placed his bag against the wall and scanned the modest hall. "We'll be sharing a prison until Father returns. I suppose you will sleep behind that partition?"

"Actually, I don't sleep there, but someone you should meet does. I was told you were coming, and asked him to give us a moment of privacy before introductions." She folded her hands at her lap and called toward the rear of the hall. "Finn, you may join us."

Finn emerged from behind the partition screen of deer hide stretched in a light wooden frame. His freckle-splattered face was bright and hopeful, and he had recovered enough from his injuries to stand straight. He faced Aren and raised his hand in greeting. "I'm glad to meet you," he said. "Your father has spoken often of you."

Runa watched as Aren blushed and lowered his head and gave a short nod. Despite his intelligence Aren had never done well in social situations, and now with a bruised and battered face Runa feared he would withdraw. He turned to his bags while Finn looked to Runa with his hands turned out. She shook her head to dismiss his concern, then went to Aren's side. Lightly touching his shoulder he flinched, but she did not step away.

"I've been helping Finn recover from his wounds, and he has told me all about your father's life in Iceland and his time at with traders. Did you know your father spent an entire winter at Yorvik in England before his ship came here?"

Aren released the sack and faced her. "I want to talk about Konal. He's more important than history now."

She touched the silver amulet of Thor at her chest, and searched Aren's eyes. He swallowed hard, then pushed past his mother. He pulled a table from the side of the hall, then dragged benches. Both Runa and Finn waited until he gestured they be seated. All the while Runa wrung her hands and bit her lip.

"When Hrolf's men came to fetch me, they said it was because Mother feared my safety. I expected nothing but rage from Konal, but allowed me to leave without protest, nor even a word of parting. When I left men were boarding his ship, putting sails onto the mast, and looking as if they were leaving in haste. They did not have travel gear from what I could see. It means they were not traveling far."

Finn shifted between Aren and Runa, seeming to implore either of them to explain the significance. Runa did not need that help.

"Does Konal know about Ulfrik?" she asked. Aren lowered his head and remained silent. He tucked his face behind a hand, while the other made a fist atop the table. Runa let him take whatever time he needed, yet she knew the response.

"It just came out. He had smashed my face on my father's memorial stone. I was so angered. It was all I could think of to hurt him. I'm sorry, Mother."

She took his fist in her hand and massaged it. "What do you think Konal is doing now? Is he going to see Snorri?"

"I thought he might do that, but after the news he just got drunk for days. Then after Hrolf's men show and take me away, he decides to take journey along the river. Where is he going? If he wanted to appeal to Hrolf, he'd be here by now."

"So he is going to Snorri?" Finn asked.

"Perhaps," Aren said and shrugged. He withdrew his hand from Runa's without looking up. "He might want to learn the details of our meeting with Father. I asked my guards where he went and they all claimed not to know. Of course, their lies were clear to me. They knew, which means he has gone somewhere none of us should know about."

"You think he's going after Ulfrik?" Runa felt a tightness in her chest imagining the damage Konal might cause.

"Maybe," Aren said. "Since my father's visit, I've given much thought to what he said. He told me about Throst's treachery, and that has not sat right with me."

"I was there when Throst died," Finn said. "I've told this to Runa, but Throst said he had help from someone close to Ulfrik. Do you think it could be Konal?"

Runa stared at Aren, and he at last raised his eyes to hers and gave a slow nod. She had not wanted to believe it but now her head hummed like a nest of wasps. Her eyes fluttered and she felt faint. All those years when Ulfrik left Konal alone with her and her children, he had nursed a desire to be part of a family again. He had made advances even when Ulfrik had been alive, yet she dismissed them with little care. She realized he loved her, or thought he did, and when Ulfrik died everything had flowed naturally to their marriage. A great tragedy had united them again, each lost in a world without family and in need of support. But she never considered he had a part in Ulfrik's death. Now looking at Aren's battered face and feeling the tightness of her own injured cheek she wondered how she had not suspected it.

"Someone is helping Konal," Aren said. "Wherever he is going, it cannot be good. I believe he wishes my father remain dead."

"But that would risk Hrolf's son," Finn said. "Why would Hrolf let Konal take that risk?"

Aren sighed and rubbed his face. "The help can't be from Hrolf. If he wanted my father dead it would have been done already and without risk to his son. No, Konal must be working with someone in Hrolf's command. Konal may have somehow contacted Throst to betray my father, but I believe there was another involved and that person or group is helping him now."

"We should warn Hrolf," Finn said, standing as if prepared to run to his hall. Runa grabbed his arm.

"Sit down," she said. "We don't know who this person or group is. I am all for action, but only when the time is right. For now, we would do well to watch Hrolf's men and see who might be involved."

Aren nodded agreement. "We should pry for what information we can. I fear whoever arranged for my father's betrayal would have to be highly placed. To rush to conclusions would be dangerous."

"At the least we can let Hrolf know Konal has left with his crew?" Aren spread his hands wide.

"Hrolf wants to speak with me," Aren said. "I was told to be prepared within the hour. I will tell him then. After that, let's see where things lead. We can do nothing here other than alert my father's enemies to our suspicions. We must be eyes and ears for him until he can return to defend himself."

Runa patted Aren's hand. She agreed with her son's assessment, and feared the worst part of his guess was true. Ulfrik had risen high and not without upsetting a number of important men along the way. Any one of Hrolf's jarls could be an enemy waiting to pounce. All she could do now was play the role of a spy, and a poor one at that.

The three of them sat in silence. Runa stood from the table. "I'm going to step outside. You two should get to know each other better."

Outside the guard at her door gave a slight smile and inclined his head. She walked a short distance and turned her face toward the sun.

How many more traps were hidden along Ulfrik's path home? She put her hand to her mouth and closed her eyes.

39

Ulfrik rested on hands and knees in the dirt, the wind knocked from his lungs. Mail protected from slashes and glancing blows, but not against the solid thump to his gut. He considered grabbing Vilhjalmer and running, but after breaking his leg in the fall from Throst's tower he would never outrun a young man. A fight would end in his death. A quick plan of taking Vilhjalmer hostage faded when guards dragged him aside and out of his view. With so many surrounding him, he would fail in that gambit as well. One marksman with a bow would put an arrow through his neck before he could get Vilhjalmer clear. In the end, he allowed himself to be hauled up and held at spear point.

The Frank girl continued to struggle with her captors, but Vilhjalmer remained cool and still between his two guards. Ulfrik gave him a weak smile, proud at the grace the boy exhibited for one so young.

"What is this?" The voice spoke in Frankish and came from behind. Looking over his shoulder Ulfrik saw a detail of six Frankish guards from Amand's fortress. They were dressed in white and blue surcoats and carried shields of the same color. Only the leader was dressed for battle, wearing a chain shirt and conical helmet of the Frankish style.

"Caught these three running from the fortress," said the Northman holding Ulfrik. "Looks like they were helping the hostage escape."

"Dear God!" The lead Frank stalked to Vilhjalmer and grabbed him away from the others. "How did this happen?"

Ulfrik inhaled to give his story, but Vilhjalmer interrupted in perfect Frankish. "The two dead men and the girl freed me from the tower. The girl led them to me, and they wanted to ransom me back to my father, Mord Guntherson." He pointed at Ulfrik. "This man caught us and killed both of them."

"Is that true?" The Frank leader asked. The girl shook her head violently and pointed at Ulfrik, but her guard shook her to silence.

The Northman holding Ulfrik loosened his grip. "The two men were already dead when I got here. Actually, this one didn't try to run when we caught him."

"I called for help once," Ulfrik added. "But no one answered. There was no time to waste, so I killed both of them."

The Frank leader threw up his hands. "Alright, you're all coming back with us. The Count will straighten this out."

Vilhjalmer shot Ulfrik a smug look, but he turned away not wanting to give his captors any hint of cooperation. In fact, Ulfrik's chest beat with pride for the boy's quick thinking. Such a young intelligence was rare, and he had only known his son Aren to be so smart. Yet whereas Aren was retiring with his intelligence Vilhjalmer was snake-swift in putting it to use. He would be a mighty jarl one day and a fine inheritor of Hrolf's legacy.

Ulfrik was treated with a mixture of suspicion and gratitude. They confined him to a room, but provided a basin to wash blood and mud out of his face and bought him fresh clothes. They took his mail and weapons, but promised to return them upon leaving the fortress. The bed was comfortable and he dozed until he was summoned again. A bar lifted from his door, which he had not realized had been barred. Two guards gestured for him to follow, but waited for him to splash water on his face and roughly comb his hair.

They escorted him into the main building and Ulfrik noted every door and hall he passed. He arrived at the second floor where the wooden floorboard creaked under foot as they walked him into a large room with two high windows for light. Count Amand sat on a large, ornate chair, his golden cross glinting in the moonlight. He stroked his long, white mustache as he waited. Beside him stood Grimnr, dressed in plain brown pants and a green shirt which emphasized his waist-length yellow braid. He gave him a smile halfway between a wolfish snarl and a friendly greeting. A priest whispered to Amand, and seven men-at-arms ranked up behind him.

Ulfrik looked around as they led him forward, noting the high chandelier of unlit candles hanging over him on a chain. He wondered if Amand dropped it on people who displeased him. The guard nudged him and raised his brows expectantly. Ulfrik did not understand, and the Frank rolled his eyes. "Kneel to your lord."

"Of course, how forgetful." Ulfrik stepped toward Grimnr and went to his knee. "Jarl Grimnr, I am honored you should attend on my behalf."

Grimnr barked a laugh, but the Frank guard plucked his shoulder. "The Count, you fool!"

"Never mind the formalities," Count Amand said, shooing Ulfrik and his guards back. "More important matters are at hand."

Ulfrik stepped away, suppressing a smile he shared with Grimnr. He schooled his expression and turned to the Count, who continued to stroke his mustache while studying Ulfrik. At last he licked his lips then spoke.

"I have already spoken with the hostage, Halfdan Mordason, for his retelling of the story. I want to hear your account now. Tell me what happened."

"The two men had Vilhjalmer between them and the girl trotting along with them. Truth be told, I was going to the side gate to meet that girl." Ulfrik bowed his head with mock shame, then looked toward Grimnr. "She's the most beautiful woman I've ever seen, really. I know I shouldn't have left my post at the hall last night, but I had arranged to meet her at the gate for a bit of fun."

"I don't need the details," Count Amand said, holding up a hand to stop him. "You had abandoned you post for reasons we all understand. Now what did you see when the girl and her accomplices appeared. Who was leading?"

Ulfrik recognized the trap the Count had set. He paused as if trying to recall, but was actually trying to guess Vilhjalmer's answers to the questions. The safest tactic would be to stick as close to the facts as possible. He hoped an eight year-old boy was smart enough to think of that, and Ulfrik gambled his ruse on it. "The girl was leading them. I saw her first."

Grimnr glanced at Amand, who nodded and stopped stroking his mustache. He leaned forward. "How did the fight go after that? What was said?"

"I told them to halt, and once I recognized they had the hostage, I ordered them to release Halfdan. I recognized both of them, as I had once been part of Gunnvald's crew. When he scoffed at me I called for help and drew my sword."

Ulfrik then told the rest of the battle as it has happened, for the details would not be different from anything Vilhjalmer had provided. When he ended his narrative he spread his hands wide and bowed to Amand. "And that is the whole truth of it. It seems Fate put me in the way of two men who I hated most in this camp, and provided me a good reason to spill their guts."

"Yes, well, that's a vivid account of the fight. Grimnr, you've heard both the woman and the boy's accounts. What do you say?"

"I heard very little from the whore other than a lot of moaning and hand gestures. I'm sure she's accustomed to that." Grimnr laughed and Ulfrik smiled, but the Count frowned and slapped the arm of his chair. Grimnr's smile vanished. "I stand by Ulfar's account. He was on guard duty, which explains why he was armed and armored. I've seen him flirting with the whore before, and I believe when he says he was looking for a roll in the barn with her. And Gunnvald and his crew were scum that have made trouble before. There is nothing more for me to say in Ulfar's defense."

The Count nodded and began to stroke his mustache once more. Grimnr slipped Ulfrik a wolfish grin. While Fate had spoiled his plans for escape, the gods had favored Ulfrik enough to cover his treachery.

"I would like to speak to Gunnvald's crew," Count Amand said. "You rounded them up, Grimnr?"

"They were gone by the time we looked for them. Yet another reason to believe Ulfar's innocence."

With a nod, Amand fell into thoughtful silence. At length he leaned into his priest and the two conferred in whispers. Ulfrik strained to listen while appearing unconcerned, but their words escaped him. Amand finally patted his priest's arm, then made a sign of the cross and lifted the gold crucifix to his lips and kissed it.

"I believe Ulfar's story and recognize that he has done me a service. The servant will be hanged for her treachery. Ulfar, you will be awarded two pounds of silver for you aid in preventing the escape of my hostage. However, there is something about the number of incidents involving you since your arrival in my camp. Until plans with Mord are concluded, you will remain in the quarters I have provided you."

"What?" Ulfrik stepped forward, only to have both guards grab his arms.

"This is no way to treat a man who has done you a service," Grimnr said, his face turning red. "This is an insult."

Amand held up a hand. "Wherever this man goes violence seems to follow, which is not uncommon for your kind. But for Ulfar the violence is always near my person. Also, he has spent more time getting to know my fortress than any of your men. Tell me, Grimnr, how many others of your men have helped unload goods at my fortress and discovered the easy virtue of some of my servants? All in such a short space of time. Also, I believe it was his idea to attend the meeting with Mord, where he also happened to be the spark of violence. That is too much coincidence for my taste."

"That is chance, my lord," Ulfrik said. He did not wrestle with his guards, hoping manners would prevail. Yet he saw the Count's eyes harden and he gripped both of his chair arms as he rose.

Amand narrowed his eyes. "I thought you people didn't believe in chance? You will be rewarded and treated with respect. After Mord has given us victory, you will be released with your silver. Be glad you will not have to risk your life in the fighting to enjoy the benefits. I'm certain Grimnr will pay you no less than your wages, all for sitting in the warm comfort of my home."

"It's imprisonment without an end date," Ulfrik said.

"God has granted me eyes to see, and wisdom to suspect. I've been fair to you, Ulfar. When I was younger and less tired of death, I'd have saved myself a boring morning of sitting on this chair and hanged you with the whore. Now you may go with Grimnr to collect your belongings, and he will send you back straightaway. There is no more room for debate."

Amand hobbled off his chair and nodded to both Grimnr and Ulfrik as he left. Ulfrik stared at the empty chair, wondering how he would get to Vilhjalmer from behind his barred door. It seemed the gods had saved their laughter for this very moment. He bowed his head as the two guard lead him out.

40

The early morning light was cold and weak behind rolls of gray clouds. Outside the walls of Amand's fortress men were piling out of their tents or barracks to greet the new day. Others were retiring from a night of guard duty, stretching and yawning as they shambled to their quarters. Ulfrik and Grimnr stomped through the maze of tents in stony silence. In the distance a flock of black crows shot screaming into the sky, catching Ulfrik's attention.

"This is an insult," Grimnr said, punching his palm. "You prevent our prized hostage from escape and he rewards you with a prison cell."

"The room is comfortable and clean," Ulfrik said. "At least I won't be cold and wet."

"Don't be so sure of it. His captain, Remy, will probably see you to your new quarters and he hates our people," Grimnr said. Two men stepped into his path and he shoved them back with his arm. They protested but Grimnr snarled and they faded back between the tents.

Continuing to charge through the camp, Grimnr muttered to himself but Ulfrik kept watch on the horizon. The distant crows continued to scream but did not disperse, circling overhead.

The sentence Amand had passed on him made his task both

easier and more difficult. Being barred into a room frustrated his plans for quick action. However since he was not a true prisoner he had a chance to cultivate a relationship with his guard and exploit it to free himself. After that, he would be inside the fortress and closer to Vilhjalmer than he otherwise would be. He ground his teeth at the thought of further delays, but Vilhjalmer's quick thinking had spared him a far worse outcome.

"Grimnr, this is shameful to me as well. Please don't tell the others what has become of me." Ulfrik did not want others considering Amand's accusations too closely. With enough minds thinking on his actions, it would not be long before someone determined his true purpose.

"Of course not," Grimnr said. "I'll tell them you've been rewarded with a special duty from the Count. I'll find a way to get you out of that cell before the attack. No one should miss a chance at glory as big as one we're setting up."

"That means a lot to me," Ulfrik said, not insincere. Grimnr was a strong leader with a fierce pride, and Ulfrik had enjoyed his short time under his command. He regretted the betrayal he had in store for Grimnr. Once he wondered if Grimnr could be persuaded to his side, but one night of conversation with the man disabused him of the idea. Grimnr's word was gold and he had given his to Amand.

Arriving at his hall, Grimnr stopped short. "Freya's tits! Where are the guards?"

The hall doors hung open but none of the guards stood watch. Ulfrik again checked the sky, and the crows continued to circle but had drawn closer.

"Jarl Grimnr, sorry!" Vigrid trotted around the corner of the hall, holding his helmet on his head.

"Seems wandering off during guard duty has become a bad habit," Grimnr glared at Ulfrik, then back to Vigrid.

"I've got the runs," Vigrid said. "Half the men started with it last night."

Grimnr and Ulfrik straightened up at the news. An army of this size that squatted in one place too long eventually succumbed to disease. To Ulfrik's mind, an army should march to war and excite the gods with acts of heroism and bravery. When the army hunkered down the gods were insulted and sewed illness in their ranks as punishment. Men with the runs were the first sign of burgeoning troubles.

"Is it just us? Maybe something you ate?" Grimnr touched the silver Thor's hammer at his neck, and Vigrid shook his head.

"The latrines are flowing over today."

"Shit!" Grimnr spun on his heels and glared at the rest of the camp.

"Lots of that," Ulfrik said, still watching the crows. Vigrid laughed, then grabbed the seat of his pants and ran the way he had come.

"This is a bad," Grimnr said, his voice low. He laced his hands behind his head and paced. "I've seen this before. The shits begin and then half the men are dead within the month."

"Sooner than that."

"Well, aren't you a spot of sunshine?"

"It's better than what I'll say next." Ulfrik put his hand to Grimnr's back and pointed at the crows. "They took flight right after we left Amand's fortress and they've been circling. I think they're getting closer."

He did not have to explain the rest to a veteran like Grimnr. He stared at the crows in stunned silence, then growled. "If Mord is leading that attack, his son dies."

"Whoever leads it has obviously silenced your forward positions. And why are we not hearing alarms of the attack now?"

Grimnr's eyes widened. "I bet the men at the fences are at the latrines. We've been blinded"

As if in protest to Grimnr, distant horns began to sound but the crows overhead indicated the attackers were almost to the first line of fences. Grimnr charged into the hall and shouted at his men to prepare for battle. Most of them snapped to the order with whoops and cries, but half a dozen of white faced men crawled out of their beds to answer the call.

A young man, no older than seventeen dashed across the field and burst into the hall, shoving Ulfrik aside. He was out of breath, but Grimnr grabbed him by his wool vest. "You've got a report?"

"Einar's banner, the bloody ax on a white flag, it's flying over the troops. They sprang out of nowhere. They're almost to the wall."

"How many?" Grimnr shook the boy.

"Three hundred, maybe."

"Three hundred men don't spring out of nowhere. Some goat-turd was asleep on duty." Grimnr seemed to realize he was shaking the boy and released him. "Have runners been sent to Count Amand? We need his archers and cavalry."

The runner nodded and took off as soon as Grimnr dismissed him. The camp was now alive with shouts, and glancing out the door Ulfrik saw groups of men running for the fences. Inside, chain armor clinked and weapons bumped the walls as Grimnr's men prepared to escort their jarl to battle.

Einar was making a spoiling attack to further delay the plans with Mord. Ulfrik knew this had to be true. If Einar were leading these men, then Ulfrik realized he could make contact during the battle and send a message back to Hrolf. Einar might not know he was alive, but still he had to try. Trying to communicate during a battle was not only difficult, but likely fatal. Awareness on the battlefield was key to survival, and concentrating on finding one man and making peace with him in the chaos inhibited awareness. One moment looking the wrong way and a spear might pop his guts before he could react.

"You need every man who can carry a shield," Ulfrik said. "Forget Count Amand's orders and take me with you."

Grimnr thumped his shoulder. "Get a mail coat, shield, and a sword from the hall. There will be something to fit you, then follow the others to the meeting point. I have to get the rest of these men ready."

Ulfrik watched him dash across the field, waving frantically at men to head for the fences. The clang of iron already drifted over the hall, and Ulfrik watched the crows circling and screaming. They were directly over the camp.

41

Ulfrik jogged behind Grimnr's hirdmen not only to conserve strength for the battle but also to drop out of line at his first chance. The mail shirt was tight across his chest and his hair caught in the links at the shoulders, but he carried the weight easily. His helmet sat too low on his head, and with no time to adjust the leather cap inside it he found himself pushing it off his nose, though it continued to slide forward as he trotted to the front lines.

The sounds of battle washed over him. Screams, war cries, curses, blaring horns, clanging iron, crunching mail, wooden thuds. All of it hit him as square as a shield wall. Yet as he closed the distance, he found no shield wall to join. Between the black fences men clustered in groups where they traded blows with their enemies. It was like a broken shield wall, though one had never been formed. Grimnr's army had been caught on it haunches and now Einar's men came to spear them like the pigs they were.

"For Grimnr and glory!" The shout came up from the hirdmen Ulfrik followed. They charged with shields out, hurtling into a gap between the fences. None had checked if Ulfrik followed. All their training had vanished like fog in the morning sun and now they barreled heedlessly into battle. Another fault with keeping an army idle too long, he thought.

Ulfrik did not want to kill any of these men. Some of them might have been his own warriors once, and without a doubt many of Einar's hirdmen would have been his as well. Yet standing before the whirling madness of bloody axes and spears he could see no other way to break through to his old friend. Good blood would have to be spilled for the sake of Hrolf's mission. A plain wood shield before him, he raised his sword and charged into the confusion.

The first clash bought him against a man with bulging eyes in a gore-stained face, like two white stones in a puddle of blood. He screamed at Ulfrik as he blocked the passage between two fences. Their shields slammed together with a heavy thump as Ulfrik tried to plow through the man, but he only slid back in the grass. Ulfrik stabbed over the top of his shield, striking the man's face. Whether the stab killed or wounded the enemy, he fell aside and Ulfrik continued through him. Leaving an enemy alive and behind was deadly. The enemy could catch him between another foe and the two make short work of him. However, locating Einar remained his objective and until he could find him he had not time for protracted fights.

He looped through gaps of fighting men, dodging blows and deflecting others with his shield. In truth he could not tell one side from the other in this battle, but men on either side of this conflict were his enemies today. Pressing out from behind one fence he spotted Einar's banner wavering over the heads of fighting men, spears, axes, and swords swinging beneath it like a rolling tide of iron. The banner showed a bloody ax on a white field and a knot of men fought around it. Ulfrik spotted a two-handed ax rise high and chop down. A smile peeled across his face; there was Einar.

Running parallel to the staggered fences Ulfrik avoided the bulk of the fight playing out between the serried rows. The fences had been constructed to foil concentrated attacks over a wide area and provide cover for archers. Einar's men flowed around these and caught Grimnr's men in the pockets. He had dashed the length of one fence when two men charged at him between a gap. The lead man was a head shorter than Ulfrik, dewed in blood, and threw a spear. He spun to deflect it with his shield, but the head penetrated through the wood. Now the weight of the shaft pulled the shield down and he sloughed it off, jumping straight back to avoid the attack of the second man.

They broke to both sides, forcing him to leave one side exposed. Without a second thought he drew his sax, the short fighting blade worn at his waist, and with sword in his main hand he dove for the legs of the shorter attacker. They collided with a grunt, crashing to the ground, Ulfrik using his superior strength to pin the man. He shoved the sax into the attacker's neck, eliciting a scream and gout of blood, then he grasped the mail shirt and rolled over, pulling the dying man atop him.

He felt the second attacker's blade crunch through his dying friend's mail, and both shouted -- one in anger and one as his last utterance in this life. Ulfrik threw him aside as the attacker wrestled his sword free from his friend's corpse. He sliced at the back of the attacker's legs, chopping the meat of his hamstrings and sending him to his knees.

Ulfrik sprang up, drove his sword into is attacker's back, then kicked him from the blade with the heel of his boot. He whirled around, spotted Einar with another man fighting beneath his banner. The sight stopped him cold, for he thought he was seeing himself.

"Hakon!" he called out, without thinking. Over the thud and clank of battle and the screams of dying and wounded men his son heard nothing. He danced around another attacker who had lost his sword and now fought with a hand ax and shield. Beside Hakon, Einar disproved Ulfrik's rule that a two-handed ax was a support weapon. With his giant size and the reach of this weapon he kept two men at bay, wearing them out and luring them into a mistake would cost their lives.

Joy at meeting his kin in the fellowship of battle flooded him, washing out fatigue and pain and leaving only excited hope in its wake. He flew towards the battle.

He did not call their names again, fearing to distract them from the enemies they faced. Einar hooked the shield from the hand of one man, then shoved his ax to drive him back. The other attacker mistook it for an opportunity, but Einar reversed his swing and sliced into head of the other swordsman. His helmet flew off and he stumbled, but continued his attack.

Ulfrik leapt upon the man who had lost his shield, beating him down with a series of blows that sheared all the fingers from his shield hand. The man collapsed with a yelp, but Ulfrik could not allow any witness to live. A flick of his sword across the man's neck ended his life.

Something heavy slammed between his shoulder blades and he crashed over the man he had just slain. He lost his helmet as he rolled aside, bringing his sword up to deflect the next blow. No attack came. Instead he looked up at Einar's scared and bloodied face smiling down at him. Light hit him directly in the face, setting his faded yellow beard on fire.

"I always wanted to do that to you," he said through his smile. "The ax is a masterful weapon, isn't it?"

"You knew I am alive?" Ulfrik lied on the ground, though all instincts told him to stand when a battle swirled about him.

"Snorri told me, then Mord told me. Sooner or later you'd tell me yourself."

Ulfrik struggled to his feet, but Einar did not assist him. When he stood, Einar kicked a discarded shield at him. "We have to make this look like a fight."

Snatching up the shield, he barely deflected Einar's probing attack. He sliced down with his ax, sending a shudder through the shield into Ulfrik's arm. "You launched an attack to contact me?"

Sweeping his blade lazily under his shield, Einar batted it aside. "Of course not. Three hundred men aren't assembled overnight. Been planning for a week. Spoiling attack to blunt Amand. Maybe kill some of his horses."

Einar pushed him back with his ax, herding him like a goat away from Hakon and toward the rear of the battle.

"The men are sick." Ulfrik stepped inside the reach of the ax, but Einar shoved him away with the haft. Had he been serious, he could have toppled Ulfrik and hewn him like a log. "Wait a week and most of these bastard's won't be able to fight."

"Runa knows you live. She's with Hrolf."

Ulfrik feinted the same move, but Einar remembered his tricks too well and did not react. Somehow it did not matter that Runa knew now. All around him men circled each other with bloodied weapons, while others knelt in the mud clutching the stump of a hand or a ribbon of guts. Nothing but survival meant anything on the battlefield. "Tell Hrolf that Eskil and all his men were hanged. There's only me and I need help. Amand suspects me."

Einar glanced past Ulfrik, who then heard a deep bellow from behind.

"Einar Snorrason! I come for your head!"

"Shit, it's Grimnr." Ulfrik did not have to turn to see what he knew to be the giant wolf of a man charging straight for him. "Let me inside you guard."

Ulfrik slammed forward and began to wrestle Einar, all while gasping out his words. "I need Grimnr to vouch for me. Don't kill him. Get away and keep Hakon safe. Send help fast."

They staggered in a circle, and he heard the thud of Grimnr's approach. Einar crushed Ulfrik to him, using the haft of his ax to lock him. His breath was warm against the side of Ulfrik's head as he spoke. "I cried like a baby when I heard you lived. Come back to us."

Then Ulfrik was hurtling away. The sensation felt like when he fell from the tower, nothing but air flowing past him and arms flailing at his side. He crashed into something hard that slammed him the other way. The back of his head cracked against metal and snapped forward. He heard Grimnr cursing, his deafening shouts in his ear. Then he was smothered beneath iron and flesh, face in the dirt and hot blood streaming from behind his ears and into his mouth.

He flattened out, all his breath escaping, and when he thought the crush finished the body atop him slammed down again and no more air refilled his lungs. His nose clogged with dirt and his vision turned red then brown.

Another thump and he saw no more. Strangely, even beneath the welter of bodies crushing him, the last sound he heard was the shrieking of the crows above.

42

Konal stood in the prow as three ships blockaded further progress up the Seine. He leaned over the side, waving his hazel branch as if it were a wing to take flight. None of the crew on any ship answered him, but he saw the bowmen gathering at the front of their ships.

"We're only one ship," he protested to them. "Shields are still on the rails, you fools."

He continued to wave while his crew of twenty men sat on their benches, oars shipped. Glancing back at them, two rows of ten white-eyed men stared at him. He swallowed, then renewed waving the hazel.

The scent of battle still clung to the land. He had received Einar's summons the same day he received Mangus the Stone's so-called suggestion to ensure Ulfrik's failure. He was to send all available men forward to Eyrafell as a rearguard for their escape. Unable to avoid the obligation, he was forced to send all his men and use those left behind to form his crew. Now his own fortress of Konalsvik was manned by five men and all the boys old enough to hold a sword.

"I think they're moving," said one of the men leaning over the opposite rail. "Oars in the water."

"Alright, that's good," Konal said. "Remember, I have an important job here. I'm no traitor to Hrolf, and you men have nothing to fear. Just stay with the ship and be ready to leave when I return."

A few men nodded, but most looked toward the shore. Konal followed their gaze, seeing white tents billowing amid slipshod buildings. Closer to them, parties of men picked through the corpses littering the field, and flocks of crows randomly screamed into the air when they came too close to their feast. Konal shuddered, glad to have left his fighting days in the distant past.

One of the three ships pulled ahead, its oars paddling in a slow rhythm as the Seine's muddy brown current carried it forward. Konal raised the hazel branch high, a sign for peace recognized by Northmen everywhere, yet despite this archers crowded the rails of the approaching ship and all shields had been cleared from the racks. He understood their skittishness after a surprise attack, but he was only one ship.

"Tie onto us," shouted one man from the lead ship. He was the hovedsmann, a man with an iron gray beard and deeps lines in his weathered face, and he commanded his crew with a flick of his hand. Ropes flung out to Konal's ship, and he waved his own crew to grab them. Tying onto the ship was essentially surrender, but he had no chance against this river patrol of three longships. His crew knew it, and he heard grumbling behind him.

The hovedsmann stood with spear and shield ready, centered at the rail of his own ship. "Send your leader over to us. You have my word he will be treated with respect if his intentions are peaceful. Leave your weapons on your ship."

The two other ships spread out to either side, their archers standing ready but without arrows on the string. Konal felt himself trembling, having never surrendered to an enemy before. He took a deep breath, unbuckled the baldric carrying his sword and handed it to a crewman. "Do as they ask and we will be safe."

He reached for the pouch at his side, and panicked when he grabbed nothing. In all his worry, he had forgotten he had left the gems hidden back home. He had grown accustomed to their weight at his side, and to touching the pouch whenever he grew worried. The hovedsmann watched him under hooded eyes, and noted how he had reacted when missing his pouch. Konal stepped onto the rail and jumped to the opposite ship where two crewman assisted him to the deck.

Surrounded by spearmen, he tried to appear unconcerned for their gleaming blades. Behind the stern faces of the spearmen he saw their sister ship glide past, headed to cut off retreat or discover if Konal had hid other ships around the bend down-river. He smiled at the hovedsmann. "I have important news for your leader, Grimnr the Mountain. I must speak with him right away."

The hovedsmann tilted his head back and studied him. His eyes roved over the white and pink scars swirling through Konal's face and neck. Despite the long years of living with his disfigurement, he never adjusted to the reactions of others when first meeting him. He tried to remain impassive, but felt his nostrils flare and he wished he had drank more.

"Right after the ambush attack? Seems it's a little late for useful news." The hovedsmann leaned in, sniffing. "Are you drunk?"

"Only enough to get me through betraying my people." Konal rubbed his nose with the back of his hand. "I need to speak with Grimnr. I leave you my ship and crew as hostages to my peaceful intentions. Tie my hands if you will. Just get me to him this moment."

They put Einar on another ship while they arranged to guide the captured ship to dock. The new crew surrounded him with four men, and upon reaching dock these same guards escorted him ashore. The camp smelled like an open latrine and Konal put a finger beneath his nose, causing one of his captors to laugh. "It's why I prefer river patrol," said another. "Only Paris smells worse."

Guiding him into the camp, he found men laid out as if napping in the sun, yet the flies dancing on their faces showed they were dead. No sword had cut that pile of bodies, but disease had laid them out. As they wended between dirty, weathered tents he came to a long hall shaped like a hull. A side door hung open with a man squatting beside it, wrapped in his cape and spear leaning against a support beam. Thatch on the roof had fallen away and revealed the wooden slats beneath. If this was Grimnr's hall, the reality of his glory was far less bright than rumor had made it appear.

They kept him waiting outside the main doors while two went inside. Konal watched the crows screaming and shrieking at the western edge of the camp, thick black clouds of them flitting from one feast to the next. Grimnr exploded from the doorway like he expected to find a naked woman to ravish. Instead, his wide, predatory eyes dulled when he set them on Konal's scarred face. The man was as taller than Einar, but not as muscular. Both of his eyes were blackened and a three stitches held together the flesh of his left cheek.

"Important news for me? Who are you?"

"Konal Ketilsson, jarl of Konalsvik." He raised his head with pride, though his whisper-thin voice did not carry the power he had hoped. Still, Grimnr leaned back in surprise.

"Then you should've been with Einar for yesterday's attack, but you look too hale for that scrum. His head was supposed to nailed right here." Grimnr stuck a thick finger at the frame of his doorway. "But the coward ran. Right after he knocked me out with my own man and flattened my head with the haft of his ax. I guess he's leaving the real fight for later. Why would he do that?"

"I can't say. He tells me nothing of his plans, only that my men were to guard Eyrafell for his retreat."

"But you're here, and he's there by now. Bit of a problem for you, isn't it?" The men gathering around him laughed, but Grimnr's own smile turned to a wince when it pulled the stitches on his cheek.

"My hope is you will welcome me here once you have my news.'"

Grimnr nodded at his four guards and they parted, then he guided Konal toward the cleared field before his hall. "Let me hear what you've got to say before I share it with the others. We'll be fine over here."

Once they had distanced themselves, Grimnr faced him and stood with his hand resting on a dagger hilt at his waist. Konal had no weapons and fists would never prevail over this brute. He gladdened at not having to face him across a shield wall.

"There is a spy in your ranks."

Grimnr growled and shook his head. "Eskil and his men were all hanged weeks ago. You're late with that."

"No, Hrolf has sent another. If he sees me speaking with you, he will have already begun to flee."

"We're not going to a quiet, private place so you can pull a hidden weapon. Say what you have come to say or I'm adding your corpse to the pile."

Konal licked his thin lips and glanced over his shoulders, worried Ulfrik might appear at any moment. "His name is Ulfrik Ormsson, but you will know him as Ulfar the White. He was thought long dead, but had only been a captive. Hrolf sent him to free the boy hostage you keep."

He watched the lines on Grimnr's face grow taut as his lips disappeared into a snarl. The stitches on his cheek pulled apart and blood began to seep. Though Grimnr remained still, Konal felt a massive presence pressing down on him. It was as if the air between them was heating up. His jaw worked side to side and his eyes narrowed. "I don't believe you."

"I'm sure if you think back on what he has done, you will realize he has been working toward getting close to your hostage." Konal's raspy voice shook with both fear of Grimnr's simmering temper and fear of failing to convince him. "If you have not heard the legend of Ulfrik Ormsson, then I will warn you he is a clever man. He outwitted the Franks for years and has been a scourge to them since he arrived back when Paris was besieged. And the gods love him. He was thrown from a fucking tower and lived to bring his love of misery back to my hall. Tell me the gods do not favor him. Don't fret for being taken in by his deceit."

"Your words mean nothing." Grimnr's hand tightened on the grip of his dagger and Konal dropped his eyes to it.

"Gutting me won't change the truth. You are mad with yourself for being played a fool. I know. I stood in your boots once. But don't take my word for it. Find him, then tell him you've captured his son in yesterday's battle. His name is Hakon and is the very image of his father. He serves Einar now and would have fought at his side. Make Ulfrik believe he has confessed to you. Do whatever you must, but reveal Ulfar the White as Ulfrik Ormsson. Then do what I could not. Kill him."

43

Ulfrik sat up from the cold earth floor of the tent, and his head began to spin. A boxy woman in the dark robes and habit of a Christian nun worked at a table by the tent flap, golden morning light shining behind her. She saw him rise and snapped a stream of accented Frankish he did not understand. He slip back down and touched his head, working around to the back where he felt a hot, painful lump. A terrible stench suddenly registered, and at his left was a chamber pot filled with vomit that had not been emptied. From the sour taste in his mouth he guessed he had filled the pot but did not remember.

The nun knelt beside him, a cool cloth in one hand and with her free hand she lifted his head. She spoke too quickly for him to understand, so she slowed down though not without a huff and frown first. "Can't you stay still? Let me clean your head. Lift it, please."

She smelled like lilacs and her soft touch relaxed Ulfrik. She was at least his age, if not older, but no woman had touched him so lovingly since he had left Gytha in Iceland. He sucked his breath as the cloth padded the back of his head and she giggled.

"Stay. Rest. You go back today."

"Where am I?"

"Not remember? I told you yesterday. Big man and you banged

heads. Broke his face and broke your head. He crushed you until you sleep. No?"

Ulfrik shook his head. "Maybe. It's hard to remember. I'm getting too old. Where is this tent?"

"Count Amand's fortress. The injured come here after the battle. Stay away from the sick men out there." The nun swiped her hand vaguely behind her and wrinkled her nose. "I go now. But this tent, you are last one in it. We need space so you go after rest."

After the nun exited Ulfrik sat up again and braced himself for the dizziness that assailed him. The tent appeared to wobble but after a dozen heartbeats it settled. He was on a sheet laid out on the floor, one of four that had been placed in a square. Piles of bloodied rags were stuffed into a corner and rust stains on the sheets indicated his tent mates had suffered far worse injuries. A distant scream alerted him to the world beyond his tent. He heard men and women outside, saw shadows of passing figures glide across his tent wall. Moans and laughter mingled and Ulfrik guessed scores of injured surrounded him. Einar had done his job well.

Still in his mail shirt, he felt as if a dozen hands pushed down on his shoulders as he struggled to his feet. His dizziness lingered for a moment and vanished. A pile of weapons were stacked beneath the table where bowls and bandages along with knives and tongs sat prepared for surgery. Selecting his own weapon from the pile, he strapped it on, found a jug of ale on the table, guzzled from it, and exited the tent.

No one paid attention to him outside the tent. He stood amid a tiny city of white and blue stripped tents that had sprung up in Count Amand's courtyard. The front gates were open, people passing in and out in groups, and over the tops of the tents he saw Amand's fort equally unguarded. Ulfrik's heart pounded with his excitement. In the post-battle chaos, he could grab Vilhjalmer and leave. Now was his final chance before Amand's captain fetched him away to imprisonment. He marched through the maze of tents and headed straight for the entrance to the inner courtyard. Four nuns were already passing through the gate along with a half dozen workers following behind. Ulfrik caught up to their numbers and passed into the courtyard unnoticed.

He kept his head down as he walked, the ground wobbling underfoot for a half dozen strides, but he shook it off. Once through the gate he slipped to the side, hugging the left wall. The entrance to Vilhjalmer's tower was around the corner, and he slid through the shadow until he came around the other side. A steady stream of people moved back and forth across the courtyard, and he did not see guards at the other towers. Most would have been moved forward to fill gaps in defense or assist with the dead and wounded. Once turning the corner he decided if a guard was posted he would cut across the inner courtyard as if on other business, then try to lure the guard away before entering. He could not attack him in full view of the foot traffic.

Poking his head around the corner he found two men in conversation before the door. One was a short guard in ill-fitted mail and helmet, a shield too large for his arm. Talking to him was a richly dressed older man, a gold cross set against his red shirt and a white, swooping mustache. Count Amand looked directly at him and Ulfrik's hands went cold. Their eyes locked, and rather than flee he stepped out with a confident smile.

"The nuns said you would be here," Ulfrik said as he strode up to Amand. His heart crashed against his chest and he felt out of breath, but he tried to conceal his nerves from Amand, who peered at him with a scowl.

"Truly they did? Even I did not know I would be here."

"I mean the nuns passing through the courtyard said you were here with the guard."

Amand nodded and began stroking his mustache. "And so you've found me. What business do we have?"

"Well, I took a hard blow to my head and have been laid out in a tent," Ulfrik said, looking between Amand and the boyish guard, who stared at Ulfrik as if he were a giant of legend. "I'm actually hoping to be taken to those quarters you promised. That bed's a lot better than sharing tent with three men leaking their guts out."

Amand wrinkled his nose at the image. "A terrible loss yesterday. That damned Einar Snorrason has set everything back."

"I expect that was his goal," Ulfrik smiled, his mind a blur of activity. He hoped Amand would hand him off to another before he went to his prison. His ears roared with the throbbing of his blood. Something about Amand's searching eyes frightened him. Had he been caught speaking to Einar, even for such a brief time?

"Well, enough chatter. Too many good men were lost in a pointless fight. Einar may have delayed me, but he hurt himself just as badly. It's what you get putting a hand in the hornet's nest. Go back to your tent and I'll send for you later."

Ulfrik tried not to let his relief show, though his mind was buzzing with a dozen conflicting plans for his next step.

"Ulfrik Ormsson?"

He turned around, faced Grimnr, Vigrid, and five more of his hirdmen armed with shield and spears. Grimnr's face was taut with hate, a cut on his cheek open and dribbling blood onto his chest.

"By Odin's one eye," Ulfrik said. "I can't believe I answered to that."

"I can. Put your hands up and no tricks. Believe me when I say one threatening move will give me the pleasure of ripping your head off."

He blinked stupidly, astounded that a moment's inattention had cost him everything. Vigrid shook his head, and lowered his spear to touch Ulfrik's neck while others forced his hands to his back. "You played me like a fool."

"I did. Nothing personal."

"I'll be the one to set your head on a spear next to Eskil and the other traitors."

Ulfrik's mouth was dry and his hands clammy, but he steadied his voice. "Don't count on it yet. I've been killed once before, you know."

Vigrid spun his spear around and drove the butt into his chest, driving him back into the men at his back. Grimnr stepped forward, drawing his sword.

"I've got no cheer left over for a trial. I'm going to take his head now."

44

Runa watched the men from Eyrafell hurrying up the road toward Hrolf's hall. She stood in the doorway, holding her brown cloak tight against her fears. Her temples throbbed at seeing the urgency of the five messengers. The guard beside her leaned on his spear and spit in the dirt.

"Looks like dire news. Heard Jarl Einar led an attack that Jarl Hrolf was none too pleased with." The guard was a thin, morose man Runa had come to know as Smiling Lunt. He picked his teeth and leaned back against the wall.

"Did Einar win the battle? Is he alright?"

Smiling Lunt snorted and swallowed. "What do you call winning? I take it he's alive, but got banged up by some Danish monster, Grim the Rock or something like that. It's all the fucking same. Just a lot of blood and bodies everywhere. Only the ravens win."

Runa rolled her eyes at Lunt, and watched Einar's men fuss with their weapons at the hall door. "I think I should go to hear what they've to say."

"It's fine thought, but tuck that one back into your head. You can't barge in on Jarl Hrolf's audience. That'd be plain rude, and probably get me whipped."

"What happening?" Finn appeared behind Runa, stopping when he followed her gaze to Hrolf's hall. "Looks urgent."

"News from Eyrafell. I think we should go."

Aren now joined them, standing beside Finn. "It might be time to share our own news with Jarl Hrolf."

"Hey, the lot of you get back inside," Smiling Lunt said, never moving from the wall. "Is this how you repay me for the kindness I've shown you?"

Runa bit her bottom lip in thought. Days after Aren's arrival and nothing more had been learned about potential threats from Hrolf's men. She had underestimated the effort such spy work required and neither she nor the others were suited to the task. Perhaps under the stress news from Eyrafell someone might reveal more than intended.

"Let's go," Runa said, pulling the hood of her cloak overhead. She stepped out with Aren and Finn behind her.

"Wait a moment. You can't leave the hall." Smiling Lunt hurried after her, then blocked her path.

She smiled at him, shaking her head slightly at Lunt's empty hands. He had left his spear behind. "Step aside. Jarl Hrolf will want to hear what news I have."

"News? That you've chased all the rats from his guest hall? What news could you have?"

Placing her hands on his smooth cheeks, she held him still. "Dear Lunt, you are a good man, and I am grateful for you kindness. You'll make a fine husband to the right woman one day."

She kissed his forehead, then moved the blushing, stunned man aside like setting a jug on another table. Aren and Finn filed past her, and she released Lunt to mouth voiceless protests.

They approached the hall and the two guards set their spears across the doors. Runa sighed as both Finn and Aren stopped. The freckle-faced young man had recovered into his full, youthful vigor and stood ready to barrel through the guards if she asked it of him. She understood why Ulfrik would have bonded with the optimistic youth, but for this effort she slowly shook her head. He stepped aside. Aren with his face still swollen, shared a knowing smile with her.

"We need to enter this hall and see Jarl Hrolf," she said. "Save your threats, as I know you must prevent me."

The two guards glanced at each other. Both wore helmets with face plates and light brown hair to their shoulders, making them appear as twins. The one closest to Runa addressed her. "That's right. So save your pleas otherwise."

He smirked at his own wit, hitting his partner's shoulder in a show of pride.

"There's an easy way and a difficult way to do this, but I will be inside that hall with my two escorts. So either announce us to Hrolf or we do this the hard way."

"Are you going to tell us what the hard way is first?" the second guard asked.

"That's a special surprise if you choose it." Runa winked at him.

"Well, the hardest way is facing Hrolf's anger," said the closer guard. "And I can't imagine you will do worse than him."

"Shall we find out, then?" Runa spread her arms as if inviting them to test her. "At the very least he will be sorely upset when you interfered with the delivery of important news."

The twin guards frowned at each other. The second guard rubbed his nose with the back of his hand. "She has a reputation, you know. Runa the Bloody. Maybe we should just ask?"

"You fear a woman?" The closest guard turned back to her. "Sorry, you can't go inside unless Hrolf has summoned you."

"I rather hoped you'd choose the hard way. I've been bored." She reached into the folds of her blouse, but the second guard halted her.

"I'll check for you. You're news better be worth it."

The guard disappeared inside while his companion stood with his face turning red. Runa and Aren shared another small smile, but Finn stood with his mouth open and cheeks drained of color. He blinked at her in amazement.

The guard returned, slipping back outside the door. "Jarl Hrolf will see you now. Whatever you planned to pull out of your shirt, leave it outside the hall."

Runa smiled and withdrew a cloth she used to wipe her hands. She tossed it to the guard as she passed him. "It needs to be washed."

Inside the front room the other guard inspected them for weapons, his face bright red and lips drawn tight in anger. He showed them to the entrance to the main room and returned to his post. Finn tugged at her cloak.

"What was the hard way?"

"I don't know," she said. "Sometimes a confident bluff is the best threat of all."

Inside the sprawling hall, she recognized the faces of the five men from Eyrafell. Their faces glistened with sweat as they turned to face her. A savory, smoky scent lingered from a recent meal and the hearth fire still blazed to engulf the room in heat and haze. At the high table sat Hrolf with Gunther One-Eye at his right, and he raised a ring-laden hand to summon her forward.

She stood behind the men of Eyrafell, two who smiled in recognition. Aren and Finn flanked her, and all went to their knees before Hrolf.

"Off your knees," he said. "I've just received hard news that brings me great joy and concern in equal measure."

A fire set in Runa's stomach, and she feared the worst even as attempted to preserve her dignity by remaining cool. She smoothed her skirt after standing. "I too have news that I must share with you, having only just learned it from my son, Aren."

The lie slipped out easily and she hoped it would pass. However, a great jarl such as Hrolf was not easily deceived, and his expression grew dark. "Then I shall hear it now. But first, let the good men of Eyrafell complete their message."

The leader, a stout but strong man with a wild, black beard who Runa knew as Thororm, bowed to Hrolf and spoke in a clear, sharp voice. "Jarl Einar's attack has crippled Count Amand's force of traitors and cast his camp into disarray. The Frankish cavalry is still intact, but otherwise the Count will be disadvantaged for weeks. Jarl Einar himself was injured in the battle, taking an arrow to the back of his leg during the retreat. However, he was able to make contact with your spy inside the traitor forces."

Both Hrolf and Gunther One-Eye leaned forward. Hrolf's mighty hands balled into fists. "What news did the spy have for Jarl Einar?"

"He said that Amand's army is sick and they will soon be at half strength. But there was another message Jarl Einar entrusted me to deliver directly. Your spy said that Eskil and all the others are dead. The spy is alone and under suspicion. He needs swift help."

Runa's knees buckled at the news, and Hrolf leaned back with a terrible frown. Gunther One-Eye glanced at her, his single eye full of sympathy.

Thororm concluded with a bow. "That is all of the message."

Silence held the hall in an uncomfortable grip. Runa stared at the floor, imagining the horror of being among so many enemies without any chance for help. Then she thought of Konal and the fire in her stomach became a blaze, yet it also bolstered her courage. She determined to get help to Ulfrik even if she had to go herself.

"Jarl Hrolf, my news is more urgent upon learning this," she said, flashing her eyes at Thororm. Hrolf's frown deepened, but he waved at Thororm.

"I will hear this news in private. You five will be shown to hall where you may rest and be fed. Tonight you will dine with me so that I may better express gratitude for you haste."

Once Thororm and the men from Eyrafell were shown outside, Hrolf extended his hand to her. "Tell me your news, though I wonder at its late timing."

She straightened her back and met Hrolf's eyes. "Konal learned of Ulfrik's mission from my son, Aren. He did not mean to reveal it but in a fit of anger after being so violently beaten by Konal, he let it slip. He spent days afterward drunk in his hall, but when your men came to fetch Aren away he picked a crew from his men and sailed up the Seine without a word to anyone."

Hrolf's face turned red, but it was Gunther One-Eye who spoke. "When he sailed away, you did not think to tell us upon arrival?"

"I thought he was leaving on your orders. Now that Aren confessed his mistake, Konal's departure seems as if he is going to cause trouble for Ulfrik. Help must be sent to him, today if possible. Konal has had days to make mischief already."

Hrolf rubbed his eyes then conferred with Gunther, the two whispering in low voices. Despite straining to hear their discussion, she could only hear clipped and harsh mumbles from this distance. Both men snarled, though whether at each other or the bad news Runa did not know. She glanced at Finn who stood in awe of Hrolf's magnificence, then at Aren who was more collected. He quietly studied both men, and Runa recognized that contemplative face. Since he was a child, Aren was an uncanny reader of men's thoughts and intentions. Whatever these two debated he would understand and inform her later.

"This is certainly bad news," Hrolf said. "But I will have to decide the best course of action."

"Ulfrik himself told you he needs help. How much more now if Konal has gone to make trouble?"

Gunther spoke before Hrolf could reply. "We don't know what his intentions are. Maybe he went to Eyrafell. We will ask the messengers if they know his whereabouts."

The fire returned to her stomach again, and her fists balled up. "Ulfrik needs help. You must send it. Stop wasting time."

"Don't overstep yourself," Hrolf said with a raised hand. "I have loved you like a sister, but even a sister must mind her words in my hall."

Runa bit back her next words and instead lowered her gaze from Hrolf's glower. As her mind raced in search of a new tactic, the hall doors burst open once again. All heads turned to face the rear of the hall, where the same guard Runa angered earlier strode forward, looking at no one, and went to his knee before Hrolf.

Hrolf's fist struck the table, jolting everyone but Gunther One-Eye. "Do my commands mean nothing to you? Am I so indulgent that you feel privileged to enter like this was your own bedchamber? Unless my hall is burning down around me, you'll be lashed bloody for this."

The guard bowed lower. "Jarl Hrolf, the ship you have had followed since it entered the Seine has been captured and brought to dock. On your order, I am here to inform you that the crew has arrived."

His fists unclenching, Hrolf subsided and smoothed out his beard and shirt. "This is good timing, in fact. Bring the crew's hovedsmann to me immediately."

The guard swept away without a word or glance and anyone. Runa's chest tightened and she blinked at Hrolf who now smiled at her. "Should we leave?"

"On the contrary, you must remain. You will want to meet this man, if he is who I believe him to be."

Looking at Aren and Finn, both returned a blank stare. "Who would that be?"

"Another man you thought dead, your son, Gunnar the Black."

45

A numb tingling spread across Runa's face as she watched the doors to Hrolf's hall, waiting for them to open and reveal her first born son. Her mind raced with a dozen thoughts but none of them completing. She wanted to flee the hall and hide. She imagined the fading bruises on her cheek and placed a hand over it, feeling heat radiating from her skin. Gunnar could not see her like this, not with both her and Aren beaten at Konal's hands. The door loomed in her vision, as if all the world lay behind it. What was she going to do or say? She never believed he was dead, but could not believe he had never returned. Why had he abandoned her? Her own son, the best of part of her and Ulfrik, and he had left her when she needed him most.

"Mother?" Aren tugged on her sleeve, and she turned to him. His wide, swollen face was filled with the same fear and instantly she forgot her own.

She touched his glossy hair and smiled. "You were only a child when he left. He will be proud to see you growing into a man. Do not fear."

"I don't want to see him like this." Aren bowed his head, and Runa slipped her arm about his shoulders. He was still her youngest, and though many called him a man at his age she could not help but coddle him. He was more sensitive than normal men, both a blessing and a curse.

"I am intruding," Finn said. "Maybe I should go?"

Runa shook her head. "From all you've told me, Ulfrik treats you like family. Stay and meet his first-born son."

The hall doors opened and Runa yanked Aren closer and gasped. The two guards entered first, but Runa could already see the wavy black hair of her eldest son behind the guards. They looked at her expectantly, and Runa stared back. Aren pulled back and she realized Gunnar, if it was him, must present himself to Hrolf first. She retreated to a wall with Aren and Finn, a spectator to the return of her own son.

When he entered the tears flowed from her eyes and her knees buckled. Aren held her straight as she fought against sobbing. Gunnar stood as tall as his father, walked with his purpose and determination. Though his second brother Hakon looked like Ulfrik, Gunnar was truly the inheritor of all Ulfrik's gifts. Runa marveled at his power and authority as he followed his escorts to Hrolf's presence. His vision did not waver, and if he recognized his family huddled against the walls he made no sign. He acted as if Hrolf was his equal, and for all Runa knew it could be true. He was dressed in fine clothes, with new leather boots and a rust colored cloak held with a golden pin. At his side a sword slapped against his leg, though it was bound tightly in its sheath with leather peace straps to prevent it being drawn. His right sleeve hid the stump of his missing hand, but three gold bands adorned his arm.

"Jarl Hrolf the Strider, I am honored you have taken such an interest in me." Gunnar went to his knee before Hrolf. Even his voice carried the hint of Ulfrik's own powerful tones. Runa wiped her eyes with the back of her hand, and sniffed.

"No ship enters Seine without my knowledge, and when you named yourself to my men there I had to learn who you really are." Hrolf spoke but Runa only stared at Gunnar, heart thudding in her chest. He did not waver before Hrolf, arms resting at his sides and his head tilted up in pride. She wanted to rush to him, but he did not turn to her.

"I am Gunnar the Black, son of Ulfrik, and I once knew your hospitality. I beg it again for me and my crew."

"You shall have it. But where have you been and why return now?"

"I have been everywhere, yet none of my travels matter. I left to find revenge for my father, but failed. The tale is too shameful to repeat. As to why I have returned, perhaps you know already. My crew and I arrived in Yorvik only recently, seeking our fortunes only to learn that a man calling himself Ulfrik Ormsson had spent a long winter there and made friends among the traders and merchants. I heard he had only recently departed for Frankia, swearing an oath of revenge on those who had betrayed him. I wanted to believe it was a trick of the gods, for I had seen my father's shattered head and heard Einar tell the story of his murder. Yet men who knew him swore to me the truth, and described my father's likeness and habits in details that leave no doubt he lived. I am here to find him, to bring this news to you and my family, and return to my rightful place...if I will be welcomed back to it."

Gunnar lowered his head and Runa saw the regret on his face. She glanced at Hrolf, who smiled at her and extended his jeweled hand. "Your news is a joy to hear, but as for assuming your rightful place, that is for your mother to decide."

Both Runa and Aren swarmed Gunnar, who turned to them with his own eyes shining with tears. They embraced and Runa sobbed into his shoulder. He smelled like the sea and smoke, and though her cheek pressed hard muscle beneath his shirt she held him as if he were still her little boy. No matter what happened or how much time passed, he would always be her beloved first-born son. He finally pulled her back with a gentle hand.

"I am sorry for all the pain I must have caused you. No words will undo my thoughtless cruelty." He cupped her face in his rough, warm hands and smiled. She saw her brother, Toki, in his expression and in the dark pools of his eyes. "Will you forgive me?"

Shaking her head, she pressed her face back into his shoulder and cried again. She lost count of the time and soon Gunnar peeled her away again. Sniffling, she dabbed at her face with the cuff of her sleeve. Gunnar's eye shifted to the bruises on her cheeks, and his lips tightened but he said nothing more. Now he turned to Aren, and the two embraced with a ferocity that told Runa they would be whole again.

"Your timing is a sign from the gods," Hrolf said, stepping down from his high table. "Your father has returned to us, and we all now know it. He is in need of swift help, and I believe you are the one to deliver it to him."

Hrolf welcomed Gunnar with an embrace, then stepped aside to allow Gunther One-Eye to do the same. He thumped Gunther's right shoulder. "One hand hasn't kept you from grabbing an armload of gold, I see."

Gunnar smiled, the same boyish grin Runa remembered from his childhood, and he shook his head. "Fate has been kind to me in that regard, and my crew does not go hungry for wealth."

"You sailed the same tides as your father," Hrolf said. "And found similar fortunes. There will be a time for that story, but not today. Be seated, and hear all there is to be told of your father's story. This young man, Finn, can tell you of his days in Iceland and I shall tell you of his condition today. Then we shall lay plans for you to aid both him and me."

Gunnar lowered to a bench and as promised sat with rapt attention through all the stories Finn either experienced with Ulfrik or had relayed to him. At the description of Throst's death Gunnar lowered his head and closed his eyes. Runa wanted to take his hand and comfort him, but realized such a display would shame him. When Finn completed his stories, Hrolf detailed his own and concluded with the news of only a few hours prior.

"Someone must get to Ulfrik and render what aid he needs," Hrolf said, then paused to drink from a mug of mead servants had provided to all of them. "Worse still, if Konal would do as Runa fears, then not only haste but fighting prowess is required."

Rubbing the back of his neck, Gunnar winced. "I loved Konal like an uncle once. Yet even before I left on my long journey he was a changing man, and now the evidence of the worst change is battered into the faces of my mother and brother. If he could hurt Aren so, then it is no feat of imagination to see him betraying my father to the Franks. It is not the choice of a reasonable man, but he must be beyond clear thought."

"Even without that worry, there is the urgency of his own message," Runa said, driving her fist into her palm. "No one is happier than me to have you return, but I believe as Hrolf does. Your ship and name are unknown to these Northman traitors. You could join with them as your father did, but bring a whole crew of fighting men to his aid."

"Such a large number of men cannot maintain a secret for long," Hrolf said, standing from his bench. "Witness Eskil. He grew his numbers too large and exposed all of his doings. You would only have a handful of days to contact your father then extract him and my son. The good news is they are reeling from Einar's blow. You should be able to achieve this."

Gunnar went to his knee before Hrolf and bowed his head. "I swear before you and all these witness I shall not return without my father and your son, alive and whole, or my own life be forfeit."

Hrolf raised Gunnar to his feet, and then embraced him. "Bring them both back."

"We must leave as soon as your men are refreshed and provisioned," Runa said, also getting to her feet with the others.

"Reunions are for later, mother," Gunnar said. "You should remain where it is safe."

She grabbed his handless arm and pulled him close, his eyes widening with surprise. "I am still your mother, and no matter how mighty you've grown you will obey me this once. I go with you."

"And I shall come as well," Aren added, his face red. "Though I cannot fight I can row or tie a rope, whatever you need done."

"Tie a rope?" Gunnar cocked an eyebrow at Aren.

"I'm not being left behind," Finn said. "You'll want me to find Ulfrik for you, since none of you have seen him recently. Besides, I was a hunter once and know how to sneak about. Ulfrik will tell you that himself once he's back."

Gunnar gave a helpless look to Hrolf, who shrugged and laughed.

"You see how well I've been able to confine your mother to her guest home? By now, she is better off with you than with me and I'm sure these fine men will be of service somehow."

"Gather your belongings," Gunnar said, a small smile creeping onto his face. "Let's go meet my father."

46

The audience room of Count Amand's fortress was as large as the halls Konal had seen of the greatest jarls, only Hrolf the Strider's hall being larger. As he waited for Grimnr the Mountain and the old Count to finish their whispered argument he scratched his chin and studied the room. Christian symbols adorned all the empty spaces, from crucifixes to statutes of their small gods. Candles guttered in silver holders and above him on a great wheel. He folded his arms, both against the evening chill of the room and his worry. Grimnr had not killed Ulfrik outright, and now he sat in a prison awaiting execution. If the Franks decided to press him for information, it would just give Ulfrik more time for his luck to work him out of the trap.

The argument reached a peak, hissed whispers rising to a sharp shout from Amand and his guards lowering spears. Grimnr the Mountain looked like a wolf about to pounce on a flock of sheep, unafraid of the guards and their spears. Konal held his breath for the heartbeats they stared down each other, and Count Amand finally waved them back with an irritated sweep of his arm.

"Enough posturing," he said. "Let us reserve our decisions until we've spoken with this one."

"Konal Ketilsson, come forward," Grimnr said, his voice little more than a growl. His hulking form heaved with anger and his mouth was bent in a frown. He held up a hand when Konal stood beneath the wheel of candles. "Close enough. Your information on Ulfrik was correct. He answered to his own name."

"Did he? That seems unlike him to make such a simple mistake."

"Well, I caught him off guard attempting to get close to Halfdan."

Konal frowned at the name, then recalled Halfdan was the false name Vilhjalmer used to disguise his true identity. "Still you allowed him to live?"

Here the Grimnr's eyes shifted to Count Amand, and he folded his massive arms. The Count stroked his mustache as he reclined in his chair. His voice was airy and aloof. "I need to learn whatever I can from him. He will be spend some time with one of my more ... energetic men, and if he has not told me all I want to know before his teeth are gone then we shall work on his fingers until I get it. Then he will be killed."

Konal's repulsion must have been plain on his face, for Count Amand smirked. Grimnr shook his head and his gaze fell to the floor.

"It's a mistake to torment him," Konal said. "I can tell you all you need and more. Besides, I promise you he is the luckiest man I've ever met. The longer he lives the more likely he will elude your justice."

Amand raised his brow and his hand went still on his mustache. "By now I trust the words of no Northman besides Grimnr's, and after this I begin to doubt his judgment." Grimnr snarled but did not take his eyes off the floor before him. "Yet I do have your ship and crew as hostages. Tell me what else you know."

"Only on the condition you execute Ulfrik immediately."

Pushing himself straighter on the chair, Amand gave a playful smile. "You are setting conditions with me? Is that all?"

"I want protection for me and my crew and a promise you will allow us to leave unharmed. It is a fair trade for what I will offer you, I can assure you."

Grimnr glanced at Amand, who slowly nodded. The giant man turned to Konal, his smoldering gaze setting a fire at the pit of Konal's guts. "You have terrible scars on your face and hands. Did Ulfar ... Ulfrik, give you those?"

"He gave me scars of another kind," Konal said in his hoarse, whispering voice. "My history with him is deep. It was much easier when he was dead." Both the Count and Grimnr expressed confusion and Konal waved his hand. "As I warned you, he has escaped death once already. Do not linger in your decision to execute him. I assume you asked about my scars because you wonder why I betrayed him. Let me make it clearer to you. I married his wife and sit in what would be his hall. That should explain my actions."

"By now Einar must know you are here," Grimnr said. "How will you return to your wife and hall when he knows you for a traitor?"

"I have a plan for that. Your concern flatters me, but do not think of it."

"The prattle of you barbarians is enough to try Job's patience." Amand slapped the arm of his chair, a gold ring clanking against the deep brown wood. "Tell me what you know, or perhaps I'll have you hanged alongside Ulfar."

Konal narrowed his eyes at the old Count, but Grimnr tilted his head in challenge. Konal swallowed, trying to recall a time when such a threat would have sent his hand for his sword rather than a skin of ale. Still he found himself wishing for a drink under that feral gaze. "I assure you Ulfrik is alone. He was sent specifically by Hrolf the Strider to contact his spy, Eskil. His mission was to break out the hostage you know as Halfdan."

Grimnr nodded as if he had known this all along, but Amand showed only confusion. "I knew Mord was close to Hrolf, but never expected him to take an interest in Mord's son."

"You never gave your word on my demands," Konal said. "Before I say another thing, I want to know you will execute Ulfrik tomorrow and allow me safe passage out of here."

"Only if your information has value and is true," Amand said.

"I already revealed Ulfrik to you. How much more assurance of my honesty do you demand? I work for myself and none other. I want him dead, and to give Hrolf a black eye as well. Now do I have your word?" His voice was scratchy and faint, but no less powerful for it. Again Grimnr nodded and Amand let out a long sigh.

"You have my word on both demands. I swear it before our Lord God. Satisfied?"

A smile swept Konal's ruined face. "Very. Now, you know all there is about Ulfrik. Only you do not know the one you call Halfdan's real name. He is not Mord's son, but Hrolf's. He was Mord's guess when he slipped away to find adventure. His name is Vilhjalmer, which I believe you people call William. You have in your custody Hrolf's first and only son, the most precious person to him in the whole circle of the world. All the jarls know it, from Mord to Einar to Ull the Strong. They all play for time for Ulfrik to rescue the boy. Otherwise, imagine how you could make Hrolf bend knowing his son is at your mercy?"

Count Amand now sat back in his chair as if slapped into submission. Grimnr's mouth hung agape, making small, noiseless movements. Konal smiled and folded his arms. "Put your so-called energetic man to work on Vilhjalmer and he will soon confirm what I've told you. You have as a hostage what your people call a prince. Is learning that worth my demands?"

Count Amand nodded, though his eyes remained fixed on some distant landscape in his own mind. "Worth it all. You may leave with my blessings, but are invited to remain for Ulfrik's execution. We'll hang him at dawn."

"I wouldn't miss it."

47

"I heard Hrolf's orders," Gunnar said, spitting over the rails of his sleek longship. "But on my ship my commands are all that matter, and please, Mother, try not to speak to me as if I were a child. I will hear no end of it from my crew."

Runa sank back with a smile trembling on her lips. "Of course, I overstep myself. It's fear that rules me, makes me worried that your father is so close to us, but might as well still be in Iceland."

Gunnar leaned on the rudder with a grunt and the ship angled around a bend in the Seine. "I know how you must feel. Attempting to join with Count Amand's men is not a good plan for what we must do. Hrolf has never been a thief, and does not know how best to steal from an army of angry Northmen. We send in Finn, learn what we can of Father's situation, then offer him help from the outside. He will need a ship readied to sail at a moment's notice, and we won't have that ability if we are being tested by suspicious enemies. Besides, we are sailing up the Seine and could not have come this far without Hrolf's permission. Of course they will not trust us. We just have to stay out of sight, which the bends in this river makes simple."

She inclined her head to her son's decision. She could not find fault with the idea, and liked his reasoning. Gunnar worked the tiller as skillfully as a man with both hands. He had strapped a hook to his right arm that he claimed held the tiller just as well as a normal hand. The ship still had the glow of fresh wood, and creaked and popped as it plied up river. He had twenty oars, ten on each side, each manned by fierce men with broad shoulders and battle-scars. The water splashed as they grunted at the oars, Gunnar shouting a curse whenever he thought the pace slackened.

"I will want a sword and shield of my own," she said to Gunnar, her voice edged with defiance. To her surprise, he grunted agreement.

"Pick a shield from the rack. There are more than I have crew for. You can have my sax, since I guess Konal has continued to forbid your practice. Am I right?"

She watched the dark line of trees glide past, and her silence answered for her. "After I thought your father died, I let everything go. He did not need to forbid practice, since I would have been glad to die under the sword. It wasn't until I learned Ulfrik returned that I realized I too had been dead."

"Hard words. Do not think so lightly of yourself. You are still a shield maiden."

Runa laughed. "At my age I am more a shield matron. I suppose my arms remember what to do in a fight, but if pressed I will be in trouble."

"Stay near me. No enemy will harm you."

She watched Aren and Finn review the rigging, and only the clipped conversation of the crew and the swish of water along the hull made any sound. Her hand groped for the silver Thor's hammer hanging from her neck and she spoke under her breath. "I pray we will not fight at all."

They fell into silence, and Runa took stock of the ship. Clustered about the mast were casks and crates, creating an island that forced men to the sides of the ship when crossing the deck. She pointed at the pile. "You do trading?"

Gunnar shrugged. "I do whatever makes gold for the crew. Those are casks of oil from Lundene, which I bought at a price little better than thievery. The crates are filled with spun wool on top, but gold coins on the bottom. I thought I'd have to pay my way back into Hrolf's graces. Looks like Fate had a better plan."

Runa winced. "A problem solved with gold is better than one solved with blood."

"I've missed your wisdom, Mother." He smiled at her and they both shared a laugh.

At length Gunnar guided his ship to the shore and Finn prepared for his task. Men leapt the rails then hauled the ship to the shore, and Runa had to grasp the rails with both hands or fall on her face. Gunnar set a gangplank for Finn, then slapped his back. "Tell my father I am impatient to see him again. Bring him and Vilhjalmer as fast as you are able."

Finn's bright, freckle-splattered face lit up with a smile. "I'm excited to see him again, too. I owe him my life for the second time, so I hope this will pay for one."

Aren clasped arms with Finn, then frowned as if confronted by a puzzle he could not solve. "Good luck," he said.

He leapt onto the rail, paused and unbuckled his sword baldric. He handed it to Aren. "It's too big for the sly work ahead of me. My sax and dagger is all I need. If I have to pull this out I'm in a lot of trouble. So you hold it for me."

The sword dangled before Aren's wide, swollen face and he looked sheepishly at Runa. She smiled and pointed at the sword with her chin. He took it into his hands as if it would break, then slipped it over his shoulder. "I will keep it dry and safe for you."

"Use it if you have to. Swords need to be bloodied or else they bring bad luck. That one's been clean a bit too long."

Runa let him amble down the gangplank and flit away into the trees without a word. A lump caught in her throat and she did not know what so say.

Gunnar posted a guard at the bend to check for approaching ships. Other guards watched the tree line and opposite shores. Runa felt as if everyone had a purpose but her, and soon she felt foolish for having joined this trip. She gave Gunnar space to lead his crew, but she stole glances at him. He ruled his crew with a blunt ferocity that was not characteristic of Ulfrik. His gruff, harsh words motivated them, but it reminded Runa more of Ulfrik's father Orm or his brother Grim and she did not care for that change.

After a long morning of idleness she had settled onto the beach to stare thoughtlessly into the cloudy sky. The shout of the guard at the bend roused her.

"A ship," he cried. "Full sail, twenty oars."

Men began to rush back to the ship, several of them already pushing it back into the water. "Hurry!" Gunnar shouted a from the prow. "Mother, get back on the ship. We have to leave!"

She scramble up the gangplank, artlessly falling over the gangplank. Aren helped her up, his newly acquired sword swinging loose on his shoulder and unbalancing him. She heard the splash of water and the pop of the sail unfurl. She staggered to Gunnar, who pulled hard on the tiller making the ship tilt and moan with the strain.

"We can't afford to be caught now," he said through clenched teeth.

"But what of Finn? How will he get Ulfrik to safety? We have to return."

Gunnar shook his head. "Not too soon. They'll see a ship beached recently. I'm a thrice-cursed fool for doing so. The patrols will become more active."

"They'll know we were here just from that?"

"Any hovedsmann worthy of the name will know how large a ship had beached there and when." Gunnar growled at the strain of holding the tiller in place as the ship lurched around and caught the wind. She threw her own hands atop his and pushed as well. Gunnar laughed. "I've got it, Mother. Save your strength for picking Aren off the deck. I think he needs to steady himself."

Runa twisted back to see Aren on hands and knees at the middle of the deck. Finn's sword held him down like an anchor stone. She felt heat rise in her face for his shame. "Konal never trained him properly."

"Father will mend that problem," Gunnar said, then as the sail filled and the mast creaked forward he bellowed at his crew. "Row, you dog-loving turds or I'll strip the skin off your ribs! Keep the pace."

From her position at the stern she peered down the river toward the bend, but still saw nothing. The crew continued to drive hard, and she turned toward the prow and saw nothing but straight river until it shaded away to a bland misty horizon. "They'll see us no matter what."

"True," Gunnar agreed. "But if these bastards row like real men we sail close to the wind we'll out-pace them."

"We'll have to return to Hrolf, then?"

Gunnar shrugged, easing off the tiller with a sigh. "If they pursue us, we will have no other choice."

"We could fight them, make sure they never get word back." Runa stared at him, hoping he would agree, but his face twisted into a scowl.

"That's not how it works. If a ship doesn't return they'll send three more out to find it."

Runa's hopes fell as she saw the enemy sail round the bend. It was far enough away to seem no bigger than a toy ship, but to her the ship seemed a giant blocking the river. "We're leaving them all behind."

"For a short time," Gunnar said, his voice far less fierce than it had been. "We'll return in another day. Finn will wait for us if we are not there when he returns. Don't worry for it."

She leaned on the rails and watched the enemy ship's oars lift and fall like the legs of dragon crawling over the water. She closed her eyes and swallowed hard. "He is still without help."

48

Ulfrik sat in the blackness of his dank cell, the scent of mold heavy in his nose. Black iron bars framed a window in a heavy wood door, and a square of orange light filtered in with the rotten scent of burning tallow candles. The floor was cold beneath him, all hard packed earth with any rock larger than a walnut dug out of it. He had pried at the dirt, but found it impossible to lift more than a fingernail's worth of it at a time. He flicked the grime out of his nails now, and rested his head against the stone wall.

"Are you still there?" he called out in Frankish, and when no answer came he tried again in Norse. His guard had only appeared to him once with a mug of gritty water and a wooden plate of hard bread and stale cheese. Time disappeared inside this cell but judging from the growl in his belly a day must have passed since that poor meal. He had not lose hope for a way out of this trap, but one had not revealed itself to him yet.

If Count Amand had not stopped him, Grimnr would have struck off Ulfrik's head in one blow. That was his mistake, and Ulfrik waited like a spider on a dark web for his moment to strike. He feared death and knew it was near, but the gods would not have taken him this far merely to dangle him from a rope before a gawking crowd until he pissed his pants in death. Just like his imprisonment in Iceland, the gods would present a path out that led through pain and blood. He would tread that path willingly and set the gods to dancing for joy at his exploits.

Until then, he tried to forget the reality of being stuck into cell with no chance of escape.

When no voice answered him, Ulfrik shifted to the door. He banged on it with a flat palm. "Talk to me, you fool. No harm in that, and I just want to know how much longer I've got to live. You can tell me that, at least."

Someone shushed him from outside the door, then a familiar voice whispered. "Be quiet while I get the key for the lock. I've never seen a real lock before."

Ulfrik began to laugh and his limbs trembled with excitement. He clapped his hands and spun around inside his cell. "Finn, your voice is a song to me."

Metal scrapped against the door and Ulfrik attempted to peek out the small window, seeing nothing but stone walls and the glow of candlelight. He glimpsed the top of Finn's head against the door.

"So, this is how it works." Ulfrik heard a click and then more metal shaking against the door. "Time to get you out."

The door swung into the cell, sweeping Ulfrik away, and Finn stood framed in the center. His innocent freckled face was splashed with drops of blood as was his gray linen shirt. A sax and dagger hung from either hip and he threw his arms wide, throwing back his dark brown cloak. Ulfrik embraced him with a slap on the back.

"Hrolf sent you?"

"Jarl Einar sent word to him, and he sent me to you. Here's a dagger for you, in case we have more killing to do on the way out."

Ulfrik searched his surroundings, finding a narrow stone hall lit by candles and several rows of doors matching those of his own cell. When Grimnr dragged him down here, he was hanging upside down between two guards and was flung head first into his cell. He never got a look at the prison. "The blood, from the guard?"

Finn rubbed his cheek, smearing the blood into a streak. "There was only one for this entire hall. I got him from behind and shoved him in the first cell. This place is empty but for you."

Tucking the dagger into his pants, he clapped Finn's shoulder. "We should get Vilhjalmer and leave. We're already beneath one of his towers, not sure which one. But Vilhjalmer is in the southwestern tower on the top."

Frowning, Finn shook his head. "We've got to get you out of here. It was a lot of work getting inside and every guard in this place is standing on his toes looking for an enemy. We'll have to come back for Vilhjalmer."

"After I escape, they'll move his location, maybe out of this fortress altogether. We take him now."

"With a two daggers and a short sword between us?"

"That's one blade of each of us then. Besides I thought you dreamed about being a hero?"

"That was before I understood how bad it hurts to get your guts sliced open. Now we've got to move before another guard shows. There's a back gate out of here we can exploit. It's where I got in."

He let Finn lead, and kept his hand on the hilt of the dagger. At the end of the hall stone steps lifted up toward a mellow light of an opened door. A splash of dark blood glistened on the wall beside the stairs. "I know you want to get to Vilhjalmer," Finn said. "We won't be able to talk much after we get out of here. So I want to warn you I'm not alone. I've met your wife, Runa, and she's waiting on a ship nearby to use in our escape."

Ulfrik stepped back as if he had been slapped. "She found out from Snorri, didn't she?" Finn nodded and he growled. "Why tell me now?"

"In case we've got a bunch of angry Franks chasing us to the ship, I don't want you so surprised it causes you to make a mistake."

"Good thinking. Let's go." Finn barred him with an outstretched arm.

"The ship belongs to your son, Gunnar the Black. He returned after he heard about you from our time in Yorvik. He looks a lot like your wife and is a bit scary, to be honest."

"You're a world of surprises," Ulfrik said. "I'm glad he's not dead, but this is the wrong time for a family history chat. We've got to hurry."

Finn opened his mouth to say more, but Ulfrik grabbed his shoulder and spun him around toward the stairs. With a gentle shove, Finn swooped up the steps, keeping low as he peered out the door. He remained motionless like a cat watching a bird on a fence, then without looking back he waved Ulfrik forward.

The two piled out into a room where another man lay face down on a bed, a line of blood dripped from the side and pooled by a set of boots. Finn whispered, "He was asleep already, just made sure he stayed that way."

The candles lighting the small guard room fluttered and danced as the two shuffled to the door opposite them. Finn peered out, again staring like a predator on the hunt until he turned back. "I can't see the whole courtyard from here. The southwest tower is directly opposite and is also the wrong way for us to escape."

"This is not about rescuing me," Ulfrik hissed. "We need to take Hrolf's son or you should've left me to die."

Finn's normally sunny expression went dark, but he nodded once and cautiously opened the door. He slid against the wall beside the door, and his hand appeared to wave Ulfrik outside. As he exited into the predawn darkness, he pulled the door closed and flattened against it. His legs trembled and his breath was short, but a smile creased his face. Only a moment ago he was a helpless prisoner and now he was again a skulking devil preparing to sew confusion among his enemies.

"There are no guards around," Finn whispered. "We might be able to do this."

"They're about. We just haven't spotted them." They waited on Ulfrik's suspicions, but when no one appeared they began to slink along the darkness of the courtyard edges.

Pausing at the last stretch, Ulfrik drew his dagger. "That tower door is guarded inside, and I'm sure it's locked. We might have to find another way inside."

"You're telling me this now?" Finn's eyes were bright in the murky black.

"I'll try to door, and you hang back. These towers all connect at the higher levels, though maybe not that one." He scanned the walls around them, but without a moon he could not discern anything more than a darker patch on the night sky.

They stared at each other, and Ulfrik set off for the door.

Torches flared into light and men rushed into the courtyard. Ulfrik froze and for an instant believed if he was still he would remain unseen. Only he was the cornered rabbit and the fox was Grimnr and two dozen guards, half of whom had arrows stringed and pointed at him.

"I'm right here," Ulfrik called, hoping to distract them from Finn. Grimnr stepped forward with his sword drawn, and it flashed with torchlight as he pointed it directly at Finn.

"We saw him enter the prison," Grimnr said. "So you're working with others after all. Put down the dagger. Even if you throw it through my neck you'll get ten arrows through your own in return. Not a good bargain. Same for your companion."

Ulfrik's blood roared in his ears and his head grew warm. He ranged the dagger before himself, snarling at Grimnr. "You're a traitor to your people."

"Don't you think I've heard that talk before?" Grimnr asked, approaching with his sword held low. Behind him the points of arrow tips gleamed with orange light. "I am loyal to my word, and I give that to whoever pays me the most."

"Mord will pay anything you ask for that boy. Give him up and you will be wealthier than that old Frankish turd you serve."

Grimnr's feral smile widened, and he tilted his head like a hound trying to understand a new command. "Mord can pay so much? Are you sure it's not Hrolf the Strider who would pay?"

Ulfrik's hands went cold, and Grimnr laughed. He stopped before Ulfrik just as his sword point touched Ulfrik's dagger. Somehow he had discovered Vilhjalmer's true identity. Time had run out and Ulfrik had failed. He glanced at Finn, who resolutely held his sax against a dozen archers.

Throwing his dagger at Grimnr's feet, Ulfrik lowered his head.

"Set my friend free. He's here just to save me and knows nothing of what I intended."

"Oh, he'll be freed," Grimnr said. "But he's leaving with you on the hanging tree as soon as the sun rises. You've got about an hour until the two of you can greet each other again in Nifelheim."

49

Ulfrik sat on the dirt floor and rubbed his face. The small shed smelled like sweat and urine, much like his old cell beneath the fortress but this one instead was outside Grimnr's hall. Three men might have fit into the space, but Finn had been separated from him, leaving Ulfrik with enough room to lay down if he had wanted. Instead he sat ready to face whatever came through the door in front of him. Currently it was only the stains of morning light, and he heard the roosters crow with the day. Through the rear wall of his shed, he heard low voices of men but their words were indistinct.

He sucked his bottom lip as he considered the events of the morning. His chest burned with the anger and frustration of being caught yet again, and now he had Finn's welfare to consider. He tried to rethink where all of this planning had gone wrong, but soon shook the thought from his head. He could worry for the past once he survived the mistakes that had led him to this moment. As the deep voices beyond the walls of his prison shack grew louder and more numerous, he realized time for planning was at an end. He had to decide the next move or else end up swinging from a noose.

That Grimnr held him in his own camp rather than turning him over to the Franks indicated Count Amand had either lost interest in questioning him or did not know of the escape attempt. Ulfrik believed it was the latter, and Grimnr was eager to erase the embarrassing stain on his judgment by hanging him at dawn. Nor had he bothered to tie him or Finn. Seeing how they were surrounded by hundreds of enemies, binding them would have been a waste of rope.

As he rested his head against the wall he closed his eyes and inventoried his choices. He could save himself and Finn and forget Vilhjalmer for another day, or, he could still attempt to free Vilhjalmer. Freeing Hrolf's son seemed an impossible task now that he would have to wade through a camp of hostiles and break into a fortress guarded by men well-aware of his intentions. Yet returning to Hrolf in failure may mean he had saved his own life but ruined any value in living it. Hrolf would have no mercy on him, especially now that Grimnr and Amand knew Vilhjalmer's true identity. Any plan to escape had to include Vilhjalmer or it would not be true escape.

No other choice existed but to save Vilhjalmer. Now the gods merely had to show him his moment and he would act. They had left his hands free, which was a sign they would place a weapon in them soon. He only had to watch for it.

A shadow fell over the light seeping between the planks of the door and someone pressed his face to the crack in the door jamb. "They're getting the noose prepared. Won't be long before you're swinging like a common thief."

"Is that you, Vigrid?" Ulfrik leapt to the door then pressed his ear to it. The answer did not come, and he banged on the door.

"You used me to get closer to Grimnr," Vigrid said through the door. Ulfrik could feel him leaning against it, the two of them separated only by the planks.

"That's true, and I'm sorry for the deceit."

"I doubt you would have been sorry were you not caught. Grimnr would've killed me in your place, just because I spoke for you."

Ulfrik slid from the door and stepped back. "He is not that sort of man."

Their exchange stultified and Ulfrik began to pace the small, empty room. Flies buzzed around him, attracted to the waste left by former captives in the corners. He paced until his leg grew sore then realized at some point the voices outside had fallen quiet. He turned in time to hear the bar lifted out of the door and have it sweep open. Mellow dawn light framed him against the wall as he faced Grimnr, his bulk filling the doorway.

"As I promised, hanging at first light." Grimnr was a shadow that turned from the door to allow two others to point their spears at him. They barked at him to exit, which he did.

Outside the fresh air hit his face like an open palm, and the two guards herded him at spear-point toward Grimnr and Vigrid. Ulfrik's eyes swept past them to the throng of men at their backs. What seemed every Northman in the camp that was not bed-ridden pressed from all sides. For such a crowd, their silence was more awesome than their numbers. Grim faces stared out at him, some old and scarred and inscrutable, some young, dirty and curious. Rank upon rank of fighting men, survivors of Einar's surprise assault, had gathered to see him die.

"The name Ulfrik Ormsson is well-known here," Grimnr said.

"Not all of them know me," he said, so quietly his voice was faint to his own ears. He searched the crowd for familiar men, but saw nothing more than the same beaten and bent faces common to all warriors. "Do men even remember my name?"

"Time is a battle that fame always loses," Grimnr said. "But you have not been gone so long that the land has forgotten you. I was not here for your days of glory, but I am here for your death. I've kept your hands unbound and expect you to act with honor. Do not be foolish in the final moment, when so many have come to witness how a hero goes to his death."

Another guard shoved Finn beside him, and his young companion fell to the ground with a grunt. Ulfrik did not bend to help him, but allowed Finn to struggle to his feet. He clutched his side, the wound from the bandit camp still troubling him. His normally smiling face was contorted in fear and his freckles stood out like brown sand scattered over snow. His eyes were wet, and the threat of tears Ulfrik saw there set a fire in his gut.

"Straighten yourself," he snapped. "A man will not die until his hour is at hand, and if it is, no tears will keep it at bay. You know this."

"But I don't have to be happy for it."

"It is not our time," Ulfrik said. "The gods have not seen us this far to hang us like slaves."

"But like oath-breakers," Grimnr said. "The gods have no love of false men. Now enough foolishness."

The crowd parted as their guards shoved them forward. Ulfrik held his head up and back straight, hands loose at his sides. Even if he could grab a weapon, he had no hope of fighting out of this press. He fixed his eyes on the distance and allowed himself to be herded toward the Seine, where over the heads of the crowd he spotted the crowns of oak trees and the masts of ships at the riverside. The crowd started a low murmur as they funneled Ulfrik and Finn to the hanging tree. As they drew closer, a few voices called out but Ulfrik did not hear what they said.

The hanging tree was the tallest of the hoary oaks that had defied the encroachment of the camp. Pines, elms, and other trees had once populated this stretch but now were either stumps or holes in the earth. These three trees stretched out their thick limbs like the Norns themselves, reeling out their skein of Fate to rules the lives and deaths of men. One shape already dangled and twisted from a limb. The mute Frankish girl's neck had stretched an impossible length. Her glossy, beautiful hair hung over her face, but he did not need to see it to know crows had already pecked out the soft parts. The black birds clung to the branches around her, staring down with what seemed hunched shoulders and greedy black eyes.

"Not me. Not today," Ulfrik muttered at them. The crowd gathered tighter, but gave the hanging tree a wide berth. He would not escape back toward the camp, of that he was certain. The only route lay toward the water, and he could never launch a ship in time. As his guards held their spears at his back, Ulfrik scanned Grimnr, Vigrid and the other hirdmen for weapons. Their swords were tight in their sheaths, impossible to grab without a struggle. All of them wore daggers at their waists, and were simpler to draw. He would have to take Grimnr as a hostage and bargain his way out. It was not the best plan, for one good archer could solve that stand-off. Ulfrik had done it himself with a throwing ax. But desperate as he was, he saw no other way. His palms itched at the thought of seizing the dagger when Grimnr approached.

Then he froze.

Over Grimnr's shoulder he locked eyes with Konal. The angry white and red scars that flowed across half his face made him stand out among the others. Konal's expression was tight and focused, and a group of men stood shoulder to shoulder with him that must have been his crew.

Grimnr broke in between them, and grabbed Ulfrik's arm to lead him to the tree. "I liked you as Ulfar the White. It's a sad thing to hang a good man."

"Then don't." Ulfrik struggled to turn toward Konal again, but Grimnr held him firm and laughed.

"You earned the noose." Grimnr held him still while others set ladders to the trees then climbed up to secure the ropes to the limbs.

Ulfrik felt the hilt of the Grimnr's dagger press into his side. Finn stood like a wilting reed, his white face staring in defeat at the ground. Konal had come with a crew, and now Ulfrik had a true chance at escape. Whatever differences they may have over Konal's treatment of Runa, they were sword-brothers once. Such bonds were stronger than iron and just as enduring. Konal had come to his aid and now waited for Ulfrik's signal.

He leaned away from Grimnr, who frowned up at the hanging trees. Finn still hung limp, Vigrid at his side.

Striking like a snake, he slammed into Grimnr's ribs and yanked the dagger from his belt. In the same motion he slipped his foot between Grimnr's and collapsed him to the ground.

Vigrid and Finn stared in amazement, but Ulfrik already leaped Grimnr's prostrate body. He swept up with his dagger, slashing Vigrid's throat from collarbone to ear. His eyes rolled back and he crashed into Finn.

"To me!" Ulfrik shouted at Finn, then he spun toward the crowd. Only the front ranks reacted, most with astonishment but others falling away if charged by a bull. Konal did not waver, but drew his sword and his crew followed. The scrape and hum of blades eager for blood filled the air and Ulfrik roared in joy as he bounded to Konal. "To your ship! Hurry!"

The crowd rippled with confusion, men pressing forward while others retreating. In four strides he reached Konal, and put his arm out in greeting. "I can't remember a day I was happier to see you."

Konal's blade flicked to his throat, catching him under the chin and pressing into his skin. He backed up, and Konal pushed closer as his crew flowed around him.

"You should have stayed dead." The voice was a ragged whisper, but the words cut no less deeply.

"Wait!" The voice from behind was Grimnr's. "He's mine."

Ulfrik stared into Konal's pale eyes, and realization plowed into him like a ship crashing into an iceberg. His hands went cold and his muscles slackened. Before his death, Throst had taunted him with a warning that someone within his hall had participated in his betrayal. Ulfrik had suspected Hrolf, and even as he risked everything to save his son Ulfrik still suspected him. Yet Konal stood with cold iron pressed into his neck, scarred face tight with anger and baleful eyes glowing with hatred. He was unrecognizable now. He was the traitor. He sold him to Throst, then stole his wife and hall. A man he had named a sword-brother and friend.

Then he was sailing backward, the sky a pale blue above him. He crashed on his back and a rock dug into his spine. Grimnr loomed over him, his bulk blotting out the sky and his long braid falling over his shoulder. "You murderous pig! I'll gut you myself!"

50

"What do you see?" Runa asked, tugging at Gunnar's arm. She cursed her poor sight, but the distant shore was nothing more than green and black smudges.

"Two nooses, and one body already strung up." Gunnar stepped back, and his face was as hard as winter ice. "A massive crowd has gathered around the hanging trees. It must be for Father and Finn."

Runa's first reaction was to collapse into tears, but she grabbed the rail and dug her fingers into it. That Runa, the weepy and powerless woman, stayed married to Konal. Runa the Bloody has returned once more. She had led men in battle, killed for her home and family, and helpless tears did not befit who she was. She stood straighter and met Gunnar's dark eyes with the same icy determination.

"We will aid them, even if it is our handful of crew against their army."

Gunnar smiled. "I agree. What that herd of sheep needs is a wolf to scatter them. Set a panic among them and we will not have to fight. They will fight themselves."

Runa strained to see the opposite shore, but the river was wide and clusters of ships blocked the view. It seemed every ship had gone to dock, explaining why they had slipped upriver without any deterrents. How Gunnar planned to scatter this many enemies eluded her.

But as she counted the few masts not blurred from her poor sight she snapped back to him.

"Burn their ships!"

"It's like setting their children on fire."

They both turned to the casks of oil. Aren sat atop one and picked at the hem of his cloak. Gunnar started to shout orders to his crew. "Take the short oars," he said. "We'll be getting close to those ships on the other shore. Aren, start moving those casks to the sides."

"What can I do?" Runa asked. Gunnar stared at her, then smiled.

"There is touch-wood and a striking steel in my sea chest. You get the kindling started so we can set the fire with haste."

The ship lurched and creaked as the crew rowed back into the river. The sails were drawn but the wind still buffeted from the east, which would aid them greatly in escape but hinder their crossing of the Seine. Gunnar groaned as he worked the tiller, but he managed as well as any man with two hands. Runa fumbled through his sea chest, pulling aside clothing, a seal skin cloak and boots, and layers of blankets. She removed a small pack and shook the contents into her hand. A dirty cloth doll spilled out along with a delicate silver chain that had a silver pendant of Thor's hammer attached. She held these in her palm and the implications sunk in.

Could I be a grandmother? she thought. The incongruity of the joy she experienced at realizing this shamed her. Unless Ulfrik were alive to share that news, then she did not want to know. She stuffed the contents back into the bag, then found the striking steel, flint and touch-wood. The pungent scent of the fuzzy touch-wood filled her nose as she cupped it in her hands. Beside the chest was the tinder box, blackened with soot and filled with dried twigs. Blocking the wind with her back, she broke the touch-wood into pieces and sprinkled it into the tinder box, then using the flint and striking iron she struck sparks onto the kindling. Aided by the swift-burning touch-wood the kindling started to burn. When she stood again they had crossed to the first ships.

She strained to see up the shore to the three trees, but only saw one body dangling there. She let go her breath when she realized the hanged corpse wore a dress. The crowd had disappeared behind the rise of the land but she could hear the mass off onlookers as a murmur of voices and clanking iron. She bit her lip and narrowed her eyes at the nooses on the trees, then turned to Gunnar.

"The fire is ready," she said.

Gunnar grunted at her as he pulled on the tiller. Aren hung over the port side and called out the distance to the first ships. They were coming in close enough for boarding. Runa joined her son and watched the muddy river water slap against the hull as they glided to a stop before the enemy ships.

"Let's burn everything at this dock," Gunnar said. He grabbed a cask of oil and the rest of his crew did the same. "Were this another day, I'd steal every one of these. What kind of confidence do these men have? Leaving ships unguarded!"

His boast was answered when two men on the closest ships popped over the rails. Both appeared confused, but one turned and fled. The one who stared like a fool died with a spear hurled into his chest.

"Get that bastard," Gunnar shouted and three men leapt the rails to the dock.

One shirtless man of rippling muscles and dozens of tattoos used a two-handed ax to hook a ship and anchor the boat while other men crossed with their casks underarm. Runa grabbed a shield off the rack, then stopped Gunnar as he prepared to cross to the dock. "I'll take you sax now."

She drew it from the sheath at his waist and then he leapt the rails. A man screamed in the distance and Runa prayed it was the fleeing man who died. Aren followed the men, a flaming brand in his hand.

"Be careful," she shouted after him, but Aren did not seem to hear. He scampered after the men while she waited on deck. Flitting along the rails she wished she could do more, but getting over the side with any dignity in a dress was impossible. She gripped the sax in hand and practiced two or three strokes.

The flames leapt up at the far end of the dock. The men were racing back, and as they went more ships took to flame. By the time Gunnar helped Aren over the rails, all but the closest ships were ablaze. The tattooed man released his ax, and the ship began to drift. Aren flung his brand as the men began to row and when it hit the deck of the enemy ship, fire blazed into the rigging and rails.

"It will take a moment for the fire to burn high enough to catch their attention," Gunnar said. "We can escape and burn other ships down-river."

"Did you kill the runner?"

Gunnar nodded as he took up the tiller again. "We did, and there were more. Some were ill and moved slower than snails. No need to worry for them now."

He hollered at the crew to row, and the men were full of exuberance from their exploits. They pulled hard, laughing at the destruction they had wrought. Nearly a dozen ships were blazing and Runa heard the first cries of terror drifting down to the river. She stared hard at the oak trees and the two nooses remained empty.

"Did you see how fast they burned!" Aren said. His face was bright with a smile and his face shining with sweat. "We burned a fleet! Just us. That's going to be a song one day, don't you agree?"

"It will." She placed her hand on Aren's shoulder as they watched the flames strengthen. "Let's hope we bought your father time."

"More ships!" Gunnar called. "On the shore, let's burn them to cover our escape."

Again they glided to ships, but now the enemy was on alert. Guards emerged on the decks and Runa squinted at the dark shapes.

"Arrows!"

Runa did not hear who shouted the warning, but crashed to the gunwales and raised her shield overhead. She pulled Aren down. "Get under the shield, unless you want a hole in your head."

A smattering of shafts plunked into the deck. One of the crew roared in pain.

"Give it back to them!" Gunnar bellowed. A second sprinkling of arrows landed and Runa's shield buckled as a shaft pinged off it. She felt one thud into the wood of the gunwale.

Beneath the shield, she saw feet of men gathering beside her. Aren pulled tighter to her side, and she threw her sword-arm around him. The twang of bowstrings was Gunnar's answer to the attack. The crew sent another shaft immediately after the first. All the while the starboard bank of oarsmen rowed and Gunnar turned his ship to face the attack. Runa remember the tactic. Gunnar was narrowing his frontage to deny the enemy targets, then he would board the ships and clean out their crew.

"The bastards are running!" Gunnar shouted and laughed. His crew joined him and the ship banked hard, sending Runa and Aren falling against the gunwales.

"It's safe now," Aren said, then pulled himself free from her protective grip.

Standing, she saw five men dashing up the slope toward the safety of the tree line. Three ships were beached and tipped to the right in a close row. Gunnar pulled alongside these.

"We should capture one," said a man close to Runa.

Gunnar left his tiller and approached the man. "We should, but let's not test fate today. Hrolf will reward us for each ship we burn, of that I'm certain. Now to kill these fat seals and be gone."

Crewmen jumped across to splash oil on the ships and Aren fired up another brand. Runa went to the stern and saw the enemy upstream swarming the docks like ants. Their angry cries were clear from this distance. Untouched ships launched into the river like rats fleeing a fire. Such destruction of so many ships would become a legend, but her part in it had not mattered to her. All she saw was flaming ships and black smoke. Unless it aided Ulfrik in his escape, the glory of it was nothing. She leaned her shield against the rail, tired of bearing its weight, and sighed.

"How will Ulfrik and Finn find us in this madness?" she asked, shouting over her shoulder.

When no answer came, she turned back to see most of the crew including Gunnar had boarded the other ship. Aren stood with his brand guttering beside his bother. The crew was shouting back and forth, the man who had wanted to claim a ship jabbing a finger at Gunnar's chest.

The shouting continued, and the crewman's face turned bright red. Runa knew they were fighting for the ships, and Gunnar's expression darkened with each poke from his crewman's hand. At last Gunnar knocked the arm aside and the crewman grabbed Gunnar's shirt. In response, Gunnar slammed his cask of oil into the man's belly and kicked him back. In one fluid move he snatched the brand from Aren's hand and threw it on the oil-soaked crewman. Flames engulfed him with a whoosh, and his former companions jumped away.

His screams bought a weakness to Runa's knees. As casually as if they had done nothing more than set fire to a bale of hay Gunnar and his crew crossed back into their ship. Gunnar did not look at his mother, his face dark and tight with dark anger. Now she understood why they called him the Black, for it was not just for his dark hair and eyes. The horrid stench of the man wafted to Runa's nose, bringing back terrible memories of hall burnings and death. The crewman stood up and staggered to the rail, then flopped into the water with a splash and hiss.

Aren fired two more brands and tossed them onto the other ships, setting all three aflame. He moved as if groggy, all of the former excitement gone. Runa let him go, and decided to keep to herself. The crew was reserved, but they seemed indifferent to the murder. That though made Runa's skin tingle. Her son had murdered a man for disagreeing with him. Ulfrik had been tough on his men, but he always erred with mercy and never with violence. What had the long years away taught her son?

A shout from Gunnar shattered her contemplative mind. "Thrice cursed gods! A ship!"

Runa and the crew followed Gunnar's pointing figure to a fast moving ship with full sails bearing down on them. Oars beat the water, making long and powerful strokes such that the ship seemed a horse galloping at them. Before she could join her son in a curse, another ship peeled from behind to the center of the river.

Men scurried to their oars and to unfurl the sail. The best she and Aren could do was to stay out of the way. Runa retrieved her shield and wiped he sweat from her hand on her skirt. "Fetch a shield," she said to Aren. "You have Finn's sword."

His puffy wide face was white with shock. "Gunnar's ship can outrun them, do you think?"

One look over the rails and she realized the lead ship seemed to fly as if the gods themselves blew into its sail. She scooped him toward the rail with her shield. "They will shoot arrows as they close, then they will tie to our sides. If both ships lash onto us, we are doomed. Cut free any hook that bites the our ship."

Her heart pounded and Gunnar gave the tiller to another man while he pulled on his shield. It had straps and a leather socket where he pushed his stump into, then he pulled the buckles tight on his arm. In his left hand, rather than draw his sword, he retrieved an ax from beside his sea chest. He pointed it at Runa, "Stay near me if we are boarded. Do as I say and we will prevail."

The chase was short-lived, for the leading enemy ship came within bow range and arrows thudded into the deck or splashed into the water. Gunnar realized he would not break away, and ordered the oars shipped. The long poles slid back through the tholes and were tossed into the rack. The men pulled on their shields and grabbed spears from a rack at the mast. As the enemy ship approached, the first hooks sailed across the gap of muddy river. Runa watch one thud off the rail and plunk into the water. Another gouged into the rail as the long ship slid into position. Her sax was not strong enough to cut the rope. "Aren, cut that hook!"

Now spears and arrows slashed the air in both directions, and Runa shielded Aren as he hacked at the rope, finally breaking it free. An arrow tore the shoulder of her blouse, and a warm stinging pain tore through her skin.

"It's off," Aren shouted, but at least four others had found purchase. Angry men in dirty clothes and armed with flashing iron crowded the rails, and as their companions hauled the ships together they prepared to leap the gap.

"Get back," she said, grabbing Aren's shirt. "Let the men fight up front and we'll watch the opposite side."

Men jumped onto the rails while Gunnar's crew set spears against them. The first eager waves spent themselves on the attack, either falling into the water of impaling on spears. At least three landed on the deck and began cutting into the crew. That gap was all it took, and soon all the enemy were swarming their decks.

Runa and Aren held on with their shields up and blades forward. Gunnar howled his fury and hewed his enemies like rotten wood. He was a marvel to behold, fighting with the wrong hand but with such grace it seemed unfair to the enemy. His ax hooked the enemy shield, then he punched out with his own shield. Runa notice now it was not lined with leather but with iron, and it shattered the face of the enemy as he rammed it home. He then stroked up with his ax, letting the other horn of the blade slice into his opponent. The body flopped overboard, and he repeated the same steps, hooking with ax and slamming with his shield.

Then three men were upon them. Aren hid behind his shield, and aimlessly slashed out. Runa deflected the first hit from one attacker, and cut down for the inner leg as she had known to do from years of practice. She missed.

A flurry of blows backed her against the rails, when she realized her attacker had stopped and stared wide eyed at her. "It's a woman and a boy!"

Her sax plunged beneath her shield and she felt the blade plow into the man's guts. He groaned and blood flowed from his mouth. Aren was on his back, hiding under his shield like a blanket while his attacker raised a foot to smash it down on him. He would be crushed.

"Gunnar, help your brother!" She saw Gunnar's head snap around, then the third man charged her.

"You bloody whore!" She flung her shield at him, striking him in the face and sending him skittering aside, then she leapt onto the back of Aren's attacker before he could bring his foot down.

The two screamed, Runa stabbing him in the chest while he clawed at her. He got one hand into her hair and pulled. She fell back.

For a moment she saw the sky.

Then she saw the brown water and plunged into the cold, mute world beneath the Seine. Her dress tangled in her legs and she clawed at the water as if she could climb out. But she could not swim.

51

Grimnr's hand reached for the hilt of his sax, then he stopped and his head snapped up. Ulfrik used the moment to kick him in the crotch then head-butt him. The collision sent Ulfrik falling back with a lance of pain through his eyes. Yet in the next instant he was on his feet and facing an oncoming rush of the entire crowd.

He feared they were converging on him, but they shoved past. Ulfrik spun around and found Grimnr retching on hands and knees. Three feet away Vigrid's corpse leaked brilliant red blood into the grass as Finn filched the sword from his hip. Swarming around them, men scrambled toward the Seine.

Flames and smoke rolled skyward from the masts of ships at dock. His heart flipped in his chest and his limbs filled with power. He howled in joy. "Gunnar the Black! Runa the Bloody! The skalds will sing of you forever!"

Finn forced his way to Ulfrik's side in the same moment Grimnr rose above the flow of bodies charging for the docks. "We've got to go."

"I must free Vilhjalmer. Now's the perfect distraction. You go and I will find you along the riverbanks."

He turned to push through the crowd, and Finn joined him. "I didn't think we'd meet Konal."

"So you knew of his treachery?"

"Your wife suspected it. Where is he?"

The crowd plowed into them, panicked faces flooding past them for their burning ships. Ulfrik strained to find Konal but saw nothing more than rows of men in their drab colored shirts pressing forward. "He's lost to the chaos. Let's head for the fortress and worry for him later."

At the rear men who did not have ships milled in confusion. As they dodged between these idlers they heard fragments of worried talk. "Are we under attack? Should we man the fences? Is this a feint?"

"Raise the alarm," Ulfrik shouted. "Mord comes with his army! Hurry!"

Finn laughed and repeated the same false warning. Within moments horns blared and orders to guard the western approaches were shouted. A new current of men flowed toward the plains where Einar had attacked. Across the camp, echoes of warning horns blared from Count Amand's fortress and the gates swung closed.

"That's not good," Finn said.

"They will man the front walls and not be looking for two men at the rear. Now come with me."

They stopped at Grimnr's hall and Ulfrik slammed open the doors. At least six men were laid out on the floor and the interior stunk of human waste. Finn coughed and held his nose. "What are we doing here?"

"Arming ourselves for the task." The sick men did not protest, only one raising his arm as if asking for help. Ulfrik did not spare a glance for them, instead finding his mail coat, sword, and all his other belongings. Grimnr had piled everything on his bed, probably to be divided among his men after the hanging. "Help me get this chain shirt on, then we will find one for you."

"I'm not used to that weight," Finn said, as he helped Ulfrik slip the heavy links over his head. "A shield and helmet is enough."

The familiar weight on his shoulders felt good and he strapped on his sword and sax, daggers and his shield. He threw his pack to Finn, then rummaged deeper in the hall. "Here's what we need. Finn, take these."

He pulled out a two-handed ax and a rope tied to a bucket. "Cut off the bucket and coil that rope. It's how we're getting over the walls. Be fast about it."

Guarding the door while Finn worked, he searched for signs of anyone returning to the hall. Every man raced west, sprinting through the fields with shields and spears ready. "I'm ready," Finn said from behind.

No one paid them any attention as they ran against the current. He continued to shout encouragement to those lingering. "Every man is needed to fill the line. Go now!"

They skidded to a halt by the front walls, and Ulfrik struck to the right where wagons of empty barrels and crates had been left. "More carelessness for our benefit," he said. "Hide behind them as we pass to the rear."

At last they came to the back of Count Amand's fortress and as predicted all men were stationed facing the imaginary attackers. An enemy could not approach in force from the rear, so at best a sentry or two might have been left behind.

"Have you ever scaled a wall with an ax?" Ulfrik asked. Finn's face was now full of color and his bright smile returned.

"Like the skalds sing about? That's what we're going to do?"

"How's your side?"

Finn covered it with his arm and lost his smile. "I'm completely healed. I can do this."

Ulfrik looked from him to the wall, which was twice as high as a tall man. "These Franks have built high. I'm not sure I can leap that distance. You're younger but that wound could tear."

"Hrolf's healer told me I was the strongest lad she'd ever met and that I had no business surviving as well as I did. I can do this."

Shaking his head, he took the ax in both hands and stepped back for a running leap. "I'll toss you a rope when I'm at the top." Finn groaned in protest but Ulfrik had already started his run. His legs hurt with each pounding foot-fall, and just before the wall he launched himself with the ax pulled back. The black timbers flew at him and struck hard, but he did not reach the top. His feet broke the collision and he tumbled back to the ground, landing on his shield.

Bright pain lanced through his body and he stared up that the blue sky.

"Are you hurt?" Finn's concerned face hovered over his.

"Just old. I think I have seen the last of my days leaping walls."

"That's right," Finn said, snatching the ax from the ground as Ulfrik lay motionless. "Time for me to try."

"I've got a better idea." Struggling to his feet, his head swam as he steadied himself. He pulled the ax from Finn's hands, then tied the rope to the head. "Give the rope a strong tug to test the knot."

Satisfied it would hold, he carried it to the walls and held it overhead. "Get back. If I miss you're likely to be split down to your crotch."

He sized up the throw and everything returned to him: the balance of the ax, the controlled breathing, the power of his stance, everything his old mentor Snorri had taught him since he was a child. Some things a man never forgets. He let the ax fly with the ease and grace of releasing a dove to the air. The weapon spun in a circle even with the rope thrashing behind, and it thudded home into the wood at the top of the wall. Finn gushed his admiration. "I can't believe that! How did you do it?"

"Forty years of practice. Now test the rope and up you go." Finn clambered to the top, lay flat over the edge, then waved to Ulfrik before he hung from the opposite side and dropped. He spoke to him through the wall, his voice muffled.

"There's no one here. I can open the side gate if you want."

Ulfrik considered the plan, and the throbbing in his left leg begged him to agree. "Alright, but be on the watch for guards."

As he rounded the corner he found Finn waiting for him in the small gate as if he had been there all morning. "What kept you?"

"This is no time for play. We must be swift." Together they fled into the main buildings, the hallways now familiar. They heard shouts and confused speech, and had to wait for a line of guards to pass as they hid in a pantry, but soon arrived at the inner courtyard.

"No one at the tower doors?" Finn asked.

"I don't like it, but there's no choice." With the morning sun filling the courtyard they were denied shadows, so they sprinted to the tower where Finn was held. Only one woman scurried through the courtyard, head down and oblivious to them. Ulfrik tried the door and it opened. "Another bad sign."

The rushed inside, daggers drawn for a close quarters fight, but the room was empty. With a curse, they trudged up the stairs to find every room vacant, including Vilhjalmer's at the top. Finn stared at the simple bed which lacked any blankets, a sign of no one having slept there. "What now? He's gone!"

"They must have moved him, but where?" Ulfrik rubbed the back of his neck and began to pace. "We'll go to the source. Let's find Count Amand."

"Are you mad?"

"Yes, but I'm also right. I'm taking him hostage in exchange for Vilhjalmer."

"Won't he have guards?"

"Of course."

"Lots of guards?"

"We'll be smart about it, Finn. Now unless you plan to overwhelm him with your worries, we are going to find that old bastard and slam his head off that pretty throne of his until he gives us Vilhjalmer. Let's move."

The threaded back down the stairs and into the main fortress. They encountered servants who blanched at their drawn daggers, but none cried out or raised an alarm. Ulfrik had been to the Count's hall once but he remember the path. On the second floor, after tramping up steps that bounced under their feet, they came to the closed double doors. "Shouldn't there be guards here?" Finn asked.

"Not if they've gone to the walls. Let's just find out what has happened."

He slammed open the doors. An elderly man with fly-away white hair stood frozen in the center of the room beneath the giant wheel of candles. He cradled a silver crucifix in his arms, and appeared to have been wrapping it in blue velvet. All around boxes were laid out and the Count's belongings were in various stages of packing. The old man's dull eyes met his, then he bolted for the opposite door.

Ulfrik clomped across the wood floor, his footfalls like hammer blows, and he collared the old man before he reached the door. He hissed at him in his poor Frankish. "Stop, and don't shout or this goes badly for you."

He whirled the old man around, and put the dagger to his neck. The servant's eyes hardened in defiance and he held the crucifix to his chest. "You'll have to pry this out of my dead hands."

"Now that's a poor invitation to a Northman. I've splashed your god's crosses with blood far holier than yours." Ulfrik emphasized his threat with his dagger. He glanced at Finn, who was exploring the wood boxes piled around Count Amand's throne. "Good for you I'm not interested in the silver. Where's Vilhjalmer?"

"I don't know who you speak of."

"The Norse boy. He was Amand's hostage. Where is he?"

The old man's face bent in a frown. "I will not tell you."

"You're waiting for help to arrive. If you tell me, I let you go. If help gets here before you do, I'll slit your throat."

He appeared to consider Ulfrik's threat. "They left yesterday. The Count took his personal guard and the barbarian child. I don't know where they went."

"That's a good start." Ulfrik hooked the old man's leg and pulled it from under him. He crashed to the floor with a feeble cry, the crucifix still held to his chest. Ulfrik put his boot on the man's head and began to press. "If I squeezed your brains from your nose, would that help you remember where they went?"

Finn shot Ulfrik a surprised look as he wandered behind the throne. Ulfrik shook his head; he believed the old man but wanted to be certain. There was no honor in abusing the elderly when it served no purpose. To the old man's credit, he wormed and struggled but revealed nothing more.

"Get your foot off me, you loathsome toad."

"Tell me where they went." He shifted more weight onto the old man's head.

"They went to Paris."

The answer came not from the old man, but from the double doors. Ulfrik whirled and recognized Amand's captain standing in it with five other guards. They wore mail and conical helmets, and carried spears and shields. The captain had his sword drawn and was as heavily armored as the others. Ulfrik removed his foot from the old man's head, who immediately scrabbled away.

"Will you let me draw my sword at least," Ulfrik said, holding out his dagger. "It's not much of a fair fight otherwise."

The captain snorted in disdain. "Fair fight? I think not, my cunning barbarian friend. I save such things for men, and not animals."

Ulfrik began to shift toward the throne, where Finn stood transfixed. The captain strolled into the room, bringing his guards in a tight rank behind him.

"Now you're calling me names?" Ulfrik slid closer still to the throne, and the captain continued forward.

"It is what you are. All of you. The Count has shamed all of Frankia for consorting with your kind. He goes to Paris to beg forgiveness by offering the King an important hostage. Maybe then he will redeem himself."

The captain and his guards had crossed halfway to the throne and Ulfrik now stood beside it. The Captain stopped and pointed his sword at him, his guards lowering their spears with wolfish grins.

"I will delight in sending you and your friend to hell."

"What is it you Christians do for the dead? Yes, I remember now. I'll light a candle for you."

Ulfrik swept back and up, Finn shrieking in surprise as the dagger flashed past him. Ulfrik cut into the rope that held aloft the wheel of candles and was secured behind the throne. The rope resisted only a heartbeat, but it was so taut that one cut unwound it.

The captain looked up in horror as the massive wheel of candles crashed down, slamming him and his guards to the floor with a wooden thump.

"Finish them," Ulfrik shouted, then leapt onto the pile and began stabbing, Finn right behind him. Whether from the crushing wheel or their stabbing the captain and his men were dead. Ulfrik stood back from the bloody carnage and regarded the pile of bodies.

"Looks like we're headed to Paris."

Finn turned a blood-splattered face to Ulfrik and scowled. "Can we at least get back to Gunnar's ship?"

"Of course, I wasn't planning on walking." Ulfrik turned to see the old man seated against the far wall. He stared at the bodies as if he could conceive of nothing more terrible. "I think we can use the confusion to escape back to the river. Let's go."

52

Runa did not know how her head broke the surface, but she sucked air into her burning lungs then coughed on the river water dragged in with it. Her arms and legs thrashed in all directions. The hull of Gunnar's ship filled her vision but she had no control over her body as she flailed in the river. Water filled her mouth and nose, and her hair clung to her face like a mask. Panic gripped her and she could think of nothing but breathing, yet her head continued to dunk beneath the water. Her legs grew heavy and she felt as if two icy hands were hauling her down to the muddy bottom.

A shadow fell across her, and she heard a splash. She saw a man with a broken spear shaft protruding from his back bob on the water until it swallowed him. A bloom of red marked where had had fallen. Runa kicked and flapped her arms, but again her head went under and now she could not bring herself up. The water bubbled and gurgled in mute world. Her eyes opened but she saw nothing but watery light and the green shape of the dead man floating for the river bottom.

Then she stopped fighting. Her limbs grew leaden and she needed all her strength to hold her breath. Her chest burned and the urgency to breath gathered like a volcanic pressure ready to burst.

Muted, dull sounds of bumping wood and splashes surrounded her. Her mouth slipped bubbled over her face.

This is how I die, she thought. Down to the river mud. Alone.

Then something warm enveloped her. She opened her eyes again and but the man was too close. His hair swirled over his face, masking him, but the grip around her waist was firm and comforting. She began to rise toward the light. Her legs kicked as she flailed against breathing. The light drew closer, but she felt as if hours had passed and no time was left to escape. Her chest burned and her head shook in protest. The surface was so close. The world began to grow dark and she went limp.

Air slammed her face and her mouth opened with a massive gasp. The world of sound crashed back into her ears, the clash of weapons and shrieks of the dying. Men shouted while others fell into the water. She gripped the man with her, who in turn held a rope. They both dragged through the bloody water to the hull of the ship. The man in the water lifted her up to waiting hands that grabbed her clothes first. Her shirt tore and one man cursed. She was paralyzed with fits of gasping and coughing to help herself. They dropped her into the water and she squealed, but then the man below shoved her up once more. They caught her now and hauled her over the side as inelegant as a porpoise dragged to the deck.

She crashed on her face and water flooded off her onto the deck. Closing her eyes, she shivered with terror and cold, watching feet shuffle around her and hearing them thump on the deck. Her mind could not hold a single thought other than she was breathing again. Hands flipped her over and a bedraggled face peered down into hers.

"Are you alive?" The voice was hoarse with fear. She shook her head, staring through him and not understanding what happened. The man wiped the water from his face, then untied the rope fastened under his arms. "Get her a blanket."

The voice was familiar, and she tried to focus on him. The man collapsed to the deck and one of his crew threw a dry cloak over him. More hands lifted her and wrapped her in dry cloak. She looked to thank the man but he already abandoned her. A man lay on the deck as if napping, then she noticed the white-fledged arrow sticking from his back and the runnel of blood beneath his corpse.

Her eyes widened and she looked at her rescuer. Konal sat smiling at her, his disfiguring scars bright against his bloodless flesh.

"I saved your life," he said, his voice barely audible over the crash of battle.

She struggled to stand, glimpsing Gunnar's ship lashed to the enemy before Konal pulled her flat.

"Your crew might shoot you as readily as me. Stay down."

"And your only son is on that ship. Your allies were about to kill him before I fell overboard."

Konal's smile fell and he turned aside, his wet hair hiding his face. She darted to the side and began to crawl over the rails. Gunnar's ship was only ten feet distant. She would either drown or reach the ship, but she would not be carried away by the man who had turned her into a weak, dependent worm.

"Gunnar! Aren!" she cried, throwing her leg over the rails. Her wet skirts tangled her legs and the best she could hope to achieve was to plop into the water.

"Mother?" Gunnar came to the rails, his ax and shield slicked with blood. Aren joined him and screamed when he saw her poised to fall into the water. He darted back into the fray swirling behind them.

She was about to call back when two hands dug into her shoulders and hauled her back. Konal's wet breath assailed her ear as he leaned into her. "What madness is this? You want to drown?"

Before she could answer, both she and Konal froze in place. Aren charged out of the screaming battle and leapt over the rails, flying like a cat across the gap and landing on the deck in a crumpled heap. Crew ran at him with spears, but Konal dropped Runa to the deck and intercepted them.

"Get back! He's my son," he cried, and the crew fell away.

Runa clawed back up on the rails but now she had Aren with her. The ships were already plying apart as Konal's crew manned the oars and began to row. The sail unfurled and the ship lurched ahead. She searched for Gunnar, but the battle on his deck had sucked him back into the fray. Turning to Konal and Aren, she found her son wrestling with Finn's loaned sword while Konal's men held him at spear point.

"You fool," she yelled, then charged for him. "What are you doing leaping onto an enemy ship with no one to help?"

"I came to rescue you," he said, even as enemy spears prodded him.

"Enemy ship?" Konal said, whirling on her. "Is that what you call me now? What happened to husband?"

"I divorce you, Konal Ketilson!" Her declaration drew sharp looks from the crew. Konal's scarred face crunched into a murderous frown, then he backhanded her.

She slammed to the deck and saw a white light as her head struck the wood. Konal dragged her by the feet, exposing her legs to her hips as he did and shouted to his crew. "Tie her down!"

"Konal," she heard Gunnar screaming from his ship. "You murderous coward. I'll kill you myself."

Runa heard no more as two men handled her no better than a wet sack of grain. One held her down while the other tied her legs together. He patted her thighs and winked at her. She spit at him, but only drew their laughter. In the time it took to dredge up more spit they had tied her legs together and her hands at her lap then dropped her back to the deck.

Men were already at their oars, rowing furiously and ignoring the corpses at their feet. Konal leaned on the rails, ducking when a smattering of arrows chased his ship away. Aren growled in frustration as his captors removed his sword and bound him in ropes. Runa set her head down and watched the clouds slide past. The ship rocked and creaked and the men cursed. The corpse of a sad-eyed man lay an arm's length away, staring at her as his blood ebbed and flowed with the motion of the ship.

"You should have thanked me for saving your life," Konal said, reappearing over her. She turned her head aside and stared at Aren as he sat against the gunwales with his hands tied and head bowed in shame. Konal waited then sat beside her with a groan. His whispering voice set her teeth on edge. "What were you doing on that ship?"

"I should ask you the same," she said. "But I know what you were doing with the enemy."

"You don't know anything," he said. "And was that Gunnar?"

She faced him now, a cruel smile on her face. "It was and he will not rest until he frees his brother and me."

Konal snorted then laughed. "I taught him how to fight. I've nothing to fear from him."

"He's no longer a child, and I've seen him in battle. You would do well to let us ashore and sail as far away as you can."

They sat in silence while the crew rowed, the splashing of the oars loud in her ears. The man at the tiller called out that they had escaped pursuit. Konal groaned and stood, brushing debris from his wet pants. "I will sail as far as I can, but I'm taking you two with me. Time to return home and introduce my son to the land of his father. Ireland is far better than this rat's nest."

As he stepped away, Runa closed her eyes and clenched her jaw. She would never see Ireland, no matter what Konal believed.

53

Ulfrik awakened to Finn shaking him. A shapeless dream skittered away as he rose with a gasp, but Finn's dirty hand clamped over his mouth. He had drawn his sword, smeared with mud to prevent it from shining in the dark. Ulfrik's own blade remained sheathed and laying in the grass beside him. Finn pulled back Ulfrik's cloak and slid the weapon up to his side.

Contented that Ulfrik would remain silent, he removed his hand. In the blue gloom of the crescent moonlight Finn was a blurry lump wrapped in a cloak. He pointed hard to the east, then held up three fingers. Ulfrik nodded, then he placed each approaching enemy by chopping the air at their location. They were fanned out and approaching from Count Amand's camp.

He stood and strapped on his sword, unhitching the loop that kept it tight in the sheath. Finn hunkered and watched the trees. Ulfrik shook his head, still unable to see their pursuers. These Franks were persistent, even working through the night to find them. He expected Grimnr to set a large bounty for their capture, driving every man with gold lust to search for them. They had spent all day running along the Seine searching for Gunnar's ship, yet finding nothing but burned ships and the mast of one ship sticking out of the shallows as if it had sunk only moments before reaching shore.

They leaned their heads together to whisper, Ulfrik laying out his battle plan. "You're more skilled at field-craft. You go wide to the right, and herd them toward me. I will make myself a target they can't miss."

"It's three to one," Finn said.

"They're expecting us to be unaware. We have all the advantage, plus I expect you to make it an even fight before they get me. Make it a noisy kill, and they won't know which way to turn."

He released Finn and he flitted away into the dark. Ulfrik had slept in his mail, and now without a cloak it gleamed in the moonlight. He leaned against a tree as if he were on lookout and bored, but his senses stretched all around him. At first nothing stirred but for an owl hooting in the distance. Rustling of woodland creatures on their nocturnal adventures had ceased, and that alerted Ulfrik to nearby danger. A silent woods was a dangerous place. He heard a muffled snap to his left, but he resisted the urge to turn for it. He gently rotated his head until he saw a darker shape amid the shadows of bushes and trees. The form observed him as if it were holding his breath, and he nearly dismissed it as imagining until he saw it move. The shape slipped something from its shoulder, and Ulfrik's heart began to beat harder. He heard a creak, then realized the form was carefully lifting a strung bow to point at him. He continued to feign ignorance, but his hand slipped to the hilt of his sword.

A scream broke the silence. The shape in his peripheral vision jolted, and Ulfrik broke into a charge.

His sword was out and gleaming with blue fire of the crescent moon. The bowstring snapped and a shaft zipped past his head. The shadow cursed and dropped the bow for another weapon. Ulfrik felt his blade carve into flesh then bite into bone. The form before him howled and Ulfrik kicked into the black shadow of the man's face, his heel slamming into something hard. With another stab, he drove his sword into the soft flesh of the man's stomach and he groaned in death. Unable to see more of the victim, he searched for the third attacker.

A black shape suddenly sprinted in the dark. Ulfrik bounded after him, but only took five long strides before his foot slammed into rock and sent him crashing to the ground. With a curse, be struggled to his feet, the heavy weight of his mail saddling his effort. He growled in frustration, seeing nothing but hearing the crunch and snap of the enemy darting away.

"Finn?" he called out. "Tell me you're alive."

"I'm here," Finn answered from close to his back. He stumbled toward Finn's voice, eventually finding him hunched over in the gloom. "They were our people. This one has a silver armband."

"Take it for your own," Ulfrik said. "Anything else?"

"Nothing we need." Finn stood and dusted down his pants. "The last one escaped. So we have to keep moving, and I didn't get a chance to sleep yet."

"Well the few hours I had were hardly better. We'll have to keep traveling west until we reach Hrolf's lands. I don't think we will meet Gunnar on these shores. Burning those ships was like beating a hornet's nest."

Finn laughed. "We added to that, didn't we?"

"We certainly did. I think Grimnr figured that out, too."

"So it was more like throwing a rock into a bear's den."

Traveling the woods at night was a slow and frustrating process made worse for their unfamiliarity with the geography. Ulfrik knew his position but did not know the folds and nuances of the land, leading to smashed toes and at least three solid falls for both of them. The cursed, knowing they left an easy trail but counting on the distance solving the issue of pursuit. Horses could not navigate woods, and so Grimnr's men would also be slogging along the same terrain.

By dawn, Ulfrik's eyes were heavy with sleep and Finn yawned incessantly. Yet in the early morning he saw a ship anchored in the river, tugging against its anchor stone sunk into the river bottom. Finn stumbled up behind him, leaning against a tree and studied the long ship with bleary eyes.

"You're going to be angry," Finn said after a long pause. "But I don't remember what Gunnar's ship looked like. I suppose that might be it."

Pinching the bridge of his nose, he let out a long sight. "Then you go hail them and find out who they are. My eyes are not what they once were and I can't see that far, or I'd tell you if that was my son."

Finn grumbled and looked around for a tree branch. "There are no hazels?"

"They'll get your meaning. Just be careful and ready to run." Ulfrik watched Finn trot out to the shore, waving a long branch he had cut from a thin poplar tree. He shouted at the ship and leaned back as if ready to run. At first no one answered but then Ulfrik noted a few blurry shapes waving from the deck. Finn called back to them, and soon tossed aside the branch and motioned Ulfrik forward. The ship came to life at the same time, men drawing the anchor stone while the sails were lowered.

"That's Gunnar's ship," Finn said. "That's Gunnar in the prow. Interesting fellow, he is."

Ulfrik strained to see Gunnar, but at this distance the shapes were still indistinct. "How is he interesting?"

"He's a lot like you, but there's something I don't trust in him. Sorry, I know he's your son. But something tells me he'd spill my guts if I told him it might rain tomorrow."

"Then don't talk about the weather." Ulfrik watched the ship approach. As it drew closer his experienced eye took in all the details that turned his blood cold: arrows in the mast and hull, missing shields from the rack, a grappling hook stuck in the rail that still trailed rope. "Odin's balls, they were boarded."

As the ship nosed onto the bank, men jumped out to lead the ship onto a safe mooring. Gunnar jumped into the shallows and waded with his arms thrown wide. His shirt was torn and collar to boot was splattered with brown stains. His wavy black hair flowed to his shoulders and his dark eyes gleamed with happiness. Ulfrik's heart lifted with pride and he blinked away tears.

"My boy," was all he could say as the two embraced on the muddy bank. His ship moaned as it slithered to a halt on land next to them. Ulfrik pulled back and studied Gunnar's face. He had new scars and his skin had grown leathery and hard from life at sea, but it was his boy's face nonetheless. "You've grown to be quite a man, Gunnar the Black."

"And you look solid for a ghost," he said, clapping his father's shoulders. "I never dreamed I'd see you again, but when I heard the stories in Yorvik I knew you lived. You did well to spread your tale, for it led me home."

"We both have tales to tell," Ulfrik said, then searched over Gunnar's shoulder. "But now's not the time nor the place."

"Not while standing up to our ankles in river mud."

They laughed and embraced again, but now Ulfrik turned toward his ship. "Finn told me your mother was aboard. Is she too shy to greet me?"

Gunnar's smile vanished, and he put his arm on his father's shoulder. "Really, let's not speak any longer in the mud. Come with me up the shore and I will tell you what has happened."

"You were boarded," he said, trying to keep the trembling out of his voice. "Is she alive?"

"Yes, she and Aren both are alive, but during that fight she fell overboard. Konal was aboard one of the ships pursuing us, and he picked her out of the water. I know he saved her life, but you haven't seen what he did to her. Her face --"

"Just stick to what happened next. I will deal with Konal when I find him." Ulfrik thought of Konal's betrayal, and knowing how close he and Gunnar had once been did not want to describe how he intended to kill him. Gunnar nodded as they mounted the short slope. A gentle breeze rustled the grass and birds sang in the morning light. The river was placid and on the opposite bank deer ventured to the water's edge.

"Aren saw she had been taken aboard Konal's ship, and that it was shoving off from us while we were tied to another enemy. So he jumped the gap and landed on Konal's deck. I couldn't see what happened to him. Konal had already beaten Aren's face out of shape, so I must believe he would be less gentle with him now."

Ulfrik pressed his temples and squeezed his eyes shut. "I don't understand what happened. What drove him to this? I trusted everything to him when I was away. He was like a brother."

"Well, brothers can turn on one another," Gunnar said. "I did with Hakon, though not so badly as that. Our differences drove me to leave him and everyone behind. My part in all this is big, Father. When this is settled I will ask your forgiveness, but I would not give it were I you."

Waving his hand to dismiss the thought, he said, "That's because you have no children of your own, or you'd understand how easy it is to forgive one's blood for these mistakes."

Gunnar stared at him without expression. Ulfrik let out a long sigh, and punched his fist into his palm. "This is so frustrating. Vilhjalmer has been taken to Paris, and Runa is gone with Konal, Fate only knows where. I can't go in both directions at once, but choosing one path almost guarantees the other path will close. I can afford to lose neither my family nor my future."

"It is a hard choice," Gunnar said. He glanced back at his ship, which had not disembarked. "With either choice, we cannot stay here longer. Whatever ships we did not burn will be upon us now that the sun is risen. I delayed in hopes you would show, but we cannot risk another boarding. My crew does not warm to risks without immediate rewards and they have no love of my family."

Ulfrik stared west over the Seine to where it vanished around a bend. Geese splashed down into the water as he watched. He wished he could fly as they did, and head straight to Paris before the sun reached the peak of the sky. His landbound feet could only take him so far, and Paris was at least two days away on foot. He took a deep breath and faced Gunnar.

"I'm going in both directions," he said. "I ask for two of your crew to accompany Finn to Paris. He is skilled in fieldcraft and will be able to reach the city on foot and get inside. I need to have him scout the city while he awaits me there. I just hope the Frankish court moves slowly and Hrolf does not learn what has happened."

"You'll have the men," Gunnar said. "Now what about Konal and mother?"

"I will pursue them first. There is no sense in saving my future with Hrolf if I let my wife and son be stolen from me. I will find them and there will be no doubt that I have returned to bring an accounting for all of Konal's crimes."

He stared into Gunnar's eyes but was surprised to find no

wavering or regret, only a hard look of satisfaction. "You intend to kill him?"

"He was behind my betrayal to Throst. He came to witness my hanging. There ends whatever loyalty I may have had for an old friend. The best I will do for him is make his death swift."

"It is the right choice. Now where do you think they have gone?"

"I don't think he planned to find Runa as he did, so he was probably not ready for a sea voyage when he left Grimnr's camp. He must have returned to his hall to prepare. Can you take me there?"

Gunnar smiled, "Nothing would make me happier."

They broke up and Ulfrik described the plan to Finn, who was excited to lead an independent adventure into Paris. Gunnar provisioned him with food and enough mead for a few days on the road, and then he set out. Gunnar's ship sailed further west for Konal's fortress and Ulfrik prayed he had not already slipped away.

54

Runa paced in the hall that had been her home and now served as her prison. She and Aren sat alone by the hearth, the squalid light of a bleak day dribbling in from the partially opened smoke hole. Every shuffling footstep, every frustrated sigh echoed in the emptiness. Looms sat abandoned against the wall, baskets of thread sitting beneath them. Konal had chased everyone from the hall upon his arrival and tossed her and Aren in like two sacks of old clothes. She paused at the front door and tested it. They were still barred from the outside, a spear unceremoniously shoved through the door handles.

"How long will he be gone for?" Runa asked, her pale hand trembling against the door.

"He's loading however much as he can take from this place before he flees. He could be hours yet." Aren tossed scraps of thread into the hearth fire, watching them burst into flame and float up with the smoke.

"At least he untied us," she said, massaging her wrists as she turned back to the hall. "That gives us an opportunity to act."

"I think he's aware of that," Aren said. "He won't return alone to face the two of us."

Runa glanced around but found only makeshift weapons, the best one being the iron poker for the fire. "We have to escape long enough for Ulfrik to find us."

"What makes you believe he will?"

She stared at her son, and read the defeat she saw in the slouch of his shoulders and the downcast eyes. "Because we bought him time to escape. Gunnar will find him and send him here."

"Do you see the future now, Mother? We are within a walled fortress of enemies. How will he find us here?"

"Then on the water," she said. Aren turned aside and she grabbed his arm, pulling him to her. "You are only defeated if you surrender. I speak from my own experience. Look at my life since I believed my husband died. I gave up and earned the scorn of the gods for it, and they were sure to make me miserable. But all of this has awakened me to fight again. You must learn this lesson now, that no man may defeat you until you have defeated yourself."

He shrugged and continued to look away. "But still we are barred into this prison and await Konal's pleasure. There can still be defeat even if we choose not to believe it."

Runa let him go, not wanting to push his already sour mood. In time he would see the truth of her words, and for now was not wrong to see only their capture but not their escape. Even she did not see the end clearly, but trusted Fate was in motion and on her side. She had seen this too many times before to not recognize the gods at work.

As she continued to pace, the door trembled as the spear was drawn from it. She stopped, her hands cold and clasped together beneath her chin. Aren stood, stumbling back as if he wanted to shrink beneath the benches lining the walls of the hall. The doors swung open and Konal stood framed within, two men at his back. No one moved, until at last Konal stalked into the hall, a wavering shadow in the gloom. Runa stood beneath the high table where in happier years she presided over a full hall. Now she strained to keep her body from quivering as she watched her former husband pause beneath the milky light at the center of the hall. She could smell the mead on him.

"With all your plans you still found time to get drunk," she said, forcing herself to sound strong. Aren stared at her with warning eyes, but she did not heed him. Konal did not deserve any less and if he would hold her captive then she would make his miserable for it. "Maybe with luck you'll fall overboard and drown."

The words bounced off him, and he merely shook his head. He had shed his mail shirt and now wore a white shirt and black pants with a blue cloak. His face was red from drink, making the pale whorls in his burn scars more evident. Runa's eyes brushed across the sword at his hip and the daggers in his belt to find the pouch of gems reattached to his hip.

With a flick of his hand, he dismissed his men. "Stand outside and no matter what you hear do not enter."

The two guards shared pained looks, and one pointed to Aren. "Should we take him outside?"

"He's nothing." Konal wavered on his feet as he peered at Aren shrinking against the wall. "A good jumper, but otherwise not even as useful as week-old shit. At least you can burn shit for fuel. He just eats my food and drinks my mead, nothing more."

Runa bit back on her protective instincts. Aren was old enough to deal with his father and did not need her sheltering him. She bit her lip as Aren cringed and Konal laughed, but she remained silent. When drunk Konal either wept for joy that Aren was his only blood kin left in the world or cursed him for a wasted life. Given recent events, he was not likely to see much good in his son.

The two guards gave Runa a sad look and shuffled out of the hall. Not all of Konal's men were beasts, and as these two had not been part of his crew Runa figured they might be his most honorable men. Still, they closed the door behind them leaving Runa trapped with the wolf. She turned her chin up in defiance and folded her arms.

"You divorce me?" he asked, his voice full of disbelief. "In front of my crew, you shame me so?"

"It is my right under the law. You have publicly humiliated me at least three times --"

"When? How? This is outrageous." He stepped toward her, his face gleaming with sweat and his eyes fever-bright. He stumbled in his drunkenness, but steadily approached her.

"Look at my face. Everyone knows how you beat me. Ask Groa or any of the other women. They all know."

He nodded appreciatively, taking one deliberate step after the next. "So that is reason for divorce. But where will you go?" He mimicked deep though, putting a hand to his brow. "I know. You think your dead husband is still alive. He'll take care of you, won't he?"

"You went to make sure he was dead, didn't you?"

Konal paused at the edge of the hearth, staring at her. "What do you know of where I went and what I did? How can you know anything?"

"Snorri and Einar both know of Ulfrik's return. Aren knows. It does not take much imagination to realize why you've done as you have. I only wonder at the timing of it. Who else are you working with, Konal? You want Ulfrik to stay dead to me and the rest of the world, as does someone else. Someone in power. But who?

She saw Aren step from the shadows, waving his hands to stop her, but she did not want to. It felt good to grind this shame into his face. "You look amazed. Do you think yourself so sly that I wouldn't guess? Are you --"

He was upon her in an instant, faster and more accurate than even his sober moments. He grabbed her by the throat and began to throttle her, his face a red mask of fury. "You know nothing, you arrogant bitch! You are my wife, and should keep your fucking mouth shut."

Her foot collided with his crotch and he collapsed backward, falling onto a bench and screaming in rage and pain. Runa collapsed in a fit of coughing to the table behind her, then Konal began to stagger to his feet.

Snatching an earthenware jug from the high table, she turned into time for him to leap on her. She slammed the jug against his temple with a loud clunk, but it did not break. His fist connected with her cheek and she crumbled to the floor.

"You dare fight with me? I am your husband, and I do not accept you divorce." He grabbed her leg and yanked her flat. "You cold-hearted bitch. You haven't given me a good fuck in years and then claim humiliation at my hands. I took you in when you had nothing."

"I had nothing because of you. You killed my husband to take his place!"

He kicked her side and she balled up. Her hands sought the jug she had dropped but her fingers only brushed the smooth side of it. Konal shoved up her skirt with one hand and began working his belt with the other.

"Give it to me now, woman. Give me what you would have given to him." His destroyed voice cracked and broke as he bathed her with the smell of stale mead. "You belong to me. All of this belongs to me."

Runa's hand grabbed the jug again, and she flung it into his face. This time it shattered in a tinkling crash and he staggered back without a sound, his pants low on his hips. She scrabbled backward, sticking on the table legs and searching for anything to use in a fight. Konal was on his knees, his face bleeding. When nothing came to hand, Runa pushed off the floor and darted past him.

Aren stood pale and slack-jawed, and she yelled at him, "Run, get away from here."

Konal caught her ankle and she slammed to her face, narrowly missing the stone edge of the hearth. He dragged her into her arms, then pressed his lips to hers. Blood and sweat mingled on her tongue as she clawed at him, tearing his shirt and ripping his skin. Nothing stopped him, and he slammed her to the floor. White flashes of pain blinded her and her ears rang. Her skirt was over her chest now and she felt the cold on her bare skin.

"One last fuck, like it used to be. Remember that?"

"Get off me," she screamed. She punched at his head, but his strong hand caught it.

"I'd rather kill you than give you up," he said through bloody teeth.

Konal's eyes went wide and he dropped her hand. His mouth opened but no sound came. Runa pushed back, batting down her skirt to cover herself. Aren stood above Konal, tears flowing freely over his swollen, red face.

"You killed me?" Konal said, struggling to turn around. "With my own dagger? I'm...your father."

Aren stepped back as Konal reached for him, but his hand

dropped to the floor, then he toppled to his face. Runa saw the dagger sticking out of Konal's back, a dark stain blooming across the white fabric of his shirt.

She stared at Aren, whose lips trembled to speak.

"You're not my father. You're a gutless bastard, and I killed you."

55

Ulfrik leaned on the rails next to Gunnar, who worked the tiller of his ship with as much ease as man with two hands. The hook he wore was sufficient for the calm river waters, but he wondered at Gunnar's ability on the open seas. His mind wandered from thought to thought, for he could not fix upon what he knew must come next. The splash of oars in the water was a calming rhythm, and the dark green of the trees pressing the river banks was a balm to his sight. Yet his pulse throbbed knowing the final confrontation with Konal was at hand. He had killed scores of enemies in his day, but never one who had been such a trusted friend.

The Oise river was half as wide as the Seine at this point, and the afternoon sun glittered off it as they cleared a bend. Ulfrik strained to see the fortress over the serrated tops of pine trees. At first it seemed distant but as Gunnar's ship sailed closer he realized it was only a small fort that dominated a low hill.

"Not much of a fortress," Ulfrik said. "This was newly built by Konal?"

Gunnar nodded. "In the year after your death, the Franks drove back all the western border. Only Ull the Strong, that miserable old bastard, wouldn't shift. We had to surrender Ravndal, and Einar built a new stronghold in Eyrafell and Konal placed himself here. This is to hold the river against the Franks should they try to sneak an army up river behind Eyrafell."

"This fort doesn't look as if it would hold against a flock of doves."

"The Franks haven't come this way, so they must believe otherwise."

Both fell silent as the ship nosed for the shore and the empty dock. Ulfrik's stomach tightened when he saw a thin trail of black smoke rising from Konal's fortress. It was a thin ribbon like a streamer proclaiming the site of troubles.

"What is it you said about the Franks?" Ulfrik said, not taking his eyes from the smoke. A faint scent of burnt wood reached him.

Gunnar swallowed and shouted at his crew. "I'm taking us to the docks, then I want ten men with me and the rest of you to guard this ship with your worthless lives."

After docking the ship and selecting his ten men, Gunnar led them along the trail through the woods that ended at the hill rising to Konalsvik. None one spoke, but all were wary for an attack. At the walls they found the gate opened and unattended. The scent of burning wood was heavier in the air here, and from the top of the hill Ulfrik scanned the surrounding dark green carpet of treetops but saw no signs of an army.

"I don't like any of this," Ulfrik muttered to himself. Gunnar, pointing with his war ax, ordered men to open the gates as wide as they would go.

"Well, there's your fire," he said, again using his ax as a pointer. A building with blackened, smoking thatch sat opposite the gate. A dog with three arrows in its side lay in front of the building's opened door.

"Konal wouldn't attack his own men?" Gunnar asked.

Ulfrik did not answer, but drew his sword and entered. No one guarded the front gates, but once inside he saw the hall appeared to have men stationed outside. "Three at the hall doors," he said.

"Rank up," Gunnar ordered. "Shields out."

Gunnar walked at the front, unable to match his right-handed shield to anyone in line. Ulfrik joined with him and the two approached the guards, who upon noticing them disappeared inside the hall.

"Faster, while no one's about," Ulfrik said, and they broke into a jog. Once the guards re-emerged, they were not alone.

Runa stood between them.

Ulfrik stumbled to a halt, blinking in disbelief. His mind was a beehive of confused thoughts, all conflicting for his next action. No matter how much time had passed, she was the same beautiful vision he had carried in his heart for all these cold and lonely years. Her hair was still full of tight curls that splashed over his shoulders, though now brushed with gray. Her back was straight and the years had not creased her face, other than to work lines between her brows. Yet best of all was her smile, a warm and welcoming smile that took away all his confusion.

He thrust his sword back into its sheath, stalked up the incline to the doors where she stood, then he grabbed her into her arms.

"I'm home."

Their kiss was deep and he forgot his surroundings as he drank in the familiar scent of his wife. All the memories flooded back to him in that single kiss, and when she pulled away he looked her straight in the eyes.

"I did not want you to see me like this," she said, lowering her head. As if the words had removed a spell from his sight, he noticed the bruising and swelling on her cheek. An ugly red lump under her left eye was red and hot. He brushed her hair from it.

"I have dreamed of this moment every day. Nothing can ruin it." He kissed her forehead then set her back. "But for now I have to put it aside. What has happened and where is the bastard who did this to you?"

"Gunnar told you about how Konal found us?" She glanced past him, then placed her trembling hand on his chest. "He took us here and got drunk. He flew into a rage and ... did things."

"Like beat you?" The anger seeped into his voice and a red haze was already forming at the edges of his vision. She nodded in confirmation.

"I thought he would kill me."

Ulfrik saw the bruises on her neck and his hands itched to draw his sword and cleave Konal's head in two. "But he did not?"

She shook her head. "Aren stabbed Konal with his own dagger. It stopped the attack, but then his men went mad at this. Eleven of them had more honor than the others, and they protected me and Aren in this hall. The others ransacked the fortress and left. I don't know where they went. The craftsmen either fled or joined the looters. I don't think they will return."

"They took Konal's ship," Ulfrik said. "There was nothing at dock nor did we see it on the water. Runa, my soul, I would have killed him myself had Aren not done the deed."

Gunnar joined them, and hugged his mother. "Killed by his own weapon and by his own son. I could never imagine a more disgraceful end to a life."

"He is not yet dead," Runa said, placing a hand over her mouth. "He lingers at the edge of life. We bandaged his wounds and placed him in his bed."

"Why?" both Ulfrik and Gunnar asked at the same time. Runa backed up a step, eyes wide with surprise.

"We just couldn't do it to him. After the fires of anger passed, that face is still the same face of a man who... it's not so simple...he does not deserve mercy, and yet." Tears began to roll down her cheeks and Runa stomped her foot then covered her face.

"Don't be ashamed," Ulfrik said, taking her hands in his. They were small and cold, skin hard and rough from work at the loom. "I have dreaded this reckoning as well. No son should have to kill his father, and no wife her husband."

She looked up at him suddenly. "I have divorced him. He is not my husband. He never lived up to the word."

He stroked her hand, then kissed it. "Take me to him, and leave us alone. Worry no more for this."

Runa turned inside without another word, the guards parting to let Ulfrik pass. Gunnar paused, and when Ulfrik turned he found him red-faced and staring at the ground. Gunnar and Konal had been as close as kin, and for years he idolized Konal's stories of adventure. "Wait for me here," Ulfrik offered, and he bowed his head in acceptance. He needed a face-saving excuse or his reputation as Gunnar the Black might suffer with his crew.

Inside the hall the rest of Runa's men waited around a table, their faces solemn. Four of them stood but the rest only leaned back to regard him with indifference. They were unfamiliar, except for Aren who sat at the head of the table. His face was puffy and misshapen with bruises. When he smiled his front tooth showed it had been chipped. Glancing back at Runa's injuries and the vestiges of Aren's, his resolve strengthened.

"Where is he?" Ulfrik's voice was like a lead ball dropped in the smothering silence of the room. Aren pointed at the door behind the high table, a typical location for a jarl's quarters.

He clomped across the hall, then stepped onto the rise where the high table sat. He faced the men and placed his hand upon his sword. "You have protected my wife and son, and for that you have my gratitude and in time you will have a reward to match it. You are all still sworn to Konal, and I must know if you will hinder me in what I do next. Your jarl has revealed himself as the foulest sort of traitor, one who posed as a friend. Today I will avenge myself and claim what was once his as my own. Jarl Hrolf the Strider will support me in this."

The men lowered their eyes and stole glances at one another. With his hand upon the hilt of his sword, he waited for a challenge but none came. Ulfrik narrowed his eyes at them and inclined his head, then he turned for the door to find Konal.

Ulfrik recognized Runa's touch in the small, dark room with it's neat organization and freedom of clutter. Hanging on the opposite wall a silver crucifix that had belonged to her brother Toki was tarnished black. The revolting scent of a tallow candle filled the room and mingled with the iron tang of blood. Konal lay on his bed, a red stained wrap about his torso and his hands folded over the hilt of his sword which had been tied into its scabbard with leather peace straps. His chest rose and fell with his labored breathing and his forehead glistened with sweat.

Stepping up to his side, he stared at his former companion's face. The burns scars had always been his defining mark, but otherwise he seemed a different man. His eyes were closed and sunken, his face pallid and gaunt. Ulfrik's lip curled when he thought of the violence he had brought to his family, and how he had betrayed him to Throst. He swept Konal's hands from the sword, so that when he died it would not be as a warrior but as the gutless coward he had become.

Konal's eyes fluttered open, rolling wildly until focusing on Ulfrik. He frowned, then coughed. His usually strained voice was even thinner now that he lingered at the edge of death. "My own son did this to me. Can you believe it?"

"There is little I won't believe anymore," Ulfrik said. His pulse beat in his temple and his chest felt tight. "It is no less than what you deserve."

"What I deserve?" Konal choked a laugh that turned to a fit of coughing. Blood splashed from his mouth as he did. "Fine words from the man who deceived me all these years. I found the jewels my brother and I spent our lives seeking. You lied to us about them, denied us our share."

"I returned that share to you tenfold. I gave you a home, a family, and a fair share of all my war spoils. And you repaid me with treachery. You sent word to Throst and connived to have me murdered. Then you stole my hall and my family. I lost everything to your petty jealousy, and your anger over a few stones."

"A few stones? Those gems were a gift from one king to another. They must be worth a kingdom. You could never return my share."

Ulfrik leaned close. "I killed Throst. I threw him from the tower where he had contrived to murder me. But unlike me, the gods hated him. They smashed his body to pieces so that when I found him at the bottom I could not tell where his head should have been on that twisted lump of flesh."

Konal's frown deepened. "Do you think to threaten me? I am already dead. What worse can you do?"

"You're right," Ulfrik said, stepping back. "Just tell me why you did it."

He waited but Konal closed his eyes and folded his hands over the sword. The silence stretched until Konal's wheezy breathing overwhelmed Ulfrik.

"Once you had everything you wanted, why did you mistreat it? Why did you hurt my wife and son?"

Eyes flicking open, he bared his red-stained teeth. "She was my wife and he was my son. Not yours! You were dead and should've stayed that way."

"That doesn't answer my question."

"Because she is a stupid whore and he is a monster!"

Ulfrik clamped his hands onto Konal's throat and began to crush. He grabbed Ulfrik's arms in feeble grip, but he was too weak to dislodge him.

"This is for me, and all my family," Ulfrik hissed through gritted teeth. "This is for all the lost years of my life and the broken body you left me."

Konal gasped and kicked, the sword slipping to the floor with a dull clank. His eyes were wide with terror as his face darkened. Ulfrik drove his thumbs into the base of Konal's throat, squeezing with all his force.

"This is for the ruin your petty greed and jealousy has wrought. I curse you to Nifelheim. May worms eat your corpse until Ragnarok!"

His hands flopped to his side and his body went limp in Ulfrik's grip, but he continued to squeeze. He crushed until the pain in his hands traveled up to his elbows, long past the moment when Konal had grown still. Only until he was sure Konal's last breath had been chocked off did he release. His hands burned from the effort. He felt for a pulse in Konal's neck and detected nothing, nor did he breath or otherwise move. He lay on the bed as peacefully as if he had fallen asleep. Only that his legs and arms were splayed out did he show any sign of a struggle.

Konal was dead. Ulfrik wiped the sweat from his brow and blew out a long breath.

"My revenge is done," he said to the corpse. "Now to find my new life."

56

Ulfrik's footsteps in the hall were the only sounds despite Gunnar having joined his ten men with the others already inside. The hall was again full of warriors and each one turned a dour face toward him as he took a seat at the high table. Runa sat in opposite the corner with Aren, both holding each other's hands. Gunnar studied him with arms crossed and face expressionless. Ulfrik sighed and leaned on his elbows at the table.

"It is done. Konal is dead and justice is satisfied."

Runa stifled a sob and buried her face in Aren's shoulder. Gunnar provided a slow nod, but otherwise he and his men demonstrated no care for the announcement. Only Konal's men seemed moved, each one staring at the other with wide eyes. At last one of the men stood. His brown hair was stained with gray streaks and his short beard was interrupted with a white scar at his cheek.

"Now we are men without a lord, little better than bandits. You say Jarl Hrolf the Strider supports you?" Ulfrik nodded. "Then we shall serve you, if you will lead."

"I will be honored to have you. Swearing of oaths will come when the arrangements are formalized with Hrolf. Until then, I'll charge you with the protection of this fortress until I return. No one, not even your former companions, may enter without leave from me or Runa."

The man inclined his head. "I speak for all of us when I say we had no love of our former companions. They were leeches, not warriors."

With the men settled, Ulfrik gathered Gunnar, Aren and Runa to his table. He guided his wife with a gentle touch on her shoulder, and she flashed a smile at him through teary eyes. He understood the history between her and Konal, but did not understand how she could grieve for a man who had treated her with carelessness. He hoped time would heal those wounds. For now, he had more pressing needs.

"It was a hard thing I did," Ulfrik said quietly. "Even after all the pain he has caused all of us, he was once a friend."

His family kept their eyes lowered, but Gunnar frowned. "Some deeds can never be forgiven, and he made a list of them. I don't regret his death. It was a service to the world."

Aren nodded and sighed, patting his mother's hand. Runa blinked away more tears but could not speak. Ulfrik let them remain in silence, his own head clear after bringing justice to Konal. He had dreaded the moment, but now that it had passed he found himself sharing Gunnar's sentiments. He felt loose and excited for the next step in his plans.

"I sent Finn ahead to Paris, where Count Amand has taken Vilhjalmer. I will meet him there and rescue Hrolf's son once and for all."

"From Paris?" Runa asked, wiping tears from her cheek with the back of her wrist. "That will be even harder than the camp, and look how long that took you."

Ulfrik waved in dismissal. "That's because I had to infiltrate the ranks and sneak about the fortress. Paris will be much simpler. It is the hugest city I've ever seen. Only cities like Lundene in England might rival it. People of all races move within its wall, Norsemen included. We will only need gold enough to bribe my way through any guard curious enough to ask questions. Otherwise, no one will fear the arrival of a lone man."

"You don't really plan on just you and Finn doing this?" Gunnar asked, his dark eyes flashing with curiosity.

"More than a handful of men will just arouse suspicions. I've learned much about skulking among enemies from my time in Amand's camp. One or two are better suited to tasks such as this. But I have a role for you, if you can convince your crew. Hrolf will reward them, of that I am certain."

Gunnar sat up and grinned. "My men crave gold the way other men crave food and mead. Name the task and we shall carry it out."

"Sail me down the Seine to Paris. That means we will have to portage around Amand's camp and right now that will be dangerous."

"And on the return trip?"

Ulfrik turned to Aren. "You and your mother take four men and make haste for Eyrafell. I need Einar and Mord to launch another feint at the camp. Only a distraction to keep their eyes from the river as we pass. Without leadership, they may even surrender. Half that camp is wracked with disease and without strong leaders they may crumble."

Aren nodded eagerly but Runa shook her head. "How will we time it to coincide with your passing?" she asked. "It seems unlikely to succeed."

"The attack is all we need to break up that camp while they are distracted with Amand's sudden absence and the spread of disease. Count three days from the time you have left before Einar attacks. He won't have time to gather all his men for a full assault, but only a distraction is needed."

"What about inside Paris?" Gunnar asked. "How will you find Finn."

"Finn will find me, no doubt. He should have already located Vilhjalmer, for the Count probably holds him in a church. Any one of the big ones will do, and Finn will have scouted them all. After that, I will create my own distractions and deceptions." He smiled and tapped his head. "As I've gotten older, I've gotten craftier. The years have taught me some hard lessons about how people react to danger. I know how to make them do what I want."

"You make is sound simple," Runa said. "But the years have also taught me some hard lessons, one being that your schemes usually involve the greatest risk to your life."

Ulfrik laughed, and took his wife's hand once more. It was wet and warmer now, and he clasped it between his. "If the gods are not entertained they will not bless me with victory. If I do not take risks that bring blood and glory, they become bored. That is my fate, Wife. I will be in the heart of the enemy's power, walled in by those who would kill me if they knew my heart. But I will walk out of Paris, and so will all Finn, Vilhjalmer and any other who goes in with me. This I swear before you and all the gods."

She pulled her hand back. "Do not swear lightly. This Count knows the value of his hostage, and Vilhjalmer will be guarded like a king's treasure."

"True, but unlike gold or jewels, Vilhjalmer is a smart and courageous boy who will aid in his own escape. One other thing to consider, Paris is like a giant walrus. It is fearsome when roused to fight, but it is a slow and ponderous beast. You can't tip over a hay cart in that city without soiling the finery of some nobleman. All those leaders makes Paris slow to react. I just need to be fast and confusing. We will be gone before they know what they have lost."

He scanned their faces, and his boys were ready to aid him. Runa pursed her lips, but relented under his assuring smile. "I should trust you more than I do, yet I can't help but worry. I don't want to lose you so soon after finding you again."

"Everything will be fine," he said, then stood. "I will have Konal's men bury him with his clothes and a sword. That will be a token of our old friendship, and from this day that is all I choose to remember of him. If any of you wish to place anything in his grave, see it is done before you leave."

Again all of their eyes fell to the table, and Ulfrik grunted. "Let's prepare for the journey. We've little time to lose. Paris is slow, but they are not at a standstill. Every day gives more time for Count Amand to take action against Hrolf."

After they broke up and Ulfrik dispensed his orders to his new men, he stepped outside to clear his mind before departing. He stared at the dead dog with three arrows running along its side like a spine. Despite all his assurances to his family, he feared this attempt would be the most foolhardy plan he had ever assembled. He wished he had something to sacrifice to the gods for their favor, but in the end all he could offer in sacrifice was the risk of his own life and the lives of his family. It would need to be enough.

57

The stench and noise of Paris overwhelmed Ulfrik. It was no ordinary experience of foul odors and commotion, but a near debilitating crush of sensation. Fish, garbage, sweat, smoke, dung, and half a dozen other scents he couldn't identify filled his head upon entering the city walls. His ears throbbed with the cacophony of life, the only thing louder being the clash of shield walls. Hawkers cajoled him as he passed; people seemed not to speak but to yell; the endless procession of carts and horses followed by streams of people flowed around him; craftsmen hammering; goats, chickens, dogs, and horses bleating, clucking, barking and snorting; pigeons swooping in great flocks from building to building. He wanted to fold into a dark corner and cover his ears, but knew he could never escape the assault.

He seldom entered large cities, and when he worked as a trader he spent his days aboard the ship. The largest he had ever entered was Yorvik in England, and it was a mere corner of this vast city. It was no wonder he and his fellow Northmen were unable to capture it, for swallowing a whale would have been an easier task. Yet not only the physical size of the city amazed him, but also the mass of people crammed behind these walls. Buildings leaned together over cramped streets, and he wondered how one unattended oil lamp or errant spark from a cooking fire had not burned the entire city to ashes. He had considered setting a fire as a distraction during Vilhjalmer's escape, but now he revised that plan. He might trap all of them within an inescapable inferno.

People jostled him through the streets, funneling him along their path of travel whether or not he desired to go with them. No one had patience for his delays, and when he halted someone would shout at him to move or simply shove him aside. His boots were already thick with animal droppings, which littered the roads. The city was a playground for fat, black flies which boldly landed on his face or buzzed around his head.

He angled toward the large church where the two men from Gunnar's crew said he would wait. Neither of them entered Paris, but had waited outside for Finn's report. Ulfrik told them how Gunnar had moored his ship upstream and to return with news he had entered Paris. He left all of his weapons and mail aboard the ship, knowing he would not be allowed inside with anything more dangerous than a dagger. He carried three, one in each boot and one at his hip. Paris was a city of churches, and he had visited one already and not located Finn. This final one was taller than the others, and in the location fitting the description. Though there were roads to follow Ulfrik still found it easier to navigate by the sun to determine east from west.

At tap at his shoulder brought him around to face Finn, who stood smiling at him. "Welcome to Paris," he said in Norse. The use of the language drew a glance from passers-by but they continued on their way. Ulfrik looked Finn over from head to toe.

"You're dressed like a beggar. What happened?"

The dirt on his face hid his freckles but did not diminish his bright smile. "I ran out of silver in the first day. I had to carve up my new armband and that's gone. I hadn't thought about money when I came here. So, I'm a beggar now. Got anything to eat?"

Ulfrik laughed and slapped Finn's shoulder. "The gate guards took a good chunk of my silver. They think our people dress in it."

"Well, they should stop putting it in churches for us to take."

"I think I can buy us some food, if you can show me a place where we can buy it. You can tell me what you discovered, and we'll finalize our plans."

"Lots of places for food and drink, just not many allow our people. I've been all over this city, day and night. Got nothing else to do, really, and it has been exciting. Had a few close scrapes too, and these Franks don't fight fair. Ten friends come out of nowhere when the fighting talks starts."

They wandered through the crowded streets, Finn happily chirping about his adventures. Despite all the danger, Finn's boyish enthusiasm made him smile. Finn led them to a place where the owner of a stall spoke enough Norse to demand a ridiculous price for mead and a plate of cheese and bread, and then demanded the sit outside. Finn did not care, and devoured everything with relish.

"You really haven't been eating well, have you?"

"Didn't expect that in a city," Finn said, then belched. "I found our boy. He's being held in some fancy church, biggest one ever I think. I saw him with a priest and five guards surrounding him."

"You know what he looks like?"

Finn paused with his mug halfway to his mouth. "We're not personal friends, but I'm pretty sure a lone Norse boy with a priest and a bunch of nervous guards is the right person. You said he'd be with a priest and that Count Amand was an old arrogant bastard with a mustache like a walrus. I saw him too, though not with the boy. He seemed to be trying to impress some very rich looking man. I thought the rich man would make him lick his shoes. You know, that would've been something to see."

Finishing his drink with a gulp, he sat it down and smiled at Ulfrik, who slapped the table with a smile of his own. "Alright, you found him. Gunnar is down-river and ready to shove off as soon as we arrive. What else have you learned?"

"Remember those fights I was telling you about? Beggars have them all the time, and I offered my fists in service to a few of them. Made a few friends who had other friends, and I learned about a tunnel out of the city."

Ulfrik sat up, hands frozen over the loaf of bread between them. "Have you seen it yourself?"

Finn nodded. "Just this morning, it goes from a small church in the northeast section, and comes up in a patch of bushes on the island where a rowboat is stowed. The monks sneak in country girls through it, or so I'm told. Not sure what its original purpose is, but it's simple to find."

"So it's not guarded?"

"Not this morning, anyway."

Ulfrik pondered the utility of the tunnel while Finn stuffed bread and cheese into his mouth. "Anything more about where our boy is hidden?"

"Haven't been inside, but there's two priests who go to fetch water but spend a lot of time talking instead. Same time every day. Maybe they're a way inside."

He settled back with hands folded over his stomach and belched. Ulfrik thought of the priests and his plans solidified.

"Let's visit the priests. Are you finished?"

"Unless I can eat the plate, I'm done."

They dived back into the chaos of Paris streets and Finn led them along twisting lanes that all seemed the same to Ulfrik. All the while, he explained to Finn the details of his plans. By the time they arrived at the church, Finn was jumping with excitement.

"I've never seen anything like it," Ulfrik said as he stopped before the church, and he meant it. It was a mountain of rock carved into shapes and spires he scarcely believed possible from human hands. "Their stonemasons must know magic."

"You should see where Odo makes his palace. I couldn't get close but it makes this a pig pen. We've got time before the priests arrive, and the well is around the back. We can hide in the bushes there." Finn pulled Ulfrik by the sleeve and lead him around the side of the church. The small courtyard was filled with green grass and red flowers unfamiliar to Ulfrik, and their dazzling colors were a stark contrast to the brown-gray of the church stone. The well was covered with a wood roof and likewise surrounded by yellow flowers. Hedges and trees filled the small square.

"They don't come out until a bell rings. Seems like everything changes with the bell, and that doesn't happen till the sun is directly above."

"While we have time, let's get ourselves properly outfitted for the task ahead." He winked at Finn, and the two left their prepared positions.

Finding a quiet area was not as difficult as Ulfrik expected. He backed into an alley where he picked up a stone brick slick with slime and moss. Finn stepped into the road and promised to return with their quarry.

"Try not to return with more than two," Ulfrik said. "This is not about a challenge."

With a wink of his own, Finn disappeared from view. The alley was ripe with garbage and the odor of refuse sickened him. Across the street a cart filled partially with hay sat abandoned and three empty barrels stood beside it. Someone moved past the partially opened door, but no one emerged.

Then he heard the shouting and heavy foot falls. Ulfrik backed up to let Finn have room to enter, and he hefted his brick. Finn dashed into the alleyway and the first guard was right behind him. Ulfrik flattened against the wall to let him pass. The following guard crashed into Ulfrik as he slammed the brick into the guard's face with a sickening crack. He crumpled with a whimper, but a third guard followed.

A stream of Frankish curses flowed, and Ulfrik flung the brick and clipped the guard's shoulder. He drew his dagger and plunged for the guard's gut. He was faster than Ulfrik expected, but he could not draw his weapon. Instead, he seized Ulfrik's knife hand and punched him in the side of the head. Ulfrik pulled back on the dagger, but the Frank resisted. This was a fight he needed to end fast and without injury. Nor did he want severely bloodied guard uniforms. They were face to face, and the guard snapped at Ulfrik's nose as if to bite it. He pulled his head back, and shoved the Frank to the wall. He drove his knee into the guard's stomach and pinned his other hand with his own. They wrestled over the dagger, twisting wildly in the struggle to drive it into flesh. The blade slipped down and cut Ulfrik's knee. He stifled his cry and the Frank grunted in effort. In the end, Ulfrik prevailed. In one instant the Frank's strength broke and the dagger plunged into his chest.

Ulfrik fell back with a curse as the guard slid down the wall, pulling at the dagger even as he died. Finn stood over his man, dagger dripping blood.

"That went worse than expected," Ulfrik said through his ragged breathing. "Can we put together two clean uniforms from this mess?"

Finn began pulling the surcoat from his guard. "I got this one through his ear, so he's not bleeding on himself."

"Mine was much sloppier, and I'll need his pants now that mine are cut."

Working quickly, they assembled uniforms of blue and white surcoats and short swords fastened to fine leather belts. Ulfrik tried to brush away blood drops but only smeared it across the fabric. Finn dashed across the street and dragged the hay cart to the alley entrance. Again passers-by paid no mind, and they loaded the bodies into the cart then returned it without question from anyone. Giddy with success, Finn laughed as they returned to their positions at the church.

Within moments the bell rang at the top of the church and the sleepy building sprang to life, with black robed priests emerging from different doors and the sounds of loud conversations from the rooms beyond. The crouched behind bushes and after all the others had cleared out Finn's two priests with emerged from a side door. One shouldered a water carrying yoke and the other held two large wooden buckets. They set their burdens by the well and began to chat in the shade of the grassy yard. Their voices were full of cheer and gossipy excitement.

"They're like two women," Ulfrik whispered to Finn.

"They've done this every day I've been here. They won't even start drawing water until moments before the bell rings a second time."

"Let me do the talking," Ulfrik said, loosening the sword in his sheath.

"Sure, I don't speak Frankish," Finn said, his freckled face shining with his excitement. Ulfrik rolled his eyes and then emerged from hiding.

The two priests did not notice them until Ulfrik was upon them. He drove the point of his sword in the soft belly of the closest priest. Finn circled behind the well and cut off the other's retreat.

The first priest was an old man with a fringe of white hair, an beak nose, and sleepy gray eyes that widened in shock at the touch of Ulfrik's spear point. "What is the meaning of this?"

"Call for help and you die. You two will lead us to the Norse boy Count Amand is hiding here."

The old priest shared a look with his younger partner. "I don't know what you're talking about."

"I figured that'd be your first answer. You get one lie and you've used it up. Next lie sends your friend to the bottom of that well without his head. The lie after that I start dropping your fingers down the well after him, one for each lie. Are you ready to try again?"

"Don't say anything, Englibert." Finn drove his fist into the priest's gut, crumpling him like a stack of old straw. Ulfrik smiled at Finn's improvisation.

"So Father Engilbert, you will escort me to Vilhjalmer and speak for me to anyone who questions us. And to keep you on my side, your young friend is going with my young friend. If I do not return to him within the hour and with Vilhjalmer, your friend will be carved up and fed to the dogs that rut in your filthy streets. You will protect me and lead me safely wherever I want to go, or you can blame yourself for the death of a dear friend."

The old Father Engilbert recoiled in disgust. He did not answer, but Ulfrik prompted him with the point of his sword. The priest blinked, then lowered his head. "You are not a Frank. I can tell from your horrible accent. How can I trust a barbarian?"

"You can trust we're always happy to gut a priest. So cooperate and you at least have a chance that I may be a man of my word. Otherwise, you've definitely killed your friend."

"Don't do it, Engilbert," the younger priest pleaded and Finn struck him again.

"My word is my life," Ulfrik said. "I just want the boy and nothing more. Your friend will remain unharmed and in good health if you aid me."

"He's on the second floor, two guards are with him always. We are at afternoon chores and so now is a good time to seek your boy."

"Take the priest for a walk," Ulfrik said to Finn. Then he grabbed the younger priest. "Also, don't speak a word to anyone or endanger my friend. If I don't find both of you where I expect, Engilbert dies."

Satisfied at his arrangements, Ulfrik watched Finn and the priest walk away as if enjoying a deep conversation. With a little distance it seemed Finn was actually conversing with his priest, but in reality he was likely cursing him in Norse. He sheathed his sword and gestured for Father Engilbert to lead the way.

They got as far the small side door when it suddenly opened and an officious seeming priest in white robes and a gold crucifix on his chest appeared. He was also old with a clean-shaved faced and bushy eyebrows of startling white. He glared at the priest and then at Ulfrik.

"Father Engilbert? Where is Father Wibert?"

The priest bowed low, "Your Grace!"

Ulfrik's hand fell to his sword. This must be the bishop, he thought, and everything just went to shit.

58

The bishop's dark brown eyes shot between Father Engilbert and Ulfrik, and his bushy brows lowered threateningly over them. Ulfrik forced his hand away from the hilt of his sword, fearing he would alert the bishop, though his neck throbbed with anxiety. The bishop, or whatever these Franks called their head priest, could mobilize the entire church with one word.

"I asked you a question," the bishop snapped. "And what is this fool doing besides staring at me as if I were Christ returned?"

"Father Wibert had to relieve himself, Your Grace." The old priest bowed lower, keeping his eyes averted.

The bishop waved his hand before his nose as if he had just smelled Father Wibert's relief. "Such detail is more than I care to know. Now who are you and why are you disturbing my priests?"

Ulfrik blinked, not knowing how to behave in front of a powerful holy man. He began touching his forehead, shoulders, and stomach randomly like so many Christians did, but this generated a look of revulsion from the Bishop. Father Engilbert nearly jumped atop Ulfrik as he brushed his hands down.

"This man is dumb, Your Grace. He knows not of speech or manners, nor even more than the rudiments of Our Savior's teachings. In all respects he is a brute, employed to terrorize men into obeying the law. But I have seen a kinder side to this man, and so I have taken to instructing him in my spare moments. I know this is odd, Your Grace, but if ever there was a soul worth saving it would be this man's. I was about to take him inside, probably his first time in many years, and show him how to properly pray at church."

The bishop raised an eyebrow and then regarded Ulfrik as if he were a jewel on the merchant's table. "I'm certain he donates for the time he consumes, and that donation finds its way to our coffers. Father Engilbert?"

"Most generously," he bowed again. "He has learned that to support the church is to support himself."

The bishop grunted, then eyed his priest. "Send Wibert up when he's done with his business. And do be sure to fetch that water. They're waiting for it in the kitchen."

Disappearing back into the door, both Ulfrik and Engilbert stared at the yawning blackness. Ulfrik smiled and nudged him. "Inspired work, Father. You lie with a practiced tongue."

"You have damned me to hell," he said dryly. "Let's make haste. We will have to cross one large room where many of my brothers will be at work. Do not look at any of them, nor speak. Follow me and we will be up the stairs. From there, we may exit another way. God have mercy upon me."

"God will reward you with your own cloud when you die," Ulfrik said. "But I will reward you with your life and that of your friend's."

"May you burn in hell, you heathen bastard."

Inside the dark church Ulfrik did as instructed and kept his eyes lowered. The cloying scent of oiled wood and burning tallow filled the spacious room they entered, which appeared to be the main hall where Christians gathered. While he did nothing more than stare at the wood slats of the floor as he followed Engilbert, glints of gold and silver danced at the sides of his visions. For the brief moments he passed through that hall with its rows of well-worn benches he imagined a king's trove of wealth must be stacked within it. It was no wonder Hrolf and Sigfrid had been so eager to knock down the walls of this city if this was the abundance of one church.

In back rooms black robed men with young attendants stopped

their sweeping or scrubbing to stare at their passing. One called to Engilbert but he mumbled a reply and pushed through the room to wide stairs. Their feet made hollow thuds on the risers as they climbed. At the landing the old priest stopped and put a frail hand on Ulfrik's chest.

"Two guards will be at the door. The boy does not come out except for exercise or for prayer. Did you know he is a Christian? Even your people can understand the truth when they choose to."

"Well pray that you get me past the guards without trouble," Ulfrik said. He had known Hrolf's marriage to a Frankish woman had converted him to Christianity, but it was a meaningless gesture. In practice, Hrolf held to the old faith and sacrificed to the old gods and got better results for it, at least to Ulfrik's mind.

"Maybe it's best you wait here for me. I can explain the boy is coming with me for prayer, which is not unusual. If they see you, I will have a harder time explaining it."

Ulfrik stared hard at him, but the priest's impassive face was inscrutable. "Remember Wibert. If you betray me or whisper a warning to those guards, he will die. I'll be listening to everything you say, and my hearing is excellent."

"No betrayals from me. I will get you the boy and take you to wherever you want to go. Just spare Wibert. I know your kind will try to kill us even if we keep our word to you, just so there's no witness to your crime. But if you have a conscience, Wibert should be freed. Keep me as a hostage as long as you need to feel safe of your secret."

They stared at each other for a moment, and Ulfrik patted the priest's arm. "Your loyalty to your friend is admirable. Be good, and I will do as you ask. Now fetch me the boy."

The priest climbed the last flight of the steps and Ulfrik strained to listen to his conversation with the guards. This was a large risk, as Engilbert could pass the guards nonverbal warnings or a hushed message. His hand was ready at his sword, and he half expected two guards to charge him with lowered spears. Instead, he heard doors creak, distant murmuring, then the footfalls of two people on the stairs.

Vilhjalmer was in front of the priest, who guided him with a firm hand on his shoulder. Hrolf's son was freshly clothed in a new outfit befitting his royal status. His hair was combed and neat, framing a clear and proud face with a strong nose and jaw. His regal composure held for a moment before it melted in recognition.

"It's you!" He rushed to Ulfrik and hugged him, all the pretense of royalty gone and nothing more than a child left in place. "Have you come to take me from this horrible place?"

"It is my sworn oath to save you from these Franks." He gathered Vilhjalmer to his side, then pulled a sheathed dagger from his boot. "I bought one of these for you. From hence forward no man takes you against your will."

Vilhjalmer accepted the dagger with wide-eyed reverence, the stashed at the back of his waistband. "Father was right to send you. I thought I'd never live beyond these walls again."

Engilbert cleared his throat. "Whatever you two are babbling about, you need to save it for later. If anyone finds him out of his room, they might realize what we're about."

"Can I trust him?" Vilhjalmer asked, raising his eyebrow at the priest.

"No, his friend is held hostage to his behavior. He will only help you as long as he believes his friend endangered." He turned to the priest, switching back to his Frankish. "How do we get out of here without going through a room of priests?"

"At the bottom of the stairs, turn to your right and follow the corridor to a room that will let us out on the other side of the church. There is a courtyard similar to the one you found me in."

Ulfrik gestured the priest to lead the way, which he did with a disdainful sneer. At the bottom of the steps he turned left toward another door. "That's the hallway. Don't look into the rooms along the way, but go straight to the end."

The door swung open and the Bishop again appeared, his bushy eyebrows rising in surprise. He was not alone this time, but at his side was another old man dressed in a rich blue shirt that offset a gleaming gold crucifix. His hand was occupied stroking a swooping white mustache, and it froze in place as he locked eyes with Ulfrik.

"Count Amand," Ulfrik grumbled under his breath. For an instant he thought the Count would not recognize him, but his hooded eyes shifted from him to Vilhjalmer and back again.

"They're trying to take the boy," Amand shouted, pointing with finger bearing a gleaming red gem set in a fat ring of gold. "Stop them!"

Ulfrik launched himself at the Count while drawing his sword. Behind the count a group of guards swarmed forward in the doorway. Ulfrik slammed into the Count with his shoulder, sending him back into the door which crashed shut in the face of the advancing guard. One man tried to stop it, and his hand was caught between the door and the jamb. His screams reverberated through the door. The bishop side-stepped as if avoiding a puddle of mud, but before he could scream Engilbert clamped his hand over the bishop's mouth and wrestled him away from the struggle.

Count Amand's hand sought to grab Ulfrik's dagger while he kept the door pinned shut with the Count's body. The hand fought against the door, four fingers wriggling like fleshy worms, and others battered from the other side. Ulfrik's actions had led to a stalemate, and his priority now became keeping the guards at bay. He raised his short sword and hacked at the fingers. Two flew away and blood sprayed over Count Amand's head, brilliant red flecks in his white hair. The guard beyond screamed, and Ulfrik cut again, shaving off another finger and finally slamming the door shut. He had to release the Count for a his next move.

"Vilhjalmer, help me," he called over his shoulder. "Use your dagger."

He released Amand, who toppled away in his struggles. Ulfrik then slammed the door tight and fed his sword through the arms used to hold the bar lock of the door. He whirled around and caught Vilhjalmer losing his wrestling match with the Count as he bent Vilhjalmer's dagger aside. Ulfrik drew his last dagger from his boot and plunged it into Amand's back. The old Count stiffened with a howl and toppled onto his face. Vilhjalmer scrambled away then turned on the prostrate Count to drive his own dagger into his back beside Ulfrik's.

"Good work," Ulfrik said, breathless. "You're a man today."

"I am!" Vilhjalmer said his blood-flecked face brightening. "I'm glad the old bastard is dead."

"Help me," Engilbert hissed. He danced around with the Bishop, and Ulfrik would have laughed at the sight of two priest in black and white robes wrestling. The bishop's eyes were wide with horror as Ulfrik yanked the dagger out of Amand's back. "Sweet Jesus, don't kill him!"

Flipping the dagger around in his grip, he slammed the pommel into the bishop's temple. The old man went slack, but was still conscious. Ulfrik hit his two more times before he slumped. Engilbert fell back and made the sign of the cross. The bishop seemed dead, but Ulfrik guessed he might be dead. He had no time to decide as the guards at the door were battering it.

"Where's the bar for that lock?"

"That door hasn't been locked for years. I don't know."

Ulfrik cursed the loss of his sword, as well as his disguise. His guard surcoat was splattered in gore. He grabbed Vilhjalmer and leveled his dagger at Engilbert. "Show us the fastest way out. Now!"

The old priest yelped and began running back the way they had come. Once inside the main hall he ran for the front doors where a few people had gathered in thoughtful silence. All along their route priests fell aside in horror, clutching their chests as if their hearts might fall out. They sprinted down the main aisle of the prayer hall and burst out of the double doors. All the sounds and odors of Paris slapped him in the face as they spilled down the stairs, Engilbert trailing behind. "Don't lose me. Wibert must be freed."

They dashed into the street, and Ulfrik's bloodied appearance caused people to fall away, and a group of three women screamed. He was about to tear off his surcoat when a guard in the same uniform ran up to them. He was a tall man with a narrow head and untrustworthy eyes, and he halted in front of Ulfrik with a look of horror. "What has happened to you?"

"No time to explain," Ulfrik said. "We must get this boy to the north gates."

The guard stared at him in confusion. "What accent is that?"

"I'm a Burgundian, alright? We can trade family history later. We have to hurry."

The guard stared at him then to Engilbert. "What's this about?"

"As he says, the boy is in grave danger. Help us clear the way." Engilbert placed a hand on the guard's shoulders. "You are doing god's work, son."

The guard glanced at Vilhjalmer then turned on his heel, drawing his sword and roaring at the crowd. "Get back! Clear us a path."

They rushed along with their new guard. Ulfrik appreciated the escort but needed to shake him before he attracted less gullible guards. As they trotted along, the sea of people parting for them, Ulfrik pulled at the guard's surcoat. "Wait, we can cut this way. It's faster."

Pointing at a side alley, he smiled hopefully at the guard, who stared down the alleyway. He slowly turned toward him, sword held against his leg. "I don't know what they call a short-cut in Burgundia, my friend, but this is not one. Are you a guard and you even a priest?"

In answer to the question, the bell from the church began to clang wildly behind them. The crowd remained parted but did not disperse. Like ravens they anticipated violence and a dead bodies for picking over. The guard tilted his narrow head at the sound, and his eyes lit up in understanding.

"You fucking liar," he said, lifting his sword with both hands on the grip. "Stay where you are."

He dropped one hand to his side and began patting his leg. When he did not find what he sought he glanced down. Vilhjalmer instead lifted a horn up to him. "Looking for this?"

The guard's alarm horn had a cut strap that trailed from Vilhjalmer's hand. He smiled triumphantly, but the guard merely scowled then shouted. "Alarm! Call for the guard!"

The crowd closed in on them, and Ulfrik drew his dagger. "Nice job, Vilhjalmer. But next time lift his sword instead."

59

The guard stalked closer to Ulfrik while Engilbert cowered behind, babbling to God for deliverance or some such nonsense. The warning bell tolled and the cluster of people drew closer for a better look at what they supposed would be the uncommon spectacle of killing a guard and priest then arresting a boy. Ulfrik thought the guard's form was an insult, holding his sword too high and exposing himself to an easy strike.

Rather than mock the guard as he might have, he had to recapture lost time. The surrounding crowd was not deep but calls for guards had rippled out like waves on a lake. He slid his feet wide and felt his center of power low in his hips, and when the guard inched closer Ulfrik struck like a flash of lightning. He ducked under the sword, drove his dagger to the hilt in the guard's ribs, then relieved him of his sword. The guard collapsed with a gasp and blood rushed into a puddle on the street.

Engilbert cried out. "God, please no more killing!"

Vilhjalmer clapped his hands together. "Marvelous! I want you to teach me how that is done!"

With a laugh, Ulfrik tore his surcoat off then ranged his newly acquired sword at the crowd. "Back away or you'll get cut."

The crowd melted like snow before a torch, but one large man stood his ground. He was wide with a nose broken too many times and a flat head made flatter by greasy hair clinging to it. "You're not one of us. You can't kill our people."

Ulfrik flung the bloody surcoat over the brute's head and in the moment of confusion cut deep into his leg. The brute growled then crumbled, and Ulfrik yanked Vilhjalmer into the alleyway. The crowd screamed in indignation, and four or five of them gave chase. Ulfrik had no idea where he ran, only that he had to put distance between his pursuers while keeping Vilhjalmer in his grip. The boy laughed in glee as he kept pace. "This is fun!"

"Gods, lad! Our lives are at stake!" He also gritted his teeth the pain in his legs as he ran, but held that to himself.

Engilbert dropped behind them, and then there was a huge crash. Ulfrik turned to see he had knocked over barrels and crates into the alley they had just exited. They continued to run until the stitch in Ulfrik's side became unbearable. They rounded a corner into a quiet street and regrouped. Engilbert collapsed to the ground while Ulfrik leaned on his knees. Vilhjalmer, with his youthful vigor, danced in circles around them. "What an adventure! My father will not believe all we've done."

"Keep the details from your father," Ulfrik wheezed. "No need to give him more gray hair."

Pedestrians stopped seeing Engilbert on the ground, but Ulfrik grunted at them and hoisted Engilbert to his feet. The old priest dusted off the seat of his black robes. "Take me to Wibert now. I've done all you've asked."

"You've done more than I expected," Ulfrik said. "If I live through this, I will be sure the skalds add your name to the songs that will be sung of this deed."

Engilbert's lips wrinkled in a disgusted grimace. "Dear God, have mercy upon me."

They returned to the streets, joining the flow of traffic until Ulfrik felt anonymous once more. The bell tolled in the background, but no one around him paid it any attention. At last, he stopped and got his bearings. "Priest, I do not know this city well. We are to meet Wibert and my young friend in the northeast section by a row of destroyed buildings. I'm trying to navigate by the sun, but these cursed streets funnel me in the opposite direction."

The priest gave a long sight and began to trudge back the way they had come. "Wibert had best be alive after all I have done."

"Bold words," Ulfrik said, sticking close behind Engilbert with Vilhjalmer at his side. "What will you do if he is dead?"

The priest remained quiet but Ulfrik saw his ears turning red. Time was running out and the alarm bell might have put Finn on edge, particularly with all the other tasks Ulfrik had left to him. It would be a shame if he had killed Wibert given how arduously Engilbert had worked to save his friend's life. As they wended through streets the bell stopped ringing and only the hum of city life remained. Ulfrik remained alert of betrayal or discovery, but pedestrians flowed around them while lost in their own concerns. At last they came to the row of burnt-out buildings.

"These have never been rebuilt since your kind failed to defeat our city years ago." Engilbert tilted his chin up in pride as they regarded the row of jagged timbers and piles of debris.

"Then your people are lazy," Ulfrik said. "That mess has been sitting there over ten years."

They circled the ruins, having to dodge a pair of guards rushing through the streets. By now Ulfrik expected the bishop had recovered to tell his story and guards would be combing the city for him. It was still early afternoon and the guards had plenty of light by which to search. They stepped out from behind a corner and approached the ruins. Finn whistled within the most intact building.

"You made it out," he said, the excitement in his voice straining to remain hushed. "Guards are looking for you everywhere. What happened?"

"We had a few diversions but here's Vilhjalmer." Hrolf's son stood straighter and Finn bowed low, then his freckled face reddened when Ulfrik smirked at him.

"Well, his father is the strongest jarl in the land. Well met, Vilhjalmer, you'll be remaining close to me."

Hrolf's son turned a skeptical eye at him, "I prefer to stay with Ulfrik, if it's all the same. He's an amazing fighter."

"Where's Wibert?" Engilbert brushed past Ulfrik to confront Finn. "You had best not harmed him."

"He's fine, if a bit bored." Finn motioned him forward. "He's against the post in here."

The priest grew still and seemed to shrink. Ulfrik grabbed Engilbert's arm in case he decided to run, and he yelped. Ulfrik dragged him to where Finn gestured, and Father Wibert sat tied to a post with a cloth in his mouth and a welt under his left eye. Finn put both hands on his hips. "Told you he's fine. He just got a little hard to handle, so I tied him up."

"Well untie him," Engilbert said, his courage inflating him back into form. "I've done everything you demanded."

"That you have, but you can't be reunited just yet."Ulfrik tightened his grip on Engilbert's arm. "I've got to get out of the city, then you can be freed. Wibert will remain tied here for you to release later."

"How long will that be?"

"Of course, I will need the cover of night to mask my escape. I'm sure he'll be fine until then."

Father Engilbert sagged once again and Wibert struggled against his bonds. Ulfrik turned his attention to Finn. "You've done as I've instructed?"

"Everything is ready."

"Then show me to the passage under the wall."

"You know about that?" Father Engilbert asked.

Ulfrik nodded. "Is that passage widely known?"

Father Engilbert fell quiet, and Ulfrik yanked him hard to loosen his tongue. "Well, some of the priests know of it. I've known of it for a while."

"No matter, the plans are already set. Vilhjalmer, you must do what Finn instructs. Everyone depends upon your doing exactly as he tells you."

Vilhjalmer straightened up and patted his dagger, looking like a miniature version of his father. "We will have nothing less than victory."

"What will Wibert do?" Engilbert asked. "It's dangerous out at night. What should he do if he's discovered?"

"The same thing we will do," Ulfrik said. "Pray."

60

Ulfrik cursed the bright moonlight that flooded the city in silver light. Where the streets were in shadow the darkness was so complete he could not see his hand before his face, and where an opening appeared the moon blazed like cold fire. Without the benefit of torchlight, he had to inch along with a hand on the walls of buildings, and Father Engilbert and the others behind him clutched the hem of the man's shirt in front. The darkness of a city at night was more complete than even the thickest forest, and Ulfrik had discovered another cause to detest these large cities.

"Hold," he whispered, facing a small church. It sat across a wide street that was bathed in light. "There's the door, but we'll be completely exposed while getting to it. Stay in formation, but move swiftly."

He waited for Engilbert to tap his shoulder then they scurried across the open street like a giant centipede, four hunched shapes linked together. Ulfrik crossed into the darkness of the door, and checked that the others had disappeared into the shadows of the wall. He saw points of orange light from towers and had seen torchlight in the distance, but for now no one approached. He pushed on the door and it opened with a gentle swish.

Again Father Engilbert had proved invaluable; he had negotiated payment to this church for use of the passage this night. So not only was the door opened, but inside he found an candle burning in a dull iron holder next to the trapdoor on the floor. Ulfrik patted the priest's arm. "You know, you have served me well. I'd say your life here is ruined. Why not continue on with me? I could use a man of your skills."

In the fluttering light of the candle, Engilbert's face contorted with a frown. "A life among barbarians is worse the penance the Bishop will assign me."

"You aided the murder of royalty," Ulfrik said as casually as if discussing a favorite hunting spot. "I bet the Count's family will want blood for that, and it sure won't be mine. Wibert might get away with the hostage excuse, but not you. Well, it's your choice. You go down first."

He popped open the trap door and held it for Engilbert, who stared at the quiet darkness in absolute defeat. Ulfrik had not meant to ruin the priest's life, but he was honest in his appraisal of his chances. Killing him outright might be kinder to him if he refused to join. For now, he watched the old priest clamber down the ladder with the candle held in one hand. The globe of light shrank until he reached the bottom, where it swayed around as Engilbert checked the room. His whisper echoed in the tunnel. "It's just me and rats down here."

"Alright, you two next," Ulfrik said, helping the cloaked and hooded figures down. When they were halfway, he drew his own hood over his head, and disappeared into the tunnel.

At the bottom all four of them were crowded into a space large enough for three men. Engilbert had been pushed into the small tunnel. "Give me the candle and I will lead the way. He drew his dagger, a sword useless in such cramped quarters, and squeezed into the lead position. The candle smoke filled the tunnel that must have been dug by children. It was all dirt, supported at intervals with wooden beams, and plunged down into darkness. Ulfrik imagined dwarfs living deep in the earth, and a chill came to his hands. He had not considered how the restricting earth and unremitting darkness would gnaw at his guts as he journeyed deeper underground. Soon the tunnel leveled out for a dozen feet before sharply inclining. He doubled his effort to climb out of this evil place and promised himself he would never travel under the earth again.

"We're at the end," he said, his voice flat and dead in the tight earthen confines. "I can't imagine smuggling women through this. Their hair must be full of dirt and worms by the time they get to the church."

He placed his hand against the ladder leading up to a trapdoor, then tested the rungs with his foot. He handed the candle to Engilbert. "I'll go first, then help the rest of you out."

He scaled the ladder without difficulty, though the rungs sagged under his weight. He stretched to place his ear against the trapdoor, but heard nothing other than the beating of his own heart. With a gentle shove the door opened a crack and sand fell into his face. He turned aside as the trapdoor opened, dropping more dirt, then climbed out into the promised cover of bushes and trees. The gurgle of the Seine and its mucky scent greeted his arrival. He let the trapdoor down carefully, then leaned his head into the opening. "Pass the candle to the man behind as you climb out, then the last one extinguish it. The walls are close, and we don't want to mark ourselves for the guards."

"They look away from what happens here," Engilbert said as he climbed next. "I believe they actually anticipate activity since they extort the church for their silence."

"You know much about these dealing. I wonder if you have your hand in the pot as well?" Ulfrik hauled Engilbert out, then the remaining two, until all were hooded dark shapes crouched in the bushes. The rowboat was beached ten feet away, and the Seine was a glistening black strip behind it.

He stood straight and motioned for them to follow. No sooner had he stepped out of the trees did the dark shapes of other men follow him out as well.

His heart skipped a beat and his stomach burned. A dozen men had crouched in the same bushes, waiting patiently in ambush. He heard the clink of iron, saw the flashes of moonlight on drawn blades, and realized a perfect ring had formed around them. The dagger in his hand also caught a spark of moonlight, but it was the wrong weapon for a fight against the swords and spears arrayed against him. Engilbert shouted in surprise and tripped back into the bushes with a rustling crash.

The laughter was cold and deep, and the giant shape of one of the men stepped into the moonlight. He was broad-shouldered in a shining mail coat, and he moved like wolf on the prowl. A long braid of hair hung to his waist. Grimnr the Mountain had found him.

"How did you find me here?"

Grimnr laughed again, putting a giant hand over his belly. "From you, of course. My men spotted your young friend over there," he pointed past Ulfrik. "Earlier in the day and it did not take me long to guess where you planned to escape. The gates are all watched and the entire city is looking for your group. An old Northman with a boy, a priest, and a runt make an easy mark. Where else could you flee?"

Ulfrik bowed his head. "I knew I should not have trusted this way out."

"You didn't leave yourself any choice," Grimnr said as if he sympathized with Ulfrik's plight. "Killing a Frankish Count in a church gets a lot of attention. The nobles don't want to believe they're that easy to kill. They're burning for justice."

"And you'll give it to them?" Ulfrik glanced at the rowboat. While he could reach it, he'd never get the boat launched fast enough. He might be able to back down the tunnel, but not with everyone else to consider.

"I don't care about justice for nobles. I am here for honor, something you wouldn't understand."

"It is honor that has carried me this far. I have sworn an oath to Hrolf to see his son saved. A man who cannot keep his oath is worth less than dust."

Grimnr inclined is head. "We both agree on that. But it seems you won't be keeping that promise. I've taken my best men with me, and you're surrounded. If you cough too hard you'll stick yourself on our spears. You've made a worthy effort, and you can be proud of it. But now you will hand over Vilhjalmer to me."

"Why? The Count is dead and you owe nothing to anyone. Join

with me and return to Hrolf. Strong men are always welcomed to fight the Franks."

"Don't imagine Hrolf would be forgiving of me."

"I will vouch for you and Hrolf will understand. These Franks, you must realize, they are defeated. You fight for the losing side, no matter how many Northmen say otherwise. Our people have been set back in recent years, true. But we are the strongest of any nation. Our people are taking over the world, Grimnr. I have traveled almost all of it, and everywhere we chose to make our own we are victorious. Frankia will be no different. Hrolf will sit inside these walls one day soon, and a wise man would befriend him now."

Ulfrik searched the shadows of Grimnr' men, but they remained cloaked in darkness. Grimnr himself had not shifted, holding the point of his drawn sword in the ground. He raised it to point at the boy. "You make a fine speech, but that boy is worth a prince's ransom. I'll take Hrolf's gold and conquer some other land. No more delays. Hand over the boy."

Grimnr's eyes glittered in the dark as he waited in triumph. Ulfrik, however, began to laugh.

"What do you to laugh at?"

Ulfrik cleared his throat then beckoned the boy and his guardian forward. "I knew men would be watching us, and guessed you might have joined such a hunt. I have hard news for you. Both Finn and Vilhjalmer left via the West Gate this afternoon. By now they are on a ship sailing back to Hrolf. No one was searching for a man and his brother returning to their country home, but for a priest with two men and a boy."

He thrust the two figures forward and pulled back their hoods. "Here you have two beggars. The small one is actually a girl. I paid their mother in good silver to risk their lives in this gamble. Any spy watching for us would see exactly what he expected, and I would misdirect him to where I wanted. As long as my pursuers chased us through the city, Vilhjalmer would never be in danger."

Grimnr stared, his eyes wide in the moonlight. He roared like a bear, his voice echoing off the walls of Paris. The two beggars shrank to Ulfrik's side and he gathered them behind, even though the ring of enemies grumbled with anger.

"You cunning bastard!" He punched the air with his free hand and swung his sword in frustration. "You played out this ruse to the very end, even tried to convince me to join you."

"That offer still holds. You should serve me, Grimnr."

"Serve you?" Grimnr pointed his sword at him. "You should be begging me for your life."

"You left your camp with your best men," Ulfrik said, slowly herding the beggars behind him toward the trap door. "Before I departed for Paris, I sent word to Mord and Einar to attack again. Perhaps only the Franks will resist, but the rest of your army will scatter, at least those who have not died from disease yet. I would guess this handful of men with you will be all that remains of your command. I wonder how you will pay them for their loyalty? Count Amand's coffers will be closed to you now."

Grimnr bowed his head and his sword lowered. For a moment Ulfrik thought he would surrender to common sense, but the giant man slowly raised his head and a snarl contorted his face. "I hope you enjoyed your victory, for now you die."

61

Father Engilbert and the beggars behind Ulfrik screamed in terror as the surrounding enemies closed their ring around them. Their voices filled the moonlit night, and if this did not bring attention from the wall guards nothing else would. He had no chance to check the wall, as Grimnr closed with his sword flashing blue light. Ulfrik, still holding only a dagger, dropped to a fighting crouch.

"Is this how a man of honor defeats his enemies?" he asked. "Surround him like a wild boar and letting his dogs do the dangerous work."

Grimnr pulled up short as if awakening to his actions. "Halt," he called to his men. "He's right. This is for my honor, not murder."

Ulfrik relaxed his stance. "You'll allow me a real sword, not this cheap knife?"

"If you have one, draw it. Don't expect me to give you one."

Satisfied, Ulfrik sheathed his dagger and drew the Frankish short sword. He tested its weight and made a few cutting arcs to learn its balance. Franks made good weapons, but those went mostly to their nobles. This blade would serve for one fight, but not more. "This is between us. Let the priest and the beggars go."

"More conditions? You are an arrogant man."

"Actually one more condition. If I kill you in this duel, I want your men to swear I will be free to leave unharmed."

Grimnr's chuckle was slow and deep. "I've seen you fight. You're good but not better than me. Still, it is not an unfair request." He turned to his men, and pointed his sword at them. "The priest and beggars are not our concern, so leave them. If I am killed in this duel, none of you avenge me and leave Ulfar the White unharmed."

Speaking in Frankish, Ulfrik repeated Grimnr's promise to Engilbert. "You are free to do what you think is best," he said to the priest, then glanced at the rowboat. He scanned the ground and located what he sought, then turned to Grimnr. "It is dark and the footing poor here. I suggest we hold our duel over there where the ground is more level and the moonlight falls evenly."

Grimnr did not check, but merely agreed. The giant man was stronger than Ulfrik, had a better reach, a better sword, and wore a mail coat. He did not need to check since no rational man would imagine Ulfrik defeating Grimnr the Mountain. He was a fierce warrior who cut a bloody path through his enemies. Grimnr the Mountain was a king of the battlefield, and it showed in his swagger as they relocated to the spot Ulfrik had chosen.

"I'm sorry we could not have been friends," Ulfrik said, gripping his short sword with one hand.

"As am I. But too much has come between us. It's a sad day when one so skilled must be sent to his doom. Now prepare to journey to the feasting hall."

Grimnr struck in a flash of moonlight reflected from his longsword. Ulfrik knew Grimnr's penchant for a decisive killing strike, and knew a man of his strength and size could deliver one from the start. So we faded left and the blade cut the air. Grimnr had too much experience to overextend himself, but Ulfrik had repositioned him.

They squared off again, this time Grimnr placing both hands on his blade and taking a careful measure of Ulfrik's stance. He jabbed at Ulfrik's outstretched sword, testing his guard. Each time he gave a little ground and Grimnr closed it. Ulfrik returned a low strike, forcing Grimnr to block, but it was a diversion for Ulfrik unpin his cloak. He now held it to his neck with his left hand.

He struck a flurry of blows at Grimnr, none striking flesh, but forcing him to watch his sword as Ulfrik continued to shift back. Grimnr charged in with a roar and his blade shoved Ulfrik back as he parried. He felt his heels strike the knee-high, jagged rock he had found earlier.

Rather than stumble, he smiled, then waited for the follow up strike. When Grimnr jabbed again, Ulfrik tore the cloak from his shoulders and slung it at Grimnr's sword.

The heavy wool wrapped the sword and dragged it down. Ulfrik dropped his weapon, grabbed the other end of the cloak, then leapt up on the rock behind him. Grimnr stumbled forward, still entwined in the cloak, and Ulfrik jumped off the back of the rock.

Grimnr's chest crashed onto the rock with a crunch of mail and his face struck with a wet crack.

Ulfrik lifted his foot then stomped down on Grimnr's head. He heard bone snap and Grimnr's grunt as his neck broke. The men around them, formerly silent, now groaned with sympathetic pain. Ulfrik brought his foot down a second time, and he saw the rush of blood black in the moonlight and heard the gut-churning crunch of Grimnr's skull breaking.

Ulfrik stepped back and stared at Grimnr's form slumped over the rock, his cloak-wrapped sword dropped to the grass beneath his limp hand. He felt for a pulse in his neck, but Grimnr the Mountain was no more.

"That was not fair," said one of the men. Others began to grumble as well.

"You didn't even use a sword. What kind of duel was that?"

Retrieving his sword from the grass, Ulfrik started for the river. "Remember Grimnr's promise. I'm to be let free."

"Not for killing him like an animal," said one and the others shouted in agreement. Ulfrik dashed for the water, sinking into the mud and wading out to the Seine.

A spear flew after him and splashed into the water, but already the rowboat emerged out of the dark. Ulfrik flopped to it, and threw himself over the side.

"I thought you might abandon me," Ulfrik said to Engilbert, who was frantically rowing.

"If you die your friend will kill Wibert." A spear thudded into the side of the boat, then dropped into the water. Engilbert threw himself flat. "You row!"

Ulfrik grabbed the oars and left Grimnr's men stranded on the shore, screaming for justice. "I guess the guards really don't care what happens beneath their walls."

"Just tell me this nightmare is over now," Engilbert said, his voice muffled as he huddled against the bottom of the rowboat.

"It just might be done." The oars were like the wings of a gull taking off from the water and their rowboat sped toward the opposite shore. "Pray to your god those men don't find another boat to cross the river. Otherwise, Father, we both have our prayers answered this night."

62

By dawn of the next day, Ulfrik had journeyed up the south bank of the Seine to rendezvous with Gunnar's ship. He rowed up to the hull where Finn and Gunnar both hailed him from the rails as a crewman extended an oar aid him in climbing aboard. He stood in the rocking boat and steadied himself with the oar before turning to Engilbert. "You won't come?"

The priest lowered his head. "Wibert needs me."

"You'll be blamed for what happened. Can you help your friend when you're dead? If you stay with me, then you have a chance to do some good."

"No, I am returning to Paris. God knows the reasons for my sins, and His judgment alone is all I fear.'"

Ulfrik nodded. "What is Wibert to you? He is more than a friend."

"He's my son," Engilbert said, looking toward the far shore. "You are the first one to know that truth, and I don't even like you. Even Wibert doesn't know."

He clambered over the rails of Gunnar's ship to welcoming pats from Finn, then he leaned over the rails to salute Engilbert. "I wouldn't have guessed that, but protecting a son is a noble task. Good luck to you. I don't think we shall meet again."

"God willing I will never see another of your kind for the rest of my days." Engilbert began to row for the shore, and Ulfrik turned with a huge smile to greet Finn and Vilhjalmer.

"No troubles getting out of Paris?"

"It was boring," Vilhjalmer said, hands on his hips. "We just paid a gate tax and walked out. You had all the adventure."

Ulfrik laughed but both Finn and Gunnar gave him a serious look. "Grimnr the Mountain has fallen. As expected, he had men watching us and waited in ambush when we emerged from the tunnel. I killed him in a duel."

"There should be a few good stories from that," Gunnar said. "But save them for Hrolf's hall. We sail straight for it."

They hugged the southern shore of the Seine as they approached Count Amand's camp. Already they founds ships in disarray and depleted. Smoke hazed the river, filling their noses with the scents of burning wood. As they glided past the docks, they were ignored by any Norse ship still on the water. The camp was heavy in smoke, but the fortress beyond it appeared unscathed and blue and white pennants still fluttered from the towers.

"Einar and Mord either finished the traitor camp or they revolted," Gunnar said.

"Probably both," Ulfrik said, leaning on the rail beside Gunnar as he worked the tiller. He stared down at Gunnar's hook hand and nodded. "That seems to work quite well. Made it yourself?"

He shook his head, his dark curly hair falling across his eyes. "Gunther One-Eye had a blacksmith who helped design it for me. Even in a storm it holds fast, maybe better than a real hand."

"Gunther, eh?"

"He helped with a lot of things after you died. He lost an eye and knows how losing a body part affect a man. Seemed like he was the only one at that time who understood how I felt after I thought you dead. He understood how hot the fire of revenge burned, and how missing a hand made if feel like I would never lead a crew of my own."

Ulfrik nodded, then held out his left hand. "Well, I lost a finger."

"I noticed. That's must have hit you hard. It was your favorite one to stick up your nose."

They laughed together and Ulfrik's heart was feather-light for the rest of the journey to Hrolf's hall. By late afternoon they arrived to a throng of guards waiting for them at the shore. Once in safe waters, Gunnar let the current and wind carry them the rest of the journey. Fishermen they met along the way sped ahead to relay the news. Now Ulfrik stood with Vilhjalmer between him and Finn, and placed a hand on the boy's shoulder.

"Are you excited to return home?"

Vilhjalmer shrugged. "There were some boring parts, but this was an excellent adventure. I don't think my mother would ever let me do this again."

"Nor would your father," Ulfrik said, patting the back of Vilhjalmer's head. "Nor would I, for that matter. A lot of blood was spilled on your account."

"But they were the enemy, so no matter."

"Spoken like a true noble," Finn said dryly. He exchanged a glance with Ulfrik over Vilhjalmer's head.

"Your mother still believes you were with Mord," Ulfrik said. "Or at least that was how I left matters. I think it's best you keep this adventure a secret between us."

"Then how will skalds sing of our deeds?"

"That will be for you to solve if you succeed your father one day. For now, enjoy the secret."

At last Gunnar steered his ship to dock and set the gangplank down. Hrolf and his wife, Poppa, waited at the end of the dock with rows of armored guards behind them. Always the giant in any crowd, Hrolf appeared especially tall next to his petite and retiring wife. Ulfrik helped Vilhjalmer to the gangplank, then let him proceed ahead. They walked together, Ulfrik's chest bursting with pride at the fulfillment of his task. Hrolf struggled to keep himself in check as Vilhjalmer bowed dutifully. "Father, Mother, I have returned."

Hrolf simply patted his son's head, but Ulfrik was certain he caught a glimpse of wet eyes. Poppa, his wife, gathered Vilhjalmer to her side and enfolded him with graceful arms, then she turned toward the hall with a dozen maids and as many guards falling in behind him. Now Ulfrik approached Hrolf and went to his knee.

"Your son is returned unharmed," he said. "And I have other news as well. Both Count Amand and Grimnr the Mountain are no more."

He dared to glance up. Hrolf studied him with a furrowed brow. He seized Ulfrik with both hands and lifted him to his feet, gripping him by his shirt so close that Ulfrik could smell the faint scent of mead on his breath.

"He got to Paris?" Hrolf's face was incredulous, and Ulfrik could only nod in confirmation. "And you slipped inside to complete the task I assigned you?"

"And I killed Count Amand in a church and broke Grimnr the Mountain's neck over a rock beneath the walls of Paris."

Hrolf's face trembled, then he crushed Ulfrik into an bear hug. He squeezed hard enough to drive out Ulfrik's breath. "Gods, man, I love you. You have done all that I asked and more, and kicked those Franks right in the stones while you did it."

Hrolf led Ulfrik with an arm over his shoulder at the back of the procession to the hall. For the evening's welcome feast Hrolf slaughtered a heifer and invited hirdmen and tradesmen both to the celebration. Vilhjalmer's kidnapping was kept silent, but Hrolf positioned the event as a celebration of Count Amand's defeat and the dissolution of the traitor camp. Ulfrik sat at Hrolf's left hand, where Gunther One-Eye had traditionally sat. Gunther had apparently gone to help Mord with the surprise attack. Runa, Aren, and all the others yet remained at Eyrafell.

By the time the reveling had calmed, a cool night breeze was blowing through the hall. Ulfrik was hot with drink and the roaring hearth fire that bathed the room in a golden glow. Hrolf had been gregarious throughout the evening, talking with everyone and toasting everything he could imagine. Now with Gunnar and Finn having joined them at the high table after Poppa and attendants had retired, Hrolf gathered them close.

"I promised you a reward for your service," Hrolf said. "You deserve more than I can give you right now. But take over Konalsvik, give it a new name and a new garrison. I will send men to seed your ranks, but in time you will find more. It is an important location, but it has seen no action. Do not get comfortable there, as I will move you closer to the borders where honor dictates you should be. As for gold, take whatever Konal left behind, then tell me what it was and I shall match it. You will not be poor, not for all you have done for me."

Ulfrik blinked at the generosity. "You do me too much honor."

"Don't say it. Who else could have freed my son while cutting the legs out from the Franks?"

"That credit should be placed at the feet of Einar and Mord. They led the attacks that routed the enemy."

"And you cut off the enemy's head. Do not underestimate what the loss of leadership does to them. The fortress still stands, but without an army to occupy it and ships to protect it from flanking attacks, we'll smash it to splinters."

Ulfrik looked between Gunnar and Finn, both smiling like two children receiving Yuletide presents. Gunnar rapped the table before his father. "Will you allow my ship to dock with you while we figure out what to do next?"

"Of course, but I hope your plans involve raiding Franks and not sailing off again. I'm going to need experienced fighters."

"If there's gold to be had, you won't find any protest from my crew."

They spent the rest of the evening in celebration. Once men had crawled away to sleep in a corner, Hrolf stood and stretched. "I will retire now. Tomorrow, I expect you will want to rejoin your family. Give them my thanks, especially to your wife. She is a rare woman, and as brave as she is unruly."

"That she is,' Ulfrik agreed.

Hrolf paused and placed a warm hand on Ulfrik's shoulder. "I can scarcely believe you still live. No man returns from his own funeral, but you did. Since we first met so many years ago, I have always believed you brought me luck. These years have been hard. I've lost territory and allies. But you have returned and already brought me a victory, I think the gods have shown I will prevail in this struggle. No matter how long it takes, we will drive the Franks back and make this a place where all our brothers can live united under a king of their own kind. Your return is the start of that time."

He squeezed Ulfrik's shoulder and staggered toward his room. Ulfrik watched his king go, but thought only of finding his home once more.

63

Eyrafell had seemed much smaller when Ulfrik had first visited Einar's fortress. He attributed that to his narrow focus at the time, but today he saw how large it actually was. High walls encompassed four quadrants packed with buildings filled with tradesmen and warriors, and the town bustled with life. Einar led him through the streets, pointing out buildings or other points of especial pride. He walked with a crutch, the arrow wound in the back of his leg still raw. He often stood on one foot and pointed with the crutch, swinging it in an arc that made some of his men duck. Finn was close at his heels, asking all sorts of questions about the town that Einar was too happy to answer.

They made for the main hall, with Einar between him and Gunnar and a line of crew and guards behind them. Ulfrik had more time to note the similarities between Ravndal and Eyrafell. He agreed with some of the changes to the design, while other things he would have chosen differently. Since Eyrafell had held the borders against the Franks, he could not be too critical.

"Runa and Bera have been preparing a feast all day," Gunnar said. "Our wives must be the two best cooks in the entire world. Do you smell that from here?"

"That's a taste I've sorely missed."

"My mouth is watering," Finn said from behind. "I could eat a whale."

The doors to the hall were opened and arrayed before them was his family. Their memories had been all that had sustained him for so many arduous years; to see them in the flesh again made his legs weak. Runa stood before his sons, Aren and Hakon, and she welcomed him with opened arms. He began walking, then jogging, and finally grabbing Runa into his arms and lifting her into the air with a squeal. The people gathered at the hall cheered and Ulfrik kissed her like he had on the day of their wedding.

He set her down, embraced Aren, then grabbed Hakon by his shoulders. "Gods son, you do look a lot like me. You grew into a man while I was gone."

Hakon had no words, but hugged his father and slapped him on the back. Behind them Snorri hobbled out of the dark hall, leaning on a walking staff.

"Here's a day I never dreamed of, lad. I'm glad these old eyes still see enough to welcome you home."

Ulfrik braced arms with his oldest friend and mentor. Snorri appeared so old and frail that he might shatter in a bear hug. Yet he pulled Ulfrik close and squeezed him with all the strength of a man half his age. Ulfrik laughed. "It is good to be home again, old friend."

A long night of feasting and stories ensued. Finn, who had befriended Runa and Aren, assimilated into the family like an old companion, and shared every embarrassing story of Ulfrik that he could recall. Of all the feasts he had ever held, this was the sweetest. So when the night grew quiet and only moonlight lit Eyrafell, Ulfrik stood in the doorway of the hall contemplating the long journey's end.

"What are you thinking?" Runa slipped her arm around his waist as she joined him in the doorway. They both stared up at the summer moon.

"I've spent much time remembering," he said. "So much that I've forgotten how to think for tomorrow."

Runa chuckled. "I doubt that very much. Your heart has ever been set on tomorrow."

"Yes, but I am starting over again. It will take years to climb back to where I was before Konal and Throst tore me down. I'm getting older, and the wounds don't go away like they used to. Actually, injuries I had thought gone have returned."

His wife squeezed him but kept her thoughts hidden. He kissed her head, enjoying her sweet scent.

"Hrolf was generous in his reward," he said. "But it is nothing compared to what I had before all this happened. I visited all my treasure hoards, but they've been looted or lost. Even my grave was dug up, and so the best part of my fortune gone with it."

Runa pulled away, then took his hand and placed a leather pouch in it. She folded his fingers over it, and he felt the hard gemstones underneath. His heart leapt and he stepped back, staring at the pouch. "Is this what I think it is?"

"I kept them, but did not know what to do with them. I was going to split them among the boys. Konal found the jewels eventually, and either kept them on his body or hid them in a loose rock in the well. Everything is in the pouch, every gem. Konal called it treasure enough to build a kingdom. That should help restore some of the wealth lost."

Ulfrik blinked, weighing the bag in both hands. "I think it won't be long before I retake Ravndal. You will dress in gold and jewels and sit on a chair inlaid with walrus ivory. I am certain with you at my side again, the future is ours to rule."

Runa's laughter was like the chiming of silver, and he kissed her again. When they pulled apart, she cupped his face in her hands and whispered, "Welcome home."

AUTHOR'S NOTE

Hrolf the Strider was said to have taken Poppa of Bayeux as either his mistress or wife. He was to have captured her while on raid in Bayeux sometime between 885 and 889. Poppa's father is assumed to be Berengar II, making her Frankish nobility. The details of Hrolf's relationship with Poppa are not well known. Hrolf would eventually take a second wife, but this marriage might have been for political reasons and in fact might not have ever occurred.

Poppa did bear Hrolf two children. The firstborn was a son, Vilhjalmer Langaspjot Hrolfsson, better known to history as William Longsword. Years later she would bear Hrolf a daughter named Geirlaug who would go by the name Adela and eventually marry the future duke of Aquitaine. Vilhjalmer was said to have still been a pagan in his youth, though his mother was clearly Christian. Little else is known of his life or attitudes of his younger days. His role in history would come many years later. Hrolf's most famous descendant, however, would be William the Conqueror.

The entire account of taking Vilhjalmer hostage, Count Amand, and the gathering of a Norse "traitor" army along the Seine is entirely fictional. However, during this period the Viking position along the Seine was at a standstill. The Franks had not succeeded in ejecting the Northmen, and the Northmen had no significant progress against the Franks in this area. There are still many years of struggle ahead, but the dawning of Normandy is now closer than ever. Ulfrik will be heading into a period of tumult just at the time he could use stability to rebuild himself. His future is fraught with peril, both from within and without.

∼

If you would like to know when my next book is released, please sign up for my new release newsletter. I will send you an email when it is out. You can unsubscribe at any time, and I promise not to fill your mailbox with junk or share your information. You can also visit me at my website for periodic updates.

If you have enjoyed this book and would like to show your support for my writing, consider leaving a review where you purchased this book or on Goodreads, LibraryThing, and other reader sites. I need help from readers like you to get the word out about my books. If you have a moment, please share your thoughts with other readers. I appreciate it!

ALSO BY JERRY AUTIERI

Ulfrik Ormsson's Saga

Historical adventure set in 9th Century Europe and brimming with heroic combat. Witness the birth of a unified Norway, travel to the remote Faeroe Islands, then follow the Vikings on a siege of Paris and beyond. Walk in the footsteps of the Vikings and witness history through the eyes of Ulfrik Ormsson.

Fate's Needle

Islands in the Fog

Banners of the Northmen

Shield of Lies

The Storm God's Gift

Return of the Ravens

Sword Brothers

Descendants Saga

The grandchildren of Ulfrik Ormsson continue tales of Norse battle and glory. They may have come from greatness, but they must make their own way in the brutal world of the 10th Century.

Descendants of the Wolf

Odin's Ravens

Revenge of the Wolves

Blood Price

Grimwold and Lethos Trilogy

A sword and sorcery fantasy trilogy with a decidedly Norse flavor.

Deadman's Tide

Children of Urdis

Age of Blood

Copyright © 2015 by Jerry Autieri

All rights reserved.

No part of this book may be reproduced in any form or by any electronic or mechanical means, including information storage and retrieval systems, without written permission from the author, except for the use of brief quotations in a book review.

❧ Created with Vellum

Printed in Great Britain
by Amazon